PENGUIN BOOKS
Dunstan

Conn Iggulden is one of the most successful authors of historical fiction writing today. He has written three bestselling historical series, including the *Wars of the Roses*, a remarkable period in British history. His previous two series on Julius Caesar and on the Mongol khans of Central Asia, describe the founding of the greatest empires of their day. Dunstan is a stand-alone novel set in the red-blooded world of tenth-century England. Conn Iggulden lives in Hertfordshire with his wife and children.

Dunstan

One man will change
the fate of England

CONN IGGULDEN

PENGUIN BOOKS

PENGUIN BOOKS

UK | USA | Canada | Ireland | Australia
India | New Zealand | South Africa

Penguin Books is part of the Penguin Random House group of companies
whose addresses can be found at global.penguinrandomhouse.com

First published 2017
Published in Penguin Books 2018
001

Copyright © Conn Iggulden, 2017

The moral right of the author has been asserted

Set in 11.88/14.11 pt Garamond MT Std
Typeset by Jouve (UK), Milton Keynes
Printed in Great Britain by Clays Ltd, St Ives plc

A CIP catalogue record for this book is available from the British Library

PAPERBACK ISBN: 978–1–405–92151–0
OM PAPERBACK ISBN: 978–0–718–18145–1

www.greenpenguin.co.uk

MIX
Paper from
responsible sources
FSC® C018179

Penguin Random House is committed to a
sustainable future for our business, our readers
and our planet. This book is made from Forest
Stewardship Council® certified paper.

To Louise Moore

Acknowledgements

My thanks to Shelagh Broughton, who did a vast amount of research on this one. Also to Mauraid Moran, who was kind enough to check the manuscript for matters monastic. Any remaining errors are all my own. I should also thank Clive Room, who asked questions in obscure churches and came back with some extraordinarily useful information, surprising us both.

Finally, I must thank my agent, Victoria Hobbs, and both Louise Moore and Jillian Taylor of Michael Joseph. I do love to tell stories like this. Thank you all for making it possible.

Æthelstan, Edmund, Eadred

Edwy and Edgar

Edward and Ethelred

Three brothers

Two sons

Two grandsons

It is clear this manuscript was never intended to be read. There are references within to an intention to have it destroyed, and we can only speculate as to why that did not happen. Though the recollection of events is extraordinary, almost photographic, there are gaps, as well as examples of vocabulary that occasionally defied translation. Some sections were just too damaged or faded to be made out, after centuries of poor storage. I have mended those holes as best I could.

Translation is always as much art as craft and I have endeavoured to keep the sense flowing whenever it became unclear. The author used paragraphs, but no other punctuation. That made discerning his meaning a challenge in some places. The chapter headings and separation into parts is my own. It is my hope that the result gives some pleasure and casts light on an exceptional mind of the tenth century. Despite his flaws and self-doubt, he was a great man, who knew seven kings.

Conn Iggulden

Prologue

What is a first line, but a door flung open by an unseen hand?

There, I have begun, after so long. Like a crow's foot dipped in ink and dragged across the page, my hands shake so. Shall I sand these black scratchings from this fine vellum? No grey sheets these, all overused. I see virgin fields, ready for the plough. My best ink grips the page like mortal sin, desiring to remain. Here I am. If you would seek Dunstan, I will not deny my name.

My first recollection is of sweetness, of honey stolen from a pot on my mother's shelf when I was three or four years old. I fell asleep in the sun with it smeared across my face and I do not think I have ever been as happy again. Yet I woke at the touch of some mindless creature, some fat fly or moth, struggling in the gummed mass. I sprang up, dashing at myself, feeling the hum of wings on my lips.

My mother came when I called, blotting out the sun. I have not forgotten the sensation of it, the strange thrill of fear and disgust – and I recognise it now. My oldest secrets rustle and climb to the edge like those winged things, wanting to be said. Like prayers, they wish to be wrenched forth, quivering wet in their birth.

I have broken my vows. I have betrayed those I loved and those who loved me. I have murdered innocents. There, in the bare English tongue all those with eyes can read. Too many know their English now. I look upon my words and I am afraid, though I have had my three score years and ten. I should fear nothing. It is true my hand shakes, yet my heart trips in my chest and I am light. I am all light.

Perhaps I will consign these precious sheets to the fire. No one will disturb me now; I have earned that much. These hands that hold the quill are just bones and paper-skin, so like vellum themselves as they whisper against each other. Brother Talbot once said they were a workman's fists, all scarred and thick. Well, time served him well, didn't it, with his delicate scribe fingers? I have trod down the soil over his dead face with my bare heels, and only the moon as witness.

I have worked my whole life, from six years old when I first piled bricks for workmen on my father's land, in exchange for crusts of bread and a draught of cider. I have prayed and I have dropped my sweat onto the forge. I have made swords and I have used them. I have made a cask or two of wine in my time, taking grapes from different vines. I have pissed in a bottle once or twice as well, when I did not like a man – and I have watched him smack his lips and tell me it was so smooth and extraordinarily fine that I was half tempted to try my own vintage. I have loved a woman and she ruined me. I have loved a king and yet I ruined him. And all I have gained in return for my lifetime of labour is fame and power and servants and an abbey.

Still the creatures brush at me, the words crowd my lips. I will set my tale on calfskin, with ink and feather, seated on English oak, dressed in black wool and smooth flax linen. I am a man of this world and the next, but you will not see deception in me. All my deceptions are behind.

I believe I took my first breath in the year of our Lord 920. My parents were mismatched and somewhat more concerned with their own safety than with registering my birth. They fled from the older sons of my father, so my mother cooed to me later, the daft old hen. Four of them opposed the match and threatened to spill the old man's blood.

I was born when King Edward the Elder was still on the

throne, son to Alfred the Great and father to King Æthelstan. Those three men took our small kingdom of Wessex on the south coast – and by war and wit and cunning, they made it into England. That is what matters. Edward the Elder ruled as I grew, and I thought then that he always would be there, like a great oak in the forest. Well, I was wrong about that. His sons and grandsons would mean more to me.

Of all the estates of man in the world, the best is to be born the fine, shrieking son of a king. I have seen mighty lords fall to their knees at the sight of a babe, all for a crown painted on its crib. Yet there are more men than thrones and it does not come to many. If you can't be born a king, be *made* a king, though that has thorns. When violent men secure your crown, they keep a knife at your throat ever after. Last, and not the least of these, is this: if you can't be born a king or made a king, you might still anoint one.

In some ways, the third path holds sway over all. I chose the Church. I could be glib and say it came about because my father made a poor match, denying his future children the halls of power for the sake of youth and a saucy laugh, but a man can run mad winding his life back – and it is always more tangled than a single thread. There is never one truth, one love, or one enemy. I wish it had been so simple.

The calfskin sheets are smooth under my palm. The door is open and yet, somehow, I hesitate. Settle, Dunstan! These halls are the place for truth, much more so than the confessional. No, never there, though I have bored a priest or two in my time. A man must confess or be considered an unrepentant sinner, but only a fool would expect the seal of the confessional to hold. I would not whisper these words to any crouching priest, much less the open congregation. Should I tell a man who might one day consider me for high office that I lay alongside a woman and was taken with a strange sickness? Vows can be broken. God knows, I have broken them all.

There never was a sin I could not learn to love. Yet here I sit, with a quill and a vial of oak-gall black, and I scratch away. The ink is called encaustum, or 'the biter', for the way its acid eats the page and lasts for ever. Words can bite – and memories can worry you like a dog. The flames leap merrily as I write. They must consume all when I am done. They may take me too, in the end, but they will keep me warm first. Perhaps I will be found like poor Brother Severus, whose body vanished into ash and left only his feet and one hand still in the chair! What devil took him so, that charred him before he even went to hell?

Am I afraid of the other place? What fool is not? Yet I have raised great churches to set against my sins. It is my fervent hope that there is no eternal torment waiting for me now. How they would smile then, the dead, to see old Dunstan cast down! Made young again, perhaps, to be torn and broken for their pleasure. I could bear it better if I were young, I know. How those saints would laugh and shake their fat heads. I wonder, sometimes, if I can feel them clustered around me, all those who have gone before. Like bees pressing on a pane of glass, I feel their souls watching. Or perhaps it is just the wind and the scratching of woodworm in cantilevered joists.

Settle, Dunstan. Tell the story.

PART ONE

Behold the Boy

AD 934

'Remember not the sins of my youth,
nor my transgressions.'

Psalms 25:7

I

I could have hung on that cliff all day, if they hadn't broken my fingers. My hands have always been strong, but when bones crack, there is no true anchor, not even for an ocean of rage. Yet I clung on for a time even so. Near the end, as I glared at them without pleading or begging, all their laughter and mockery died away, which gave me some small satisfaction. That little crowd of men and women stood around the edge, just waiting for me to fall. They watched me hold on to crumbling earth with torn and swollen hands and yet remain to spite them.

I saw Encarius abashed then, he who had become my friend. I tried to form the words to tell him I forgave him, because I had no other way to take revenge and I wanted him to wince when he recalled me ever after. Vengeance is a fine thing, but forgiveness can be just as cruel.

I did not fear death. In my youth, I do not think I could imagine it. I ground my teeth as my fingernails tore on the stone, and I remember trying to look down between my outstretched arms as I felt my grip fail. Bones splintered and I was still there, thinking of all the things I would do to them if I survived. I was fifteen years old, but I had broad shoulders and black hair on my arms and I looked more of a man than some of those twice that age who stood and wound their priestly fingers together like beggars. Oh, their pious faces! I can see them still.

When I knew I could hold on no longer, I called to Encarius, asking him to make the sign of the cross on my forehead so that I would more swiftly pass through purgatory and on to heaven. He came forward at that, of course, willing to do so little when it meant so much. I watched him bend and our eyes met, though he did not want to look on me. He was the architect of my destruction, my accuser, yet he shook his head at me as if I were at fault.

'I would change your fate if I could, Dunstan,' he said. He touched his tongue and took up a smear of dust, rubbing it in spit before he pressed his cold hand to my skin.

'You are a good fellow, Encarius,' I whispered to him. 'Will you allow me to confess to you?'

He saw how my arms trembled and yet he still looked askance at me, as one who did not trust me even then. I said nothing more until he leaned in, just pleaded with my eyes. As he bent to me, his wife or some other drab called in warning, but it was too late. I reached up and gripped his robe, pulling him over the edge and falling, oh, falling, like Lucifer before me.

My father took me first to old Glastonbury, my beloved isle, sailing through the mists. It was where King Arthur had his end, where Excalibur was thrown into the salt marshes that surround it. My father sought a miracle for his son, possessed or eaten up by devils as I was. I was given to fits and rages then.

I sometimes think the old man was as much a pagan as he was a strict follower of Christ. He kept some odd charms sewn into his robes and mail, I know that. Glastonbury is far older than the true faith's arrival on these shores. Thousands of years of witchcraft and worship have seeped into that damp ground. So they say. I went out on the midsummer a few times, all a-fevered and looking for the naked women. I never found them, nor caught even a glimpse of breast or leg. It was ever thus, with me.

The boat had slopping black water in its bilges, I recall. I was thirteen years in the world and I kept tugging my father's sleeve and trying to draw his attention to it. I could not understand how a vessel could float and yet take on water, and I was afraid it would rise up and swallow us along with the poleman, who was red-faced and seemed somewhat addled in his wits.

My father pulled his sleeve from my grasp and I left him alone. I'm told Heorstan had been a great barrel-chested fellow thirty years before, when he was made thane to King Edward of Wessex. In his own youth, to me then as far off as the days of King Arthur, my father Heorstan had known Alfred Magnus, the Great, the man who made Wessex the kingdom that would one day rule all of England. Reigns were longer then. Nowadays, it seems a man cannot turn round without finding a new face wearing the crown.

My younger brother Wulfric stood up in the prow as the boatman poled us along.

'Be careful, boy!' my father snapped.

Wulfric tried to look abashed, but he was too full of wonder at the strangeness of the island and the mist that lay all around. Creeping things dropped into the still waters as we passed through reeds. Those dark marshes stretched all the way to where the sea had broken its banks, some dozen miles away. They rose and fell with the tides, so thick with salt that not much grew.

Once or twice, some sleeping bird would be startled and rise in a mad flurry. The waterways lay like veins around us, unseen, so that the sounds echoed oddly and were changed.

As I watched, Wulfric reached out to wisps of white fog, unable to understand how it could seem so thick and yet vanish before his eyes. I will say I loved him, but his head might have been a block of polished bone for all the good it was. Wulfric seemed sharp enough in speech, but he could not master his letters. As his older brother, I tormented him for it.

9

In so many ways I am not the boy I was, with my spites and quick judgements. I was so sure then that I was surrounded by enemies! It has taken generations for me to understand I made them come at me. Yet when I think back to my own cruelty and torment of Wulfric, well, it still makes me laugh.

Wulfric tried to jump from the prow to the dock and I saw my father snatch him back, more concerned with him falling to drown than he had ever been with me. The old man must have been seventy then, just about, his two boys born to a woman forty years younger. Heorstan gave my mother a fine home on twelve hides of land, good coin in exchange for her youth. Perhaps he needed a nurse and I was the happy result. Or perhaps she plucked and stroked him back to life.

The isle of Glastonbury did not get so many visitors in those days, nothing like it does now. We were greeted on the docks by two boys to carry the bags and two Irish monks who spoke only Gaelic, which I did not know. In the mists, that liquid stream of sounds seemed strange to me, almost magical, as if I only had to listen hard enough and it would no longer sound like someone choking to death.

My father bowed his head to give them honour, he a thane who had known kings. I kept my silence, though Wulfric bounded out amongst them, exclaiming on everything while I winced and wished he would just keep his peace.

I could see the porter boys were amused. The two lads nudged each other and grinned, and of course, poor Wulfric smiled back at them as if they were his equal.

I pulled him roughly to me and was bending down to whisper that they were no friends of ours when I caught a sickly odour wafting up from him. I shoved him away then with a sound of disgust. It had been a long time in the boat and Wulfric had soiled himself. Yet there he was, skipping along as we took to the path and headed to the little abbey they had there then, where miracles were an almost daily occurrence.

The rest of our party trudged on and the mists thinned as we climbed onto a higher path. No one was listening and the only noise was from our steps.

I whispered, 'You have *shat* yourself, Wulfric.'

I said it in a furious hiss, because he was so cheerful, but I felt even then that he was a reflection on me and especially my father. Heorstan seemed oblivious to such things in his later years, but I could protect his dignity even so.

Wulfric looked wounded, as if I was the one in the wrong rather than him. He flushed deeply and glanced at the two boys carrying our bags. They seemed to have noticed nothing, but they surely would.

'Go ahead, Wulfric,' I said. 'The wind is behind us. Go on ahead of the rest so that we cannot smell you.'

He looked close to tears as he did as I told him. I think I hated him then, for his weakness. One of the Irish monks called out to him, but no one spoke their strange tongue and my father barely looked up from his travails. It was enough of a struggle for the old man just to keep up with the rest of us, his furs and mail weighing him down like a millstone around his neck.

Looking back on it, I know I should feel ashamed that Wulfric fell off the path. He vanished from sight as he stepped off an edge and broke a bone in his heel, landing too hard on a stone. We had to wait, though we were tired and hungry, while the two monks climbed down and brought him back up. They muttered to each other when they saw him limping, though we would not know till later that he had actually cracked his foot. He was weeping – and looking in accusation at me, if you can believe it. I was ashamed for him. If he had fallen into the marsh and been drowned it would have been a thing to grieve, but I would have forgotten him by now. I always tried to protect Wulfric, but some lives are touched by dark.

The sun rose on my right shoulder as we went on, clattering along a wooden walkway that must have been as old as Caesar. I found myself at my father's side, scowling at Wulfric as he limped and made more of his injury than he should have. My father was breathing hard and sweating like a dray horse. He nodded in relief to me as we came to the outer wall of the rough place they dared to call an abbey in those days. Even after the peace of Alfred and King Edward, monks still knew the value of a good wall. It was fine, golden Wessex stone too, none of your stockade camp. Yet the gate they heaved open for us was made of wood and had to be lifted by the two Irishmen, to keep its trailing foot from dragging in the mud.

Nowhere was truly clean then, at least where men worked and slept. The passage of our feet turns grass to a quagmire, which is the way of the world and means nothing more than that. In time, we take that mud and make bricks and tiles, so you can keep your damp peasant huts and shiver as I warm my hands in the dry.

Wulfric was given into the care of a tutting matron. I watched the woman put her big, pink arm around him to help him along. I was still scowling when he looked back. I raised my head sharply, trying to remind him to keep silent and to be watchful and to remember his name and line. I saw Heorstan greeted by a man in plain black wool, his scalp like a brown knee, with knobs and freckles and odd planes to it. I waited patiently, content as they talked just to stare around the abbey yard. I looked up to where some men were labouring, and my entire life changed with that glance.

There was a cart piled high with grain sacks and four young monks stood on the cart bed. Above those working lads, two more gestured from a high window cut in what must have been a grain store. I didn't know. What caught my eye and held it was a double pulley, with ropes that whirred in polished wooden grooves. I swear to you I felt hair rise on my neck.

I have told this story a dozen times and there's always someone to laugh or scoff and tell me it couldn't have been the way I remember it, but I will tell you the truth here. I saw those pulleys and I understood them in the instant, that turning a rope over the spinning blocks would halve the weight. I saw a device, a machine so extraordinary it looked the work of angels. I knew nothing then of Euclid's mathematics, nor the engineering of Archimedes. I was just an empty sheet, waiting to be bitten deep.

I stood there, though my father was tugging my sleeve as I had done to him before, trying to break my perfect concentration and introduce me to Abbot Clement. Yet I saw it all: how four pulleys would be better still and give a ratio of four to one, while the rope would travel four times as far. My mind lit up, and if you have never experienced such a thing, well, I am sorry. There are many wonders in the world, if you look.

I know them all now. Even today, these old hands could make the six great engines of the Greeks, that built the modern world and in combination will make wonders for a thousand years to come, if the Day of Judgement does not interrupt all our labours. The lever, the wheel and axle, the inclined plane, the screw, the wedge – and the wonder of the pulley, which sailors call the block and tackle. No great sail can be raised without the last. Those six, simple machines have given us dominance over all the natural world. I saw my first at Glastonbury Abbey and I stepped onto a new path.

'Dunstan! His head is in the clouds, I swear it. Dunstan!'

'Yes, Father, I'm sorry. I saw . . . the pulleys, how they raise the bags.'

13

He didn't understand my wonder, of course.

'Well, pay attention now, boy! Bend your knee to Father Clement or I will redden your ear for you.'

I knelt, though I felt my mind aflame. I bowed my head, but still tried to glance over to the pulleys and ropes even as I felt the abbot pat my shoulder.

'Boys, Heorstan, eh? Always distracted at that age. Yet there are worse things to tempt a boy than pulleys, is that not so?'

My father smiled, as if accepting the point. I saw he was flushed and I realised he was truly annoyed with me.

'I am sorry, my lord Abbot,' I said, looking up. I did not dare to rise without my father's permission. 'My name is Dunstan of Baltonsborough. I give you honour and I am pleased to meet you. I have never seen such a . . . contrivance before. Please forgive any hurt I may have caused.'

The abbot raised his eyebrows at that, then grinned at me, revealing just three brown teeth of unusual length.

'You must call me Father Clement, boy. Your father and I were friends so many years ago it seems another age. I am astonished to see him once more with young sons – and you are welcome here, of course – a local lad brought to follow Christ.'

'Thank you, Father Clement,' I said, dipping my head once again. He was in earnest, I learned later, one of the true old believers who lived with God on his shoulders and thought evil could be beaten out of a boy. He lived only another year and almost all my memories of him are bitter. Still, he smiled away, all nut-brown and healthy from a life working under the sun.

'Perhaps you should go and see how Wulfric is faring, Dunstan,' my father said. 'And leave me to discuss our stay at the abbey with Father Clement.'

'I would rather speak to those men by the cart, Father, if I may,' I said. The reply was thoughtless and innocent enough, though I saw from the tightness of my father's expression that it was the wrong thing. There was a hint of thunder in the abbot's eyes as well, though I did not see the danger then, as I did with my father. Heorstan was too old and slow to catch me, but then I was too young to know I could dodge. So I stood still as he backhanded me across the face and sent me sprawling.

'See to your brother,' he snarled at me.

I scrambled back up, my cheek flaming as I stood and bowed carefully to them both. Only when my father dismissed me with a sharp gesture did I actually dare to leave. He'd shown another old man he still had authority over a lad, which was important to him. I accepted it out of love, if that makes any sense. I would certainly have borne a thousand blows from him rather than see him reduced in front of strangers. Looking back, I think so still. If he lived, I'd back him so today. Not the abbot, though. I'd strangle that old bastard and put him down the privy.

2

Wulfric was sitting on a little flat bed in the infirmary, chattering away to the matronly sort and calling her 'Mother Aphra' as she wrapped his foot. I noticed she was careful to add small blessed medals under each layer, so my brother would heal twice as fast as some poor churl without them. She sprinkled holy water on him as well. It had great powers of healing, she said, when I asked in suspicion what she was doing.

The abbey was an oddly relaxed place then, with a few married and unmarried women tending the brothers, and half the men not ordained nor even formal Benedictines. The cellarer was paid a wage, if you can believe that. They had a small grant of land, but it was hardly enough to raise food to feed themselves. For the most part, they survived on gifts from wealthy families. I think they would have withered in a generation if I had not been taken by shaking sickness and brought amongst them to be cured.

I edged closer to my brother, honestly just to see if Wulfric had managed to clean himself while he'd been away from me. I don't like to talk about my own illness. It was a nuisance for a while, then. I fell down on occasion and I twitched and shook. I'm told I stuttered as well each time, before. Strange, but a vital part of me is one I do not experience and cannot recall. It does not happen often, thank God, though it unmans me and makes me a child when it does, so perhaps they are all one time too many. Yet of the two of us, I did not feel the weak brother. I sat there in a room of cool beech benches and piles of folded linen, watching a woman make an invalid of Wulfric while he simpered and pretended he could not see my glower.

'Father says my brother Dunstan can be cured here, with the relicts you have. He says the abbey has bones from St David and St Patrick – and a blessed sapphire.'

Aphra seemed pleased the boy knew so much. She patted his leg as she split the bandage and tied it in a neat knot.

'Wiggle your toes for me, blossom. There, you'll be right as rain in a few days, or sooner if you pray at the shrine. I'll get a crutch for you.'

'There's no need, ma'am. I can walk well enough,' he said, showing her his courage and yet somehow still making a little squeal as he put his weight on. I saw her slip him an apple as well and I watched where he put it, though he thought he hid it from me.

'There are dozens of crutches and walking sticks down in the cloisters, from those who came here and were healed.' She whistled up one of the urchins from the water-landing, all snot and elbows. 'Fetch one of the crutches, James, one of the good ones for this dear lad.'

He raced off and the great, bovine creature turned her head towards us once more.

'We could make a bit of coin selling them, I dare say, but Abbot Clement says they're to be left where they are – to carry word of what we do here, so more will come. They are evidence of our faith, he says. God knows, we do need the money the pilgrims bring, just to keep body and soul together. Canterbury gets them all, of course, from Rome even. If the faith had come first to Wessex instead of Kent, we wouldn't be struggling to feed ourselves each winter, I tell you that!'

She rattled on and I nodded and smiled, irritated by her. The boy James returned with a rough-carved crutch that was a little too large for my brother, so that Wulfric had to stand lopsided, with his bad foot tucked up behind. I saw a gleam

17

of devilment in the urchin's eyes as he looked him over and I took it as an insult. I gestured for young James to go ahead, then helped him along with my boot. He rubbed the tail bone down there and glared, but he knew then to be wary of me – and that I wouldn't take kindly to Wulfric being mocked. God knows, Wulfric was a trial, but he was also my brother.

We were taken through some open cloisters with a chill wind nipping at us, then through a great refectory where a dozen monks sat with heads bowed over their plates. One of their number stood at a lectern to read Augustine's sermons at them. I took it all in as best I could, but I think my decision was made even then. My father had been a thane to kings. My uncle was a bishop. We were not royal ourselves, but still so far above churls or slaves they might have been a different breed. Earls, churls and thralls make our Wessex England. Or thanes, common men and slaves – with kings above all, as God ordained. Yet Heorstan was long retired, too far from power, too old to place me with a court household, or even in a position to be noticed by one. He had no titles to grant the second batch of his sons, and my life would be one of hard labour and working someone else's land. The abbey was a place where learning lay – from pulleys and Latin to secret alchemies. I could hear the sound of a smith beating iron somewhere not too far away. It was my bell, and it rang for me.

I considered my future as we ate that evening, honoured at a long table where the abbot sat and engaged my father in talk. Every other seat was filled, of course. The monks desired to know anything they might hear of the world, informed of it by visits like ours. I had thought the marshes cut the abbey off, but Abbot Clement talked with energy and interest of King Æthelstan and all he was doing to secure the realm and keep the Danes out of it. Across from me, Wulfric chewed with his jaw so widely open I could both hear and see each mouthful being made to paste. I tried to kick him under the table, but it was too far.

I would have found a way on my own to broach the subject of joining the classes at the abbey, but there was no need. I had no inkling the talk was in part for my benefit, innocent that I was. I suspect my father had sold me before I even broke bread that night.

Clement described the dozen boys who attended the school there, keeping the hours of the abbey day and learning their prayers, as well as plants and all manner of crafts. The words were like gushing water to me, and I turned to my father and found he was already smiling at my expression, his eyes lost in wrinkles. It is how I remember him best, that affection.

'Would you then have room for another, Father Clement?' Heorstan said.

I stopped breathing. The abbot inclined his head as if in thought, the old fraud.

'For both lads, my lord, if you would have it so?'

This had not occurred to me, that I might have to share the wonders of this place with Wulfric. I began to shake my head, but my opinion was not sought and the two men continued to discuss the arrangement as if they sat alone.

Abbot Clement went a little pink around the gills after a time. He cleared his throat, drawing one finger through a puddle of ale on the tabletop.

'My lord Heorstan, if it is your will, I will undertake to add your boys to our classes here, to instruct and discipline them, to return them to you as young men. Yet . . . I recall St Augustinus taught Latin in Rome for a time. His classes were always packed, but the custom then was to take payment on the last day of the term. On that day, his benches were always mysteriously empty. It has been good habit ever since to collect the fee on the first day rather than the last, though no insult is intended, on my very honour.'

I turned to see a frown darken my father's expression. I knew Clement was on shaky ground, though it was the poverty of the abbey driving him to it. To risk even a suggestion that we might not pay was a perilous path. I turned a look of scorn on the abbot, just as I imagined my father doing. At my side, I flinched from a sharp movement from him, but it was just a pouch being tossed the length of the table.

Abbot Clement did not open it, barely fondling the coins as he made it disappear. I am sure he made a fair guess by weight alone. My father's pride would have doubled whatever he might have been asked. Perhaps that had always been Clement's intention, for he was a cunning man – and sharp enough to cut himself. He and my father exchanged a nod and the matter was not raised again.

Wulfric was gaping, his eyes wide enough to show the whites as he turned from Father to me to Abbot Clement, with no sense of decorum at all. I did not care. Joy filled me and I pushed my wooden plate away with food still on it.

My father left the following morning. Wulfric and I awoke at dawn, though the monks had been up and working long before. We rubbed water on our faces and peed in a half-barrel the monks used for bleaching wool. Wulfric splashed the floor, of course. I cleaned it up with a rag, so that he was first into the sun.

Abbot Clement stood with my father, still a big man in his furs despite his age. Both of them were smiling at something as Wulfric and I came into the yard.

'I will see you again at Christmas,' Heorstan said sternly to us. 'Work hard in the meantime. Behave. Pray every day and do not neglect your souls, though your flesh withers. Tell the truth, boys. Do as you are told.'

Wulfric and I stood side by side and stared at our sandals in the dust, just waiting to be dismissed. I didn't know I would never see the old man again.

I wish I could make my young self look up that last time, to hold every moment of that morning as a jewel – but I cannot. That lout, that thick-headed clod of thirteen, was thinking of all the things he might learn at the abbey. Our family home was not a dozen miles from Glastonbury and it did not seem too far. I think boys are never truly away from home when they can walk back.

My father did not embrace either of us. I do not think he ever did, which is only right when a man is preparing sons for the world. My mother embraced me all the time and it is true I miss her with more tenderness, but we are given our roles in this grief-ridden vale and there is no changing them. A father gives strength and makes a man. A mother tempers that iron with tears and her love. Too much of either makes weakness.

Heorstan was too old to survive another winter, that was just the truth of it. He did not live to see the next Christmas. He gave me a good start. A man cannot ask for more.

Abbot Clement gave me over to the care of a Brother Caspar, who loomed thin, but even taller than me. He took me to a little empty schoolroom, where he settled himself as I stood there, with much clearing of throat and fussing with quills and papers.

It broke my heart to look through the window and see Wulfric tripping nervously off to the Prime service. I had to stand there and listen to a cadaver in his thirties scratching a blunt quill, sharpening it poorly, all the while breathing through a softly whispering nostril.

I was asked to describe my illness in more detail than I ever had before. I made the mistake of saying it came on sometimes when I was weary and hungry. I should have said it was worst when I slept well and ate like a lord.

Brother Caspar wanted to see one of my trembling agues, and of course I could not produce one for him. My hands were steady, my mind relaxed and unclouded, as he stared and waited, tutting to himself and smoothing a quill through his hand, over and over.

'Your father fears a curse,' he said, 'or perhaps that a demon has you in its grip. If the last is true, the creature would hide from us, just as it seems to be doing now. Oh, I see your insolence, boy – and I wonder at its source. I wonder if he hears me, your friend.'

'I have no friend, Brother Caspar,' I said, looking to see if I might get past him if he leaped at me. There was always that sense in Caspar, that madness might lurk in him, that he might go for a man's throat with no warning at all. He was too bright in the eye to breathe easily in his presence.

'I can't waste days and weeks on you!' he snapped. 'We must bring him out. Up, boy, from your slothful waste of a morning. Run around the yard for me, while I read.'

I have never been slow to hate a man I thought a fool. In my innocence then, I took his words as a challenge. My body had not once let me down and I could not imagine it doing so. I believe I smiled as I began to run, which was the last such expression for quite some time.

I set off while the monks were still in the Prime service. I was sweating freely by the time the brothers trooped out of the chapel to breakfast, passing me with curious glances as I ran, though saying nothing. It seemed not long before they were streaming out once more, heading to the workshops and gardens. St Benedict's Rule is for work and prayer. It makes for healthy, long-lived men, though admittedly liable to ill temper.

I ran on, consumed by pride, while the morning passed, with no sign of Brother Caspar noticing as I began to stagger. Again and again I rallied my will. I counted in dozens and hundreds and reached four hundred circuits around that yard, eventually six hundred or thereabouts. I lost count. The sweat fell like coins from me, while my eyes stung so with salt that I could hardly see.

I ran until the Terce prayers were called around nine, three hours after Prime. I had been waiting for that bell to toll, telling myself I would hold on for it, even if I had to run on bloody bones. When it sounded, I felt such a wave of relief it was almost an ecstasy. I drew to a halt and, without a warning or a sound, there was Brother Caspar standing before me in his black robe. He said not a word at first, but raised my eyelid with a cold thumb and peered at me like a man examining a horse for sale. He shook his head in disgust and, as I heaved for breath, he kicked my legs away.

'Show yourself, creature,' he said softly, looking down on me.

I tried to scramble to my feet when I saw a stick in his hand, but he laid about me with as much force and energy as a madman. After a time, I recall the stick splintering and breaking into sharp pieces, though he still flailed and whipped in a frenzy, almost shrieking with his own exertion. Spittle gathered in the corners of his mouth. It looked like the white froth you see sometimes in spring grass, where creeping green things protect themselves from the sun.

'Show yourself,' he said again, panting almost as hard as me.

I remember seeing his spittle and then the world became too bright and I fell away. I suppose I did show myself to him in the fit that followed, so bright and huge it was a kind of death.

In the infirmary, I ate soft-boiled eggs and green cabbage soup until I thought my bowels might burst for the noxious wind they produced. I remember my irrational fear that such foul odours might be taken as more evidence of possession

23

by devils, or some evil thing rotting away the heart of me. I did not want to earn the attentions of Brother Caspar again. When the air became oppressive, I clenched myself tighter than a drum, then hobbled over to the open window. Gently, I prised my buttocks apart to expel the bad air in silence, or with no more than a soft whistle. Aphra had a dozen duties and bustled in and out. I was always safely back in bed when I heard her steps coming.

I must have done it a dozen times over the course of that afternoon. I was not quite in my right mind, I think. My vision was blurred and my left eye was swollen. I saw only the bright window. I did not know there was a classroom across the yard. The boys at their lessons had a very good view of me creeping stealthily up and turning round, then parting my cheeks to the open air.

It was Brother Encarius who was teaching that class across the way; it was his lesson I disturbed by reducing his pupils to hysterics with my antics. I believe he had to cane every one of them, and it was that exertion that gave him colour when he came to see the cause of the disruption. Perhaps he thought I was doing it for a lark, then, a wilful, vulgar boy. He came to stand over me and winced visibly.

'Ah,' he said. 'I'd heard, of course, in this small place. Brother Caspar is . . . a right enthusiastic seeker after truth.' He sounded almost apologetic, but I did not reply, having learned to be wary. Encarius waited for a time before he went on.

'The shaking sickness is fascinating, is it not? My own brother was overtaken and made senseless by fits, not too different from yours, I believe. He came to them after he was struck in a raid on our village and left for dead, at just a few years old. His skull was oddly dented ever after. He used to rest his thumb in it while he read. Just here.' He indicated a spot, while I glowered in silence. 'When it came, his fit would leave him senseless and weak for a whole day.'

Still, I stared at him. I would give them nothing. He seemed to sense the rage behind my glare and flushed a shade deeper.

'Dunstan, is it? I have made a hobby of the physic. If you tell me you have suffered any similar wound in your life, I could petition Abbot Clement for permission to study you. Instead of you continuing your work with Brother Caspar.'

He gave me no clue at all that he wanted me to lie, leaving it up to me to catch his meaning. I liked him then, Encarius. It is hard to believe he was only twenty. I was seven years younger and I thought of him as grown, not one who blushed like a girl and did not yet shave all his jaw, but just the top lip and the point of his chin.

'My mother said I fell when I was young,' I told him. 'She said I struck my head on the hearthstone, hard enough to knock me out for two days. She used to tell me she thought I would never wake.'

He seemed delighted, did Encarius. He reached out and examined my forehead, looking for some sign of the old wound. I imagine he was disappointed. He patted my leg as well, though I pulled back in case he was one of those who liked lads in the way of women. I was wrong about that, thank goodness. He didn't like boys; he didn't even like women.

'What happened to your brother?' I asked suddenly. I maintained my scowl, but I had never met another who had seen something like my shaking and I wanted to know. Encarius bowed his head and I guessed before he spoke.

'He died young, just a year older than you are now. He would wrench his joints apart in his fits and had to be tied down . . .' He trailed off as he considered his audience. 'Yet for all his roaring and pain, I never saw a devil in him. I know they can be invited in by some unwary soul, but my brother was so young – a good boy. Did you ever give up your soul, Dunstan? I see great anger in you today – instead of penitence and forgiveness. Did you ever rage aloud and wish destruction on your enemies, no matter what it cost? If you did, your shaking could be unholy, an abomination. I could not help you then, except at peril of my own soul.'

I was too used to dissembling to look at him in surprise, though he had called me right. 'Never,' I said, holding his gaze. 'I confess I am a poor sinner, but my soul is mine.' That is the key to the lock, with monks. If you claim to be an innocent, they will suspect the sin of pride. Claim instead to be a lowly, wretched creature – and they will love you for it, knowing you for one of their own.

'Then in the name of St Luke, patron of healers – and the angel Raphael, whose name means "God heals" – I will attempt to help you, as God wills it, with prayer and the medicines of plants and natural earths.'

I did not like the sound of the last part. When I look back on that morning, with my choice to be beaten by Caspar or dosed by Encarius, honestly there is a part of me that wishes I had chosen the beatings.

'I will pray with you now, Dunstan, then leave you to rest and recover. When I am gone, please don't go to the window again. The boys find it amusing.'

I looked up at him in appalled shock, my face burning. There was no twitch of mockery in his expression, only stern interest. He was always a humourless man.

Brother Encarius laid his hand on the crown of my head and I was content to stare down at the coarse blanket, ashamed and furious. He prayed over me for a time, while I planned vengeance on Caspar. I did not know then what it would be, only that it would be terrible.

3

I was three days in that infirmary after my beating, so I missed the beginning of Wulfric's troubles. I was not fully well even then, but at least I did not need a crutch. I could imagine the mockery if both Heorstan's sons had to hobble about like cripples. If I had spent those first few days in the classroom, I might have been able to prevent what came later. As it was, I made my entrance when all the boys had already set themselves against Wulfric – and so, all unknowing, they had set themselves against me.

Had I not been yellow, black and blue, I might even then have established my place and warned them off from tormenting us. I don't know. A white blackbird will be killed by its flock – a stranger causes fear and anger in those he meets. Joining the boys in that little wolf pit would always have been hard.

There was a great range of age and degree of birth in that abbey class. The youngest was James at nine, whom I had already booted once through a doorway. If I had known he was an earl's son, I would have been more conciliatory. His father had an army, after all.

The eldest was Godwin, then fifteen and broader than anyone had a right to be on what they fed us. If Brother Caspar had owned the wits of a babe in arms, he would have seen the devil in Godwin, not me. 'Show yourself, creature' indeed! The man was an idiot.

I entered that small schoolroom on a day where sunlight dragged a beam of gold across the desks, shining thick with motes. I bowed to Master Florian, who would teach us Latin, joining boys from Ireland and Wales with those of Wessex in one tongue – introducing us to Virgil and Livy and Cato and Pliny and Caesar's commentaries. Ah, old Florian held the key to a gate of wonders. I still recall his first words, when I knew almost nothing.

He spoke slowly, as if to a fool – not that it helped me.

'Dunstan! *Italia . . . pæninsula est. Britannia insula est!* Dunstan: *Estne Britannia aut . . . insula . . . aut paeninsula?*'

I had no more idea whether Britain was a peninsula or an island than I could speak Aramaic. I had sensed the tone of a question and every eye was on me, so with a grin, I repeated a nonsense rush of his words back to him.

'*Britannia . . . insula pæninsula est . . . aut Italia?*'

There was laughter in that room and Master Florian struck my ear with his switch, so that pain seared across the side of my head. I yelped, of course, only to hear that sound mocked in turn by Godwin, made higher and longer, like the squeal of a butchered lamb. Master Florian seemed not to notice. He returned to his raised dais, already mumbling through some correction with another boy. I could see a glitter in Godwin's eyes. I would learn he was the son of Prior Simeon – the second in authority over our community after Abbot Clement. I knew, in something like joy, that I had found my enemy and he had found me.

I welcomed foes, in those far-off days. For a man to become my enemy now, he must work so hard to be noticed that he will surely exhaust himself.

Wulfric turned round to commiserate with me and earned a smack with the switch across his hand for doing so. Master Florian never seemed to take especial pleasure in hitting us, but he was still remarkably free with his stick and kept a little basket of them by his desk, of different thicknesses. The narrow ones hurt worst, but the thick ones left bruises that took longer to heal. I think he was a good man, was Florian. I liked him.

While my poor ear continued to throb and sting, I was given a three-panel wax slate and a wooden stylus. We recited and chanted, and the switch snapped across desks and hands and the backs of our heads as the morning droned on and the groaning of empty stomachs could be heard in the silence, the strangest of sounds coming from a dozen starving boys. Even Godwin lost his lazy smile as he waited for the Sext bell to sound. The air filled with the smell of stewed mutton gravy, suet dumplings and turnips, so rich and thick that we dribbled like hounds. We were always hungry then.

When the bell rang, we rose from our seats and stood in perfect silence. Master Florian was as sharp-set as we were, so dismissed us without delay to the chapel. We trooped past the door, placing our slates into a box, ready to be snatched up the next morning.

To those who have not lived a monastic life, it may sound a burden to be scurrying off to prayers at all hours of the day and night. Well, it was. I admit it became second nature to me, so that I cannot sleep more than four hours even now, always finding myself upright and ready to chant Matins, or to sing it on a feast day, though my voice would always have shamed a crow.

We memorised services as quickly as any other lesson, under the sharp eye and sharper punishment of the monks. I understand a little better now that it gave us moments of peace in busy days. Our prayers became the hum of bees; the air became still. Each morning at Prime, we stifled yawns as the sun rose through glass, splintering colours on the stone floor. There are many worse ways to begin a day.

After the brief Sext service, we were released to the dining hall at last. I remember running down the cloisters, my discomforts vanishing at the prospect of food. Wulfric was just behind me and then his crutch was kicked away and he went down with a yell, barking his knees on the stones. I came to a stop, though my stomach protested.

Godwin was there, grinning at me in challenge.

I looked down at Wulfric and saw his hurt and shame. Though I was still sore injured, I threw myself at Godwin, with only rage as my armour. The cloisters were empty and there was no one to see as the older boy began to batter me with his bony knees and fists, grunting all the while like a pig at the trough. I thought he would kill me, by accident or of a purpose I did not know, but I felt it coming.

I will say that Wulfric jumped up and tried to hold Godwin's arm, though he was no great weight and earned only a buffet across the jaw for his interference. Wulfric fell dazed or senseless and I struggled for breath and blew speckles of blood, though I did not weep. I was exhausted, finished, could barely raise my hands, and yet Godwin measured the distance and tilted his head and swung again, trying to rob away my senses in one huge blow. I learned later that Godwin had knocked out a number of the smaller boys and considered it his finest art. He was never satisfied with mere bruises. His entire aim was to bring about that kind of small death. I am told he would stand and crow then like a barnyard cockerel.

If he had managed that with me, perhaps our fates would have been different. Instead, I flinched away and swung wildly. Godwin stepped into a blow that broke his nose and made blood flow like a bubbling stream. I gaped a little, more in fear of what he would then do than from any sense of triumph. In turn, Godwin stood stunned – an instant of perfect stillness in that empty corridor. His eyes glittered. At first, I thought he was crying, though it was just the reaction. If I had my time again, I would break him in those few, precious moments when he was blind with tears.

As I watched in horror, Godwin reached up to his face and stared at fingers marked in blood. A single tear spilled down his cheek and he wiped at it in rage. There was an ugly light in his eyes as Wulfric spoke behind me.

'Go on, Dun! You've marked him! Give him another!'

My heart sank at the words. Godwin made a growling sound, all his jeering cruelty replaced by something more dangerous. He reached for me with splayed fingers. I tried to avoid his first grip, but then we all froze as a man's voice snapped out.

'You boys! What are you doing there? Stand!'

I dare say a group of village urchins would have scattered, but there was nowhere to run where they could not find us and Wulfric could only hobble. We shuffled into line to be inspected, with Wulfric and me on either side of Godwin and all staring at a point on the wall. Our obedience seemed natural then, though blood still dribbled from Godwin's nose and my eye was slowly swelling shut. The white of that eye went red for a time, so that I did look a little demonic. I missed the effect of it when the clot finally faded.

Brother Encarius tutted as he peered at us.

'Well, boys. You had the choice to eat or fight – and you chose to fight. It looks as if the honours are even. So I will watch you shake hands and beg each other's pardon.'

We did so, mumbling. Encarius nodded seriously.

'Well done, lads. I hope you can put this behind now. You are not saints – no one expects you to be, but neither will we allow you to brawl like peasant boys. Now, you have missed the serving, but it will not hurt to go without a meal. I can see too much flesh on all of you as it is.' That last was just a lie, by the way. Wulfric and I were growing like runner beans. You could tell all our bones.

Encarius let us sweat for a few moments longer as he glared at us, then the fire went out of him in a sigh.

'Dunstan, Wulfric. I must say I expected better from you, if not from Master Godwin here. You two go and assist Brother Thomas in the garden. He was just saying he needed someone to load marrows into boxes, then to help him row the boat across.'

I dipped my head, sick at the thought of going hungry when my stomach was aching, but pleased to be allowed to go. I dawdled even so, wanting to hear what he would say to Godwin. Unfortunately, Encarius was no fool.

'You have been dismissed, boys. On your way,' he said. 'If I see you fighting again, I will send you to the abbot.'

I had no idea what that involved, but it sounded as if Encarius considered it threat enough on its own, so I took his word for it. Wulfric and I rushed off then, away from the wondrous smell of gravy and carrots, away from Godwin's sour glare. We grinned at him, of course, as we had escaped punishment and he had not.

'Thank you, Dun,' Wulfric said as we rounded the corner and paused to pant and wince. 'He torments the small ones. I told them you would defend me when you came.'

I rolled my eyes at hearing that. It seemed Wulfric's weakness had brought about my fresh bruises and the taste of blood in my mouth. I detested him anew.

'Well, you were wrong. You cost me a meal and I am starving. Anyway, I was defending myself, not a baby like you.'

He looked hurt at that, though I knew he would get over it. He was always a sunny boy, my brother. No matter what happened, he could put aside his troubles and smile. Like a dog, I suppose, coming to cringe and beg at its master's knee even after a beating.

'The gardens lie beyond that arch,' Wulfric said as I bustled past.

I glared at him and he fell silent. I didn't say another word as we found our way back to the dormitory. There were three in all, unnamed rooms of no great size, with barely enough space for six beds in each. Wulfric was in the leftmost, while I had been given a cot and a small shelf in the second.

Sacks of onions and leeks were stacked in the corner of my little dormitory, suggesting the original use before Abbot

Clement discovered the true value of teaching was in the income it brought in. My bed was rough oak, with splits in the honey-coloured beams I could put my hand into. There was a straw-filled pallet no thicker than my thumb and a single blanket made from what appeared to be some evil mingling of nettle and briar. I hadn't spent a night in it since my arrival and it seemed a stranger's bed. Perhaps because of that, I took out my knife and began to carve a 'D' on the post, down low where it could not easily be seen.

'I don't like it here,' Wulfric said from the doorway.

I think we sensed even then that time alone was a rare thing in the abbey. There was always somewhere we should be, or a service, or stacking wood and making food, or working in the gardens with the monks and other boys. We were alone in the night's darkness, though that was not always a comfort. I heard a few lads snivelling sometimes, in those early days. If I wept, it was when no one else could see. My tears flowed, my pain eased and when I was done, when the storm had passed, I splashed water on my face and went on with the day. I never choked and grizzled and hoped someone would hear and take pity on me. I did not need pity.

'Learn to like it,' I told him. 'Father has paid for you to be turned from a pathetic baby into a young man. Your red eyes, your cringing, your stink and your whining little voice shames us all.'

His face crumpled and I stood in a temper to grab his arm, not truly aware of the knife still in my grasp. He flinched from the blade and I think that enraged me more. I shook him, like a dog with a rat, taking out my anger as he wailed and tried to pull away. His legs folded and I was supporting his full weight, so I let him go with a cry of disgust.

'Go back to your room, Wulfric. I am sick of the sight of you.'

'Dunstan, please! We must stand together in this place.

The rest of them are Godwin's creatures. I have no friends amongst them. Come on, Dun. We're brothers! Please!'

I took the door in my hand and slammed it in his face, a crack of sound that echoed a long way. When I thought of another stinging insult, I opened it again, but he had retreated and I could hear my classmates returning from their meal. I remembered then that I was meant to be in the gardens. Being late might earn a few welts from a cane, but not turning up at all would bring much worse punishment.

I began to run, then cursed and came back, putting my head into Wulfric's room as the corridor grew noisy behind me.

'Come on. We have work to do in the gardens before the None service.'

He scrubbed his hand across a tear-stained face and I rolled my eyes as I understood he had been weeping into his pallet, the noise smothered.

He scrambled up and I spat on my hands and wiped at his eyes.

'Don't let the others see you've been crying, toad-eater,' I murmured. I was always too soft on him, I suppose. My heart overbrimmed with kindness then.

I don't think Godwin liked the way I watched him after that. He sat ahead of me in class and he reacted to my gaze on the back of his neck like a draught. When Florian asked him to decline a noun in Latin or Brother Encarius asked him the name of some plant – when he could not reply or spoke his answer poorly, I would snort to myself, always the same noise and just loud enough for him to hear as the master turned away. It does not sound like much, but I would watch the flush spread on his neck then. I played with fire, with very little understanding of what I was doing. I thought it was just a game.

It did not help that I was sometimes so ill I could barely

stand and had to spend a half-day groaning and sweating over the privy. That long shed was a marvel of design, with a stream diverted through a lead-lined trough that ran the length of it, washing away whatever fell from above. There were a dozen seats on the bench and it was common for us to find a few doleful monks wedged into the wooden seat-holes, waiting for nature to complete the work and staring off into the distance. Conversation was considered ill-mannered there. It was a peaceful place, though I saw too much of it in the first months.

On Wednesday and Sunday evenings, Brother Encarius would summon me to his little apothecary and grind ingredients while I watched, explaining the nature of each one and what effect they had on the humours of the body. He wrote everything down in his black book, next to my initial. I saw names to conjure with, from the innocent-sounding lily of the valley to garlic for the lungs and vervain for the bones. I have never met anyone else so well informed, nor one so casual with his herbs as to the effect on my bowels.

A herbalist was vital then. Despite our Roman drain in fired clay and lead of which we were so proud, the smell of forty men, eight women and a dozen boys all crammed together was never pleasant. Beyond my face and hands, I did not wash from one spring to the next, and only then because my neck went grey or one of the monks found my rank sweat particularly oppressive. Encarius would grow herbs to strew on the ground, or to hang in bunches. If I press my face to lavender or mugwort even now, it takes me back to that silent young man, working his mortar and pestle.

When he was done with his grinding and mixing, he would dose me with some horrible concoction. His aim was always to either bring on a fit, through heating my blood, or reduce their frequency and power over me. He was an earnest seeker after truth, but the reality was that I missed a number of morning classes, spending those hours in stunned disbelief on the wooden privy seats. There is a particular horror to seeing the door swing open on some merry soul, only to observe the change in their expression as they wave a hand and back away. I cannot say those doses did me much lasting harm, but I do not think they did me any good.

I did, however, learn herbs from Encarius. He sent me out at intervals to collect what plants clung on in the sulphurous marshes around our abbey. I gathered wild garlic there, crushing it in my hands as he taught me, to be sure it was the right kind. Unfortunately, the smell lingered, which was how I ended up preparing a salad with lily of the valley – and lost a day vomiting. Still, such knowledge is useful and the form of the lessons made me keen to learn. When he gave me a pinch of powdered foxglove, for example, I thought my heart would surely burst in my chest.

Encarius did not trust me with books or paper, not then. Yet I watched and I listened, as he dissolved and boiled and cut and burned, holding crystals in iron tongs and showing me how they gave off strange colours and scents. From him, I learned of nitre and aqua fortis, of a dozen wonderful vitriols and the extraordinary sal volatile.

Even to say those names brings me pleasure. We took the world in our hands and ground it fine. Like an innocent, Encarius described poisons so potent they could dispatch an army. I wrote nothing down, but my memory was a vault.

4

That first summer seemed to last for an age, and then suddenly it was gone and it rained as if our little abbey had been chosen to serve as an ark. I do not usually note the seasons, especially now that I have seen so many. Yet I recall my pain, and making a cocoon around myself where I could not be hurt. Alone, neither Brother Caspar nor Godwin would have been able to touch me. Together, it seemed I had enemies on all sides. At least Godwin remained wary as his nose healed. It had to be rebroken by Aphra and Encarius to let him breathe, and for a couple of months, it gave him a weak spot he feared I might grab. I certainly mimed twisting it once or twice, in case it hadn't occurred to him. He left me alone and I thought we'd somehow agreed a truce between us. I was wrong.

While storm gales battered the abbey walls, Godwin and a few of his acolytes sought out Wulfric and slapped and punched him until he was in tears, snivelling like a ruined girl. I found him later, crammed into a cupboard and blowing his nose on a fine altar cloth, though that too would have earned him a beating if he'd been found.

'Did Godwin put you in here?' I asked him, already growing full of wrath.

'No, it's my hiding place, for when I am afraid or I miss home.'

I reached out and turned his face, seeing a fat swelling on his lip and a bruise along his cheek. He was protecting his ribs, I saw. I imagined there were marks there as well, from hard feet.

'Was that Godwin?' I asked, pointing to his wounds. I felt a terrible coldness come upon me and I welcomed it.

'No! Why do you have to keep asking? Leave me alone, Dun. You'll only make it worse.'

He was a terrible liar, but I had the truth of it later from another boy. Godwin could not come at me in the night for fear of my knife. I was not in that place for friends and so he could not turn others against me. My only weakness was Wulfric – and I detested him almost as much as Godwin did.

'Stop your snivelling!' I told my brother, gripping his tunic. 'He doesn't care about you. This is all because you told him I would protect you, in front of the other boys! By God, Wulfric, you've made an enemy for me.'

'You would have been enemies anyway,' he said, in perfect truth. He knew me well. I do not like to lead, but I will not be led. That is the heart of me.

Do not think I was immune to sneers and pinches and scornful laughter. Godwin mimed the way I'd expelled air on my first day, in the infirmary. He did it well and had our classmates hooting. They wore me down. Such things weigh on a soul when there is no escape. The abbey was a very little world and at times it seemed as if there was nothing else beyond the foetid waters lapping at our fields, with the great hill of the Tor stretching above us all in the mists.

Godwin was a true leader, I suppose. Though he used us ill, the boys of that class adored and followed him. If some of them met me in private and apologised, they were only one or two. The rest were as bright-eyed and cruel as a family of rats. In some ways, Godwin taught me more on the nature of boys and power than King Æthelstan ever managed.

Just before Christmas, Abbot Clement called Wulfric and me to his little office and asked us to sit down, a suggestion that made me wary from the start. When Clement handed me a thick white fold, clasped with a coin of blue wax, I knew it was not going to be good news.

My father had always worn a ring with a wyvern carved intaglio, so that its image stood proud when pressed into warm wax. He loved words, did Heorstan. Most men would have seen nothing strange in the wyvern crest of old Wessex, the two-footed dragon. Yet it was said to have a poisonous bite – and the name came to us from *vipera* in Latin, a viper. In my family, we used that ring as a warning.

I broke the seal like a wafer of unleavened bread, with a crack that sounded loud in the silence. I knew it had to be news of treachery or death, but there was no way of knowing who had been taken. Age was no guide then, nor is it now. The old and the young defy their endings, while others go too soon. Neither is it good or evil in the veins that seems to protect them. This is a brief and bitter life, the mere proving crucible for what lies beyond. That is all that makes sense of it, or I would rage at the heavens themselves.

It was my father, of course. I knew as soon as I saw the few scratched lines in childish lettering. My mother's hand.

Wulfric and I were dismissed in silence, allowed to take the paper with us. We read it over a score of times, but could tease no further meaning from the words. What goods we owned or had made in the abbey were easily gathered into a single sack of hessian.

I hardly remember the boat across the marsh, or walking the dozen miles or so with Wulfric snivelling beside me, as if his grief was so sharp it could not be held in. I told him to be quiet and he only wailed the more.

We arrived at our home, stepping onto Heorstan's twelve hides of land as we crossed a gate of whitened beech, made into bones by a hundred summers. A rowan tree loomed over that gatepost, its berries red, though the air was chill and winter had come.

I heard howling down the track, and in the distance I saw my father's dogs, yelping and staring in their excitement. They raced at us then and I believe any wolf or thief would have turned tail and run from that pack. As it was, Wulfric and I were near bowled over. Hounds leaped four-footed into the air around us, bouncing like hares, shivering with excitement, hardly able to believe we had returned.

The house was long and high, of oak and thatch and plaster. My father's home was no stone keep, though it was solid enough and comfortable. A dozen thralls and servants had beds under his roof, or in small cottages on the land. We had other farms around us and there had always been food on that table. We had never gone hungry, my father used to say. I remember his pride.

I thought it looked just the same as it always had, with Threefingers and John of Ower coming out of the barn at the noise of the dogs. Both men carried huge bundles of dried meadowsweet, that queen of herbs. Those were put down and they walked together to intercept me. My father's men were not young. They had served him for thirty years or more, as I'd heard it, coming with him in retirement for their food and a little pay – and for the companionship. They were free men and they both had families living there. In some ways, my father's house was a village.

Threefingers put one knee to the dust with a grunt. John of Ower glanced aside at him and did the same, both men bowing their heads. I blinked at them, wondering if they were making mock of me, before I understood. Though I was barely fourteen years of age, they assumed I was the head of my house. That was natural enough, except that my father had four older sons as well. When they heard, there was every chance I would see those men striding around that very yard, kicking over the buckets, judging the worth of every beam and iron nail.

Young as I was, I did not know how to respond to two old servants kneeling to me in my father's yard. I cleared my throat and Wulfric just gaped.

'Is . . . is my mother inside?' I said, blushing and pointing at the door as if I had not seen it before. Both men nodded. The dogs continued to fuss around us, whining for just the touch of a hand or a glance.

'Welcome home, boys,' Threefingers said. 'I'm sorry it had to be for this. Your father was a fine man, a great thane.'

'We all depended on him,' John of Ower added, though I saw Threefingers wince. Of course they were worried about their homes and futures. They'd been happy and secure, and now all that had been thrown into the air.

I reached the kitchen door and paused, feeling the intensity and grief of that moment – the change that my father's absence had made. Wulfric could not help himself and ran in, calling for his mama. He was very young then, though I remember being annoyed at him even so, for spoiling my entrance.

My mother had heard all the howling and barking. Those dogs were hunters for the most part, able to run a wild boar to collapse so that a hunter could stroll up and dispatch it with just a knife. Yet they were howlers as well. I do not know the breed, but they were noisy hounds and they walked through their own muck, tracking it all over our home. I have never owned a dog since.

Mother had Wulfric pressed into her skirts as I entered, so deep into the folds the little sniveller almost vanished from sight. A white veil covered her hair, but the red dress was bright, the colour of new madder, fixed with seethed moss mordant. It seemed an odd colour for mourning.

She gathered me in and I went to her like one of the dogs outside, pleased to be held. After a time, I stood back, watching her remove Wulfric's grip on the cloth with more gentleness than I would have used.

'I am glad you came home, Dunstan. Your half-brother Aldan has sent word that he will be arriving tomorrow or the day after. I fear it will not go well.'

'Where do you stand, with the law?' I asked, in all my innocence. I know a little better now that the rules of men are whatever we claim them to be. I thought then that they resembled a tool handle: hard and unbending. I was very young.

My mother sighed. Cyneryth must have been around thirty then. Her skin was unlined and her eyes were bright, though there was no sign of tears in them.

'I have sent a maid to the king's Witan to ask for a judgement, but Threefingers says I might be turned out and should prepare for it. If you or Wulfric were younger than ten years of age, I would have a stronger case.'

I began to grow angry on her behalf. My father had adored my mother, I knew that much. It would never have been his will to see her made homeless.

'You must have talked about it with . . . Dad,' I said. It was like picking at a wound to speak of him, seeing a drop of bright blood or pus swell at the edge. I still expected to see him in his chair by the fire. I dared not look over at it.

'Yes, of course. I will not starve, Dunstan. Your father's will leaves me wealth enough to live quietly and at peace, though perhaps not here. Do not fear for me, or for your place at the abbey. If you wish to continue your studies, there is coin for that.'

'I want to come home!' Wulfric wailed suddenly.

I rounded on him in a temper, though it vanished when my mother touched my face, smoothing it with a thumb as if she could rub away the rush of angry colour.

'Be gentle, Dunstan. Wulfric is your kin and he'll need you now, more than before. I only wish I could have brought forth sisters to temper you a little. You were always iron in the cast, not iron wrought. Yet I would not see you break.'

I don't think Cyneryth had ever set foot in a forge, but I understood her and nodded. I did not accept her judgement of me, however. Cast iron will break before it ever bends, that is true, but what of it? That is the whole point of being iron!

That night, I slept in my old place under the attic eaves, wrapped tight against the frosty air. When I woke, the house was very still. I broke ice on the surface of the water jug and poured some into a bowl, waking myself with a double-handed splash, so that I shook and cursed and even laughed, before I remembered my father had gone.

When I opened the shutters, I saw a cart coming slowly along the track, raising dust behind, turning in through the gate and setting all the dogs off once more in a great cacophony.

I felt a touch of fear at the thought of my older brother. Aldan had grown to manhood when my father had been much younger. I'd hardly known him, and when he'd described Heorstan from those days, it seemed I hardly knew him either. The father I'd loved, the man of wry amusement and patience, who lay beneath the earth in the graveyard of St John's Chapel not a mile from his home, had gone.

The house felt strangely small to me then, after the vast spaces of the abbey. Yet that too is reduced in my memory. Perhaps the greatest of wonders can become ordinary in time. Or perhaps we just grow out of old places, like hermit crabs finding new shells, one after the other.

Aldan looked around as I came out to greet him, still smoothing damp hair with my fingers. Wulfric was behind me, more solemn than usual. I felt a prickle of dog-like resentment, as if another hound stood on the verge of my land. Yet as I came close, I saw Aldan's eyes were as red as mine. He held out his hand and I took it, feeling a hard, dry grip.

'I cannot believe the old man has gone,' he said. 'My goodness, Dunstan, you have grown so – and you, Wulfric, both of you. Dad loved to be tall, I remember. He must have been delighted for you both. I know he spoke of you with great pride in your accomplishments.'

I remember his words because, even then, I understood for the first time that my older brother was truly a man – and that I was yet a boy. I would not have thought to put two grieving children at their ease, to speak with fondness of a man we'd all revered.

'Will you come in?' I asked him. 'You are welcome, Aldan. Threefingers and John of Ower are here, with . . . Mother.'

I hesitated over that last, not quite sure how to refer to the woman who had been my father's second wife. My mother, yes, but not his. Aldan nodded and I thought I saw tears shine in his eyes before he knuckled them away, surprising me.

'I will break bread and take salt with you, of course. Perhaps later I'll walk over to see the grave and sit a while with him alone, if you wouldn't mind.'

'Of course not. Wulfric, bring in his bags and have one of the lads see to the horse. Wulfric! Move, would you?'

Wulfric didn't want to be dismissed, I could see. I gave him a push and he began to complain and shriek. I am afraid I pushed him more roughly then in my temper. It was a solemn moment, of grief and dignity between older brothers – and he ruined it with his high voice. I smacked his head and he ran off with a great screeching wail that made me clench my jaw almost in pain.

Aldan chuckled and shook his head.

'Ah, Dunstan. I never see my brothers now, do you realise?'

'That sounds . . . bearable,' I said.

44

'Well, it is not. It is a hard bond to break, but once it is gone, Dunstan, there is no getting it back. Now, may I enter?'

I bowed in answer. It was strange, but I accepted his authority because he was my older brother and because he looked a little like my father. I did not do it lightly.

As Aldan ducked his head to pass under the lintel, I saw he wore a sword on his hip, in a scabbard of well-worn metal and leather. I felt a touch of cold at that and considered that I truly did not know him that well. Yet he was alone and we were many. Such was the world I lived in then, that I suspected my own brother of planning murder. I am ashamed.

5

Aldan was fairly awkward as he embraced my mother, perhaps because they were quite close in age. Had she been sixty, I think he would have been content to leave her the house and the land until she passed on. I saw no real cruelty in him. Still, he was his father's eldest son, so there was not much weakness either.

He brought up the matter after we had eaten, as we sat and sipped at hot wine, enjoying the scent of Italian bay leaves, all the way from the markets of Turin. Wulfric and I had been given our own cups. We felt as if we were grown men, and looked suitably sombre and reflective. The farm lads came in after the meal, to sit around the fire and talk of the old man. They had eaten with their families, though on less formal occasions my mother might have simmered a stew on the fire for them all. She was always soft-hearted, which was part of the reason we had so many dogs.

Aldan agreed easily that it was too late and already too dark to put his pony and trap back on the road. He seemed to relax a little in the firelight, speaking memories of our father and listening to stories from Threefingers and John of Ower. Heorstan had been loved by those who knew him, feared by a few, respected by his enemies, so they said. Over the next month, some thirty men and women came to tell a tale or pay a debt, or share a memory of him to my mother. They were not all friends to us, but she fed them and many stayed the night. I hung on every word they spoke, and I learned a great many things about how they saw him. It was not such a bad passing, I think. The old man would have been pleased by our grief.

Aldan, though, had a true claim on the land we owned, not just the memories of an old king's thane. The very table and the company itself proclaimed that wealth, in bread and fish and meat – enough from hill, field and river to support twelve families. We had eaten goose, and spelt bread, with fresh sage and rosemary, dill and mint, all grown despite the frosts in our sheltered herb garden. My mother had a rare touch for teasing green things from cold earth. Perhaps she brought the old man to her bed in much the same manner.

'My lady,' Aldan said softly. 'Some would say it is too soon to talk of my inheritance, though my father is in the ground. Yet I must away in the morning, to Winchester. I should therefore speak of what my father left me as his oldest son – and whether he wrote a will at the end.'

'He did,' my mother said. 'There is a copy kept in the archive house at Winchester, or you can read the one I have here if you wish.'

Aldan nodded slowly and she fetched a leather fold and untied the thongs on it, drawing out a piece of fine vellum. It bore my father's signature and it was crammed full with tiny letters, no spaces between the words – the work of some miserly law clerk who had wished not to incur the cost of a second sheet.

My mother watched Aldan read for a time and her kitchen girl refilled all our cups from a jug. I noticed Wulfric was becoming a little glassy-eyed and I tried to wave her off, but he only glared at me and held his out, the bold boy.

After an age in which empires might have risen, known glories and finally fallen into dust, Aldan folded the sheet, staring into the gloom by the fire. My mother was not a woman to fidget, usually, but she could not keep silent in the face of that perfect calm.

'I have no claim on this land, Aldan,' she said. 'Your father, may he rest in heaven, saw fit to provide well enough for me even so. I could take rooms in town, or pay rent to my sister in London. I will not starve or be sore reduced, God bless him. Yet it . . . was my hope to remain in this place while the boys grow to be men. Perhaps as your tenant. Does . . . er, is that what you wanted? Would that fit in with your plans?' Her movements were quick then, her smile brittle. She looked like a bird watching a fox pad closer to her eggs, helpless and afraid.

Aldan closed his eyes for a moment, as if he had slipped into a drowse by the fire. He looked the image of my father in that dim light.

'Cyneryth, I know the old man would be furious if I turned you out. Yet this was my father's only house, God rest him. He sold the one I knew as a boy and I have not had much from his hand. I have not complained, nor asked for some better share. His wealth was his own – and we must all make our way in the world. I understood he had two young boys and a woman he loved, who made him happy.' He paused to raise his cup to my mother and she dipped her head, pleased. 'I found a path for myself, in trade and land and fishing crews on the coast. I have wealth enough now to marry and make my own way. I tell you this not out of pride, but so you will know there is no spite in me, on my oath.'

There was pride, though, oath or not. I could see his delight in himself. He knew very well that we were all waiting on his word – and that only his word mattered in that room. I learned something from him then.

Aldan paused to sip his wine. Even at such a moment, I was somehow distracted as Wulfric held out his own cup for a third time as our brother went on.

'But I knew my father when he was in his prime – and I saw that man slip away, to become a kinder fellow, less given to temper and calling down the heavens on those who crossed him. I believe you knew a gentle man, perhaps a better one.

48

If that is true, you made him so, Cyneryth. Yet the one who raised me would want his son to have the land. You know that is no lie.'

He looked up then, to meet her eyes. After a time, my mother nodded. He seemed to relax a fraction more, stretching out his legs.

'You are still young, Mother. I do not doubt you will marry again, perhaps even to bear sons and daughters with a different man. If I left you this house and these acres, would some new husband cross his feet by this fire in a few years? Would he draw a blade on me if I came to collect my inheritance? We cannot know what will happen, so we must be wise today – and not store trouble for the years ahead.'

'You will turn me out, then,' my mother said, her voice a breath.

He did not look up from the flames for a long time.

'My father's will gives you the silver dishes, the tables, the horses – the marriage bed. I could make you an offer from my own coin, if you wish – or you can sell it all in the markets. The house and the fields and pastures are mine, though, with all that grow or live upon them.'

'The thralls are freed by your father's word,' she said. 'You'll pay them a wage if you want to keep them.'

'As I said, he was a kinder man than he used to be.'

Aldan's tone was grudging and I saw that the news had not pleased him. Still, he could have come into that house like a summer storm and thrown us all out. Instead, he gave my mother honour, for all she was a stranger to him. I could not dislike the man. He was in the right and my father would have known exactly what his will meant when he made it and had it witnessed. There was no question of misunderstanding – Heorstan intended his first son to have the land along with his titles.

*

After Aldan had gone, we enjoyed our last Christmas in the old house, with candles lit along the drive and a great bonfire on the old hill. I imagined the sparks flying up like souls and I knew my father was at peace.

On the road that passed by our white beech gate, I bade my mother farewell. Threefingers had loaded a cart with all she owned and he stared off into the distance as we all embraced. The dogs slunk around us in the road, woebegone curs, with tails all tucked up. Wulfric and I were to walk back to Glastonbury and the abbey school. It was strange to think we would not return to that house, that it would be a place of memory and nevermore our home. I remember I felt great sorrow at that – I have always loved the land, far more than any people on it.

Threefingers had his old sword on his hip and a horn-handled knife under his seat that had been a gift from my father. He promised he would see Cyneryth to her sister's in London, though the roads were safe enough then, with Wessex all armed and ready for enemy ships.

Wulfric and I stood in the road and watched until the cart became a smudge and then just part of the dun line of hills heading east. We had bread, cheese and a pot of blackcurrant jam that we shared as we walked the fields back to the marsh around the Isle of Avalon. The day was cold but clear, with blue skies behind the hill of the Tor. I could see for miles and, to my surprise, I felt a rising excitement. I had not left home to come to that place. I had come home. I was where I was meant to be.

We waited half a day on that muddy shore for Brother Guido to pole across to us. He was not one I liked and I suspected him of pederasty, for the way his eyes gleamed whenever his gaze fell on boyish skin. I recall one winter game of football in the rain when Wulfric was hanging back from the mass of kicking, yelling boys. Brother Guido came out from the cloisters and scooped up a handful of mud and dust. He rubbed it on Wulfric's knees and said, 'There, now you are dirty, boy. Get in!'

He sat in the stern and rested while we rowed, glancing at us with greedy little eyes as we heaved and grew pink. The waters slipped under us. Glastonbury Abbey grew at our back – still the largest collection of buildings I had ever seen, with windows rounded like the arches of a Roman aqueduct. It was a stone oath in a whole world of rotting wood, thatch and plaster. I welcomed it, as well as the sight of new scaffolding and ropes. There had been rumours of a proper bell tower for months. The very idea of that, the mathematics and the measuring and the pulleys – ah, I remember! It was a window into joy to me as I bent my back. When we'd tied up the boat, I almost ran along the paths in my delight.

Wulfric had been quiet over the last stretch of our journey, becoming aware that he would soon meet Godwin once again, and masters he did not like. As my spirits rose, I'd seen dismay settle on him like a cloak, growing heavier, so that his shoulders drooped. I could not understand it. The abbey was the place where they took empty jugs and filled them with crystal water, or gold coins, however you wished to see it. They grew green things from the ground and new faith in the boys.

For my part, I wanted Pythagoras and Euclid. I wanted Archimedes and, dearest of all, Thales of Miletus. I would read his words, that gift of God, and I would know that when two lines cross, the opposite angles are the same – or that the base angles of an isosceles triangle are always equal, always! It was my greatest joy, though I had not then experienced the temptations of the flesh.

One by one, we met the monks and the secular clergy, dipping our heads to them like solemn adults. Wulfric and I bowed to Aphra and, for the first time, to her daughter. I learned that Alice had joined our merry band to learn the skills of the infirmary that spring. Ah, gentle reader, I had so little experience then. If she had looked like a smiling sack of turnips, she would still have filled my feverish imaginings. If she had looked like her mother, even. Yet Alice was a fine, strong slip of a thing, with broad shoulders and a swan neck that met her collarbone in lines like sails. Well, I have never been a poet. I do not have words to describe the way my heart quickened, the heat I felt leaping up in me. I only know I glanced upon her and lost my heart in an instant.

I left Wulfric to unpack our things and then raced around the hill to the new tower. I stared for a time at the masons, trying to discern their secrets as they wound string onto spools and held up their thumbs outstretched, with one closed eye staring past. Walls grew on deep foundations, straight and true and square on the corners, woven about with plumb lines and lead bobs.

I beamed at the workmen and more than one ruffled my hair as they passed, sensing a fascination for their craft. It was not long before I was fetching and carrying stones, following their instructions and sweating, growing dusty and yet satisfied as I heard the bell for Vespers and the lighting of the evening lamps at six. The day had fled from me, the shadows grown long. I knew then that I would be a maker, a creator, to echo God in my life. When I stand naked before Judgement and I am asked how I spent my years, I will say: I built. I made. Poor shadow that I am, I am yet proud of my walls.

At Vespers, Brother Caspar saw the pale dust in my hair and on my hands. He drew me aside at the end, with Wulfric hovering nearby to see what punishment I had earned for myself.

'What is this?' Caspar demanded, brushing some piece of grit from my tunic.

I detested him, and somehow I knew he would interfere in

the deep satisfaction I had found that day. I chose not to reply and, as always, his temper was close to the surface. He slapped me across the cheek, turning my head to the side. I jerked back, glaring, ready to go for him as my own anger flared. Only the thought that it would cost me everything held my hand from striking him in return. I could not be cast out from that community, so I bit my tongue.

I saw Godwin sidling into my view alongside Wulfric, just standing there and enjoying my discomfort.

'You will answer me, Master Dunstan, or I will take you to my study and administer the discipline you lack.'

I was sullen, but not stupid. My bruises had barely healed during Christmas and I was not keen to earn any new ones.

'I was helping the masons, Brother Caspar,' I said.

'At whose order? Encarius? You seem to have fooled him with your sly humour and your lies. Did he tell you to "help the masons"?'

I blinked at the idea that I had fooled anyone.

'No, Brother Caspar. I was interested in the work.'

'Work that could see you crushed or broken, you stupid boy. Yes, that is what you are. Your fits come without warning, do they not? What if you had been lifting a stone over another's head when your devilment came on you? Should a good man be ruined or killed because of your selfish desires? No! I forbid it, whatever Encarius has allowed.'

I opened and closed my mouth in indignation.

'Brother Encarius has said nothing at all! I went to the tower scaffold because the craft appeals to me.' I knew I had flushed deep red and that tears prickled behind my eyes. I could not find a way to avoid the man's malice, though I saw it too well in him.

'Forbidden! You are not to set foot on the tower site again. Is that understood? I will not have you endangering the masons or the other men – or the boys.'

He saw the resentment in me and leaned in, so that I could smell him.

'If I hear you have disobeyed me, child, I will see you expelled from this abbey.'

'Well, you must do as you see fit,' I said, clenching my jaw. It was the closest I dared come to resisting. 'May I be dismissed, Brother Caspar?'

He stood back, his eyes glittering. I think my anger surprised him.

'Very well. Away with you now. Just remember what I said.'

I inclined my head, though I was so furious by then I could hardly breathe.

Perhaps it is not a surprise that my dreams were vivid and tormenting that first night back. They began with visions of my father and then of Aphra and Alice, which disturbed me. I sensed my sleep deepening and then I saw the tower of the abbey – complete, as if a year had passed. More, I saw a view as if I soared higher on angel's wings, so that the land around was revealed and, oh!, I saw no humble little church on a hillside, but the building that stands there today, the great abbey of Glastonbury, with towers and gables and grand halls and bells ringing out over all. I saw hundreds of monks – not just the couple of dozen that I knew, but score upon score in beetle black, making their way to the dawn service. I saw a city on a hill and I knew it had been made by my hand.

I woke, or half woke, I have never been entirely sure, filled with visions and so excited I had to rise and see. I ran on bare feet, dressed only in a shift, though I did not feel the cold, or even notice it.

The mists were thick, but I knew the way and had the bright pictures of my dream to guide me. Only once did I falter and it was because I expected a great avenue where there was none. I stumbled on, snagging my feet on sharp stones so that they bled, but uncaring, unfeeling.

I found myself at the tower scaffold, the wooden spars stretching away into the mists. I took a rope in each hand and I stood for a long time, gazing upwards. I do not know why I climbed in the end, only that a great urgency was upon me, a clear, cold desire that would not be denied. I went up like a Barbary ape, hand over hand, leaping from one pole to another with no sense of fear at the aching drop beneath my feet. The mist was thick around me and I felt as if I climbed Jacob's Ladder or the Tower of Babel – upward to heaven.

When I reached the topmost structure, my hands grasped only air and I came close to falling for the first time. I grabbed on in panic and just clung there, panting and sighing and wondering how I would get down again without breaking my neck. The fugue was lifting from me, that daze of visions and colours. I had seen a vast construction, a cathedral of God, the marsh itself drained and made into golden fields. I had climbed and survived, but I was suddenly cold and aching.

I have never known such bright thoughts and hues as when I was fourteen years in the world. I think it would drive me mad to burn so bright now. Perhaps it did, for a time.

I heard voices below, calling my name. I looked down and saw the smears of lanterns as they searched for me. I had been missed, my bed found empty. I cursed to myself then, knowing I would be beaten. I dared not think I might be sent home. My home was given to my brother Aldan. The foxes have their holes and the birds their nests, but the Son of Man has nowhere to lay his head. Dunstan too, on that day. I was alone and afraid, slumped against a wooden pole, my legs dangling over nothingness.

6

The abbey was a small world in those days. As news spread of the 'missing' pupil, I do not think anyone was allowed to rest in their bed. Abbot Clement was bustling all over, calling for lamps. Even Prior Simeon came out, blinking and dazed at having been summoned from his life of contemplation or regret. From the abbot to the lowliest urchin, they were all roused to search.

I could see their movement by following the firefly trails of lanterns and torches in the mists below. Worse, I could hear my name being called, over and over, in the high double-tone of boys and women, or the gruff voices of monks, already annoyed. They began to sound positively vengeful as the cold bit deeper. I had no idea what time it was, but I knew Matins could not have been far off. Somewhere among the search parties, Brother Caspar would be scowling, or perhaps hiding his delighted anticipation that some terrible calamity had befallen me. No doubt someone was sent down to the little dock, but I knew they would find each boat in place. On a small island in the marsh, they expected to find me.

I lay back on the wooden planks, despairing. My hand rested on a great pulley of oak, my fingers finding the grooves and pressing into them. It must have been as wide across as my chest, a great heavy thing with four channels, all polished to a shine by beeswax and use. It awoke a light in my imagination and my hand crept across that platform, trembling. I had a plan then. I had a way out.

Knowing I must not be discovered, I rose slowly to my full height, wincing at every creak of the scaffold. The tower stones were lifted to the top with pairs of these pulleys. Each one was anchored to a scaffold beam with an iron ring, and I began to untie the closest. It was not too long before I had the beam free and swung it out above the grumbling searchers, perhaps a hundred feet over their heads. The mists hid me well, though I hardly breathed, so convinced was I that they would hear me.

I lifted up the pulley and something clanked, so that I froze, wincing. No voice called from the ground, so I hooked it on and began to pull vast lengths of wet rope hand over hand.

It was difficult and frustrating, with only touch as my guide. I breathed more easily when the rope grew taut at last. I felt the iron weight shift far below. My delight was in knowledge that would allow me to step onto the air itself without fear.

That last was not strictly true. I do not think my heart had ever beaten quite as fast before that moment. The pulleys lay one above the other, with the ropes like iron rods. The huge counterweight grazed the grass below. I prayed for a silent descent and waited for the best moment, when no lights shone nearby. I knew I should delay long enough for Matins to sound, drawing them away. As I stood there, I breathed and asked for help from St Jude and St Christopher.

To my dismay, I heard Abbot Clement announce he would take the brief Matins service himself in the open, so as not to interrupt the search. I leaned out to hear, peering through mist that would surely thin and burn away in the dawn. With no warning, my foot slipped and my life rested in those few, pounding heartbeats. Below me, the counterweight rose and the ropes hissed through the pulleys. I fell, at no great speed, but as I did, someone cried out in wonder at the sight of a boy descending through the whiteness. Other voices snapped questions and instructions, but more than one saw me falling, slow as thistledown.

I landed on soft turf and tied off the rope. They found me panting and pale, as you might expect. Abbot Clement had been standing on a small mound to address the brothers. He was one of those who had caught a glimpse as I floated down and he looked at me in shock and disbelief. His gaze flickered up to the scaffold, a hundred feet above, and once more to me, unmarked, unbruised, unharmed.

My first plan had been to get down unseen and then slip away from the area of the scaffold, so that Brother Caspar could not accuse me of disobeying him. I cared nothing for being found anywhere else on the abbey grounds, as long as it was not there. Now, though, I had been seen to descend. As they gathered around me, I could not run, not with the shadow of the scaffold at my back.

Brother Caspar came through the whispering crowd like an avenging angel, grabbing me so hard by the arm that I cried out.

'See what you have done! What did I say about this place? Not hours ago, I told you not to come here and yet here you are! I will thrash the brazen out of you, with your creature! Come . . .'

'A moment, Brother Caspar,' Clement said. 'Unhand the boy, that I may speak to him.'

Caspar had not seen me descending to earth, I thought. An idea came then.

I might not have thought of it had they just clipped my ear and sent me back to bed, or marked my name for a thrashing later on, so that I would have had the morning to fear and sweat. Instead, Abbot Clement approached me with an awed expression. The brothers who glanced at him frowned in confusion at the light in his eye, but they took their manner from him and no one handled me as roughly as Caspar had done.

'What has happened here, my son?' Clement said. I saw raw need in his eyes, like hunger.

'I had a vision, father,' I said. Even then I might have faltered, if Caspar hadn't snorted in disgust.

'I told him not to come to the tower . . .' he began in anger.

Clement held up his pale hand and the monk rolled his eyes like a child, sulking.

'I saw a great abbey risen from the land around Glastonbury, a collection of towers three times as high as the one here! I flew like a bird to see them all, as if I rode the wind itself.'

I had closed my eyes, growing louder, as if overcome. I'd seen visionaries before and I'd read lives of the saints. The important thing was not to overdo it. Speaking in great passion with closed eyes is one thing; dribbling or chewing off your own lips is too far. I paused for just a beat, feeling my way.

'I could draw it, even now, before the lines fade from my mind's sight. Bring me paper and I will mark the outline for you.'

'Clement, the boy is lying to escape a thrashing, that is all,' Caspar said.

I ignored him, raising my voice.

'When I came to my senses once again, I was on the tower, high in the mists and afraid, terrified I would be plucked off and thrown down to break on the stones below. I hung there and I saw your torches, but it was as if a hand lay across my mouth and I could not cry out.'

I looked around and saw that I was the centre of a circle, that everyone had gathered to hear me speak. They made no sound and only stared, though some crossed themselves. It made me bold, that silent audience.

'I heard a whisper in my ear,' I told them, 'saying not to be afraid. "Do not be afraid, Dunstan!" I did not dare to look round, but I felt a calm come upon me – and I heard the beating of great, white wings . . .'

I trailed off, overcome by the memory, carried away by my

own telling of it. Now, yes, I admit I did not mention the pulleys, but then all that I am came from God and so my understanding was God's creation. In a sense, I *was* carried down. In telling the tale this way, I gave hope and faith to fifty souls that morning. I may have sifted out some of the truth, but the good bread rose even so.

'I was carried down and placed on the ground as softly as a falling feather. I heard the wings beat once again and the angel was gone.'

I stared into nothingness, awed by my own imagination, until I could almost see the scene they pictured, a boy borne down, cradled in white wings, wrapped all about by an angel's protection.

It occurred to me that I might faint, though I was not sure how to go about that. I considered it as a problem and, in my hesitation, Brother Caspar snorted, breaking the spell.

'I told him not to go near this tower just a little earlier! This . . . fantasy is to save him from punishment.'

I recalled then how the rope had scorched me in my descent. I held up my arm and the crowd took a sharp breath at the red marks on the flesh. It did look a little like the grip of a great hand, I think. Or two stripes of a rope scratching across my forearm.

'This was where he stopped me from falling, his light so great it burned my skin, yet caused no pain.'

'Let us pray!' Abbot Clement cried in ecstasy.

We fell to our knees and I saw that only Caspar and Abbot Clement remained standing, the senior man staring coldly at the younger. With ill grace, Caspar dipped down at last, side by side with Encarius. I noticed too that Aphra was there, with her daughter Alice. The girl was staring at me then, bending her swan neck for the abbot's blessing. I could feel her gaze like a hand on my cheek, though I knew better than to acknowledge it. I saw Wulfric looking at me in awe and astonishment and I was pleased. Pride, you see. It is one of the nastiest little sins we own.

Abbot Clement blessed my deliverance from peril and thanked God for the intervention of his most holy angel on the unworthy behalf of this most lowly of sinners. I thought that was a bit much, but kept my head down and prayed as earnestly as I could for them all to go back to bed and for it to be forgotten as quickly as possible.

Well, I have been wrong about a few things in my life, but rarely quite as wrong as I was that day. What followed was like a city market, a great rattle of visits and speeches and quills scratching on vellum as the great and the good were summoned to Glastonbury. I was examined and questioned over and over so that I repeated my story hundreds of times during the next few weeks and months. My lessons resumed, with both Encarius and the other masters, but at any moment I could be summoned away to the abbot's office to be seated before some dignitary and asked to go through it all again. I memorised the phrases after a time, so that I could repeat them without thought. It is what makes it so hard to write a slightly different account on these pages.

I did not waver, or change my tale. I understood that if they caught me out, the beatings I'd known before would be as nothing. I feared they would kill me if they learned of the pulleys.

On that first morning, I'd crept back from my bed after the monks and boys had finally settled once more and were sleeping. Though I was weary unto death, I could not rest for the image of the tied rope that held the counterweight high above the tower scaffold. The masons would hear my story as they began work. I had lost track of the hour, but as I lay there and sweated, I knew it could not be long before they came over from their little camp in the village. They would take one look at the pulleys and the weight and the tied rope and they would laugh and explain exactly what I had done.

Panic grew in me as that dawn approached, convinced my life was measured in hours. I knew it was madness to creep out again, but the rooms were growing grey and I had no choice. The floor creaked as I moved and I froze each time until I had padded to a door and rested there, my heart beating hard. I waited, listening for the slightest sound.

For the second time that night, I raced across the yard, ignoring pain from my feet. I found the scaffold by almost breaking my outstretched fingers on a beam, but could not curse aloud. It was a matter of moments to undo that rope and pass it through my aching hands until the iron block rested on the ground once again.

I was back in my bed just moments later, all doors closed behind me, panting hard and chill with dew, but exultant. No voice had cried out in anger or suspicion. I knew I had dust and scrapes on my bare feet and bruises almost everywhere else, but I was safe and they would never break me. I smiled in the darkness. I did not know I had been seen for a long time.

I cannot say I minded my new notoriety as the year unfolded after that. Though I was questioned by two bishops and an earl, I saw in them the same awe and hope as in Abbot Clement. Faith is hard work. In me, they saw a chance to lay down that burden of unknowing – and simply know. They trembled as they took my hand in theirs, wanting to believe it had known the touch of wings. By telling them it had, I gave them something of value in their lives. I cannot regret it.

My days and my lessons continued. Encarius examined the marks on my arm for an age, but he could not say with certainty that they were not the mark of an angel's palm. I think he had his doubts, but perhaps like me, he understood the world needs faith. Without it, believe me, it is a foul, cruel place.

Brother Caspar certainly did his best to make it so. Over the next months, it was rare for me to be brought out to meet some benefactor or man of the Church without being forced to stand in their presence, unable to sit on the welts that marked me. That vicious monk dared not call me a liar again, not once I had the prior and the abbot on my side – not with all the grand men and women who came to Glastonbury to meet the child carried by an angel! Yet he wore his disbelief in his anger.

He did not try to hide his punishments. I think if he had, I might have sought help from one of the gentler monks. No, I was beaten raw in full sight of Abbot Clement, of Encarius and Masters Florian and Gregory, Brother John in the gardens, Guido of the boats, my brother, the other boys of all ages, and, of course, the grinning Godwin. The prior's son always sidled around to the best viewpoint while Caspar laid on with his switch, just so I would know he was there.

Caspar laid stripes upon half-healed stripes until I was a patchwork. He flogged as if he wanted to murder me but had been given only a stick to accomplish his desire. Twice he drew my fits out, and the second time I bit my tongue, so that blood ran freely down my chin.

Encarius made a soothing balm for my wounds that helped to ease them as they healed. He applied it, tutting and whistling to himself. He muttered to me then that he had complained to Prior Simeon, as one who had responsibility for the discipline of the monks and staff. Nothing changed, however. Getting a beating was common enough, though not as often or as savagely as I endured. The other monks just assumed I'd cheeked Brother Caspar, or had committed some boyish foulness that brought his wrath down upon me.

We were constantly accused of 'dark desires' then, I remember. I confess I suffered with one or two. A linen bag of goose fat hung on the infirmary door, to help ease ordinary cuts and scrapes. I heard a rumour that Aphra would dip her whole arm into it if you were tormented, then work it back and forth between your thighs until you'd found release. She was a big, pale woman and had enormous breasts and forearms like white hams. My dreams grew quite fevered for a time after I heard that.

The strangest part of that year was that I grew used to being flogged – and more and more determined not to let Caspar see he had hurt or humiliated me. If he told me to place my flat palms on a wall, I made no complaint or sound as he laid on with his switch for whatever error I had made that day. At the end, I would smile and thank him, then carry on. I saw his frustration and it was my only reward for that stubbornness – but almost worth it. My polite thanks seemed worse than hot coals on his skin, at least for the colour it made him. As I say, I learned a great deal in my years at the abbey. Those who follow Christ have always seen value in resistance to pain, the triumph of the will over weak flesh. Some monks flog themselves, they are so delighted with the idea. It is quite difficult to punish those men, I've found.

My weakness was my brother, as it had always been. When I found my buttocks and back had grown leathery with scars, when I had developed just the right gentle and amused manner to infuriate Brother Caspar, he turned his attentions to Wulfric as well.

In class, he sneered and mocked us both. The boys who wished to earn his favour were not slow to understand. They began with pranks: breaking my slate, or stealing Wulfric's clothes so that he had to appear at lessons in his sleeping shift. Every day brought some new insult to keep me simmering. They drove me further than I would otherwise have gone.

When a master's ring went missing from his cell and was found in Wulfric's bed, it should have been clear to the meanest of them that his shock was real. Yet Caspar stepped

64

forward anyway and bore him off, wailing. Wulfric spent the next two days in the infirmary, lying face down. I do not know if Mother Aphra used goose fat on his marks.

It was a campaign against me. I sensed early on that they would not give up unless I made them, so I began to play the game. Brother Caspar raged and ranted when he found his satchel filled with turds, all across his precious papers. I looked as shocked as the others and took pride in hiding my delight from his immediate suspicion.

I particularly enjoyed stealing the abbot's silver inkwell and leaving it in Caspar's office in plain view. I had hoped to have him dismissed, but it vanished before the abbot even missed it, returned to his desk by some unseen hand. My enemies were alert by then and the whole abbey and school seemed in a state of war, at least as I saw it. It could not go on. Under the movement of such great forces, oak blocks will break; hemp ropes will snap.

7

Over that spring and summer, I learned the ways of a forge. There were only two then in the whole abbey, one large and one small bloomery that was almost a workshop size, though it was the one I came to think of as 'mine'. Encarius showed me the basics, taking me out to the forests to cut wood, showing me how to stack and dry it in our barns there, how to bake it to the charcoal we needed to reach high temperatures. Alexander the Great never knew the heat we reached with our little brick kiln. We could make iron run, yellow as a pale rose, with air forced in from bellows. Beat by beat, burned and scratched, watching my own sweat sizzle on golden metal, I learned to make simple square carpentry nails by the hundred, mastering the first skills, the anvil and the hammer. The abbey cat made its home in the warmth of that forge, spending days purring there while I worked. He was not mine, nor anyone's, but I would smile at him and saved some scraps of food until he came to my hand to be stroked.

In one of my classes, I thought the craftsman, Master Gregory, was some friend of Caspar when he handed me a thick rod of cold iron and a file and said, 'Make me a needle.' Yet he did the same with a few of the others as well. Though it took me a month and made my fingers grey with metal dust driven deep, I learned how to use a file. That was not a small thing. I liked that old man, with his pots of hoof glue that had to be heated to liquid before they could be used. He used to say that woodwork didn't really begin until you were 'bodging' it – that is, making up for some mistake. Wood was forgiving, he said, which I learned was true. Worked iron was not forgiving. Wrought iron could burn your bones black with all the heat it could hold. The metal came from the earthen ores, separated into limestone slag and molten iron in the bloomer. The forge demanded your respect and your fear. I loved it from the start.

After the great Masses of the Passion at Easter, the Trinity term came and went. I was lost in my studies then, cramming hymns and skills and the distillation of vitriols into my mind until I woke mumbling lists of rare earths; or *hic, haec, hoc*; or the range of flux temperatures when brazing brass and iron. The masters knew they had found a streak of good ore in me. I saw it in their surprise, in their pleasure at my interest. It was a revelation as important as any other in its way – that expert men love their subject. Show them interest, show them fascination, and they see themselves reflected – and then they will move the world for you.

The year aged to hærfest, that some call 'autumn' in the Roman style. I say that now, though I had no real sense of time passing. The days flew from me and it is to my shame that I ignored Wulfric's troubles. Yet even as I flourished, he began to wither on the vine. I saw the marks of tears on him many times, sometimes the stripes of beatings. I thought Wulfric would endure and be toughened, or that his enemies would tire of tormenting him, perhaps.

If I am honest, I will say that I did not care greatly, not while the knowledge of the world was pouring into me. It was a time of joy and I was young. I wanted Wulfric to love the abbey household, but if he could not, I wanted him to stay out of my sight.

In October, Father Clement fell ill, an old man's ague that brought him low. Encarius was his physician and I saw him look graver and more solemn each long day. A dozen times, Encarius sent me to the infirmary to make some concoction of herbs in hot water for the abbot.

Rosemary, mustard and lavender were the mildest of those I crushed and mixed, so that Clement could be propped up on pillows and made to lean out over milky waters with a sheet over his head, coughing his lungs to pieces in the fumes. Encarius watched me carefully in my work the first few times, but he saw I was deft and quick and I did not need telling twice. It was not long before he'd send me on my own to make a new bowl, bringing it steaming through the corridors and cloisters like a proud cook.

As the abbot's health worsened, I was excused services to aid Encarius. It meant I had the run of the abbey in those times when every other soul was praying in the chapel. There were so few of us then that no one else could slip away, but Wulfric did so anyway, choosing whatever punishment would follow in his desire to see Aphra's daughter, Alice.

I made no attempt to hide my clatter, so I did not see them in an embrace. Yet I knew from their scarlet expressions and the way Alice would not meet my eye. The service of Compline was coming to an end, so it must have been nine o'clock in the evening or thereabouts. I upbraided my brother in front of the girl, my anger made more fierce in part because I liked her myself and could hardly believe she had chosen the sniveller over me.

Wulfric stood with his head bowed, wagging it back and forth as if he disagreed, while tears streamed down his cheeks. I told him he had brought shame on our father's memory and on our mother's honour. I said he had abused the trust placed in him by Abbot Clement, that dear man, as he lay on his last bed. Even as I ranted and snarled, new lines of attack occurred to me until I had mentioned almost everyone Wulfric had ever met, as well as a number of saints who would have been appalled at his filthy, carnal appetites.

Alice fled in the end, though I had directed none of my anger at her. I suppose she took it as criticism even so, as she went wailing into the corridor. The sound choked off so quickly outside that I stopped my own finger pointing and leaned out to see if she had fallen.

Godwin stood there, facing her with his chest heaving and his eyes wild.

'What's this, Dunstan? Tormenting the servants now, is it?' he demanded of me.

I was ready to go for him then and there. Alice wailed and tried to shove past him, but he held her squirming, like a ratter does with the puppies he does not need, when he presses them down into the barrel and they bob up, shining and still. He held her in that sort of grip, not even looking as he stared at me.

'Dunstan! Where is Alice?' Wulfric said, coming out into the corridor. He too stood still and Godwin saw the way he looked at Alice and the gaze she returned to him. His brow cleared of anger, leaving something cold and uglier.

'You and Alice, is it?' Godwin said. 'Fingering her, were you?'

Wulfric trembled for an instant, his mouth opening and shutting in indignation before he leaped at the older boy, roaring.

Godwin clubbed at him and Alice ran as he let go to do it. She half-fell and then scrambled away with a keening cry for her mother. I stepped in as Godwin turned to ward off Wulfric's wild attack and I landed a great buffet on the side of his jaw that almost spun him round. It surely loosened his teeth for him and spoiled his appetite for more, either as giver or receiver. Dazed, Godwin had to raise his elbows to fend us off. He was shaking his head, over and over, making muffled sounds. I kicked his legs and when he went down, we really laid into him. It was, I have to say, one of the most enjoyable experiences of my young life.

The end came too soon. Encarius appeared to see where

my hot bowl had gone to, and of course we were all lined up and flogged that very evening. Godwin was sent to Brother Caspar, which I found suspicious. I looked to see if Godwin walked stiffly afterwards, but he only grinned at me. I'm sure the monk went easy on him, on account of his father.

We three boys were made to apologise to Alice in front of her mother, who flushed pink in shame and suspicion. I have to say Wulfric kept very quiet about whatever he had been doing before I came in. Alice too was the picture of innocence, and if she was punished in turn, it was in the privacy of her mother's rooms off the infirmary.

Abbot Clement died that night, leaving Prior Simeon to take over as head of our little community until a new abbot could be appointed by the king. Although an abbot is usually a priest, he owes no loyalty to a bishop. That can be a rare freedom or a constraint, depending on who is bishop – and who is king. In the end, there is no 'Room of Tears', as there is with a pope, where he is given time to reflect on his new status and presumably to check his robe for gravy before going out. In the Benedictines, the new abbot arrives with his papers sealed by the king's hand, makes a public oath and just gets on with the work. In its own way, that is a fine thing. Yet from that day, I was aware that Godwin's father had complete authority over me. The word was that Prior Simeon shared family with the king and would not be ousted by some newcomer from court. It meant no one would gainsay him if he chose to see me expelled. I warned Wulfric and resolved to keep well out of sight and out of trouble while our stripes and bruises healed.

Alice had brown eyes and pale skin. That is what I remember most about her. As the year grew cold and dark and I fell back into my studies, I could not avoid her completely in that small place. There were times when we passed in the cloisters, or I would see her sitting with her mother on the far side of the refectory. I thought she was aware of me then, even at such a distance. I was certainly aware of her.

It was the oddest thing, how often she came to mind. I was angry that she had chosen Wulfric, though I'd made her no promises, nor given her any indication of my interest. Yet I felt she had done wrong somehow, in choosing the lesser of us. I glared when I passed her, so that she looked at me in confusion.

I would have said, if I had been asked, that any girl who chose Wulfric would then have been tainted for me. The truth was more complicated, however. I felt light when I thought of her, or hot, or both. I gave her a bag of dried lavender and blushed as if I'd stolen it. I no longer dreamed of her mother's bag of goose fat, hanging on the door.

I think I was reading too much into our conspiratorial glances. It has come to me since that she and my brother were still risking the wrath of the prior and Aphra and Encarius to steal glances, kisses, who knows what else? Wulfric had begun to broaden just a touch since our arrival at Glastonbury. Yet he was still the boy who'd run along the path from the dock with a turd slipping down his leg, at least to my eye. I think he didn't let Alice see the child in him, somehow. When I told her about it, she just frowned and looked away, as if I was the one who had offended! Still, I wanted her for my own. I imagined Wulfric would not have known what to do with her. I used to tell him his opinion didn't matter because he had not a single wiry hair on his nethers. That year, he rounded on me in a fury and cried that it was not true, that he had twelve, actually! After that, I amused myself by whispering 'twelve' to him whenever we passed. Children can be cruel, though it makes me smile even now.

For that Christmas at the abbey, the tower was finished

and the bells rang out for the first time, sounding for miles so that the local village could hear. Abbot Simeon had some idea of penance for our sins and so he forced us out into the bitter cold. Under his instruction, monks and boys and staff all trudged to the top of the Tor, where a frozen wind made those of smaller frame stagger. We wound around and around it, to the crest, then knelt and prayed as the sun rose, welcoming Christ into the world once again. From that high point, we could see for miles, with all the ripples and ridges of the landscape revealed like draped cloth. Against that frosty blast, all heads were bowed, all eyes shut. I knew I had come to kneel close by Alice as the odour of crushed lavender drifted to me on the wind. I took it as an invitation, driven mad by the pounding of my own young blood. I cared not that her mother knelt just behind us, nor noticed. I began to reach across to take her hand and then saw she was already gripping my brother's thumb in her fingers on the other side. Wulfric had not even opened his eyes in his quivering ecstasy, and I stared at the pair of them, like pale angels on that roof of the world.

I knew several strong emotions at the sight of that little act of devotion. It was such a small thing, but I wanted to denounce them in front of all, to forgive them and shake my head in great wisdom, to bear Alice off into the woods even. Lust has sometimes been a struggle for me, though I have made it ashes now. I have denied it blood for so long, it moves not. Yet it hurts to recall that afternoon, when I knelt on Glastonbury Tor with an erection of enormous potency.

I do not know for certain if Godwin also turned and saw Wulfric's display of longing and devotion on the Tor. I imagine he did, but I must tell the story as it happened to me. My Christmas morning was a quiet walk down, huddled and shivering against the wind. Wulfric and Alice took paths far apart, I noticed, without looking at one another.

I felt the matron's eye on me as I walked, watching the ground ahead so I would not fall and go tumbling down the hillside. The Tor is steep in places, so I just bowed my head and clasped my hands into my armpits to preserve them against the cold. I looked up as Aphra came alongside, but thought nothing of it when she reached out to take my hand, examining a graze there. I was always scraped or bruised or blistered in some place. I was more surprised when Aphra pressed my hand and leaned closer to me.

'Come and see me in the infirmary, would you? I have something to ease that scratch.'

I hardly thought of her words while I was in Latin, or mixing draughts to be sold at the market, nor even in the few moments stolen between classes and service, when I watched the builders packing all their scaffold beams onto carts. The masons had produced a fine and sturdy tower, their entire labour devoted to the glory of God. I found inspiration just in watching them, and they smiled to see me, knowing by then that I was the boy who had been angel-borne. One or two touched their forelocks to me as they passed. They had faith, those men, a fine belief in good and evil – and they knew which was which, on the whole. I have heard it said that such labourers are hardly capable of sin, any more than wolves or children. Yet I think they know enough. There is courage in them that some monks do not understand.

Towards the evening, Encarius sent me to the infirmary to help Aphra roll bandages or some such chore. She had asked for me, he said. In that moment, I remembered I'd told her I would drop in that day. I hurried along the corridors.

There was no sign of Alice or my brother. I watched in confusion as Aphra put the locking bar across the only door and took the bag of goose fat off its hook. I gaped at her, thinking to my amazement that the rumour had been true. I was wrong about that, though.

'I saw the way you looked at my daughter, Dunstan, this morning. My Alice who is yet a virgin and an innocent, sweet little thing. She is not for you, do you understand?'

I stammered and blushed at her, swearing that I would never, though I had certainly thought about it, had never . . .

'I know a young man can twist himself in knots if he has no release. You might need to spend your passions, without no harm. I can help with that.'

I will not say what followed then. I cannot. Our bovine fumblings and releases both appalled and excited me at the same time. I left the room a lesser man, in every way. I had climbed her, like the Tor, though the view was not as fine.

More concerning to me was the itch that began a few weeks later, becoming quite all-consuming. I was beset with swollen patches that wept clear lymph and made me ragged. It was a savage torment, not least because it drove me to grind my teeth and almost sob with the struggle of not scratching my groin where others could see. The quick, flicking motion I made when I could not bear the itching any longer was one I had seen before, disappointingly, though I had not understood its significance then. I had seen it in Encarius. I had seen it too in Caspar.

There were once scholars in the agora of Athens who discussed whether man is an angelic soul fallen into sin, or merely dust, raised by the will of God to something worthier. I suspect I know the answer to that.

When the itching began, it opened a new avenue of research in the scrolls of Roman and Greek medicine for me. I haunted the archives in any spare hour, alone with my shuttered lamp. When I took down old tomes in Greek on the ailments of the flesh, I saw that the bound pages often fell open in those places that dealt with such intimate trials. In those moments, in the loneliness of my single lamp against the dark, I wondered how many others had succumbed to

Aphra's great enveloping arms and huge bosom. I shudder to think.

In the new year, I felt reborn, as I always do. At one lunch, Abbot Simeon stood after prayers and held up a fine white scroll written by the king's scribes, confirming him in his position of power over us. It seemed to give him some satisfaction to read it aloud. Brother Caspar congratulated him as he sat down, but Simeon just sniffed and applied himself to his food.

I had been born in December, so I was fifteen. I was strong from forge work and the gardens, so even Godwin no longer seemed a match and walked warily around me as we passed. Godwin lined up to be shaved each morning with the monks, his jaw left pink and raw by Brother John's razor. I had made my own and kept it sharp as regret, shaving with hot water and oil like the Romans.

Far stranger was that Godwin had begun to apply himself to his studies, so that he seemed less the fool with every passing day. He might have taken a different path. Instead, he earned my enmity. We all make our choices: some for good and some that lead to destruction.

The first months of that year brought storm after battering storm, tearing shutters and hinges out of stone in their ferocity. The boys huddled in rooms out of the cold, unless like me, they were made to fetch and carry, to repair broken tiles and leaking roofs. On the eve of Candlemas in February, I was called out to spend hours on a creaking ladder. Forty feet above the ground, I stood with my mouth stuffed full of nails I'd made myself, passing them up to the elderly Brother John above and trying not to catch a glimpse above his knee when the wind whipped his robe about.

It was raining, in the sort of soft drizzle that chills to the bone. I had both hands on the ladder and stood with my shanks quivering in the cold and wet. Though it was still the morning, it seemed dark, the clouds were so thick overhead. I was so numb I could not feel my lips or the ends of my fingers.

I heard a scream somewhere not too far off, muffled, but raw in its agony. I knew what it meant in the instant, some note in it. I felt the cold stab at me and I climbed down, though Brother John roared in confusion and anger above.

On the ground, I could only turn on the spot, seeking, but not knowing where to run. I remember I spat the black iron nails into my hand and put them into a pocket. Nothing teaches value like making each one.

When the sound came again, I was off, haring across the yard. The new tower loomed at me and I wiped rain and my hair away so I could make out the bundle swinging from the highest point.

Wulfric turned slowly on a creaking rope, high above the ground. For a moment, I thought he had snapped his neck. He hung slack, his head covered in blood. He could not be dead! I felt a rush of warmth race from my crown to my feet as I stared up, blinking. He was entangled somehow. I had to get him down. I had to save him.

A dozen yards away from me, Alice shrieked again. Like me, she stood staring up, her eyes wide and helpless. Encarius came running then, the man flinching at the look I turned on him. He drew to a shocked halt as he looked up, his mouth falling open. I saw Encarius bring out his horn-handled knife to cut the boy down. I grabbed his arm.

'Stop,' I said. 'If you cut the weight free, you'll hurt him worse.'

Encarius looked up, shading his eyes from the rain. I saw him bite his lower lip in confusion and realised that he did not know how to get the boy down.

'I'll do it,' I said, holding my own knife up.

He nodded, looking strangely at me.

I'd seen the huge counterweight that had dragged Wulfric sixty feet into the air. It was three hundredweight of iron and the biggest we owned in those days. I understood Wulfric had been tied on, somehow, before the iron block had been nudged off the tower. Perhaps they'd expected him to dangle and call for help. Perhaps they hadn't known the counterweight would strike his head as he passed, or that it would draw him right into the pulley, so that his arm was crushed. Or perhaps they'd known very well what they were doing.

I raced up the inner steps of the tower, flight after flight, though I grew not weary. I flew, without slowing, until I stood on the highest point and saw my brother's still form turning below. I pulled one of the ropes towards me and wrapped it around a buttress, then cut the counterweight free, so that a great snake of wet cordage went spiralling down.

The rain picked up, diluting the blood on Wulfric's face, though it still ran from a huge gash on his scalp. I could not look at him. It made me think of Christ on the cross, with water running from his wounds. I reached and strained, snatching at his robe until I was able to pull him into my arms. There was a moment when I almost fell to my death. Yet I held on.

His arm had been drawn right through the pulley by the counterweight, with great strips of flesh torn and jammed and the bones shattered. I cut the ropes around it, but with my small knife, I could not begin to free him. Instead, I lifted him onto my shoulders, pulley and all, and carried him down.

8

When I staggered out into the rain with my burden, Alice wailed as if she were the one who had been wounded. I was oddly moved by it, for which I can only offer callow youth as my excuse. Even in my grief, my rage, my aching arms, I knew I made a fine, arresting figure, with my brother held out before me under the rain.

Her mother had been summoned from the infirmary and it was Aphra who sent the girl running for bandages with a furious command. I saw Encarius take note of the exchange and sigh to himself. When men do violence to one another, there is almost always a woman at the heart of it. We are all fools, you know.

Half the monks and boys had turned out by then, shivering and whispering as they stood there in the wet. I was panting like a bellows with the effort of bringing Wulfric down and I let them take him from me. I looked for some sign of hope from Encarius, but he was almost as pale as Wulfric. They lowered him to the ground and Encarius put his ear to my brother's lips to listen for life. There was a great seam opened in Wulfric's scalp, a line as deep as an axe wound. Encarius probed it with his long fingers and I heard his intake of breath as he felt bones move beneath his hand.

'Fetch a saw, Dunstan,' he said. I blinked at him in horror. 'A saw! We'll have to cut the pulley apart to free his arm. And a hammer and chisel. Go on!'

I did not want to leave. I stood up slowly, staring at Wulfric's white face and broken flesh, all smeared in blood and rain. I saw Alice had crept back to stand with her hands over her mouth, her eyes shadowed with grief. At her side, Godwin had appeared with a few of the other boys. Young James was there, I remember, standing close enough to Godwin for me to mark them together in my mind. Godwin looked up as my gaze drifted across him and I saw he was afraid. No doubt he feared I would point him out to the brothers and call down a vengeance on him.

'What happened?' Godwin asked. 'Did he fall?'

'I think he was testing one of the pulleys,' I said, proud of the calm in my voice. Half the men there turned to hear me speak. 'It looks like he was snagged in the rope and drawn up.'

Alone on the tower, I had seen the loop that lay around Wulfric's wrist, the knotted rope. I imagine Godwin had knocked him out and tied him on, intending my brother to be found dangling and humiliated when he woke and called for help. It might have been a fine jest.

They chose the pulley and weight because I was known to love them, not because they knew them well. Perhaps they truly had no idea his arm would be drawn in and ruined. It did not matter to me what they had thought. It did not matter to me what they had intended.

I felt a great cold descend upon me, a numb calm as if I had drunk hemlock. I would not have pointed a finger at Godwin, not for the promise of a kingdom at that moment. Justice is mine, saith the Lord. Yet the flesh is weak and we are all sinners. I shook my head in sorrow at Godwin and watched the tension drain out of him, replaced by a dawning delight he could not completely hide. Not from me, who looked for it.

Encarius had been clenching and unclenching his fists, caught between respect for my grief, and anger that I had not jumped to obey him. All at once, his patience unravelled. He

79

signalled the scowling Caspar and Brother John to lift Wulfric, pulley and ropes and all. They bore him away to the infirmary, and I went at last to my little forge for the tools to cut wood and iron out of Wulfric's flesh.

When I returned, Master Gregory had been shaken out of his bed, the craftsman's white hair in disarray. He reached for the tools I had brought, but I waved him away when I came to the bedside. I knew his big, scarred hands were more skilful than my own, but it was my task. Encarius had no time for my dignity, of course.

'Take the tools, Master Gregory, quickly! I'll tighten the bind on his shoulder.'

'Let the boy work on his brother,' the older man replied. 'If that's what he wants. It doesn't make much difference now.'

He and Encarius seemed to share a moment of silent communication. I knew Wulfric's death lay in that warning glance, that the two men thought it did not matter who cut him free. I clenched my jaw, refusing to accept it. I watched as Encarius heaved a belt tight around Wulfric's upper arm. The flow of blood slowed almost to nothing. I took a deep breath and placed a saw blade on an oak spindle that could be cut through and drawn away from the rest. Gregory patted me on the shoulder and I almost gave up and let him do it. He seemed to understand and he nodded to me. I began. After a time, we passed the tools back and forth between us as I worked.

Wulfric made no groan or whimper as I cut the pulley apart, though it tore cruelly at him. Encarius and Aphra held him steady, standing over the bed like angels of judgement. At least Alice had not been allowed in. I did not think I could have borne her gaze then. It asked too much of me.

I did not look up until the pulley had been split into a dozen splinters and iron pieces, all dropped into a bucket by the bed – and me fair speckled with Wulfric's blood. I had worked quickly and roughly, tugging at flesh that moved and snagged like cloth. It was an ugly task.

When I was done at last, I could only stare at the mangled hand, torn in two, with a trench running right through the centre and the middle finger missing. The wheel of the pulley had smashed all the bones of his wrist. Sheer speed and weight had drawn his arm right through to the elbow before it jammed, a force so huge it had crushed bone and sinew and muscle in an instant.

Aphra had wiped away the blood on Wulfric's face – and stitched the deep seam on his forehead as well, making a fair hand of it. He still breathed, that was all that mattered. His skin was damp with perspiration and looked like the flesh of a candle rather than that of a man. I thought he would die then. I accepted it, for the first time, where before it had not been possible.

'The arm will poison him if I leave it, Dunstan,' Encarius said.

He was looking to me almost for permission, but as he said the words, I knew he was right, that of course he was right. I'd held Wulfric's broken bones in my own hands and felt the sharp pieces shift under the skin. Metal and wood had pierced him right through and the wounds would let in poisons from the air. There was but one remedy to save his life.

'He won't live,' I said, softly. 'Why cut more from him now?'

To my dismay, Encarius rested his hand on my shoulder, apparently unaware of how uncomfortable I was at the touch.

'Only God knows if his time has come, Dunstan. Yet he will not grow well again with a rotting arm. If I cut it away, he will have his head to heal – and one clean cut. Men have survived such things in the past. He has a chance. A small chance, I know.'

I looked down at the pale figure of Wulfric, stripped but

for a cloth across his groin. He looked like a corpse already, and yet I could not believe he would not open his eyes. I realised Encarius and Aphra were waiting on my answer. I was his older brother and the only one who could give permission.

'Very well, father. I will assist you.'

Encarius began to give orders. In a short time, the tiny infirmary was packed with as many monks and boys as could cram themselves in. An amputation was an interesting enough event to bring them all. Godwin was there, I noticed, his eyes huge as he looked around. Encarius had placed four lamps around a sturdy table, lifting Wulfric onto it so that he lay under good light. I sharpened knives on a whetstone with quick strokes, rubbing away the trace of oil with a cloth. Holy water was brought and sprinkled over the table and the boy on it. Hemlock juice was ready in a little bowl, but Wulfric's wound had stolen all sensation of pain.

The brazier was stoked and the irons to sear the wound were inspected and plunged back. Prayers were said against infection and disease and then the room fell silent, except for the breathing of monks and the flutter of lamps. Encarius made the first cut, and it was too much and I could not see for tears.

I did not sleep that night. In the dawn, I went to see my brother's body. I expected him to be cold, but he breathed yet. Wulfric looked wrong somehow, as he lay senseless, his hair unbound and spread over the cloth. His right arm had gone and his face was swollen. Alice dabbed at sweat on his cheek, but the room smelled more of sickness and urine and strong herbs. Encarius had his burners crackling, spilling out streamers of some smoke to ward off evil spirits and rot. The smell made my eyes prickle and I waved Alice away, not even looking at her. I heard her sobbing into her hand as she left. I blamed her, a little, though I could not have said exactly why.

When I rested my hand on Wulfric's cheek, I felt a deep and threatening heat that made my heart sink. The fever began that morning and built in him over the next days. He choked when Alice and I raised him up to drink soup, so that his eyes rolled back in his head and death hovered at his shoulder. Only a little went down to give him strength. The rest was spattered over his chest and over me, or left as specks in his lungs for him to cough and dribble out. Yet he endured. The heat grew in him until I expected to see the damp cloths steaming and made dry as they reached his skin. He moaned and kicked out wildly at times, but he did not wake.

On the third day, I entered the room to find Encarius and Caspar standing over my brother. I strode faster at the sight of them, feeling that I had to defend Wulfric in his helplessness.

'. . . not much longer, I think.' I heard Encarius say before he turned and saw who approached.

'Father Encarius, Father Caspar,' I said, forcing myself to bow. 'Is my brother failing, then?'

Encarius had the grace to blush, so that it was Caspar who replied. There was still spite in him, though I think I was the only one who saw it.

'His crown was broken in the accident, boy. It is a mortal wound, always.'

'Caspar,' Encarius interrupted in warning. He sighed.

'Dunstan, there is a piece of bone just . . . here.' He tapped the front of his forehead. 'In your brother, it has been pressed in, driven beneath the rest in the impact. I cannot raise it back. If I could hammer in a nail, I could lift the piece, but that would kill him with the first blow. I'm sorry. It presses on him and he cannot survive it.'

I turned away without another word and ran, my breath

caught in my throat as I scrambled down the cloisters to my little forge, my mind afire. It was cold and my hands shook as I scratched iron and flint and nursed a spark to light the lamp.

The cat came to rub its head on the back of my hand, purring as I blew on the spark and tinder I held, as if I did it for his pleasure. Slowly, I opened the toolbox I had fashioned in oak for myself. With the cat looking on, I revealed my chisels and my black pincers, my saws and my block plane. I laid them aside and brought out the wood borer I had made, with its thread based on the work of Archimedes and Archytas of Tarentum.

My hands were shaking as I took a piece of scrap pine and turned the borer's tip into it, until it bit and held. I saw the bowl of iron nails, under oil to stop them rusting. It was the work of moments to crush one in my vice, with pieces of pine to hold it steady. I took up the thinnest file I had and began to score the length of it in a single line, working back and forth to cut a screw. This would not raise water in a tube, like the one Archimedes had made, nor a mere piece of wood. This one would raise bone.

It took me all night and the following day to make four grooved nails. Wulfric still lived, though the mood of those tending him had darkened. He was a fighter, which they did not understand, not really. They saw only a thin lad, senseless and one-armed. I knew he would not give way. He would not die until death came to tear his hand from the world.

That evening, the infirmary was filled again with those who had heard we would attempt something never seen before. We lit the lamps and let the incense fill the air. I watched as Aphra cut the stitches she had made in his scalp. The blood had clotted dark and her hands shook as she took up my smallest tongs, cleaned in the fire and polished to a high sheen. She opened them in him, pushing back his scalp so that we saw his skull, with liquid seeping out of the cracks. Blood dribbled down and stained the pillow beneath.

Encarius leaned over the wound, fascinated to see what his fingers had felt before. I could see the disc of bone, smaller than I had expected, sitting beneath the rest. I swallowed, suddenly afraid it was all for nothing.

I took one of the carved nails and touched it to the bone, wincing as the thing shifted beneath my hand. Slowly, I began to turn the iron head, praying aloud as I did so. I do not think my faith, my hope, has ever been as strong as in that moment.

The point bit into bone. I could feel the thread grow tight as I turned, slow and without pressure, just letting the thing bind its way into the piece. I was shaking as I turned it, knowing that I would kill Wulfric if I went too far.

'How thick is the bone?' I asked Encarius. He was watching everything, of course.

'Not much more,' he murmured. 'Will one be enough?'

'If I am gentle, there is nothing to lose with another,' I said. We whispered as if we might wake him and find him indignant at those all around. I smiled at the thought.

The second filed nail took an age to start. I turned and turned it, wary of applying any force at all that might press the bone further and blow my brother out like a candle. When it squeaked and bit, I breathed in relief. A drop of my sweat fell into the wound and I watched it glisten there, mingling with Wulfric's blood.

When the two screws were steady, I stood back. My hands were shaking so badly by then that I could not go on. It fell to Encarius to take hold of the black iron and ease the bone up, working it a fraction back and forth until it had been raised to the level of the rest. It was Encarius who pierced the scalp and settled it back into place, leaving the nails standing out. It was he who fixed knots to them in good cord, so that they could not slip back.

Aphra stepped in to stitch the scalp together once again, then wrap Wulfric's head in new bandages. When she was finished, I swear there was a little more colour to his cheeks. Encarius and I looked in awe at each other, and Abbot Simeon called for us all to pray to the glory of God.

After that excitement, the monastery settled back into its routine of services: Matins, Lauds, Prime, Terce, Sext, None, Vespers, Compline and sleep. Wulfric did not wake, but neither did he die. As I said he would, he fought.

That small room off the infirmary saw the same scene repeated every day. Alice and Aphra and Encarius and I would visit for the hours of daylight. We changed dressings and sheets and bathed his body as it became foul. We sniffed the oozing stump of his arm. Encarius ran his knife in a flame and dug about in Wulfric's flesh until a great wash of green pus poured down his ribs. I had to leave the room then, the smell was so terrible.

After that, the wound seemed cleaner. The swellings reduced day by day, until he looked almost normal except for the black nails and the red line running in a great 'T' across his forehead and scalp. I went to all the abbey services and redoubled my prayers and promises. I made my bargains, as men do. Lord, if you can find it in your heart, I will raise a great house in your name. I will make you a cathedral. Some men promise the world and cannot deliver it. Yet my word was good, I think. I have broken some oaths, but not that one.

The days became weeks and then months. I took out the nail screws and they bled cleanly. Wulfric's skin grew yellow and stretched like canvas over his bones. I could see the hollows of his skull when I looked at him, but still he did not wake. One of the boys broke a leg around the same time. He caught his foot in a hole and went down badly, so that something snapped or twisted. He was back to running and jumping after two months – and Wulfric still lay limp and loose, weaker as the seasons passed.

Alice and I fed him each morning – we became skilled at it, as any other craft, after I had fashioned a funnel to take the broth past the juncture to his lungs. It was a small thing made from boiled cow horn and polished to a golden glow. Alice called it a miracle, and it was true Wulfric's colour began to improve.

I did not mind the way Alice looked on me. Ever since she heard what I had done to save my brother, she had softened in her glances. I was surprised when she placed her hand on mine, then blushed. We sat at Wulfric's side and I only shook my head at her as if I disapproved, though I felt such desire that I could only stare.

That summer was one of the best I remember, yet I saw it as pitiless. Blue skies and heat brought flies and sweat and made the daylight hours a torment and a misery. Encarius and I resumed our normal duties. Once more I helped him grind herbs and minerals, both for the medical supplies and for the kitchens. When I was not needed in that work, I spent my hours at the forge or working planes and chisels and files to make a harp. I shaped and prepared beams with Master Gregory, or made stirrups and learned saddlery. I was always under the eye of one of the brothers and almost never alone in that small community.

At the first touch of rust on the trees, Godwin came into the forge. I'd hardly exchanged a word with him in months, as if I had no interest in him at all. He did not announce himself that day, but just appeared and slouched against the door frame to watch me. When I noticed him at last, it was with a jolt. I almost dropped the bright iron

I held in my tongs, hot enough to burn moisture from the air.

'My father is calling for you,' Godwin said.

I could see he was pleased at the discomfort he had caused me. In the first days and weeks after Wulfric was hurt, Godwin had worn a hunted expression as he waited for some vengeance from me. Little by little, I'd seen him come to believe I truly did not know. His confidence had returned, though I wondered if he feared Wulfric waking to name him. If he ever woke, of course.

'What does Abbot Simeon want from me?' I asked. I used the man's name, always. I didn't like the way Godwin brought up the relationship, wanting us all to be reminded.

'Some fancy woman from Winchester,' he said. 'Wants to see the liar who said he flew with angels.'

I took a step towards him, though he didn't flinch. He wasn't a coward, I'll say that much for him.

'I was carried down, Godwin,' I whispered. 'And I was burned at the touch of that angel. Like this.'

He had not understood that I wore my great forge gauntlets and my leather apron. When I took his hand in mine, I was still holding the yellow piece of iron that would have gone to make a horse's bit.

I forgot myself, just for an instant. I forgot that I had promised my secret heart to make no accusation, to give no sign I held him accountable, so that when I turned on him at last, no one would suspect me.

He shrieked like a woman and flung it away, while the cat scrambled past his legs in panic at the sound. The darkening iron tumbled across the floor, making wisps of smoke rise from hay and mud. I took a moment to gather it up and chuck it into a quenching bucket. By the time I looked around again, Godwin had gone like the cat, no doubt sucking his hand and nursing a fresh grievance.

I dipped my hands into the water bucket and smoothed down my hair, stripping gauntlets and the apron to reveal my most patched shirt and a pair of woollen trews so old the crotch sagged almost to my knees. I did not inspire, but I had no way of knowing how long the abbot and his guest had already been waiting.

9

Abbot Simeon had made some changes to the little office and prayer room that had served his predecessor. Dried flowers hung at a narrow window to the outside, so that a breeze wafted scents of hops and lavender into the room.

A woman turned in her seat to face me as I made my obeisance to the abbot. No, I should not put her in the same bag as Aphra. Elflaed was as great a lady as I have ever known – and I have met so many queens I tire of the breed.

The widow Elflaed was not beautiful. Do not believe I was some lovesick shepherd, smitten as I laid eyes on her. The lady's jaw and forehead were wide, her nose upturned at the end, granting a glimpse of more nostril than is usually expected. Her eyes were heavy-lidded and had thick lashes, so that they appeared darker and far larger than they actually were. It was a face of calm and strength, certainly, but not beauty.

'Dunstan here is one of our most promising young gentlemen,' Simeon said. 'It is our hope to see him ordained as a priest, or perhaps to join the order here. He has a great gift with iron and silver, I am told. And the growing of green things. Nothing is beyond him, so his masters say. Well, one of his uncles is Archbishop Athelm, my lady. If such things are in the blood, who knows how far this one may travel in the service of our Lord?'

I blinked at Abbot Simeon in surprise. I did not recall ever mentioning my uncle to him. Perhaps my father Heorstan talked more of his family to the monks than he ever had to me. All I knew was that my father's side was packed with clerics and men of power. It was not my father's way to ever have them visit us, however.

Men like old Abbot Clement and even my father saw no great wisdom in discussing their world with mere boys. We were not real to them, I think. There have been too many times since then when I learned something of my childhood that no one bothered to tell me when it actually might have been useful.

'Father Simeon tells me your brother is sore wounded,' Lady Elflaed said, tilting her head at me. 'I will include him in my prayers this very evening.'

I thought she was studying me and I bowed to her, in part to gather my thoughts. When I rose, I was smooth-faced and calm.

'You are gracious, my lady. I'm afraid my brother has not woken now for months. None of us have much hope left, beyond a miracle.'

'Then I will pray for one,' she said. 'For the brother of one carried by angels, perhaps it is not too much to ask.'

I bowed again, a little overwhelmed by that piercing eye. She was very still, I noticed, without a flutter of her hands as she talked. I thought it would be hard to lie to her.

'Lady Elflaed has asked if you would be so kind as to show her the gardens here, Dunstan. Are you free of your duties this afternoon?'

The abbot turned a brittle smile on me, knowing I certainly was if he commanded it.

'It would be my great honour, my lady,' I said. 'I would take your arm, but I fear I am too grimy from the forge.'

To my surprise, she stood up and held out her hand even so, wrapped to the first finger in some smooth white cloth I hardly dared to touch.

'The char of the forge, or the whole world, is clean to me, Dunstan. Sin is the only mark that matters. Do you understand me?'

'I believe so, my lady. And I agree.'

As I reached out and entwined my arm in hers, she squeezed her elbow closed, welcoming me. I liked her, despite the little pig face. She guided me to the door and then drew me up as a stranger appeared there.

He was dressed in a black Benedictine robe, knotted about such a narrow waist that I wondered how much man could possibly be held inside that small snare. I glared at the stranger and, in turn, he looked scornfully at me. I had seen he held a leg of chicken in his hand, a fine piece of fat capon. His lips shone with grease from nibbling at it. I took a moment to frown, as if I had caught him stealing. It was cheek, of course, but first impressions are strange things and not always in our control.

I heard the lady on my arm chuckle to herself at my side.

'Dunstan, this is my dear companion and adviser, Father Keats. Keats, this is the young man I told you about, who was carried down by an angel in view of all the men here.'

This Keats raised his chin to me at that, though it was grudging.

'And where are you off to now with him? I told you I wanted to see the relicts.'

'Are you always so impertinent to your mistress?' I demanded.

I stepped forward as I spoke, so that I came between them. Before the old man could react, I snatched the chicken leg from his grasp. I tossed it towards the window in my anger, but it snagged on the dried hops and hung there like a garnish. The old priest scowled at me, wiping his mouth with the back of his hand.

'It is no concern of yours how I speak to anyone, boy! It does concern me how you dare to speak to me!'

He had grown red in his temper, I noticed. With no great gentleness, I moved him aside with an arm laid across his chest, clearing the doorway for Lady Elflaed to pass through. The old fellow struggled a little, but had the sense to go still as his mistress squeezed by.

I took Lady Elflaed's arm in the corridor, without meeting her astonished gaze. Nor did I look back to see the old sod retrieve his chicken leg. Instead, I directed the lady out past the infirmary, where Alice and Aphra curtsied and gazed in wonder on me, then into the abbey gardens, where the air was thick with herbs and the drone of bees on lavender.

I had not gone a dozen paces before Lady Elflaed drew me to a halt.

'Why were you so . . . brash, so hard on Father Keats?' she said.

'I did not like his manner to you, my lady. It seems to me that a monk should be humble and show respect. The way he came strolling along, waving his capon leg . . . I thought him coarse. He had no right to press you with questions either.'

I broke off, aware that I actually was sounding like a love-sick shepherd. I admired her, I will say that much. I will also say that there are many other loves beyond the act of rutting. The love of man for God, say, or for his mother or sister. Plato described it perfectly. Love can be pure, especially if the face does not excite desire.

'I see,' she said. She had gone pink and was silent for a long time as I showed her the gardens and listed all the strange things that grew there. She stopped in wonder as I described the dangers of the poison bed and told her to avoid even touching the plants.

'That ivy, my lady, if allowed to drift across your skin, will cause a blister that might take a year to heal and could tingle in the sunlight for a full year after that.'

'Why, then, is it grown at all?' she asked.

I was flattered to have a woman of great station and wealth looking to me as a tutor.

'Almost all poisons have some use in medicine, my lady. In small doses, even something as deadly as monk's hood, which we call aconite, has a use. It brings on sleep and calm in children, though the amount is no more than a thousandth of the killing drop. Or hemlock, there, which has killed more than one emperor of Rome. That will bring on a drowse where little pain is felt and less remembered.'

She pressed a hand to her mouth as she gazed around, then accepted my arm in hers once more as I moved on, over a strip of flagstoned ground to row upon row of runner beans, a September crop grown long and fat, with red flowers and our own bees sipping at them. She asked me about my time at the abbey and I drifted into the story of the angel carrying me down without really being aware of it, then of Wulfric's injury and all I had done since then. The words poured out of me and she seemed fascinated. I wonder now how many other men Elflaed had listened to and learned from over the years. I feel a twinge of jealousy at the thought of others enjoying that intimacy! Yet it was new to me then. A woman in her prime, listening closely and responding to every word I said. It was a glamour of a sort, and I fell under her spell. I was not unaware of her touch, always to the arm where I had indicated the angel had scorched me.

After a time, we came to the part of abbey land where wooden crosses marked the burial of the brothers. Away from the abbey buildings, it was a peaceful place I came to when I was weary. The grass had been trimmed back and the graves were neatly tended. I told Elflaed about Abbot Clement and showed her the carved stone where he lay beneath the sod. Abbots get a better class of grave, though the hole is just the same. She prayed at his marker with her head bowed and I took a moment to close my eyes to the breeze.

'Are you unwell, Dunstan?' I heard her ask.

I opened my eyes and shook my head.

'I'm sorry, my lady. I was a little overcome. I recalled a dream I had last night, that made no sense to me before I stood here today, with you.'

'Dreams can be sent to us, Dunstan. Did you know? They can be messages from God.'

'I have suffered visions before, my lady, as I said. They come upon me and I shake and go blind. It is an affliction to be so angel-touched.'

Her eyes widened at my words and I saw she dared not ask. I described it for her anyway.

'I saw this graveyard, but at my back was a great abbey, as tall and broad as any in England. I have seen the vision before, but last night I cried out, asking how it could be true. I was shown the graveyard once more and told that there would be a fresh plot filled in three days, by one who showed no sickness. That would be my proof that the vision was true and from God.'

I looked down at her and saw she was close to tears.

'Who will it be, Dunstan?'

I sought to reassure her then. The last thing I wanted was for her to run from that place in terror.

'A man, my lady. The voice said "He" to me. That is all I know.'

I saw relief flood her and she leaned once more on my arm.

'I would like to return to Abbot Simeon now,' she said faintly. 'You have shown me so much, told me so many things. My thoughts are in a whirl, a maelstrom.'

I worried she might faint, and then I would have to explain how her dress had crumpled and endure the suspicions of men like Brother Caspar. I hurried her back to the abbot, who glanced from her to me and looked delighted at what he saw. Father Keats stood up as his mistress entered, though she seemed almost dazed and lost in thought. Perhaps it was the heat.

The abbot summoned servants to bring cool drinks for Elflaed and Keats. I was dismissed and I was surprised when Simeon came out into the corridor with me. He patted me on the back.

'Well done, lad,' he murmured, smiling.

I could only gaze at him in confusion.

'Dunstan, Lady Elflaed is the king's niece. It does not hurt us to have friends at court. Nor will it hurt our purse.'

His enthusiasm for raising funds and supporters was somehow vulgar. I frowned.

'Jesus did not seek wealth, Abbot Simeon. I believe when asked about coins stamped with the likeness of Tiberius, he said, "Render unto Caesar the things that are Caesar's."'

Abbot Simeon's expression soured, as you might expect.

'Yes,' he said. 'I believe he did say that. Food for thought, boy, food for thought. Well, your part in this is at an end, at least. On your way then, Dunstan, with my thanks.'

His mood had turned completely as he went back in to his guests, which cheered me enormously. As he would discover, my part had only begun.

Father Keats died in the hour just after Matins, that is to say some little time after midnight. He retired to his bed after yawning through the Night Office, then was found cold and still when he did not appear for Lauds at dawn. Encarius examined his body, but there was no mark on him and it seemed he was taken by a chill. At his age, such things are a constant peril. We are all given such a brief season. I cannot say I liked him, but he was not without merit. After all, his ending aided me enormously.

It was Abbot Simeon who agreed he could be buried in our rather modest graveyard. As a Benedictine, it was not so unusual and far better than binding him up for travel while he rotted. Some towns still charged a toll for bodies, which gave rise to farcical stories of dead men and women sat high on carts and tied in place, even made to wave by their children as they rode through.

Lady Elflaed was red-eyed, of course, with all the gentleness of her sex and station. I said no word to her as we lowered Keats into the ground in his box and sang the Latin service. I let her remember my vision in her own time, which I thought would have more power than any attempt I might make.

Sure enough, she looked up from the droning abbot when I passed, taking my arm in hers as if she claimed me. I looked away as she sniffled into a fine cloth, feeling the surprise and suspicion in the men around us, but quite unable to detach myself without giving offence. I stood there like a post, while she sobbed and mopped her tears.

'He was a fine man,' she said. 'If you'd known him, you'd have seen his kindness – and his learning. He knew so much of the world. It is true he could be bitter, but he had seen so many cruelties. It is only a wonder his faith was so very strong. I do not doubt he is in heaven this moment.'

We all crossed ourselves at the thought, though my attempt was blocked by her arm, so that I had to twist my neck right down to complete it. Bad luck not to.

'And it was you, Dunstan, who told me of the vision you had, that the grave would be filled. It has been filled, just as you said! You have the gift of true prophecy.'

I was not sure quite how to respond to that, especially with Brother Caspar there in his best black, his hands twitching to lay about me one more time. I looked reproachfully at him for his angry glances, which I knew would make him wild. Indeed, he made to step forward, but Abbot Simeon took him by the shoulder, his touch enough restraint all on its own.

'I do not doubt Brother Keats is looking down on us from

heaven at this moment,' Abbot Simeon said. 'He lived a life of learning and honest labour, attending Mass every day. He would not be allowed to linger in purgatory, not with glory waiting. Take comfort in that, my lady. We remain in this vale of grief. He has gone to perfect understanding, and he sees the face of God. We should celebrate his passing, not mourn it.'

Lady Elflaed nodded gratefully to the man as I looked at him in suspicion, wondering what he was trying to do. He had certainly captured the lady's attention and she no longer grasped my arm with the same fervour.

'I believe Dunstan is due in the infirmary, my lady, to pray with his poor brother. I would be happy to continue yesterday's discussion in my office, if you wish.'

She gave me back my arm, pressing it to me.

'Of course, father. I know the work does not end. It was Dunstan who told me of a great abbey in the years ahead, one with towers to dwarf those that stand here now. Perhaps I can play a part in bringing that about.'

Abbot Simeon nodded, still smiling, though he looked less happy at including me in the conversation. I decided to leave them to their bargaining.

'My lady, it has been a great honour. I should pray with my brother this morning, as Abbot Simeon has said.'

I made no demand of her, do you see? A woman of wealth will always be approached and surrounded by flatterers, well-meaning or not. I made no claim – and she came to my hand as a result.

'I would speak to you again before I rejoin my uncle's court,' she said. Once more, her gaze was utterly still, watching and reading me. I always found it hard to lie to her.

'Of course, my lady,' I said, bowing deep as a courtier. I had taken great care with my appearance that day, removing all the soot and muck of my labours so that I appeared clean.

She turned away at last, releasing me. I thought I could detect the eyes of the monks on my back as I went, wondering what to make of my sudden rise in status. I'm afraid I preened a little at the thought of their jealousy. I should have been more wary of it.

Despite the loss of old Keats, Lady Elflaed stayed longer with us than she had intended. In the mornings, she would write letters and send them away, but she always sought me out for some part of the day. She played with the forge cat while I worked iron or wood; she prayed each evening with me, at Wulfric's side. As the sun set, she sometimes stroked her hand over his brow, as a mother might have done. Her own sons were grown and in households of their own. Still, I was touched that she would do such a thing.

The abbey settled back into its routines and if I noticed that Alice was more and more often in my sight as I went about my labours, I paid her no attention, not even when she appeared to have been crying. I had my own plans laid and a great lady of the court to bring them about. It was a happy time, I remember, filled with excitement and the prospect of leaving that damp island and seeing the world. There have been moments in my life when I truly believe I have been touched by God, despite my best efforts. Though I may be unworthy, he does love a sinner and always has. Jesus himself said that God rejoices more in a lost sheep returned than all the happy, bleating flock who never saw the open gate at all.

I was his lost sheep then – and he watched for me.

Wulfric woke while I was cleaning him with a wet cloth. I had his arm draped limply over my shoulder and I was rubbing hard at sweat and grime when I saw his eyes were open and watching me. I gave a great cry, staggering backwards and knocking over a table full of pans, so that a crash went on and on as I stared and thought my heart would burst from my ribs.

Aphra entered the room first, though Encarius was not far behind. They came to a halt in dawning wonder when they saw Wulfric turn his head to see them.

'Wulfric, I am . . .' I tried to speak and the strain of the months was released in me, so that I sobbed and could not make myself understood. He lived and he was awake.

'I am starving,' he said, then I saw his eyes widen as he tried to push himself up. I saw his stump move, but he only slumped back. 'Where is my arm, Dun?'

'It was crushed,' Encarius said, seeing I was overcome. 'We had to cut, or you would not have survived. We thought even then that you would not recover. It has been months, boy, since you were last awake.'

'My arm!' he said, reaching across and holding the stump with his other hand. He was pitiful in his confusion.

Encarius resumed his usual stern manner, putting aside the shock and wonder of seeing Wulfric pull back from the brink of death.

'Aphra, please fetch the boy something more nourishing than broth. He will need fowl and fish, with marsh samphire to continue his recovery. Yes, I will send one of the boys to collect a bushel of it! I will myself prepare a list of foodstuffs for you, all to enrich the blood. My goodness, this is a triumph! Abbot Simeon must be told. Dunstan, you have played your part in this.'

Perhaps Wulfric had done some of his healing in the months he was asleep, I do not know. Once he was awake, it seemed he grew stronger each hour.

We asked Wulfric what he remembered from the night of his injury, but it was fruitless. Not only had he no memory of being hurt, he seemed to have lost days before as well. He had no recollection of the tower and little even of the previous Christmas. I wondered then if the blow to his head could have taken some memories, which was a strange thought.

He was slower of speech, though he did not slur or speak as a child. He just took a moment to think before he answered back. It broke my heart to see him do it, so that I wondered if he would ever again be the quick and laughing young man I had known. It was hard enough for him to lose his right arm and have to relearn eating and getting dressed and writing with his left. I saw his determination, but I also heard him weeping and cursing when he thought he was alone.

Alice was a help to him. Just by waking, he had won her back from me, though I could not resent him for it. I knew my life was about to change, the moment Lady Elflaed realised I could replace old Keats and return with her to the king's court. Wulfric had been the last thread holding me at the abbey, keeping me back. Now that he had woken and was recovering, I knew I could leave him, that I could leave them all like a chrysalis, dead and flaking on the branch. I waited for Elflaed to ask, and I bit my tongue whenever I thought of prompting. It had to come from her thought, her lips. My bright future rested on it.

The end of the month approached and news spread amongst the monks and boys that the king's niece was leaving us at last. She would return to London or to Winchester, wherever King Æthelstan lay his head. More than one of the monks wanted to know if I was going with her and looked surprised when I said I did not know. If it was so clear to them, I was certain she would alight on it.

On the last day, she came to my room, where I lay reading speeches by Cato the Elder. Every one ended with the words 'Carthaginem esse delendam' – Carthage must be destroyed! It did not matter if he spoke about slavery or the drains, he could not resist that final barb on his favourite subject. I liked the man's determination – and in the end, Rome destroyed Carthage so completely that even the ruins are lost.

I leaped from my cot as she appeared, bowing deeply as

Elflaed stared around at our little dormitory. I could see she was fascinated at the cramped space where we slept.

'Dunstan, I have come to pray that God watches over you . . . to urge you to complete your work here. I only wish . . . no.' To my surprise, she touched a cloth to the corner of one eye. 'It has been a great honour to have met you and I will speak well of you when I see the king.'

She seemed in earnest, and I did not like it at all. I waited for her to ask me to go with her, but she only rattled on, oblivious.

'You were so kind to me when I was in grief at the loss of poor Keats. Perhaps in a few years, you will honour me with a visit to the court. I would be proud to be your host, the man who was carried in wings.'

I blinked at her. I was being left behind. I had packed a bag! Wulfric was walking about in the infirmary, stretching his stick legs a little further each day! I had been so sure she would ask me, my mind leaped to horrible suspicions. Someone had reached those pink ears with jealous whispers. I wondered if it had been Caspar, or Abbot Simeon. The abbot saw me as a lure for Glastonbury, bringing pilgrims and their coins. Caspar only liked to see me suffer, so that if I wanted something, he would work to deny it to me.

'My lady, I have thought long and hard on the visions I have been granted, of a great abbey rising in this place.'

'Yes! Oh, yes, Dunstan. You could be the one to build it!'

'My lady, it would take more years than one life if I use these hands. I believe my path lies away from here. I have sensed it. One man alone cannot build my visions, my lady. I must find the path, even if it takes me from my beloved forge and my offices here, even if it takes me from Wulfric and my dearest friends. God's work will not be denied.'

I looked at her, willing it, staring into her eyes as if I had lost a penny in them.

'Oh, Dunstan, Father Simeon told me you would not be happy if I asked you to leave. When I asked for his counsel on the matter, he said you had taken the abbey as a bride and that you would wither away from this place.'

The cunning bastard, I thought. For my own good, she would leave me behind. I nodded as if agreeing, though I seethed.

'That was true once, my lady, before the great visions came. Now I know I am drawn away to other paths. Glastonbury is my home – and always will be – but I must leave, as a boy leaves home to become a man. I will return to build the dream I knew, with God's help I will.'

She brought her hands together in delight, almost in prayer.

'And mine, Dunstan! With my help as well! Oh, I am so relieved to hear it. I was sick at heart when I thought I had to leave you behind. Will the abbot not be angry with you?'

'I am not ordained, my lady, nor yet one of his monks, though I sense that path lies ahead of me. He will lose a poor pupil, but perhaps gain more when I return.' I thought for a moment, considering how the abbot and Brother Caspar actually might react. 'Perhaps, though, you should wait a mile down the road when you leave tomorrow. I will come to you.'

She clasped my hands in hers and kissed them, then pressed them to her cheek. I liked Elflaed, I really did. When she left my dormitory, it was with tears of happiness shining in her eyes. I put down my Roman speeches and lay for a while in thought. After a time, I stood up and went to the infirmary. If that evening was to be my last in Glastonbury, I would not leave Wulfric to the wolves.

10

Deep in the night, I was shaken awake, by Brother Caspar of all people. A lit candle rested on the shelf over me, where Caspar had placed it. The monk was red-faced and his hair stood up wild around his tonsure, like a halo. I blinked up at him, confused and a little afraid.

'Is it Wulfric? Is my brother all right?' I asked, fearing the answer.

'What? How should I know that? The abbot's son is dead, boy! Godwin!'

Though he had his fist entangled in my sleeping shift, I came upright, my mind sharpening.

'I thought he looked feverish,' I said. 'You have examined him?'

Caspar just looked at me, his eyes narrow as he weighed my responses. I knew he was searching for guilt, and so I frowned at him, showing a trace of anger at being ignored. I knew too that I could not acknowledge his suspicions. An innocent man would not guess himself accused. I showed him nothing.

'We must not delay here, Brother Caspar. Thank you for coming to wake me.'

He had come to point a finger, but he was not sure. He kept silent as I went on.

'Encarius will want me to assist him, of course. Abbot Simeon must be distraught. He will need to be dosed and made to rest, I have no doubt.'

Brother Caspar's colour began to fade, though he chewed one part of his lower lip and still watched, as if he thought I might yet give up my charade and run mad. I could see he was full of doubt, but the truth was that death was never too far away. We saw rather less of it at the abbey than in the villages and towns. Yet even in our small community, any one of us could take a chill, or eat and drink too much and never wake again.

'Brother Caspar?' I prompted, when he continued to say nothing. 'Should I go to the infirmary, or is poor Godwin still in his room?' I spoke gently, as if to one bemused by grief, or as we speak to the very old. 'Brother Caspar? Is Encarius with him?'

'He is,' the man replied at last, strangled. 'The whole abbey is awake now. I don't know how you could still have been asleep.'

I heard the other boys and young men rising from their beds around us as he spoke, listening to every word. Yet Caspar could make no accusation. All he had were his suspicions – and they were not enough. Caspar's dislike was all too well known, and no one would believe him if he wailed it to the heavens. I tried not to smile at the thought as I gathered my wrap of tools and belted it on. My last morning in the abbey would be a strain, I was certain. Yet I would shake its dust from my sandals before the sun went down.

They had taken poor Godwin to the infirmary, as Caspar finally admitted. I found that place almost as crowded as it had been for Wulfric's amputation. I resolved then that if I ever did get the chance to rebuild the abbey, I would include more beds for those taken ill, or the dying. The world is harsh enough when we are well. It does not have to be cruel as we pass from it.

As Wulfric had been before, Godwin lay stripped, with only a brief cloth over his groin to protect him from the vulgar gaze. Yet the chest did not rise and fall, and there was no pulse beating time at the throat and wrists. More tellingly,

Godwin was a yellow gold – not dark and rich like bird's-foot or daffodils, but delicate, as are the flowers of a bladder-seed. There was no mark on him and yet there was no sense of him being asleep. His colour was simply that of death. Once seen, it is not forgotten.

I was surprised to feel tears prickle my eyes. Was he not mine enemy? My yoke and my trial? He was all those things, and yet there is something pitiful in seeing a young man's life snuffed out.

As I entered, Encarius looked up and gestured me closer. The crowd of boys and men parted. I kept my gaze on the corpse and my expression stern. I remembered the age Encarius had taken to peer into every fold and crevice of old Father Keats and I swallowed at the prospect of a repeat performance. The herbalist was thorough, I had to admit. The Church had forbidden the opening of bodies after death, but he could still prod and lift and observe. He would be disappointed. Sometimes, death just comes.

I took a deep breath of clean air and nodded to Encarius, running my eye over the tools he had laid out.

Before I could do more, a great wail went up, a sound to make any man wince. It was Abbot Simeon, who had lost his only son. I watched as he rushed to the body and pressed a hand to the cold face. I could not help thinking how poor a father he had been. Godwin had grown like a weed, untended. Perhaps if he had been pruned back once or twice, he would not have found an ending on that table.

Behind the abbot, I saw Lady Elflaed enter and cover her mouth in shock before her view was firmly blocked and she was ushered out. Some things are not for gentle eyes, and it was only her curiosity and the distraction of the monks that had given her the chance to peer in at all. I've never been surprised that it was Eve who picked the apple. Women are worse than cats, I swear.

To my dismay, Abbot Simeon refused to leave. Instead, he allowed them to find him a chair and sat staring as Encarius and I did worse work than we would have done without him there. It is hard to be thorough when you have to consider how a grieving father might react a few feet away. Forcing a little dribble of urine to judge and record its colour was hard on us all.

Despite that tearful gaze, we did our best. Encarius found no mark or bruise to explain the sudden death of a strong young man. When I was asked, I said again how I'd thought Godwin had looked feverish over the previous few days, but had thought nothing of it. No one else had reported any sign of illness and Godwin had asked for neither balm nor tonic. In the end, Encarius sighed, stepping back. God gives and God takes away.

Some of the senior men left with Abbot Simeon, perhaps to broach a cask of wine or some harder spirit. Encarius stood outside with his head upturned to the sky and his eyes shut, wiping his hands on a cloth. He had not been asked to accompany them, perhaps because of what they had watched him do. He and I shared a glance.

'I know he was no friend of yours, Dunstan, but perhaps now you will see how petty it all was. We are given such a brief time here, before eternity, to make all our choices. If he had lived, I don't doubt you would have become friends.'

'I would have liked that,' I said.

It sounded like the lie it was, but he accepted I was trying to be kind. There was no one else around and he leaned closer to me.

'Have you considered leaving with Lady Elflaed? I heard she asked for you.'

I grew very still, my suspicions flaring. I had come to admire Encarius for his skills and knowledge – and he had shown me kindness at times. I understood that was not enough, that I could not trust him. Friendship has always been a rare seam for me. I have been surprised by it once or twice, yet one thing is always true: when you are surrounded by enemies, the least cruel of them is not your friend.

'I have prayed for guidance in the matter, for a sign to show me if I should stay here and be ordained, or walk a path to the court.'

'I see. Well, you are a young man, so I imagine the idea of the court calls bright and strong in your thoughts. I don't suppose my advice matters, Dunstan, but I will say it's all fool's gold in the end. Very little is important, in this world. Not success, not wealth, not power.'

He had none of those things, so I imagine his words were a comfort to him. He lowered his eyebrows at me and gripped my arm in his hand. 'Not love, certainly, though some would have it so.'

I had also met his wife, so I nodded at that as he went on.

'Not a belly full of food and ale either – why, the sparrows and the crows eat well enough! No – not the work of the forge, nor all the crafts a clever man can win for himself. All that matters, Dunstan, all – is your soul. You have a few years in this poor place, then you are judged for how you spent them – and consigned, either to God's presence or eternal agonies.'

'Is there no mercy, then?' I said, uncomfortably.

'You may hope for it, or pray for it. Dunstan, you may not depend on it.'

'Thank you, father. I will think on what you have said.'

He patted my shoulder and seemed pleased. He'd have gone to the king's court if Elflaed had asked him. A choice is harder when there actually is one. Encarius would choose to stay, honest and uncorrupted, because no one had called him away.

Encarius and I walked together to the chapel and sat side

by side as we spoke and sang through the responses. I considered whether I should stay for the funeral. It would depend on my new patron, of course. If Lady Elflaed stayed, I would have little choice.

Wulfric came to talk to me when the service ended. He and I could exchange much in a single glance and I knew he was pleased at Godwin's fate, though he would not dare to whisper it in that place, where there were always ears to hear and condemn.

'Is it true what they say, Dun? Are you leaving us? James was saying he'd overheard the abbot and Caspar.'

'He should not creep about and listen to what does not concern him, should he?' I said. Honestly, it was difficult to keep a secret in that place. Monks are worse than nuns for their gossiping, especially those who whisper to their wives at night.

'I am praying for guidance,' I said once more.

'You should go,' he said, surprising me. 'Now that I am healed.'

I could not help glancing at his arm, or rather where it had been. He smiled and covered the stump with his other hand to shield it from my gaze. We had shaped a leather cup for it that hung from a strap about his neck and had moulded itself in sweat and oil until it was almost a part of him. He hid it, even so, from me.

'I am as healed as I will ever be, I meant,' he went on. To my dismay, he rapped his knuckles against the scars on his forehead, making me wince. 'See, Dun? No pain. I know what I owe you and Encarius. I cannot pay it back, it is too great a debt for one life. You will be rewarded in heaven, though.'

I tutted at that, thinking it a little convenient.

'What matters is that you are alive.'

I looked more critically at him, past the ridge of scar that slipped beneath his hair, or the missing arm. He was four-teen years old and looked about as healthy as a young hound. I smiled at him.

'Mother will expect you to visit her this Christmas,' I said. 'Will you stay on and join the order?'

I said it because he could hardly work the fields or do a dozen trades with one arm. It seemed to me that whatever Wulfric had wanted for himself, the life of a monastery had chosen him. To my surprise, he blushed and looked away.

'I have exchanged letters with our mother, Dunstan. She has a part share in a business in London, selling woollen coats and fine linen. I can run it for her with one arm, well enough.'

'You haven't asked me what I feel about that,' I said, show-ing him my hurt. He would not meet my eyes and stared across my shoulder.

'You have been concerned with other things, Dun. Like the lady Elflaed. And you saved my life. You shouldn't have to worry about me any longer. I can find my own way.'

'Alice will miss you,' I said, wanting to prick the happy lit-tle bladder, so full of plans. To my surprise he went a deeper shade of red.

'I have asked Aphra for her, Dun. She'll go with me in the summer, when I turn fifteen.'

'You've been busy then, all of you,' I said. 'Whispering away like mice in the corners, bowing your heads together and making your plans. Have you any idea what I have done for you, Wulfric? The lengths I went to for you?' He looked at me and I thought, yes, he does know. Yet in my youth and pride, I could not stand down from the high step I'd chosen.

'Go on then, to the devil with you all,' I said, making his eyes widen. 'Go with Alice and Mother and your small ambi-tions. I will see the royal court and the king. I will see London, Wulfric.'

'And I wish you joy of it, Dunstan. You have protected me and saved my life. I owe you everything, I know it. Let me get myself settled in the city and I will write to you, wherever you are.'

His decency and earnest appeal were irritating. I could not trust myself to speak again, so I left him there, calling after me. I yawned as I went and passed a gaggle of the lady's servants, all staggering under armfuls. It seemed Elflaed could have put an army in the field with all the goods and chattels she had brought to that place.

I was perhaps a little upset by Wulfric's happiness. I had often imagined Alice weeping as I left for the royal court, understanding at last that she had chosen the wrong brother. I had not considered her skipping off with Wulfric, hardly looking back. That did not please me, at all.

I lay down on my bed with my bag under my head to think it through. The lady's servants were still piling her bags to be carried down to the dock. I had time to rest. I was sweating and as thick with weariness as if I had drunk one of my own numbing liquors. I closed my eyes.

I came awake to find half a dozen people gathered around me. Encarius was prominent among them and I blinked at him in complete confusion, seeing his nostrils had gone white and pink in rage. Caspar took hold of me as I stared around, unsure even what day it was or if I had woken before. In my confusion, I truly thought I was dreaming or enduring some vision. It took a blow that made my ears ring to know I was awake and that they were trussing me.

I struggled mightily then, just as I imagine Joseph of Canaan did when his brothers came for him. I roared and demanded to know what they were about, why they were attacking me. Abbot Simeon leaned in when I was well bound and could not get at him. He raised his hand like an old woman, scraping at me with his nails, in a fine, screeching froth. I strained away from him, yelling murder until they muffled me with some rag, wound around my mouth. Unable to cry aloud, I merely waited, going limp.

Encarius reached into a bag that hung from his belt, pulling out the forge cat in one hand. It hung dead, and yet he trembled as if with great emotion or an ague. I goggled at it, showing them blank astonishment even as my stomach fell away within me.

'I found this on the midden pile,' Encarius said, shaking his head in foolish grief. 'Where you threw him.'

I tried to spit out the rag, but it was too tight. I made what sounds I could while they discussed my right to speak. It was Encarius who finally pulled my gag away. I spluttered at him, dry-mouthed.

'You have bound me for a dead cat?' I said.

'You were the one who threw it on the midden. You were seen.'

'What if I did? Cats die all the time!'

Encarius grimaced at me, smiling and sad at the same time.

'You dosed it, Dunstan. To test whatever gruel you made for Godwin. What was it, aconite? Death cap?'

You may be sure I gaped at him.

'That is a lie! How dare you accuse me! I have been touched by angels.'

'No more, Dunstan,' Encarius said. 'You are the illness in the wound. And we have agreed to cut you out.'

He nodded to the others. Though I continued to struggle and wail and plead and bargain, they pulled the gag back over my jaw and put a sack over my head. One of the cowards struck me then with a club, half-dazing me. The sun was high and I thought of Lady Elflaed waiting impatiently for me on the road. I've no doubt they watched for her to leave before they went after her favourite.

She would think I had changed my mind, and the tragedy was that some part of her would be pleased. She would know my labours were devoted to God and the abbey instead of her uncle's court. She would consider it a righteous decision. As I had the thought, they hit me again and stole my wits away.

I woke when they threw water over me, then dragged me to the edge of a cliff, so that I could hear small stones skipping and sliding down beneath my feet. Master Gregory of the workshop was one of those who lowered me until I could take a grip on the crumbling edge with my hands. I found some purchase and pleaded with him, but he only pursed his lips and muttered, 'I'm sorry, lad.' It was Encarius, of course, who had poisoned them all against me.

Master Gregory sawed the bit of rope they'd put around my wrists, leaving me hanging on my own weight, with my forearms stretched across in front of me. He plucked the gag from me and I worked dry lips.

I hardly dared look down and swallowed uncomfortably when I did. They had brought me two miles in my stunned state, to a ridge I knew well. Visible from the highest point of the Tor, it was all stone and green, where only sheep roamed. Even so, with the cold wind howling there, I could not believe my brothers of the abbey would let me break my neck.

Aphra was present, looking grim and hard-set, with some of the wives and servants in a disapproving group around her. I looked for Wulfric and was pleased they had not made him a part of it, at least. None of the boys were present, which was a relief and showed me those who were felt some guilt at what they were doing. One or two of the masters were missing as well, I noticed – Florian was not there, for example, nor Father John of the gardens. Perhaps they were teaching the boys while the rest carried me up to that place. Still, there must have been thirty men and women there to see me killed – and not a thread of proof between them, beyond a dead cat. If I would have called any one of them my friend, it would have been Encarius – and he had been the one to find it and bring the creature into the light to destroy me.

I looked at them all, just standing and watching with the sun high in the sky, waiting for the pull of the earth to put an end to my terrible sins along with my life. You never saw such cruelty as I witnessed on those closed, blank faces. Not one of them was fit to carry my tools, and yet there they were, sitting in judgement on me, without trial. I have known hate since, but, by God, I learned it then.

I could have hung there all day, making my claims in good style, my appeals in dignity. Their response was to send Master Gregory forward once more. He crouched over me and I looked up at him in hope, until he took a mallet to my hands and broke my fingers.

Still I hung on. Tears streamed from my eyes and they murmured at that, seeing guilt, where it was just agony and rage. I gave up hope and the chance that they would relent. I knew then that I would fall, I would truly fall. It was then that I called Encarius to hear my last confession.

He could not resist that and he knelt by me, scratching a cross in spit and mud on my forehead.

'Will you pray with me, father?' I said.

He nodded, his eyes large with grief and accusation.

'I know you killed him, Dunstan. Perhaps Father Keats as well. The cat is the proof I need. And . . . I saw you untie the weight on the tower scaffold. You were not carried down by an angel.'

'I would like to confess,' I whispered. He leaned closer to hear. 'I had carnal thoughts about a woman.'

'It is common enough, Dunstan, but your mortal sins! Will you go to judgement with them? You will burn if you do.'

I began to weep and mumble. He leaned right down, so that his ear was close to my lips. I heard his wife call out behind, but he was intent on my confession. I took hold of his robe then, with my broken hands.

'Come with me and see,' I said, and pulled us both off the edge, into the gaping air.

It is strange to think my desire for blood and vengeance saved my life. It seems a man can fall a long, long way and live, if he lands on a priest.

11

We fell shrieking, tumbling together in the wind with eyes streaming tears. It was an experience almost of madness until we crashed through branches and struck the hard ground. It had not been my intention to land on Encarius, but that is the way it came about. Entangled, we spun through a green canopy. I believe my shoulder and hip drove the life from him as much as the stones below.

I would like to say that life fled him in an instant. The truth is that I rolled off and ground my teeth in agony for a time, lost in my own distress. When bones are broken, our desire is to huddle around them, to protect the wounded part, not fall from a tower's height to the unforgiving earth. I hurt and yet I was filled with delight too. I laughed and laughed until I thought I would die for lack of air. They had broken my hands and sat in judgement on me. Yet I lived, despite them all.

I turned my head, in part to be sure I still could. And I saw Encarius watching me, his face like chalk. Even as I blinked at him in the silence of the forest floor, he coughed blood that ran down his cheek. He blinked and trembled. Death was there with us, in that glade. I could feel a cold wind blowing.

'I am sorry,' I said, though I was not. I began to laugh again, in relief, until I was sobbing. It was a weak moment and I felt the sting of shame. When I looked up, it was to find Encarius still watching me. I raised my eyes to heaven.

'Did you know Godwin was the one who hurt Wulfric? I think you did. Yet I saw no accusers coming for *him*! No monks gathered around Godwin's bed! That was murder, though, what he did. Only you and I made it less. We saved Wulfric, not luck or fate . . . or God. No, not you, even. These hands. These hands alone!'

I held up one broken paw to him, swollen and purpled to an extraordinary degree. I winced and put it down again.

Encarius still breathed, though blood bubbled out of him. I was unable to meet that gaze.

I was dazed from the fall, from fear and injury and exhaustion. I may have been feverish as well. I know I babbled for a time, weeping and sobbing and telling him all my sins in a great rush.

It was a while before I truly understood Encarius was dead, that he had been dead for some time. As I struggled up to my elbows, I saw his head was at a strange angle. Though his eyes were open, he did not see. My whirling thoughts settled and sharpened, so that I was myself again. I knew he was gone, but I spoke to him once more, even so. Perhaps because his spirit would hear, or perhaps just because I understood in that glade at the foot of great oaks that I was alone.

'Godwin made his own fate, father, just as a man chooses to walk to war, to face other men. Godwin chose to face me, when he hurt Wulfric unto death. Now he is gone – and I am here, broken and cast out, because I sought justice.'

My anger made my thoughts move a little faster. Would those above be scrambling down an easier trail to see where we lay? I did not want to be there when they did.

I cried out as I sat up, every muscle torn.

Around us, I frowned as I saw old, yellowed bones. It gave me a start for a moment, when my eyes first traced the shapes. I recognised the skulls and ribs of dogs in the dead leaves. They lay scattered all about on the forest floor, no doubt tugged to and fro by hungry animals when they came across them. They were all stripped bare, and I realised this was a place where dog bodies were thrown when they died. No doubt some local farmer heaved them down, his hunting hounds. I'd seen my father take a favourite dog in his arms to the edge of a steep hill near our farm, coming back alone. He was a sentimental man, in some ways.

It took me an age to stand, without working hands to help me. I heaved and inched myself up a smooth beech trunk until I stood panting, wet with sweat. They would climb down, I was suddenly certain. Encarius' wife would insist on it. They'd find him alone and they would be afraid. That was a thought to bring a little joy in all my misery and pain.

I was filthy with mud, sweat, blood, leaves and scratches. I had taken such a battering I could not stand tall, but had to shuffle and drag, with one eye stinging hard enough to keep closed. I did not dare to touch it with my swollen hands, so tears streamed from it and the pain drove me almost to weeping. Yet I moved. I would not let them take me like a child. I looked back one last time to Encarius and I said a Pater Noster for his soul. He could not say Amen as I limped away through the trees, heading east with the setting sun on my back.

I wept when I saw the carriage was still on the road, waiting for me. Her servants were ahorse, their heads bowed in boredom. They reached for swords and knives as they heard me coming, then stared at the bedraggled figure that came out of the bushes like Jonah from the belly of the whale. I heard Lady Elflaed's voice murmur an order and one of her serving women tied back the awning.

'Dunstan! My poor boy. What has happened to you?'

'My lady, there were some who did not want me to leave. Yet I escaped them and came to you. God bless you for waiting so long. I do not know what I would have done if you had been gone . . .' To my horror, I burst into tears. I was not yet sixteen and it had been a difficult day.

She gathered me in, exclaiming at the state of my poor, mangled hands. She set her jaw and gave new orders to her people all about us. The whip snapped over the heads of her horses and the whole party moved off smartly.

'You have been sore used, Dunstan. I know I am responsible for it, for trying to take you from your home, all for my own selfishness.' I blinked a little at that, thinking how oddly the minds of women can work. 'I will make this right, Dunstan. I will ask my uncle to send hard men into that place, to bring the king's justice . . .'

'My lady, no, please!' I said, filled with dismay at the thought. 'I will return to Glastonbury when I am ready to raise a greater abbey. Until then, I will forgive those who hurt me. They know not what they do.'

Her eyes filled with tears at my bravery. As well they might have done. She nodded and cradled me to her bosom. What with my exertions, my hands and the warm rocking of the coach, I fell asleep not long after that and remember no more.

PART TWO

Behold the Man
AD 936

'When I was a child, I spake as a child, I understood as a child, I thought as a child: but when I became a man, I put away childish things.'

1 Corinthians 13:11

12

Winchester was a city of wonders. Like London, it had been abandoned for centuries after our Romans pulled back their ships and turned tail for home. You cannot have an empire when your house is on fire. That is the lesson there.

Other towns and cities were still overgrown, mere ruins of what they once had been. Not there, though, in Æthelstan's capital. Fine walls protected stone streets, with buildings of three or four storeys shouting wealth and power better than any king's herald ever could. The old place had been crumbling and worn out when King Alfred took it up. His men had rebuilt the towers and the gates. His people had revived the baths and the old Roman town. Truly, he was a great king – and Æthelstan was his grandson. We knew giants then, before the wine soured.

When my lady Elflaed and I passed through the huge north gate, it was to discover the king was not in the city, had in fact gone to London to oversee some problem with the docks on the Thames there. It was Elflaed who stamped her fine-arched foot and had the king's own physician at my bedside for three days, the morning we arrived. My injuries and perhaps my distress had brought on a fit in her carriage. I can only imagine how unpleasant it had been for her, trapped in that small space as I twitched and muttered and showed the whites of my eyes. I am lucky the dear lady did not tip me out onto the cobbles. Yet I think I grew in her affections more because I was lost and needed help than because of anything else I ever did. In that way, my enemies at the abbey had brought me good fortune. From that time on, Lady Elflaed was my most ardent supporter.

On the fourth day, messengers came riding through the streets crying that the king was coming home. Elflaed was flushed with excitement as she and her servants made ready for an audience.

Still somewhat feverish, with my fingers splinted and wrapped in clean strips of cloth, I was sent tottering out into the sun as if I held white mice in my hands. There are certain difficulties to losing the use of one's fingers, some vital and some merely irritating. Like a child, I had been dressed in an itchy new shirt and belt, with fine woollen trews and soft boots. I'd argued for the black habit I'd worn before. I've always thought the colour carried a certain authority all on its own. I resolved to find one, but I was still too weak and ill when the king returned from London and his capital came alive.

Æthelstan brought hundreds of men and women with him wherever he went: counsellors and reeves, judges and scribes. The ealdormen of his roving court sealed his laws for him; hunted, flogged and fought for him; even executed in his name. The king lived at the centre of a feast in those days.

I went to the great hall in Winchester, surrounded and protected as I walked by a dozen solemn servants from Elflaed's household. Free men and thralls alike paused in their labours to see what grand person might command such a crew. I felt their scorn, but I looked ahead, to the royal estate walls and the buildings they enclosed, rising above the rest of the city. I was pleased I had seen an abbey before. If I had not, I might have been overwhelmed.

Elflaed had gone ahead to whisper in the right ears and prepare them for me. It gives me grief to remember this. My first entrance to court was a disaster.

It did not help that I was sweating as if I'd run all the way from Glastonbury. Master Gregory had thought no more of hammering my fingers than he would have of plucking a bird for his dinner. He'd gone about it with the skill and thoroughness he brought to all his tasks. As a result, it was almost impossible for me not to jar the splinted bones every other moment.

It was another mark on the list. In some ways, it was almost calming to discover I had only one aim then, one purpose – to gather whatever influence I needed to return to Glastonbury with power over my enemies. While I stood and reeked of sweat in a line of men and women waiting to glimpse the high king, I resolved to work harder than I ever had to achieve that simple aim. I would go back. I would tear that place down, brick from mortared brick. The abbey would be my Carthage; I would sow its fields with salt.

The thought was cheering, though I felt lost in the murmuring swell of that crowd. I passed into the royal hall and saw King Æthelstan for the first time.

He stood on a raised dais, slightly to the side as I entered and looked up to him. I confess my first reaction was disappointment. He did not wear the spiked crown I'd heard described at his coronation, but a simpler band of iron, set with red stones. He was blond-bearded and wore his hair long and loose, so that it made him look like the great cats I have seen in tapestry. Yet he was shorter than I had expected. For a man who summoned princes and kings to kneel to him, I had thought to see a giant.

The man at his shoulder was more the sort I had imagined. Egill Skiallgrimmson was his champion then, a berserker from lands of ice, far in the north. He too was blond, though his hair was almost white in comparison. I had seen fighting men before and remembered a boxing match of ninety rounds that my father took me to Bath to watch. Yet even those men did not have a skull like Egill. It looked to be a bone of the ancients, of giants in the old tales. It sat atop a body built along the lines of a carthorse. Egill was not a man you ever wished to face on the field of battle. He stood less than two yards tall, but a warrior is more than mere height. The short-handled mace Egill carried was one of the reasons Æthelstan had a peaceful reign. Not a single one of the small kings who knelt to him wanted to put his rule to challenge. Not that day, at least. No, the challenge would come the following spring.

As I approached the king's dais, Æthelstan's senior men were listening to the concerns of those coming in, one by one, either passing them along the line to some factor or scribe, refusing a plea entirely, or, much more rarely, turning to the king himself to rule on a petition. Æthelstan stood by a finely carved chair, with his earls and his champion and perhaps a hundred others in attendance on him. They wore an array of bright colours and the mood was light as they talked and laughed together. I was caught up in the wonder of it all, as if I approached a bench of seraphim and could only marvel at their glories. I saw my sponsor Elflaed on the dais, one of the few women among them. She smiled to me as I wound my way through to the front, patient and calm.

The man ahead was some farmer who had refused a dowry to his daughter, though the marriage had gone ahead even so. He'd delayed the payment for so long, it seemed the girl's new husband had brought a petition to the king against him. There was a council for such things, of course, the Witan, where judgements could be discussed and set down in ink. Yet some men had no trust in earls and thanes. They preferred to seek a ruling from the king himself. It was a dangerous choice, though I understood it.

Men are all the same, in their desire to follow. It is too simple a description, but men are either kings or slaves. Some slaves are kings and some kings, slaves, but that is because the world is corrupt and in ruins, no matter how high we build. Women, of course, are all slaves. I would not say this to one, obviously, not if peace were my aim.

I could smell horses coming off the farmer as he made his argument. In his passion, he flung out one of his arms and struck me with it, standing behind him. The blow twisted my fingers cruelly and I shrieked, rather higher and longer than I would have liked.

The entire hall fell silent in surprise. I was a few months shy of sixteen and I had screamed like a woman in front of every lord, lady and bishop in that place. I wanted to vanish from sight but I could not. The shit-farmer apologised, but laughter still crashed over us at the sight of my bandaged hands and red, sweating face. I saw the king grinning and saying something to his niece. In her turn, Elflaed covered her face with a palm. I knew her too well to think she would be laughing, but I had caused her great embarrassment.

'Your Highness, my lords and ladies,' I said, though I don't suppose anyone heard me. I bowed as deeply as I could. The farmer shouted something in my ear, but he was guided away down the line of scribes. He tried to protest, but the king's men were used to that and he only moved faster out of my sight.

I was left facing the king.

'My niece tells me you are the child of Glastonbury, carried in wings. She commends you to me,' he said. His voice had kingship in it, as his stature did not. It reminded me of my father and I found myself dropping to one knee.

'I am honoured, Your Grace,' I murmured, still feeling the heat in my cheeks.

'I see you are injured. It would be unseemly to make mock of you just for that.'

Across the hall, smiles vanished at his words, which interested me. Even the enormous Egill stopped showing his big teeth. It seemed Æthelstan really did rule in that place. He was my first sight of a king, and I thought they were a different breed of men, a thread of gold above the rest of us. How I wish that were true.

'Thank you, my lord,' I said.

To my surprise, I felt a strong grip on my shoulder and I too was borne away down the line. There was no question of my struggling, you may be sure. I passed the hapless farmer, counting out coins to be weighed, then found myself facing a scribe in brown wool, whose nose dripped.

'Name?'

'Dunstan, son of Heorstan,' I said, still unsure what I was meant to be doing.

'Nephew of Archbishop Athelm,' said a voice behind me.

I turned to see a man who looked enough like my father to give me a moment of panic before I understood. I did not know him as kin, but he claimed me in that place.

Uncle Athelm had my father's height, though he was no man of arms. He carried weight around his waist, like a woman heavy with child. It gave him a sense of huge bulk as he beamed at me, resting clean, pink fingers over that enormous mass. I was just pleased to meet one of my own blood. I opened my mouth to greet him formally and Athelm clapped me on the shoulder, sending a spike of pain running up from my broken right hand.

'You are truly hurt? What happened to your hands?'

'It was . . . an accident in the forge, that is all. They will heal soon enough, but it was only a few days ago.'

'The forge? Well, you'll love the royal smithies here. There are things made . . . well, you'll see. I have heard all about you, lad, from my poor brother and of course your mother, but also Lady Elflaed. She sought me out, to demand my support of you. As if I would not have come.'

I was armoured against weakness by my earlier humiliation. I think he sensed that coldness in me, so that he reached out and patted my cheek.

'I know you've had a hard time of it. Your father, your brother's injury, the death of your friend. This has been a dark year or two for you, but it is in the past. We'll find a place for my own nephew in the royal court, I imagine. If half the things I'm told are true, we'll make you the king's right hand in a year.'

I smiled at him and rubbed furiously at the tears in my eyes. I certainly did not correct him about Godwin having been my friend. Still, I found myself shaking my head.

'After what just occurred, Uncle? After crying out like a child in front of them all?'

He waved his hand as if it meant nothing. Yet I know even better now what I sensed then, that King Æthelstan revered warriors in those days. He treasured physical courage above music, above wit, above even piety and holiness. I had damned myself in his court with that one great shriek – and my uncle knew that as well as anyone. He had put the crown on Æthelstan's head. He had anointed him like a Roman emperor and guided him through hard years.

Archbishop Athelm had no sons of his own and he had adored his older brother. He took me on as a pile of stones and tried to build something out of me. I was in the king's court and I had hands raising me up. So I smiled, though my fingers throbbed in agony and I could smell myself sweating.

'I would like to see those smithies and forges, Uncle, if you don't mind showing me.'

'I would be delighted. This evening, we'll dine at the king's table, but until then, I will be your guide.'

To be shown forges while your hands are splinted is a peculiar strain, almost cruelty. I could see the king's artificers had no belief in me. They thought me the privileged son of some great family, which was not far from the mark. They failed to understand my blood and upbringing were mere candles in the furnace of my ambition. Oh, they were polite enough and stood with their heads bowed in the presence of my uncle. He patted them and chuckled as he spoke, for all the world like a cheerful, red-faced shire reeve presented with a line of local children. They grinned when he told them they were the backbone of the royal household, that without such fine fellows, there would be no iron brackets to hold the lamps, no locks on the doors, no knives or nails to make anything! One of the men twisted his cap to rope in his hands while the bishop spoke, blushing like it was Christmas morning.

I looked sideways at my uncle, seeing no guile in him. Yet a man does not become an archbishop by being a fool. He becomes one when other men of power trust him enough to raise him up.

It was not lost on me that conversations were hushed as Uncle Athelm swept through the royal estate. Harsh words were stilled and great men bowed to a prince of the Church. I watched and I learned.

Those first weeks fled in frustration from me. I could neither write nor gild, nor work at almost anything. I walked the circumference of the city walls, climbing down to trot along the banks of the Itchen and see the barges, laden with bales and men. The royal city of Wessex teemed then. Ships and tenders carried coal and iron ore – and Winchester grew all around me, from those black stones and that mortar.

For a time, I filled my head with numbers and theorems of mathematics, making plans of all I might do the moment my hands healed. It took an age and my lady Elflaed had to employ one delicate young gentleman named Mannon to help me with the privy. I do not know which of us enjoyed it less, but we bore it and offered up the humiliation, as I had been taught to do.

I had already discovered I liked Winchester. If I was to succeed there, I knew I would have to learn whom to flatter and whom to scorn. It was not difficult to know which path to choose when I met the king's younger brother. Æthelstan bore no children of his own. There will always be some to suggest he had a weak seed, but I do not believe that. He had agreed at the beginning of his reign to favour his father's other sons in return for the crown, and that was all it took. Æthelstan kept his word as if he had cut the letters in iron. I wish I had known him longer, or perhaps just that he hadn't thought of me as a right lily.

I met the king's heir as my uncle was showing me the royal stables. I have never liked horses, so I was merely feigning interest as Athelm swept through row upon row of stalls, all with an overpowering smell of their ordure and sweat.

Those stables were built with columns of gold Wessex stone that would not have looked out of place on a cathedral. Fired brick and flint walls made up the rest, the work of hundreds and no expense spared. Racing tracks had been cut and laid with wood chips, so that at any moment of the day there could be a dozen horses trotting round in the sunshine, mending their wind or being trained for war. It was a town within the city, almost. In some ways, it was the iron heart of Winchester, lit by forge light when the sun set and darkness came.

As I turned a corner in conversation with my uncle, I was almost knocked down by a big rangy fellow striding fast around it. I flinched from a shape in dark leather and wool. I am pleased to say I made no sound or cry of surprise, but I jerked back to protect my poor hands from further insult. Yet the boy moved well. His gaze was steady as he came to a halt, without so much as touching, though he had been moving at a fair gallop.

'My lord Edmund,' Uncle Athelm said warmly, bowing his head.

The young man looked across and dipped one knee as soon as he recognised the archbishop. Athelm chuckled, a rich and throaty sound. He always spoke as if he was finishing a mouthful of milk pudding.

'Please, my lord, dear me, please rise.'

Both of them were smiling as Edmund sprang up, delighting in his youth and strength.

In later years, when Edmund was full-grown, he would be called 'the Just', 'the Deed-doer', by some, 'the Magnificent'. Edmund could have been the great king of the age, more so even than Æthelstan. His story is a hard thing to tell.

When I met him, he was sixteen, with the look of eagles. A rook will chase away a red kite, though the kite has twice its reach and speed. Fighting spirit matters and Edmund had it. He stood tall and lithe, in perfect balance. My fat uncle was an ancient compared to him, but still they chuckled and exchanged pleasantries. The prince had that gift as well – he could talk to anyone. Add to it that he used a blade like a cat uses claws, as if it was part of him, and that he had a great soul. He was born to rule. Why not? Like his brother Æthelstan, Edmund was the grandson of King Alfred, the son of King Edward the Elder. When I think of a king, I always mean him.

'May I present Dunstan, my brother's son,' Athelm said.

I bowed, though I was of a height with Edmund and not sure then who he was.

'What happened to your hands?' Edmund said to me.

I found myself challenged by calm brown eyes, so did not want to lie. Equally, I did not want to be drawn on the events of that cliff edge.

'I tried to make them fireproof,' I said. 'It did not work.'

He blinked at me, caught between delight and suspicion.

'Oh, you did not! That is not true,' Edmund said, though he hoped it was.

'They were bitten off by a wolf,' I said. 'I am growing them back.'

He grinned then, understanding it was a game.

'You sharpened them into claws,' he said.

'I did,' I replied. 'But it made me hungry, so I cut them off and fried them.'

'How did they taste?' he asked.

'I could not pick them up to find out.'

He laughed and his merriment set me off, so that I could no longer keep a straight face. For a few moments, we howled and snorted, delighted by silliness. I doubt it will amuse when written down. It was funny then – and I had met Æthelstan's brother and the heir to the throne. I was never again a face in the crowd to Edmund after that morning.

'Do you ride, Dunstan?' Edmund said, still chuckling.

In answer, I just held up my hands, showing him the wrapped fingers.

'Ah, of course. You prefer puppets,' he said.

Well, I confess that set me off in gales again, Edmund with me, until we were giggling and snorting. I liked him, I really did. He is the great failure of my life, but God forgive me, I was young. I thought we would all live for ever then.

13

In the gleam of lamps, I stood in the shelter of my uncle's arm, a gosling under his wing. The last of the splints had come off that morning and I flexed my hands with a wince.

The Witan council on that frozen night was the first of its kind I had seen. I was in awe of those who'd ridden or sailed to Winchester from all over the country. Great lords of the north were there, taking seats by men of Kent and Essex, of Mercia, of Wessex, all come at Æthelstan's call. They were far too many for the sort of round table old King Arthur had known. In the Witan hall, thanes, reeves, earls and family of the king sat in rows like teeth, all facing inwards to the heart.

Æthelstan remained on his feet to welcome them as they entered. I saw how his servants guided men to particular places around the central aisle. It was more subtle than the old custom of sitting by the king's right hand, but there were some who were left far out, and some seated so close they might have drawn and attacked if they had so chosen. I supposed those were the king's most trusted men and I was pleased to see Edmund among them, sitting with his brother Eadred at the front.

I had seen little to like in Eadred. He was a sickly-looking lad and I did not expect him to live long enough to be of interest to me. I was mistaken, as it happens, but I will tell that in time.

The white-haired Icelander, Egill, sat on the king's left, a position that allowed the man to watch all those close to Æthelstan. The berserker seemed always to be cheerful, but his eyes were very pale and I could never quite tell what thoughts drifted under the ice of them. Needless to say, the king's champion was well armed. All the men wore knives or short-handled axes out of habit. Egill rested some sort of serrated spear on the bench where he sat, as likely to take the eye out of those behind him as anything. No one else wore his weapon as an outright warning. I understood that Egill was Æthelstan's hound, the violence that underpinned the king's orders. I was fascinated and turned back and forth, watching everything.

Æthelstan himself wore a cloak of white over some darker cloth, perhaps in blue. I would not usually trouble to describe a man's choice of colour, but on this evening, I saw the crown of England for the first time. Before Æthelstan, kings had worn battle helmets for hundreds of years. It had been his idea to reach much further back, to the crowns of gilded laurel worn by Caesars. It caught the light in gold spikes, like the rays of the sun. All eyes rested on it and him as the last seats were filled. I smiled to see a piece of forge artifice and craft that defined him as king in that place. My hands had been made weaker for a time, but they itched to work again.

As archbishop of Canterbury, Uncle Athelm had a place reserved for him that actually was on the king's right hand. I had hoped he might bring me forward, in the way a family can present a new child to the court and have him acknowledged. Instead, Athelm patted me on the shoulder. As I stayed on his heels, thinking to accompany him, he stopped and leaned in.

'Find a cushion for yourself, Dunstan, before they are all gone. Pay a small cross penny if you must. I still remember how my backside ached after sitting on cold stone for my first council. The king is in a rare temper and these Witan assemblies can go on for days. Make yourself comfortable.'

I stared, but he was already moving away like a boat leaving the shore. Two of his servants fell in beside him, appearing out of the crowd so that he was flanked and protected from the elbows of others still finding their place.

I was left beyond the lamplight, under the fall of darkness outside. My low rank, my youth and lack of importance were written clearly. I did not exchange a glance with those others who were so far from the centre of power. I cared not for them! Rather than seek out some low spot where I would be able to see nothing, I chose to stand, certain in my youth that I could remain utterly still for hours if needs be.

I spent much of that first session of the king's Witan in careful thought, planning my own future rather than listening. I tell this because there are times when it might seem as if I enjoyed extraordinary fortune, as if the stars had my name written bright amongst them. They did not, or if they did, I never knew it. Instead, I worked hard and I looked ahead, for obstacles and tumbling stones. And I stepped aside before I could be brought down. Those who did not, were crushed.

One or two of those stones were pushed by my hand. When heaven or hell lie before us, what does it matter really when we leave the world? It is all an eye-blink. Perhaps if I denied a man his chance to repent and be forgiven, so that he spent eternity in flames, then yes, he would have the right to curse my name. Beyond that slender balance, though, I have merely hurried some to their eternal reward, just as they deserved. Perhaps they thank me now, and bless my name. If we knew heaven from the first, truly knew what lay ahead, we might ask to be killed as innocent children, to speed our path.

The Witan had been noisy while the last found their seats: two hundred and forty men of influence who knew each other, clattering their boots against the wooden floor and chairs, all talking and laughing. Perhaps another two hundred were crammed around the edges to watch the king's council. There were as many degrees of power in that place as there were souls. Yet they were all subject to the king. As soon as Æthelstan raised his head, every voice dropped to whispers and then to silence to look to him.

'You are all granted safe passage and stand under the seal of the king while you are in this council. Any blood shed during the period of the Witan will mean execution for those I judge to be guilty. My peace will stand, my lords. Your lives are forfeit if it does not. Raise your voices if you must, but not your swords.'

If you could see the first king of England standing there in the light of flames and glass, the hair would stand on the back of your neck as it did for me. He was four years over forty then. Every head bowed in response, as well they might have done, grim as he seemed, with his gaze watching for the smallest sign of dissent. Æthelstan knew very well that some of the men there were kings in all but name. He was the only one standing on the heartstone of Winchester; they looked to the high king as if he were the source of the light.

'You will have noted two empty seats in this hall. Seats close to my right hand. I name those men who are not here: Constantin of Alba in the Highlands. Of all of you, I called him first. He had furthest to come. I gave him time, yet his seat remains empty. I name Owen of Cumbria also. Neither man has answered me.'

Æthelstan bowed his head for a moment, in prayer or mourning. I saw the eyes of all remained on him. I think I was the only one there who looked around the room. When the king spoke again, his voice had roughened, as if he restrained anger.

'I am *Rex totius Britanniae* – the king of all Britain. These men gave oath to me. They swore that oath on my own relict, the very spear that pierced Christ's side. Yet they are not here, in my halls, in this council. Instead, I hear they consort with Wicingas, the "Vikings", the robbers of old, who have brought so much fire and blood to English villages! They have abandoned their oaths; they have abandoned the true faith, returning to crow-sign and wolfskin, to vile superstitions and dark spells. They have left their Christian honour in the filth of a midden and taken up arms against me!'

That news brought a ripple of sound as dozens of men grumbled either astonishment or anger to each other. Iron and leather creaked as they shifted, leaning in. Some cleared their throats and coughed in those few moments, but no one called out to deny it, no one rose to leave. I watched as Æthelstan held up his clenched right hand, a great scarred fist that looked itself a hammer.

'The lord of the Highlands and the lord of Cumbria have joined our enemies to defeat us: Anlaf Godfreyson, who calls himself the king of Dublin. Some of you will know his line. He whose cousin held my city of York for a time. This Anlaf has peered over that salt sea for an age, sending his messengers, watching for his chance to remake the Danelaw that meant we were ruled in our own land. Never again, my lords, my Witan. When you made me king, I told you all I would not bow my head to any man, only to God. Britain is mine. England is mine. I choose to fight – and I call the levy.'

The silence vanished in a laughing roar as they leaped to their feet, raising their arms to him in support. I do not know if some cried out against the rash course. I could not see them in the tumult and there were too many shouting and bawling to hear dissent. This was a Witan, a sober council? This was the beating heart of Æthelstan's rule? I had expected muted talk of appointing new reeves, of land disputes or setting taxes on the moneylenders – not a summons to the battlefield. England was at peace!

I gaped at them all, rocked by the sound, the more so to see Uncle Athelm red-faced and bellowing alongside bearded warriors. He and the king's champion Egill grasped each other, howling like wolves, while I could only look in astonishment at such madness erupting. It was as if they had merely been waiting for the king's words to throw off the trappings and forms of civilised life.

I felt it around me, as I was buffeted by the moving crowd. They all stood and Æthelstan was at the heart of them, smiling like a Christ figure, as if he had kindled the fire but not been touched by it.

The king's officers had to enter bearing spears before the room settled back to peace. They came jingling in, and the first reaction was as if to a threat. Just about every man there dropped a hand to some weapon or other, so that their joyous rumblings were interrupted. God save us from big men. They believe themselves invincible.

When they had quietened down, Æthelstan broke off from a conversation with three or four of his lords to address the group once more. He grinned suddenly, almost boyish as he looked round at them.

'I see many among you who remember my father. You were not always so sure of me – some of you wanted my brother Edmund to take the throne as his right, though I was of age and the Vikings were destroying our people, our land. I am my father's son, first-born to King Edward the Elder. He who was the first-born to King Alfred the Great. Yet I spent my youth in Mercia, not Wessex. My mother was not of a royal line – and I was a stranger to most of you when I asked to be named king. On that day, I gave my oath to the Witan that I would not marry, that I would instead devote my life to England and bear no sons of my own. I have kept that oath, in Christ's name.'

I swallowed drily, hearing that. He'd taken the crown to give him dominion, but it had not corrupted him. I tell you, there have not been half a dozen like Æthelstan since the beginning of the world.

Many grey-haired heads nodded and a few murmured their assent. I began to understand that they loved him, those ealdormen of the Witan. I had not heard the circumstances of him becoming king before that day. It seemed they had chosen well – and that his honour had held.

'I have served England and kept her safe for my brother Edmund.'

The king indicated the young man I had met with my uncle. Across the hall, his lords called 'Hear him' in a rumble.

'Now it is true I feel the touch of winter in my joints, in my old wounds. But I cannot pass my kingdom on to my father's son with this threat hanging over us, like another sword of Damocles. Therefore, I summon all men loyal to the king to stand at my side. Bring your forces to Winchester. I will march north in the spring. I will stand against those who threaten my realm and my peace. God will decide my fate – God and my right arm.'

They cheered him, of course. I thought of my brother Wulfric, who had no right arm, reminding myself to tell him the king's words when next we met.

My bladder had grown full to bursting and I slipped away through a side door while they thumped the chairs and called for ale and food. It would be a long night and a long day to follow.

I am not usually in the habit of mentioning each easing of my bladder, but on that particular night it became important. In the gloom of evening, I was roaming the halls and cloisters of the king's palace, seeking one of the tanner's pots. They were then set back in curtained alcoves for men who had drunk too much to hold. The pots had long necks and were well suited to anyone equipped to use them. I do not know what women did, in all honesty. I imagine they endured and suffered, perhaps to enjoy complaining about it later.

I could not find one of the alcoves that night, nor anyone to ask. Æthelstan would have been furious if he'd known, but half the servants and guards who might have kept his city safe from invaders were crowded into the doorways of the Witan hall, called by friends when they realised it would be war.

I decided, as so many young lads and dogs had done before me, to seek some outside spot, some sheltered tree I could water and lean on. I made my way to an opening that showed a promise of moonlight and the ache grew in me, only to have my hopes dashed as two women came in through the very arch I wanted.

I made a sound of surprise when I saw one was Elflaed, my sponsor and my rescuer. She and I were close friends by then, though she dwelled too much on my taking holy orders, something I was not ready to do.

'Dunstan!' Lady Elflaed said. 'It is as if I brought you out of the air. You will not believe me, but I was just describing you to my niece. Here, Beatrice, is he not exactly as I said?'

I had been tongue-tied and swollen of face from the first moment I laid eyes on her companion.

'Beatrice. Your name is "bringer of joy" in Latin,' I blurted out, bulging at the eyes a little.

She was much shorter than me, though seventeen. She had been laughing with her aunt before my appearance and a healthful colour still stained her cheeks. I felt my own heat rise as I realised I was staring.

'My name . . .' I went on quite helplessly, unable to stop. 'Dunstan means "hill stone". Beatrix was martyred, I believe, in Rome.'

Elflaed chose that moment to intervene. 'Yes, well, I see you are lost in your thoughts and prayers, Dunstan. Bea and I will not interrupt you any longer. Perhaps you will visit me tomorrow morning? I like to know you are well treated here, after my efforts to bring you to court.'

I bowed to them both, seeing a glimmer of amusement in the eyes of Beatrice.

'All bees have a queen, you know,' I said to her as I straightened.

'Really? I had not heard that,' she said. Her voice was, frankly, a delight. Beside her, Alice and Aphra were mere crows.

'Oh yes. We had hives at the abbey,' I said, warming to the subject. 'They would swarm in the spring and I had to track them across the fields, then gather them up in a mass to go into a new home. All the males follow a young queen. Wherever she went, they would go. Some of them flew until they died, but they could not stop.'

'That sounds . . . admirable, I think. Loyalty is important.'

'There, Dunstan, we will not detain you further, as I said!' There was a tension in Elflaed's voice and she no longer looked delighted as her gaze passed from her niece to me and back. 'Tomorrow, Dunstan! Early!'

I watched the two of them waft away, leaving the scent of flowers and sweat. I was not certain what had happened to me, exactly, only that I too wanted to follow my Beatrice. Suddenly, the entire world was only seen in relation to her. I was a bee, ensnared.

The moon had risen far by the time I went back to my room. I saw her face in my mind as I slept, and I dreamed fitfully until I woke in the small hours and wandered to the chapel for the Matins service. I dreamed of my father after that, which was less satisfying.

As the sun rose, I washed myself much more thoroughly than usual. I suppose I could use the word 'palace', but the king's estate was more akin to the villa of a wealthy Roman than a great royal tower or castle. Its main defence was in the guards and walls around Winchester. There was an open aspect to much of it that I enjoyed. I have mentioned the gardens and the stables, as well as the Witan and the petition hall. There were great kitchens in one part that could make almost anything in pastry, savoury or sweet. There were rooms full of scribes and stores of weapons to equip a thousand men in anything they might need. I was interested in those only for the skill it took to make them. I had no training in their actual use, nor any great inclination to take it up. If men like Egill were the sort I might meet on a battlefield, I would have to be dragged there. I saw him punch a horse once, not long after I arrived. The animal was snorting and pulling away from him. He struck it a blow meant to calm the beast down. Instead, it folded slowly to the ground, eyes turning up in its head. He looked so surprised it might have been comical in other circumstances. Yet the sudden power he had shown was like nothing else I've seen. As it was, I could only stare as he and another man tried to slap the creature's face and sprinkle water on it until it woke.

On that morning, I left the royal holding and set out onto the streets of the city proper. That too had its perils, and I knew better than to go unarmed or to carry a fat purse where it could be marked and seen. Winchester was a good town, but saints are beloved in part for their rarity. Most men are sinners, after all. I had managed to find a black robe with knotted belt and simple leather sandals any legionary would have recognised.

The streets were busy and the skies overcast as I hurried through them, worrying about rain. I knew the way to Elflaed's house, not a dozen streets from the king's estate, but all on good cobbles. Drains gurgled beneath some of those roads, while fresh rain ran in gutters of fired clay for the poor to collect and drink.

Lady Elflaed's servants were unsure what to do with a man who wore no cloak they could take. One of them rubbed my feet clean of mud while another dabbed at my forehead, until I told them to leave me alone and announce me to their mistress. At least the lady's house was laid out in simple structure, with two rooms below and two above. A good fire burned in a chimney that reminded me of a forge hearth. I could not stop to examine it and instead found myself shown to a room where Lady Elflaed and my uncle Athelm stood behind a great table, looking stern.

'My lady,' I said in greeting, frowning at them. 'Uncle.'

The archbishop dipped his head in response.

'I was not expecting to see you this morning, Uncle,' I said.

'Lady Elflaed asked me to attend when she saw you sighing at her niece yesterday evening.'

'Sighing?' I said, growing cold. Neither of them had asked me to sit and so I stood before them like a child summoned to explain why the apples had gone missing.

'Don't pretend you don't know what I am talking about, Dunstan!' Elflaed said. 'You have been here for, how long now?'

'Three months, a little more . . .' I began. One of my fingers would never again be straight, but my strength had come back like Samson's.

'I brought you to court as a young man rising in the Church, Dunstan. A man of talent who might follow in the steps of his uncle, perhaps! As I think his father would have wanted.'

'I don't understand what I have done wrong,' I said.

'Truly?' she demanded. 'Then I will say it as simply as I can. Dunstan, the robe you wear is Benedictine. It gave me hope when I saw you had found another, after your own was so cruelly torn. Yet it is more than a cloak for your back. Such robes are for those who would join the monastic order. You have been carried by angels, Dunstan! You have had

144

visions of great abbeys rising before you – and yet you have made no request to join the brothers in Winchester or London, or in Canterbury. Neither have you asked to be ordained as a priest, though your path is writ clearly before you.'

'I'm only just sixteen, Lady Elflaed,' I said, stammering and falling over my words. 'I thought to see a little of the works of men before I devoted my whole life to service!'

'You are an innocent, yet you stand there, telling me you wish to see corruption? No, no, it breaks my heart to hear. Perhaps I am to blame! I could not bear the burden if it were my fault you turned your face from the Church.'

To my astonishment, her eyes filled. I wonder now at how easily she wept, but it moved me then, that great tide of her tears.

'And now, last night, I see you blush and stammer at the sight of female flesh! I heard your lover's words of bees and honey and queens. Oh, Dunstan, you cannot refuse your fate. You must not.'

I could only blink, wondering how long this flood had been pent up within her. It is always hard to know another's heart and it seemed Lady Elflaed had made decisions for me without my even being aware of them. To my surprise, I saw Uncle Athelm nodding his big head along with her.

'I can only add, Dunstan, that I have not regretted a day of my devotion. I was ordained at fifteen and I have given almost fifty years to the Holy Church. If I had that half-century to give again, I would. I would fling the years from me!'

'I understand, Uncle,' I replied. I would have gone on, but he turned to Lady Elflaed and laid a hand on her arm, speaking in a low voice.

'My dear, there are some things not to be heard by delicate ears, that must be said from one man to another in private. If you would excuse us for a time, it will allow me to be blunt with my nephew.'

145

Lady Elflaed pinched her lips together at that, knuckling away a tear. She seemed to think my very soul was at stake, and I half-smiled as she left, expecting my uncle to at least acknowledge the ridiculousness of it. Instead, he only frowned more deeply.

'Dunstan, I have had troubling reports from Glastonbury. I imagine some of it is the jealousy or malice of lesser men, something I have known myself. Yet I am troubled.'

I braced myself, thinking how best to answer accusations now that they had come. Encarius was dead and gone, though Abbot Simeon and Brother Caspar still lived, no doubt as filled with poison as the day they had dragged me to a cliff edge and smashed my hands. Just the thought made them throb in memory.

'These shaking fits, Dunstan,' Athelm began, surprising me. He indicated a chair and I sat down, though to my discomfort he remained standing. 'Do they still trouble you?'

I thought of who might have seen and decided to tell the truth.

'At times. I taste metal, I fall, for a time I am lost, but then I return and all is well.'

'And the visions? Do they still come? It is so important, Dunstan, to know they are from God and not the ancient enemy of mankind.'

'They do, though rarely. All I have ever seen is a vast new abbey at Glastonbury – and the grave of a monk who had not then fallen ill.'

'Father Keats, of course. Nothing more?'

I blushed a little and looked away.

'I see myself as abbot, Uncle, with other monks kneeling to me. I did not want to say, because it seemed vain.'

'You were right in that, Dunstan. I wish it were not so, but there are jealous men who will always try to pull you down. Some show their spite in the letters they write, foul accusations that reveal their own base nature far more than your own.'

Caspar. It had to be him, I was suddenly certain. All I could do was try to look both modest and deserving of praise at the same time, which is not easy.

'Lady Elflaed and I have bound our reputations to you, Dunstan, in more ways than one. We have championed you here, as a man rising, as a child of Christ. With faith to melt iron and bring about true miracles. There are eyes watching us all, boy. Those who would see you fail – and through you, our stars brought low, our fires made ashes. We too have enemies.'

He raised his hand like a benediction.

'You are promised to the Church, Dunstan. I see your heart is set on the monastery, so I will not command you to be ordained as a priest under me. All I ask is that you resist temptations of the flesh, of all kinds. Lady Elflaed's niece is fallen, Dunstan. Her sins are Lady Elflaed's private tragedy, but I will say . . . she is certainly no virgin.'

The fat old gossip! I gaped a little at him as he went on.

'Women corrupt us, Dunstan, as Eve offered the apple to Adam. Instead of foul lusts, dedicate yourself to study and prayer. Make wonders in the forges and the workshops, Dunstan! Embroider and paint! Let the king's counsellors see what my brother's son can bring into the world in the name of Christ Jesus, king of heaven. You have been a novice for years now, Dunstan, but are you ready to devote yourself to God, to take the vows of St Benedict?'

'I will pray for guidance, Uncle. To be shown the right path.'

He seemed a little crestfallen at my response. He'd been building in tone and volume, and he wanted me to cry 'Oh yes! I am ready!', but I confess I'd stopped listening with my full attention after I'd heard Beatrice was no virgin. Athelm may have wanted me to embroider and paint, but I was not quite ready to put aside my foul lusts at that time.

When Lady Elflaed returned to the room, she watched for some sign our manly talk had brought about my repentance. I nodded mutely to her and she gave a great wail and clutched me to her bosom. I suppose Cleopatra did the same, in a sense.

14

The wind bit at me as I came out, so that I dragged my robe up close around my neck. Good, thick cloth is the mark of civilisation, I have always thought. Who could imagine Romans without their togas and cloaks, when they walked in these lands, six hundred years ago?

The street was already busier than it had been – and this time I noticed ranks of trudging men and mule-drawn carts, full of the sort of supplies an army needed. The king's capital was readying itself to throw a spear into the north. I was fascinated – and nervous of what it meant. For all of my childhood, there had been a threat of war, of raiders slipping inland in shallow-draught boats, scraping onto sloping shores and peering through shutters, looking for women and silver, whatever they could take away in the night. I had seen my father's men bring torches more than once when they heard some sound they could not explain, or when the dogs started howling at wolves in the darkness. I had never seen a battle, but I knew very well what violence meant. I shuddered and told myself it was the chill of winter on the air.

As I stepped off the doorstep, I turned my head and looked into the face of Beatrice. She was laden with bags, returning from whatever errands Lady Elflaed and my uncle had arranged, to give them time to lecture me. I must have looked about as aggrieved as she felt, for she smiled in sympathy and patted my shoulder, vanishing inside only long enough to drop her parcels. I waited. A team of horses could not have dragged me from that step.

When she reappeared, she took my arm as if we did so

every day, as if we were old friends. She moved me away from the house and out onto the street. I felt we'd vanished into a river almost, the crush was so bad. I was buffeted and turned about, so that I was hard-pressed to keep her arm in mine. Yet I did. I would not have let go if Æthelstan himself had commanded it.

I knew I was expected at the forges later that morning, with the master smiths. Lady Elflaed had arranged all manner of tutors and craftsmen to continue my studies. After noon, I had arranged to meet the archivist in the king's personal library, there to examine texts that existed nowhere else. If there was time, I hoped to spend the evening in the king's arboretum, studying rare plants with the herbalist there, or if that door was locked, visiting the surgery where men had wounds and cankers treated – and survived, some of them. For one of my interests, with the lady's influence and coin to back me, Winchester was a joyous place. Yet in the instant I swept into the crowd with Beatrice, all that was forgotten.

Chattering together, we bought bread, cheese and boiled eggs. I had no coin myself, but Beatrice had a pouch with change from what they had given her. She waved away my promises to pay her back, making no bargains with me. I knotted it all in a piece of white linen that was too fine for the task and carried it over my shoulder. We left the city behind us, walking out to where the cobbles ended and the road stretched into ploughed fields all around.

I saw then what I had not understood before: an army was already gathering at Winchester, waiting for the king's command in a vast encampment, invisible from inside the walls. Group after group rested or trained, or galloped horses, or worked anvil and hammer. I saw scores of banners in great coloured ribbons stretching across the hills around the city, some so far off they were no more than a smudge of mustard or sea blue. I did not know so many warriors existed in the world.

Roman eagles stood on rods of ebony, left by legions centuries before. I saw the red dragon and the white, the Wessex wyvern, the Holy Cross, the Greek fish or 'ichthus', that stands for Ἰησοῦς Χριστός Θεοῦ Υἱός Σωτήρ – 'Jesus Christ, God's Son, the Saviour'. These were the armies of Æthelstan the king – and they were still coming in. I had never seen so many souls. I felt their gaze, on Beatrice in particular, as we walked the dusty road away from the safety of the city. I swallowed nervously, but they did not trouble us. The king's peace held and we passed through without injury or insult. Though I was not ordained, I imagine my robe played a part in that. Some men have no fear of a king's wrath, but then damnation, ah now, that is for eternity. There is no way back, after that cold judgement.

The trees in the wheat stubble and lining the road were all bare, the day cold and grey. It was no stroll of lovers, but the two of us shivering as we sheltered by a bridge out of the wind, tearing fresh bread with our teeth and skinning boiled eggs by rolling them on the flagstones. Beatrice had paid for a flask of ale from one of the street vendors – it was better than the city water.

'Your uncle believes I am a corrupter of young men,' Beatrice said. I could only blink at her, hardly able to say that I certainly hoped so. 'I heard him talking to my aunt, about how important you were. How you must not be led astray.'

'Led astray?' I said, my voice muffled by egg. Or it was just that my tongue had grown thick, or perhaps that I had. Beatrice had that effect on me. She was short, but lithe in a way that made me feel clumsy and slow. Perhaps I should not dwell too long on her charms. I will say that I remember her eyes and her grace, as fine as a greyhound. Her hair curled, which I found pleasing. There was always humour in her eyes. If not for the way her breasts moved and the way my breathing deepened – if she had been a man, I mean – we might have been friends.

I have read poems of Greece that speak of beauty. That is not my purpose here, to drag a hook through old forgotten sands of my life, stirring silt back into clear water. I could describe her laugh or the way she could leap and twirl and stand on her hands, revealing her flashing legs. I liked her. That is why she was a danger to me. I might have become a merchant trader in the Winchester docks, just to please Beatrice in that year. If I had, abbeys would have gone unbuilt, tombs ungilded, great works undone.

In truth, that first day is mostly lost to me. Yet it was one of dozens that we stole together while the king's forces grew all round the city. My studies suffered and I cared not. I spent my time making her a perfect rose in iron. It had taken on spots of rust by the time spring warmed the air and the roads were dry – and by then all we knew between us had come to ruin.

I don't know whether news of our continuing association came first to my uncle Athelm or to Lady Elflaed. I was sixteen and in love. There is no other age like it, for impetuous youth. Of course we were seen. Of course we were caught.

Beatrice knew the stakes and the dangers. If we had been two village lovers, or a shepherd and a maid, I'm sure we would have eased our passions early on. Perhaps we would have married first, with some bare ceremony of simple folk. Instead, we let desire build like a river rising up against a dam, until it was far too high and crashed over. I could have been a simple man, I think. If I'd married her, she would have been beyond their reach.

I don't know if Beatrice was entranced by me, or by the thought of stealing me away from the vocation, from the oaths I might take. Perhaps it was just to prove she had power over her aunt Elflaed's influence, I cannot say.

She and I had known one another at last. In the long grasses of sweet pastures, we took eternity in our hands, and her thighs in my hands – and risked our immortal souls. And then again, in a hayrick belonging to some farmer.

As in the Garden of Eden, all things were changed from then on. No longer did we meet to sigh and talk of love. We fell on each other's necks as soon as we were alone. I tried not to think of my experience with Aphra in the infirmary, with her foul bag of goose fat. Yet I could not put it completely out of my mind. To my dismay, the old rash returned and caused me the sort of itching that maddened. It began with a pattern of tiny blisters. I thought to endure them until they went away, but of course I scraped them off instead, rubbing at them through the wool of my robe until I had great patches weeping and sticking, tearing free as I stood up. It was the price of sin, I do not doubt. I sprinkled drying powders on the parts affected and I do not believe Beatrice ever knew. There were times, in my passion, when I thrust harder to stop an itch than I would have done from mere desire.

Between my love and my most intimate torment, my studies could find little purchase. I had to duck and dart whenever I returned to the royal estate, for fear of meeting one of my tutors as they searched for me. I sweated more in my sinfulness. I ate and slept less, though I washed myself with jug and cloth each morning, the one time I felt clean.

Around noon most days, when the crowds were thickest, Bea and I had fallen into the habit of meeting at a carters' kitchen we knew well, where the food was thick with horseradish paste, no matter what meat formed the stew. The crossroads lay halfway across the city and my feet were light as I went to meet her. I knew the way so well I hardly looked around me, certainly not to see if I was followed or watched.

It was not uncommon for Beatrice to get there first, if we

had agreed to meet. We had our habits by then. If I was able to get away unexpectedly, I'd leave a flower from the royal garden between two tiles over her aunt's door. I always worried someone would take it down, but they never had. I'd left a sprig of lavender the night before, in moonlight. I suppose I had been followed then as well, though if so, they were uncommon quiet about it.

I thought the foodseller was a little curt that day. Perhaps it was just my worry showing, when Beatrice didn't appear in the first moments. I bought a bowl and took a spoon. The old woman tending the stall had grown used to me and she knew I paid, so she did not insist I take one of the chained spoons that meant you had to stand right next to her cart. Yet I finished my bowl and watched her wipe it clean for the next customer with no sign of Beatrice. I looked for my love in the streaming crowd, for the shape of her bonnet and the first glimpse of her that would spring on me with a joy that was a little like pain.

Instead, a hand clamped down on my arm and I swung round with a snarl, bristling. A sallow-faced man stood there, all grease and sharp bones. My hand dropped to my knife, only to have my wrist held in a firm grip. I jerked against that in sudden fury, pulling free and surprising us both. I was half-turned to run when he laid on once more and dragged me to a halt.

'Your sweet flower won't be coming, son,' he said.

The words stopped me cold.

'Who are you? Take your hands off me!' I said. 'How dare you lay claim to me . . .'

'Your uncle said he'll see you today, Master Dunstan. He said I was to bring you – and I will, even if I have to knock your teeth out first. He was that angry, I don't think he'd curse me for it if I did.'

I examined him more closely. He was rangy and thin, but

his face had a haggard look. I took the hand that had wrapped itself in my robe and I crushed it in a grip more used to holding forge hammers. He gasped and went a paler shade of grey under his dirt.

'Ah! You're breaking my fingers. Damn you, leave me be!'

It gave me no satisfaction to overcome him, after what he had said.

'What has my uncle done?' I said. I kept my voice soft, with the ears of the stew-seller and who knew how many others twitching behind us. Aware of that, I moved him away, though I did not release my grip and turned his hand further in mine, so that tears appeared in the corners of his eyes.

'He just told me to fetch you. I don't know nothing more about it!'

I gave him one good twist more and he shrieked.

'Please! He said she was to go away to a convent. That's all I know, I swear. On my oath.'

I felt a great stillness come upon me, as I had felt only once or twice before.

'And where is my uncle now?' I asked, as gently as I could. The tone I used frightened him somehow, so that he shook like a beaten dog.

'He's at the cathedral, in one of the chapels there. That's where I was to bring yer.'

'I'll go there, don't worry. Now get out of my sight.'

I don't think I had ever bullied another man before, unless you count Wulfric, which I don't. I felt my power over him and it was a pleasure.

I walked fast, considering what I might have to do to save Beatrice. Some women choose the life of prayer and solitude, just as my brothers did at the abbey. Those who fall into sin, who grow great with child, yet are unmarried – noble or not, rich or poor, they are shuttered away from the world. Those poor fallen creatures are our failures, made to spend their lives in prayer and hope of redemption. One thing was certain, if they had Beatrice locked away, I would not see her again.

I burned as I walked. I felt hot and ill and my skin crawled. My anger was like iron: slow-heating, but all the more dangerous for that.

I had to make my way past a queue of pilgrims as I drew close to the cathedral. The Benedictines there had a reliquary of St Swithun, very fine in gold and glass. They kept a record then of whether it rained on his feast day, when it was said to pour down for another forty if it did. They wrote too of the miracles that occurred there, in a book of wonders.

It meant that those who came to that spot were often the most deformed to be found anywhere on these islands. Children had gathered to stare at the strangest of them and I confess, even in anger, my attention was snagged by some shambling boy with one eye much higher than the other. Whether he hoped to be healed or for death, I could only guess.

A couple of them thought I was jumping to the head of the queue and hissed at me, so that I was stiff with indignation when I reached the great door, guarded by men in robes as black as mine own.

One of them put up his hand to prevent me walking past him, but the other murmured something I could not catch and they both stood aside. They were strangers to me, but I was not to them, it seemed. My uncle had left orders for me to be admitted.

The shrine to St Swithun was not a quiet place. Men and women wailed out their grief and their failures, pleading aloud for redemption. I made the sign of the cross as I passed them by, heading down the nave to one of four side chapels.

I peered into two before I saw Uncle Athelm celebrating Mass, with a dozen men and women praying before him.

My anger cooled as I waited. He had two stern-looking lads guarding the chapel against rough folk. The two fellows carried no visible swords in a house of God, but somehow I did not doubt they were well armed. My uncle was a man of power and great influence, after all. He would not walk the streets without guards to keep him safe.

When the service ended, men and women in fine cloth came out, made solemn and at peace. I recognised a few of them from Æthelstan's court and I bowed on instinct, rather than offend anyone else who had the king's ear. It took but moments for them to file out, and then one of my uncle's men bowed almost mockingly, gesturing for me to enter.

Athelm was not a fool, in forcing me to meet him there. He had privacy, but also the timbered ceiling far above and sweet incense on the air to cool my wrath. I could not stamp and demand in such a place. I rather admired him for his choice, even as I fixed my gaze and tried to bend him to my will. I had given it some thought on my stalk through the streets.

'Uncle, I wish to marry Beatrice. I will ask Lady Elflaed for her hand, as I understand she is her protector, her guardian. I am of age and I will make my life as a merchant and craftsman in this city, or perhaps in London. Beatrice is old enough to choose me and I would like to see her. No, I demand to see the lady who will be my wife, wherever you have put her.'

I felt I was running away with my anger and clamped my jaw shut on more. Uncle Athelm raised his eyebrows at me.

'Are you finished, Dunstan? Now, you have spoken your foolishness . . .'

'It is not foolishness, Uncle . . .'

He went on over me, raising his hand once more as if

about to give a bishop's blessing. It was a strangely powerful gesture.

'You have spoken, Dunstan. I believe it is my turn. You have come here for answers, have you not? Perhaps it might go better for you if you show patience and restraint instead of this, this . . . vulgar display.'

I waited, though I could feel my heart thudding in my wrists and neck. I imagine I was as swollen as a bullfrog, watching him, convinced I was in the right. As if to torment me, my groin grew an itch I could hardly bear, so strong was it. I wanted to scratch more insistently than I could ever remember before. I rearranged the rope belt of my robe and used the motion to rub the area, but it was too brief and made it all the worse.

'I promised your father once I would look after you, Dunstan, if he died. Did you know that? Heorstan was my older brother and I adored him. He was the cleverest of us and he made a fine life, with sons to make up for those I would not bring into the world. You don't remember it, but I was there in your home many times in those first years. Before my work took me to Winchester and to London, I would visit you every summer and dandle you on my knee. I told Heorstan and Cyneryth then that I would see you and Wulfric safe, if the worst came.'

He paused as I scratched myself, looking oddly at me before he went on. My itching grew worse, so I was almost trembling with it. I know now it was because I stood on holy ground. I had rotted my body with sin – and that sin was tormented in turn by the body and blood of Christ, by the centuries of prayers in the beams and stones around us.

'I tried to warn you about Beatrice, did I not? I tried to tell you she was no virgin. Perhaps I should have spoken more bluntly. She had a child, Dunstan, born dead. She would not name the father to her aunt, saying she did not know it, that she had been taken by some fellow passing by on the road. I wonder now if she tempted him, as she tempted you.'

'I will marry her,' I stammered, though he had shocked me and made me wonder.

'Oh, Dunstan! Did you think lust and sin are covered in flies? Did you think evil was unattractive? Would men be tempted by women if they were foul and not fragrant? No! Wide is the gate, Dunstan! Broad is the way that leads to destruction.'

'I . . . love her, Uncle. I will make my way with trade and the skill of my hands.'

'Skills that were given to you in the abbey and by the tutors Lady Elflaed paid to . . . What are you doing, Dunstan? Why do you keep twitching at yourself . . . Oh, son, is your flesh corrupt? Have you lain with her?'

I could not tell an untruth, not in that place, with God and St Swithun and all the saints looking on. My eyes filled with tears and I nodded, expecting him to erupt. Instead, he came forward, putting an arm around my shoulder. I shrank back from him. Lepers are unclean and I felt the same way. He seemed to read my mind and his eyes were kind as he looked on me.

'I fear it not, because I have not sinned. Come, be brave now. Let me take you to the king's doctor. He is a fine man and he has seen, well, many things over the years.'

'What about Beatrice, Uncle?' I said.

'The one who tempted you and made your skin foul? You are rotting, lad. Your sin is mortal and it will destroy you. Do you not understand? If you want to live and be clean again, come with me, deny her, denounce your sin and repent. If you do, Christ will raise you up. If you persist in your sin, in your unhealthy desires, you will know pain and anguish and death. I have seen it all before.'

He took my hands and sniffed the air as if he could smell my powders.

'Please, Dunstan. Choose to repent. I cannot force you in this. She has corrupted you, but you can still turn away.'

'Will she be taken to a convent, Uncle?' I asked. I had to know, though I could see my questions were eroding his patience with me.

'Lady Elflaed said as much. Now, there is a woman of faith, Dunstan, a fine, strong branch without rot. Her sister was a pitiful creature and the daughter . . . well, you have seen. There is a bad apple, Dunstan. I only pray it has not turned you too far to corruption and foulness, so that you are beyond saving. Now, will you come with me? Will you repent and be free of them all?'

I nodded, unable to see for the tears that blinded me. I did not ask about Beatrice again. I chose my way, my path, on that afternoon in the cathedral.

That spring, Æthelstan joined his armies. He and his elite horsemen had trained together in formations and patterns, charges and sudden wheels and strikes. I think it was some Roman tactic, rather than simply reaching the battlefield before those on foot. He had gathered eighteen thousand soldiers in his name and they rode out against three kings and all the traitors who stood with them.

When the king's men left Winchester, I went too, as my uncle's eyes and ears. Under my cloak, I wore the black robe of the Benedictines, my brothers. I had given oath as a monk and I had taken holy orders as a priest. I rode into the north, lost and raw in my grief. I never saw Beatrice again. I cannot recall her face.

15

My first days on the road left me lonely and half-starving. My horse was a foolish, skittish creature who insisted I pay attention to him. I did not want to. I wanted to let him trudge along while I sat his saddle like a pile of wolf pelts, shifting and unaware. I had lost it all.

The old Roman roads often vanished for great stretches, the stones stolen by enterprising builders. I might have grown to hate the bastards who had left us to plunge through mud and hack through briars, if I had found the energy. Instead, I felt pain as a distant annoyance, so that when I gashed my ankle on a stirrup, I let it bleed without my notice, though it seeped and dripped for a whole day. I'd known much worse.

I walked my horse as a blot of misery amongst men who laughed and sang and called to one another. They were walking straight-backed and tall, or riding in the king's own cavalry. They were warriors heading to war, and though you may hear tales of blood and terror, you must also remember that some men enjoy it enormously. It is, simply, the best and worst of us all, settled on a single day.

We were a wonder to the villages and towns we passed, of course. They came to the roadside if one existed, or scrambled up local hills to watch us pass through the fields, staying there for all the hours of daylight in their innocent wonder.

Not long after we left Winchester, a marching column disturbed our scouts, so that two thousand went to meet them, with King Æthelstan at the head. They were men of Malmesbury, a town I did not know well. They'd heard the king was riding out and sought to join him. The gesture pleased Æthelstan greatly. He brought them back to camp and paraded them around like heroes, saying it was men like these, and like us, who would destroy the enemies of England. I felt my heart beat faster as he spoke. Æthelstan had that touch, whatever it is, that made men put their heads down and quietly vow to show him what they could do.

It was on the third or fourth day that I chanced to look behind me as I rode. My mood had been fine and light that morning as my horse had grown more amenable. Yet all that went in a moment and I swallowed bile at what I saw.

How long did it take crows and wolves to learn to follow bands of men? A hundred years? A thousand? Perhaps a few loped or flew after the Brigantes and the Iceni. Perhaps they followed the legions of Rome into the north.

They had learned well, those scavengers, those devourers of eyes and flesh. The sky was dark with crows and rooks. On the hills behind us, lupine shadows moved and snarled. They knew we walked with death and they crept up in our wake.

It did not help that we were a Christian army, going to fight those who still made blood offerings. We scorned Viking gods, but then ravens and crows were Woden's servants, so the old folk said. You have to remember the faith was still new in England then. The Roman Christians all withered on the vine when the legions left. It was another two centuries before St Augustine came to Kent – and in the three hundred years since, the faith has not reached every village and dark crossroads. There was always the chance that those birds knew something we did not. They called in the air to one another, and perhaps to us. I saw men who had laughed before hunch lower as they rode or walked, stealing glances behind whenever they dared.

We passed within a dozen miles of London, but went no

closer than Clewer, where the villagers lived in caves cut into a great cliff. They peered at us from their holes and hid from the sight of so many.

By the end of the fifth day, we had barely covered eighty miles. Half the country travelled by river for a reason. We were mud-spattered and weary from wrestling carts out of great ruts and soft ground that sank them to the axles. Each one that came to a halt had to be unloaded, then lifted by four men on either side, while horses and oxen heaved at the front. I began to consider ways of using levers to make it easier on us. Archimedes said that if he were given a lever long enough, and a place to stand, he could move the world. The place to stand is the trick of it, when you are up to your knees in mud and sinking down every time you heave up.

We had swung west to take advantage of a Roman road that was still mostly intact. The going would be better the next morning and even my dark mood lightened at the prospect of really stretching out. I no longer looked back at the crows and wolves slinking about in our wake, though I could still hear them. An army leaves a trail of dropped things and the creatures would snarl and screech over them, savage in a way that we were not.

I had seen no sign of Æthelstan's personal guard. He rode somewhere in the centre, perhaps a mile from me on that rough country. I guessed we would form a column on the stone road the next day, but until then I knew only those around me. I had a place with them and they had grown familiar. Each day, I would rise and stand in line with the same faces as the stew was brought. We were meant to bring our own plates but they had spares, watched as keenly as the chained spoons had been back in Winchester. Every day I thought of her.

I was waiting there as the sun rose, my stomach making odd sounds of hunger as I stared at nothing. I was in such a daze I did not hear my name called, though I knew it had been when my arm was touched and I looked up with a start.

'It is you,' Edmund said. 'I thought it was. Who else would wear black amongst these men, eh?'

He wore perhaps the finest cloak I had ever seen, a thing of royal blue that looked as if it might be proof against a winter blast, never mind the gentle nights we knew. Under that sweep of cloth, Edmund's mail was oiled and shining, not the great sheet of rust some poor men owned. I saw too that he had buckled on a sword and belt, with a fine scabbard.

There was no actual rule that prevented Benedictines from carrying weapons in a battle. I had my knife and my tools in bags of leather, on straps I'd hung over my horse's back. Yet I envied Edmund, even so. He was the king in waiting and it showed in his bearing. He clapped me on the shoulder and embraced me, so that my tin plate clanked against his belt buckle. My mood turned grey once again.

'I know that look, Dunstan,' he said. 'I have seen it many times. Poor men we are, who can shrug off a lost bet, or the death of a favourite hound, but grow sombre as a funeral just because of love. Now, is it because she would not, or because she would?'

I blinked at him, seeing how open and honest he appeared.

'I've made my choices,' I said. I patted myself over the heart to show him my black robe. 'And my oaths. I'll live with the consequences now.'

'I'm glad your hands are mended, though I think you were in better spirits when they were in splints. Cheer up, Dunstan. You are young and in good health. A few of the lads and I have a keg of some foul draught they bought in Aldermaston. You're not forbidden strong drink, are you?'

I was not, though in the Benedictines drunkenness was certainly a matter for discipline. Yet I was not in an abbey and neither was I attached to a particular bishop. I shook my head and walked with him, leaving my horse in the care of an ostler boy.

The drink they had purchased had been brewed from lichen, so they said. I suppose anything alive can be made to ferment, with enough care. I have not tasted anything quite as foul again.

Edmund too had been born in the dark months, as so many are whose parents love in spring. He'd turned seventeen just after Christmas and seemed to have grown taller. Around him were the sons of noblemen and kings, a dozen perhaps in all, who had come to that march not for Æthelstan, but for the one who would be king after him. I saw it when they were telling tall stories and boasting about their valour. These were the young men who would make their own royal court in years to come. I realised I could be part of it.

I matched them drink for drink and I told them wild stories of King Arthur I had heard at the abbey, new to them all. Most of them cheered my tales, though there was one great brute who seemed to resent my sudden rise and the favour Edmund showed me.

Some men are petty in drink. Leofa of Kent was one of them. In truth, the same could perhaps be said of me. At one point, I do recall weeping, as the drink had a sad effect. I believe I told them of my Beatrice and how she had been taken from me. I said too much, I am sure – and I recall Leofa trying to mock my grief, until he was brought up sharply by Edmund. The Kentishman did not take well to that! I grinned at him and added him to my list of enemies, writing in the air with a finger. It was a compliment, in a sense. I have never chosen the weak to pit themselves against me. I pity those and let them go their way. No, my list was reserved for strong fools and spiteful old women.

Edmund was nursing a headache as he brought me safe back through the camp to collapse into my blankets. Now, that was the mark of him! Another would have left me to freeze where I fell, not gathered me up and brought me home. That night, I had become one of his men.

I saw it in the way the soldiers looked at me the following morning, as I groaned and rested my forehead on the cool leather saddle in the dawn light. I could not eat. I could hardly keep my own acids inside me. Yet I smiled as I groaned, recalling the laughter and the wildness. Had we run through the camp? We had, racing each other in the dark, so that I had memories of wind rushing past and my robe flapping wet against my knees.

My grey mood had burned off at some point in the night, like morning mists vanishing in sun. I spent every day from then on in the company of Edmund's band, close enough to Æthelstan and his own bearded earls to be able to watch the king and those who looked to him. Æthelstan carried himself well, I saw. In a sense, he carried us all.

After another day and night, I asked Edmund where his younger brother was. Eadred was only twelve then, but there were dozens of boys with our camp and he would not have been out of place. Edmund smiled oddly.

'If the king falls, there is every chance I will not come home as well. There will be no truce, no mercy, no ransoms when we meet these small kings in battle. My brother wanted one son of our father to survive the clash.'

I thought of the sickly little boy we had left behind. To please Edmund, I spoke once again.

'I suppose you had to tie him down to stop him riding out after us.'

He chuckled. I think he appreciated my effort, though we both knew it was a lie. Edmund was kinder to his brother than I would have been – kinder than I had been to Wulfric, in fact. Younger brothers are born weak, some of them. I know I was not the first-born of my father, but I always felt as if I had been. I grew to manhood as if I were, just as Edmund had. We shared that kinship, that subtle understanding and sense of our place in the world. I told him so as we rode on.

Æthelstan had scouts riding out for miles ahead of us at all hours. I imagine it was dangerous work, expecting to be ambushed at any moment. The roads themselves were not safe for a lone rider far from his front ranks. Never mind the enemy, we lost one scout to brigands on the eighth or ninth day. We found him stripped and battered, his horse stolen and his neck half cut through. Axes were a terrible weapon for the force they could create. The long lever of an ash handle, with a lump of iron on the end – it hardly needed to be sharp.

Some of the men wanted to scour the woods for the robbers. Æthelstan growled a few words and that was the end of it. We would go on, for however long it took to find his enemies.

England is a big country, though not wide. Edmund said we had food enough and supplies enough to take us all the way to the highlands of Scotland without needing to hunt. The carts slowed us down, but speed was not the concern of the king. His concern was vengeance. Each step he took was one further north and one we could not take back.

Perhaps two dozen scouts were ranging out ahead of us, with half as many behind. They moved in two great arcs, I discovered. The first was at nine miles or so, the next at three or four. Their task was to sight and count, then gallop back as if all the demons of hell were after them. When they came in hard, every man there knew something was up. They saw the dust cloud and the wild eyes. There was no mistaking it, and all those who had known war before turned their axes in their hands, or gripped their shields more tightly, or readied their spears.

One after the other, our scouts came barrelling in at high

speed, young men showing off as they risked their necks to bring the news everyone wanted and feared. The enemy were ahead of us. The battle would come. All the lies we'd told ourselves, that it would be just a fine spring day like any other, that we would not be called to gasp out our lives in a wet ditch, all faded away. I looked around me at men I'd come to know. Edmund's band of thanes knew they would be watched by those who followed them. They put on a fine brave face, though they snapped at one of their number who whistled, telling him to stop his damned noise.

The scouts had given us time to form and I watched as our marching army became a fighting force before my eyes. Æthelstan was the heart of it all. The orders began with him, as he leaned across the neck of his horse and spoke quietly to three large men in fine mail. They carried swords and drew them, holding them high as they turned their mounts in tight circles and gathered captains. In that way, the king's order spread in ripples, reaching more and more.

Edmund was not free of that command. As ranks formed around banners as far as I could see in any direction, the king turned his mount towards his younger brother. I felt him coming, I think. Æthelstan brought the wind with him, so that the air seemed to freshen as he reined in and nodded in greeting, gripping Edmund's shoulder with a great gauntlet of leather.

'King Constantin knows our shield walls, Edmund. He may have a counter for them.'

'There is no counter,' Edmund said with a grin.

Æthelstan chuckled, a deep sound.

'Not that we know. Your task in this, your role, is to ride the flanks and strike at weakness, before they have even formed, if you can.' He made a spear of one hand and jabbed the air with it, wanting to be understood. 'In – then out again. Do you understand? No last stand, no fighting to the end. In . . . and out. Your couple of dozen are my weakening blade, my stabbing knife, just as we've discussed. Like the Roman cavalry. You are my *extraordinarii*.'

'I am your sword. It will be my honour, Brother. I won't fail.'

For an instant, I saw there was true friendship between them. I felt Æthelstan's gaze drift over me as he turned, just long enough to be sure he had recognised me. The old bastard missed nothing, I'll tell you that. He did not seem pleased to find me at his brother's elbow, listening and watching all that went on. Still, he said nothing as he returned to his precious cavalry.

'What are *extraordinarii*?' I asked Edmund. 'It's not a term I've heard before. I thought I knew them all.'

He was watching the formations develop around us and did not turn to me as he answered. The presence of death on the field is a cold focus for those who see it. I was not fully aware of it then, and I'm afraid I chattered like a jaybird.

'Legion horsemen,' he said, distracted. 'Some were *equites*, the sons of noble houses. The *extraordinarii* began as scouts. My brother has read his history, like our grandfather before us.'

I blinked a little at the thought that he meant Alfred the Great, translator of the Psalms into English and one or two other achievements.

Edmund turned to me and smiled then, an oddly cold expression.

'Some Romans used them better than others, but my brother is convinced they can be a terror to men on foot. In normal times, our armies walk to the field of battle. The commanders dismount and draw swords – and we walk forward to settle it with shield and iron. Æthelstan has a different plan for today.'

He patted the neck of his mount as he spoke and I could see sweat dust rising from its mane into the air. I swallowed and felt the wind bite just a little colder in that moment.

I felt a presence at my shoulder and I turned and half-flinched at the sight of Egill on a stallion. The beast's head seemed at the level of mine, so that it towered over my own mount. Egill grinned at my reaction.

'I know you. Don't scream,' he said in a thick accent, chortling away to himself as if he had taken too many blows to the skull. Dear lord, his skull! I have seen more graceful lines on a prize bull. There was an odour of the dried meat he chewed about him, not completely unpleasant, though I did not like to breathe air so recently in his mouth. I decided not to reply, choosing dignity over the chance of being battered into the ground.

'Leave him alone, Egill,' Edmund said. 'Say what you came to say.'

Egill shrugged, his little eyes gleaming at me as he answered.

'Your brother says he wants you out on the left wing.' He pointed, as if we were idiots.

'My place is on the right!' Edmund said, immediately.

We both watched Egill shrug again, moving great shoulders that looked more than a little like a hog's back. Edmund set his jaw, choosing not to object further to the messenger who had not given the order.

'Tell my brother to look for me on his left,' Edmund said.

The Icelander turned away before he had finished speaking.

'Why the left?' I asked after a time.

'He seeks to keep me safe,' Edmund muttered. 'I love him for it, but I must be seen by the men, in the heart of the fight. I wanted the right wing, where the press will be hardest. I would have been happy with the centre. The left . . .' At that moment he seemed to remember it was an order from his brother the king and looked uneasily at my bright attention. 'The left is where I will stand, for the king.'

No sooner had he said the words than his thanes came

riding up. They brought some four dozen horsemen in all, bright and excited-looking fellows. Edmund spent some time greeting those who had come at the king's command, telling them our role and explaining the orders. He did not try to send me away when he moved off, so I went with him, digging my own heels in and wondering if I should ask for a sword. I had never used one, but I fancied a weapon in case I was attacked. There would be something embarrassing about going into battle with just an eating knife, that much was clear. I had already shrieked in front of the king and his petition court. I would not be the monk who merely watched. I set my jaw, suddenly certain that I must not waste this chance.

As we swung out and around the marching lines, I spotted one of the carts lumbering along, with baskets of axes as bright and shining as the day they came from the forge. I angled my horse over and snatched one up as I passed, calling thanks to the owner. I thought he might want payment, but he only grinned up at me.

'God be with you today, son,' he called. 'I have a shield as well if you want one.'

I held out my hand and he rootled in his cart to produce a fine round shield of wood and leather, with a good grip. As I took it, he returned to his mounts and eased back on the reins so that he began to fall behind.

'Aren't you coming?' I said, thinking I was making a joke. He shook his head.

'No, mate. My job's done. Yours is the work that lays ahead now. Kill one for me.'

I stared at him as my horse drew further away, until my neck ached. When I turned back, I had to canter to catch up with Edmund and his *extraordinarii*, his master horsemen. I swallowed, looking with rather different eyes at the field around me.

The carts had pulled back from the midst of us, forming up

in a great camp at the rear. I could see small fires being lit as they prepared food. In all honesty, it was where I should have been, and I considered it for a moment before dismissing the idea. Edmund was the future and I would make that future at his side, with his court. Or I would die in the attempt.

All around me, I saw vast lines in squares. I saw men marching with spears held high, with axes spinning idly in their hands. I saw the king's cavalry in the centre, fully six hundred horses and his most powerful warriors there. They carried sword and shield, and yet somehow the trained war-horses kept their line.

My own pony had no such training. In one hand, I held a nicely weighted axe that was a comfort. In the other, I gripped my shield, which left no hand for the reins. My mount wandered off to the side as I kneed it forward, trying to lean the way I wanted it to go. It was not particularly dig-nified. Yet I had greater concerns. The scouts were in, the enemy had been sighted. The shield walls were ready and the wings had formed.

'Jesus Christ,' I whispered. 'Jesus Christ! I am going to war!'

16

We met them where the sea touched the sky on our left hand, south of a vast estuary, close by the river Mærsea, which made the boundary of Mercia and Northumbria. The memory of men will never forget that place and all its horrors.

I saw the enemy shifting like wind through a field of barley, with a noise like distant howling. I remember that well, the sound that grew and grew as we marched. Æthelstan called for a song to drown their voices. We began with a few verses of 'Fortunes of Men', before Æthelstan said he found it too solemn, so we gave them 'Vainglory', bawling out lines about the proud man, the devil's son, over and over. On that day, we saw him not as an adversary. We walked with the devil in our hearts. There was certainly no forgiveness for those who had broken oath and brought us to that cold place.

Such thoughts held my attention as my horse wandered and fouled marching ranks, beyond my control. I cannot say why it did not occur to me to drop my shield, or even my axe. In my defence, it was my first battle. I could see the enemy and I was terrified of them. If you had been there, you would have beshit yourself, believe me.

Far ahead, I saw vast walls of coloured shields, the men of Anlaf. They wore Dane helmets of iron that caught sunlight and flashed. They were what I had expected of a battlefield, though the reality was not something I wanted to look upon. They stood together, and even when I looked left and right for reassurance, I could not see how we might ever break so many, how we could push through.

Huge banners fluttered all along their lines, with Anlaf's

strange trefoil dominating the centre field – a sort of three-leafed clover in gold stitching, like the coils of a snake. On one wing facing us were the forces of Constantin of Alba, traitor and oathbreaker. The man's grandfather and father had been mere chieftains to the Picts, but Constantin wanted more than that. He wanted a crown of gold, as Æthelstan wore. He wanted to rule all Scotland – and whatever else he could win for himself. Only our king and perhaps old age stood in the road against him.

Constantin was over sixty, white-haired as Egill, scrawny as an old crow. He felt the shadow of death and he was determined to go to his grave as a king and not a vassal. If he had not given his oath to Christ to obey Æthelstan, I might even have admired him. As things stood, Constantin was a damned man, still walking the earth – and a fool to take up arms against the high king. The banners of Alba were purple pennants, the heather of the mountains or some such.

The third king of that rough host was Owen of Cumbria, or Strathclyde, or wherever it was he claimed to rule. His men stood as a rabble, shifting and lunging at us. As we drew close, I sensed the sullen violence in them all, visible in jabs of iron and obscene challenge. They were ready for us and unafraid. I knew for the first time what it meant to face such men. To my marrow, I understood I might not leave that place.

Though the day was cold and a sea wind cut across the fields, berserkers capered and lunged before the enemy lines, almost naked, their manhoods flapping about. Most wore skins, with the rotting heads of wolves still attached. One or two wore slimy cloaks of black feathers, the remnant of some dark rite of Woden that made me swallow my own bile. They loped on all fours, those men, the wolfskins they wore still wet with blood. It had spattered them and dried in lines, so that they were marked like birds or wild creatures. They were brown with dead magic as they lunged and snapped at us.

They bore knives in both hands and I have seen men in mail and helmet shrink from them in terror. I have seen one biting into a throat and pulling away flesh in his teeth, ignoring his own death to laugh as another speared him right through.

Still we walked towards them, cracking stiffness out of necks and shoulders, spinning weapons in our hands to learn the weight and range. We were the tide coming in – and there was no stopping us then, no halting us. I felt it in the quickening breath, in the glare of those around me. Walking towards your own ending was hard, and there was always a chance our nerve would fail. We wanted it to begin, so that we could be free.

When we could make out the individual faces of the berserkers, when we were close enough to see the trefoil of Anlaf's banners waving in the centre, Æthelstan's harper began to slap his hand on his wooden board. He plucked the strings, but his harp made another sound – as a heart will, if you press your ear to a chest – a fine deep thumping that stirred the blood in the same way. We had no drums with us, but our men took it up even so, drowning him out, battering clubs and swords against wooden shields until we made a fair thunder.

The forces from Dublin had landed from ships to take our land, to follow oathbreakers. Wessex was far behind then, but we walked on good green ground even so.

A shield wall cannot run and keep its shape. Those in line must advance together, with their long-handled axes ready to strike in great loops. As men fall, they are replaced from behind. I heard Æthelstan's earls roaring their orders and the formations shifted, strengthening the centre. Æthelstan did not fear the untrained men of Owen or Constantin half as much as he did the shield wall of Anlaf. Or perhaps it was his insult, to show those kings that he feared them less – to make them rash when they needed to be calm.

The men of Scotland broke free at last of whatever rein had held them. They came on at the run, while we were still two hundred yards away. Some threw spears that vanished in the press of our men. Yet there was no massed attack, no sky made dark with ash and iron as I had feared. I'd read my ancient battles, but this was not the same. We roared them on as they charged, the sound dragged out of us in challenge and fear and sheer anger. The shield wall is made for men to break against.

Even over that short sprint, the lines of Constantin strung out like beads on a thread. They struck our wall piecemeal and our ranks stood firm, cutting them down. For every sword or spear or axe the men of Alba brought to our line, we answered them with three. Still they came, wailing and leaping at us, only to be struck dead, the sounds of life jerked out of them in an instant.

Sweet Jesu, I had not known what an axe could do. I'd felled trees, but had not seen what worked on oak would be so much worse on men. The handle could be swung back and forth in such wide arcs it made a wall. No one could pass and not be struck, and once it had begun, it could be maintained until the strength gave out. I saw men standing in a round of blurring steel, unable to step forward or back. I saw shield lines crash together and axes come chopping down on the heads of those who struggled and heaved. There was more blood shed in each instant than I had seen my whole life before. I had not known men died as easily as that.

The charge is a time of terror and release. Neither side gave way and the rate of killing slowed after the first rush. Men understood they had joined with the enemy and they were still alive. They began to think once more.

That was where King Æthelstan's trained men took their toll. They had round shields and knew how best to overlap them. They fought with axes that made Anlaf's Dublin Vikings raise their own shields high to protect their heads. When they did, a serrated spear would lick out from the rank behind, piercing a chest or a sword arm, knocking them back. Even if the spear missed its mark, it created fear. Anlaf's men did not lack courage. Yet they could not see the blows coming and they hesitated. Still the axes smashed down at them, each blow of such force it broke collarbones and skulls, or whichever arm was held up in fear. It was an ugly business, I will not lie.

My own part in it was hampered by my horse, whom I had named Scoundrel for his disobedience. He had not been trained to remain calm while screaming men ran at him. Nor had his rider, in fact, which meant there were some moments I still recall in nightmares. I gripped my shield so tightly my hand went numb and white. For a time, I did not even mind that my horse wandered at will through our lines, so that men cursed me as they were hampered in their advance and told me to get fucked. I could only call an apology and then, in a moment, I was glad I had not cast the little shield away.

I saw a grey blur as one of the berserkers broke through. With no warning, he was suddenly there and leaping at me. They had cut him, of course. He ran with bright blood on him and his ribs showed white from some terrible gash. Yet he was light and fast in comparison to men in mail and helmets – it was one of the things that scared those who came up against them. With only iron knives in his hands, he'd been able to grab the edge of a shield and pull it towards himself, making a gap to slip through. I saw it done a dozen times, until I began to wonder at the tactics of men who claimed to be savage wolves. Wolves do not open doors.

It was not a true weakness of the shield wall. Very few of those who rushed up and heaved an opening for themselves managed it without being speared or gashed, or spilling their brains all over our men. They spattered blood and shrieked like foxes, or children dying. It was a sound I do not want to ever hear again. Men who would have held that line all day against Irish axemen flinched from the wolves, unwilling to be touched by their magic.

Mine was dying as he reached me, I am sure. He had to have been fading, with the wounds he had taken. Yet he showed no sign of pain or death coming at him. He went for me as the only mounted man in the group. Perhaps he took me for one of the lords and not just a monk who could not control his horse and so was out of place.

I swung my axe – and I missed with the head and edge of it, or rather he came at me so fast that he passed under my blow. The handle rapped him over the shoulders and then he was clawing at me with bloody knives and I was crying out in panic, beset by a wild animal, gnashing broken teeth and spitting blood at me.

One of the men nearby reached up and took hold of him by the wolfskin, giving a great heave. No doubt he meant to yank the man down to where he could be trampled or speared. Instead, the thongs holding the skin snapped and it came away in one piece, leaving him completely naked. I cried out in terror, but something changed in my attacker as he felt the skin peeled away.

He looked dazed, suddenly unsure. His hair was thick with blood and I flinched from drops that touched me as he wagged his head back and forth, but the fire had gone.

I struck again with the axe and you may be sure I did not miss a second time. I took a grip near the head of the thing, so that it was more like a hatchet. I spread his face for him with three fast blows, then kicked as he went limp, so that he fell backwards. I nodded to the man holding the wolfskin in astonishment and he grinned at me.

'Do you want it?' he said, holding the thing up in all its rotting glory.

'It's yours. You took it to save me. Thank you.'

He seemed delighted by that. His marching rank had not yet come to the front, though it was mere yards away by then. The fighting was a great clash of noise and grunts and iron, and it was hard to stand so close and not be touched by it somehow, like a furnace. The death of one of the feared berserkers had cheered all those around me, I found.

I carried my axe with more confidence, keeping my grip close to the iron head as my horse turned with no command from me and began to walk away. The reins had fallen loose and I could not have turned back to save my life then.

On the left of the field, Edmund used his horsemen like a dagger thrust, punching into a mailed side, bleeding them hard, as he had promised. He spared neither horse nor man and I craned to see him ride. I wondered if I dared risk standing or kneeling on my saddle, but decided I did not.

I knew by then that we were badly outnumbered. There must have been eighty ships at anchor and as many boats beached on that shore, as far as the eye could see. This was no mere raid. Anlaf had brought men to meet Æthelstan's armies and to take his kingdom.

The wing facing us was at least eight thousand strong. Perhaps ten thousand. It is always a guess on the battlefield, if an enemy is not kind enough to halt in neat squares, each of a certain number, while those who wish him dead walk along with tally squares and chalk. When the sea is shifting, no one can count the waves.

Half our left wing had been drawn into the centre against Anlaf, or taken off to face the Scots. Æthelstan still sat with his six hundred horsemen in the centre, watching the battle unfold. I do not think he had even drawn his sword, but whenever I looked, he was there, pointing and giving orders, sending men away to pass them on.

Edmund took command of the left from whoever had

given orders before. His banners rose and held position in the middle of the wing, while others were brought down, rolled up and taken to the rear. Some earl or noble captain had suffered a public humiliation, it looked like. I heard men cheering the king's brother as he greeted them.

Edmund's thanes were still ahorse, marked with blood and flushed with triumph. I saw the thickset figure of his man Leofa of Kent riding hard, kicking his poor mount for all he was worth. No lover of horses, he! The man rode as if he was made of rage and violence, lost in his element. The other thanes could be seen above the heads of the shield lines, wheeling and cantering, trying to be everywhere at once, all red-faced with shouting orders and sharp gestures.

On that side of the battle, they were calling the pace of the advance, counting off each step, so that the men knew when to strike and when to hold. It lent an urgency to the line, so that no one wanted to be left behind or found wanting. The men at the front chopped and roared as they took each long pace, daring the forces of King Owen to come and take it back.

I saw my horse liked the clamour of iron and screaming men no more than I did myself. It was beginning to turn across the field once more when I cursed and threw away my shield at last, taking up the reins in a foul temper. Even then, the stubborn animal was unwilling. It became a test of strength between us. I heaved at his bit to turn his head, but in response he snorted and bucked, almost throwing me.

'There will be no more wandering the battlefield like some old ghost, you filthy bag of bones!' I shouted at it. 'Turn to face your enemy, you ill-bred bastard. Or I will kill you myself and walk!'

I was ranting at the horse as it broke into a wild trot and then a canter, straight at the fighting. Dozens of Wessex men turned at the noise of hooves clopping up behind, fearing some rear attack of an enemy. When they saw me bouncing and flapping along with one stirrup flying loose, it was probably a relief to them. Many of them gestured crudely, but I think it was meant in fun.

I would not drop my axe, but I managed to get both hands on the reins and heaved back almost hard enough to turn us over, so that the horse was forced to look straight up at the sky. It decided it could not run under that restraint and so stopped at last. The battle line was all around me and Edmund himself was there, looking on in astonishment not a dozen yards away.

The horse had pushed right through to the enemy in its panic. Even then, I could sense the beast was ready to bolt at any instant, so I laid about me with my axe, putting on the best show I could. I struck one sod as he gaped at the sight of a horse suddenly appearing in front of him. He was black-haired and had some sort of boil or canker on his gum, so that half his face was distended. I can see him now, as he fell.

A second bearded fellow tried to strike the horse with a mailed glove, making Scoundrel rear and spin. As I fought to stay in the saddle, I kicked out in a fury and missed. Yet the horse struck him with its flank as he jerked around. The press was too great to avoid the horse, with Scoundrel strong enough and heavy enough to shove men aside no matter how they braced against him. The man vanished from sight under the stamping hooves with a cry of horror.

Someone else crashed against us and that was too much for my horse. I was off again, reins and stirrups flapping, the animal whinnying and snorting and as mindless as the wolf berserkers on the other side of the battlefield.

Æthelstan's forces left aisles between their thousands, so that there were clear roads for orders – or for a horse gone mad to gallop down. I did not have the skill or the patience to stop him and we looped out from the battle, going as if the fallen angel and enemy of mankind himself was on our heels, as perhaps he was.

I quieted Scoundrel at last when we were a mile or so clear, then tied him to a gatepost. I walked back with my axe twirling in my right hand, getting used to it. Perhaps my blood had been raised by that wild ride, or by those who had come at me. I had been challenged, in the oldest way a man can be challenged. I wanted to hit back – and to be seen by Æthelstan and Edmund. I understand better now why kings must stand on the battlefield. Just being there to witness the deeds of their warriors makes those men fight all the harder. A king is worth a thousand, I think, perhaps even more.

I passed along the messenger lines, ignoring the stares of warriors who had not yet fought that day. There was a little blood on me and I spun my axe as I walked, knowing I must have made a fine sight in my Benedictine robe. Perhaps I had run a little mad myself for a while, like my horse before me. Battle will do that to a young man. I felt no pains, no aches. I was sixteen and strong. That day is bright with colour still.

The sun had passed the noon point by the time I returned to the fray. Thousands who had begun that morning in hope and health lay cooling, staring at nothing. I do not believe there has ever been such a slaughter on a single day, nor will we ever see its like again. Most battles are fought as a test of strength. When one side is overmatched, they withdraw in good order, the issue settled for a generation. The field of Brunanburh by the Mærsea was rather different.

Æthelstan bore a grudge against those who had broken oath – and still stood in arms against him. Neither he nor Edmund could forgive such men, so they were determined to leave them all as chop-bone rags. The stakes could not have been higher, nor more personal. I believe Æthelstan cried out in triumph when the banners of Constantin's son fell, raising both arms to the air to roar at them.

Constantin himself was borne away from the battlefield after that, ruined by grief and clawing to reach his son's body. I imagine the old king's guard were pleased enough to leave that field by then. It was not going well for them.

Though Constantin and King Owen of Cumbria had brought thousands of swords and men to wield them, the heart of Brunanburh was always the forces of Anlaf. Those Viking and Dublin men were the sort who had taken half of England in the past. Anlaf himself was a cunning man, no fool on the battlefield, or off it. No doubt he was the one who had whispered into Scottish ears that Constantin and Owen could be kings of the north. He'd promised much to them – and they had bolstered his forces to the point where he could challenge the high king of all Britain.

When the Scots had been driven into the ground or from the field, when King Owen of Cumbria, who called himself Owen Caesarius, had been cut down and dismembered, Anlaf of Dublin remained in the centre, facing us over a quarter-mile of murder and destruction. I arrived as King Æthelstan gave new orders – and I could not follow because I had no horse.

I could only stare in awe as six hundred riders eased across the field through their own squares and banners. The wyvern of Wessex rode high above them all. Anlaf's men gave a great growl of anticipation, knowing the man they had come to kill was on the move.

Æthelstan rode at the heart of that group on a black horse that stood like Bucephalus, as great an animal as ever lived. I saw the high king draw his sword and lower it as they reached the far edge of the battlefield and turned to the enemy, moving to a canter and then a great thundering gallop. I swallowed drily at the sight and sound of them, the shaking of the ground. Those horses moved like the wind and I had already seen what just one could do against men. I crossed myself. A thousand others did the same. The fighting almost died away across the front as men panted and watched the high king move against his enemy.

Most of Æthelstan's horsemen held spears in their hands, with two or three more ready to throw. Some of the larger men swung axes or swords, but the weapon was in their speed and their weight. Impact combines those two aspects, multiplies them so that a hammer swung hard can break anything. Give me a hammer and a place to stand – and I will break the world.

The king's charge gave a great groan as they closed on the enemy, a low note that rose quickly to a howl. I wanted to be with them and I cursed my horse once more for making me miss the greatest moment I had ever witnessed.

My foot slipped on a shield lying loose and I took it up, pleased with the weight of it on my left arm. As I did so, there was a crash to shake heaven, and Æthelstan's horsemen rode into the flank of Anlaf's forces at full gallop. From where I stood, I could see only dust rising and hear the great cry of fear and outrage from the enemy. Yet I found myself trotting forward with thousands more as the shield lines ahead began to fail and break.

Anlaf's men wanted to see what was happening to their flank. They died as they turned, so that our men walked over them, grunting and chopping with new vigour. I heard men laugh and one poor bastard was sobbing, though he had no wound on him.

I pressed in with the rest, and for a time I forgot my vocation and my vows. I can hardly describe the freedom of it. Not all killing is proscribed, but I had suffered suspicion and threats before when death was close to my hand. On that field, it was expected, desired. To win, we had to kill as many as we could. I revelled in it as Anlaf's centre collapsed.

I do not recall how many fell to me as I stalked amongst them. My presence was marked, of course. It did not go unnoticed that a Benedictine was among the line of axemen. For years, I had to deny any knowledge when I was asked about it. Yet on that day, I was proud to stand there, with my king.

Anlaf made it back to the coast, more is the pity. Not one tenth of the men he had brought were as lucky. They had come in a great fleet, landing boats on the shingle all along that coast. They needed only a few to hold the number who returned.

Æthelstan burned the boats they left behind. I think he wanted Anlaf to see the flames as darkness came, lighting the sky behind him. I imagine they could see the glow of it in Dublin, just about.

Five small kings died that day and some half a dozen earls. Æthelstan had lost much, but he'd gained peace and reminded all those who might rebel that we were strong. Constantin went into a monastery, made useless by grief, though he deserved it all and more. The throne of Scotland went to some cousin of his. Owen was taken home in pieces by a few of his servants and buried somewhere in the vastnesses of Cumbria.

Anlaf, of course, we would see again. He licked his wounds for a while, but still dreamed of coming back. He had learned he could not face Æthelstan, but no man lives for ever, not even a king. Especially a king.

17

When we returned to Winchester, I made it my concern to learn more of the wolf and crow men I'd seen on the battle-field of Brunanburh. I could not quite forget the way that young man's face had changed when his wolfskin cloak had been taken from him. It was as if he'd woken from sleep and had barely time to blink and look around in wonder before I'd smashed the life out of him. He came to me in dreams for some months after that, sometimes to claw at me and smear me with blood, but as often as not, just to speak and tell me of his life. In part, my new field of study was to protect myself against those visions. They were not an aid to restful sleep.

Æthelstan and his brother Edmund enjoyed that summer. Not only had they fought and won, but there were no other contenders for the throne of Britain then, not one. It would be a long time before Anlaf had the strength and gold to find more men.

Great feasts were held and Edmund made sure I had a place at them. Æthelstan had neither seen nor heard of my courage, more was the pity. Yet a battle of just a single day creates thousands of stories: moments of courage and shame, turnarounds, vengeances by the dozen, desperate escapes and wild luck of all kinds. War is the great engine of story-telling, from the Latin *ingenium* for 'device', keeping bards in wine and silver by the thousand.

On every holy day and celebration for months, Æthelstan would summon men of high estate and low to the front, when ale and wine had flowed as rivers and all stomachs were full. Whether they were earls, churls or thralls, if they had a story, up they went. They described parts of the day I had not seen, nor even known about.

From the king's bard, I heard that Constantin's son had called for Æthelstan's champion to face him – and that Egill had crossed half the battlefield to answer that challenge. I laughed with the rest as the bard showed us the changes in expression as the enemy watched Egill get bigger and bigger before him.

I heard too how Edmund had dismissed a senior thane on the left wing, asserting his authority over him. That man had left the battlefield and had been found hanging from a tree, dead by his own hand. Edmund told that as a sombre moment, but I knew from more private conversation that the fool had frozen on the battlefield, giving no orders for great stretches while our warriors were killed. Some men break, is all.

I heard about the king's great charge from many voices. They smiled as they spoke and looked to Æthelstan in shared memory and pride. I could see they would never forget that day. Eyes gleamed in the telling – and it was not grief, or even triumph, but just echoes of strong emotion, of having lived through it.

The country was at peace as the seasons turned and turned again. I became well known at the king's archives, so that no one minded my being there late at night, with just a shuttered lamp, gleaming dimly. Candles and bare flames were not allowed in those stacks and shelves, as you may imagine.

Æthelstan had always loved books and learning – but he took no pleasure from them, not as I did. He devoured works of faith and morals and read constantly from books translated by his grandfather or that were the result of his own scholarship. With different forebears, he could certainly have been a fine scribe or copyist. His personal prayerbook was as much his tiny black notes as the original text. What good it did him, what grace or peace it brought, I do not know.

If he had been some blockheaded lout of a king, without his fascinations, perhaps there would have been no royal library. Yet a month would not go by at that court without some book trader's cart appearing at our gates. It was a rare event to see one turned away without a full purse, even when we had every copy already and merely bought duplicates.

It was not long before I was paying a couple of Elflaed's silver pennies to the servants to tell me first when such a trader arrived. I'd been appalled to see one book destroyed, torn page from page, with all the binding threads showing like sparrow-bones. I knew there were things written no Christian king could permit. 'Suffer not a witch to live' applies also to their dark magics. Yet I did not see another book broken or burned in my time at Winchester, you may be sure. For the best part of two years, whenever I had first warning, I would gallop down to add the trader's wares to the catalogue, to settle a price and to stack them on a little wheeled cart I had made, like the ones we used at the abbey to carry bricks or heavy pots.

The archivist then was an old fellow by the name of Geraint. He seemed to know a great deal of what had once been in the royal collection, but his eyes were almost useless and the burden of keeping the catalogue fell on my shoulders. I welcomed the freedom it brought me and those years were among the happiest of my life. Yet all things perish. Rose petals fall and summers end. Lent becomes Advent, as we used to say. That is just the way of it. We are not here to enjoy ourselves, after all. The beauty of a morning is just another form of temptation, more subtle than a soft red lip, or the desire for vengeance.

I had not seen a great deal of King Æthelstan for what must have been a year. With Edmund as my patron, I had become a known figure in the king's court, though not once had I been asked to witness a Witan document, not even the minor ones where being a witness was more chore than honour. I confess I wondered why every other man and his mate seemed to be called at intervals, but never me.

I learned the reason after my third Christmas at Winchester, when I had just turned eighteen and grown a whisker shy of two yards tall. The king had his own yardstick and scales then. There was even a call to make such things the prime measures of the whole country. As if a pound of bacon in London will ever balance the scales of a pound in York. There is infinite variety in us, as it should be. Some people would put the whole world in chains.

I should have known something was up from the guard sent to fetch me. I never learned his name, but he was a pock-faced, ill-made fellow. He had certainly never been one of those who greeted me jovially when we met, whether in respect for my robe and tonsure or just good cheer, I never knew. A monk's shaven crown is something of a trial for the way it has to be scraped each morning, always by another – it is almost impossible to do neatly oneself. Yet it serves as a sign of piety and vocation, visible to all. Most men bowed to me as I walked the corridors and gardens with armfuls of my books. They did so that day as I followed the king's man, wondering idly what Æthelstan could possibly want with me.

I knew I was in some sort of trouble when I saw my uncle and Lady Elflaed in the outer chambers. Both of them rose to greet me and they looked as if they were about to witness my execution. Elflaed squirmed her hands together and yet I was ushered past them before they could say a single word, through another door that shut behind me while I was still gaping like a country boy at his first market.

Æthelstan was there, behind a great table of oak, sanded and waxed so well it seemed almost to glow with its own light. As my hands had made it, I can say it took weeks to achieve that lustre.

We were not alone in the room, of course. A king is almost never alone. Whether it is to record his words and promises, or to protect him from mad monks who might leap across a table at him, there are always men close to their master, very much like an ox in harness, straining to be let go.

I glanced behind me as I came in, fixing the position of two such oxen in my mind. I swallowed to see Egill Skiall-grimmson was also there in the corner. Though the Icelander appeared to be relaxing on a wide chair with his legs crossed and his hands behind his head, I knew by then how fast he could move. Egill could cross the room and drive me into the ground with one blow while the other two were still pulling out their swords. He raised his chin to me as our eyes met and I swallowed, turning back to the king who stood at a window and looked over the city. The shutters had been pinned back and he could watch the scurryings of his people below without actually having to touch or greet or smell them. I rather envied the arrangement and wished I could have spent an afternoon in silence on that spot.

Æthelstan turned to me and I took a sharp breath at the change in him. His right hand had darkened to a very unhealthy colour. His face had been all planes and bone under his blond beard. At that moment, it had grown softer in aspect, yet it looked to my eye to be the swelling of sickness rather than too much food or wine.

'Your Highness, my lord, I should have been called earlier than this!' I said. 'If there is some foul humour in your blood, it must be let out and balanced. It cannot be ignored.'

To my surprise, Æthelstan waved his swollen hand in irritation, as if to brush away my speech.

'I have not called you here to tend my tainted hand, Brother Dunstan. My own physician bleeds me each morning and has given much ease. It is no more than a scratch gone sour in the flesh. I will recover. No, that is not your concern.'

I blinked, waiting to be told what else it might be. The sense of relief I'd felt on seeing the ill colour in his arm and face drained away, leaving me feeling cold and shivery.

'Seat yourself, Dunstan.'

I did so, sinking into a wooden chair with a padded seat. I could feel the rounded nailheads digging into my buttocks as I waited to discover what made the king of Britain so grim in my presence. I did not have long to wait.

'I have had word from Glastonbury,' Æthelstan said. 'Some months ago, now. I don't believe I ever heard such wild accusations as came out of that place. Blasphemy, lies, fits, murders, theft – all manner of strange goings-on.'

I felt myself grow very still and once more I became aware of Egill Skiallgrimmson at my back. I could feel him watching me, so I returned the king's gaze, unblinking, unashamed. I gave them nothing.

Æthelstan was one of those who believed he could read a man. I'd heard him say it was perhaps his greatest talent – and the source of all the rest. Yet he could not read me. He frowned and began to pace as he went on.

'I sent a man to investigate in my name, to see if I had welcomed a devil into my court. Or to discover whether a good man was being lied about, traduced and ruined out of spite and jealousy. I ordered only that my servant visited as a pilgrim, to observe and question.'

I felt an urge to swallow, as spit pooled in my mouth. It was odd how such an ordinary thing became hard to do, until I felt I had an apple lodged in my throat, or just a piece of it.

'When my man returned to me, he brought reports of disarray, Dunstan. Of an abbot run wild, my own appointment, driven to fevers of the brain by grief at the death of his son. A tragedy, Dunstan, though we have all known loss – and seen those broken by it. Of course, a man of God . . . does not bear comparison with such pitiful creatures, keening after lost babes and such. Holy men like Abbot Simeon, ah . . . hermits and visionaries have concerns much greater than washing or eating.'

That interested me! I could only imagine how barking, frothing mad old Simeon must have gone to have the king clearing his throat and hesitating even to describe it! I hoped the skinny old fool ran naked round the abbey twice a day.

'The community at Glastonbury has broken apart under . . . such strain. I am told no man trusts another. It seems they eat in their cells and rooms, rather than together, believing they will be poisoned. Even the regular services have had to be abandoned, with no one attending. This, in the abbey founded by St David. In the resting place of St Patrick! Where King Arthur went to die! It is not to be borne. There was even a murder after you left, when one of them stuck one of his fellow monks with a knife and ran away.'

'Brother Caspar?' I asked. I could not help myself.

'No. Is he one who knew you well?'

The king may have thought that was a clever question, but if complaints and accusations had been made against me, I could not imagine a more likely source.

'Oh my lord, it grieves me to answer. Brother Caspar was mine enemy. Ever since the moment with the angel, he was jealous. It ate at him, I think, corroded him. I knew him first as an honourable man, but he was one of those who came in the night and tried to kill me. He seemed to . . . hate me then.'

I looked away, suddenly afraid the king would truly have a gift to see to the heart of me. It took a great effort of will to remember that the eyes are shutters on the soul. I knew he would see guilt in tiny twitches and nervous trembling. So I returned his gaze like an innocent child – and it reassured him. He trusted his judgement of me. I saw much of the tension go out of the man and he exchanged a flickering glance with Egill, at my back. I did not turn, though my shoulder blades crawled for an instant as I imagined that great white-haired troll taking my head off.

'I want to believe you, Dunstan. My niece speaks highly of you – and I have gone over and over her time at the abbey, everything she saw. She believes you were saved that day for a reason, though she does not yet know what that might be. And I trust her.'

He stared fondly at the wall for a beat – and for the first time, it occurred to me that Elflaed might not actually be the king's niece, in the sense of being related to him by blood. I felt my eyes widen. Calling a younger woman 'niece' is a term used by some men. It does not matter. I found myself blushing and I coughed violently into my hand to cover the sudden heat in my face.

'I can see you are a fellow of great promise, Dunstan, an artificer of rare ability. This very table is proof! All those who have taught or observed you say the same, that you have a mind and hands that are touched by the divine.'

I risked a small smile and bowed my head, trying to look humble. Humility is something of a pain, of course, for any man. We all claim to despise pride, but honestly, must we pretend to be unaware of our talents, year after year? Goodness me, did I make something of extraordinary beauty yet again? Well, what luck to be so blessed! It is ludicrous.

I found myself the object of the king's gaze once more as he stopped pacing.

'I must confess I have not acted with honour, Dunstan. Can you forgive me?'

I felt my heart thumping. Was it some sort of trap?

'Of . . . c-course, Your Highness, my lord. I am sure you . . .'

'I ordered you watched. And followed. For months now, I have had eyes on you, wherever you went. Whatever you read. That is my concern here, Dunstan.'

My mind was whirling with a thousand thoughts of petty sin and errors. I doubt even the saints would enjoy the thought of being observed at all hours of a day. Had they watched me as I slept? It did not seem possible. The power of such a claim is that the accused will sometimes blurt out their own guilt with little or no further effort. I have used the device successfully myself once or twice, in the years since.

'With one exception, you appear to live a blameless life, Dunstan. My men report no side deals in royal supplies, no gambling, no whores. You work and you read, Dunstan. One of my men has become quite incensed at such a simple life, which interested me. He is certain you spotted him somehow – and are hiding some great sin behind an innocent exterior.'

The king paused for a moment, to tap one of his fingernails on a tooth. I saw again how thick and dark his fingers had become. The habit clearly caused him pain, so that he looked at his own hand in surprise, wincing at the sight of it.

'I wish now that I had brought Jonah in, for him to question you directly. Yet his suspicions go some way to explain the accusations from the abbey. You are a man who inspires spite, Dunstan. Some, like the archivist Geraint, speak of you with enormous affection, almost as a father to a son. Your uncle has tears in his eyes when he speaks of your troubles and suffering. Yet others hint at sorceries, of forbidden books, of strange rituals no one else can explain or understand.'

'I am a seeker after truth,' I said firmly. 'A man of faith. That is all, my lord. I am a reflection of my maker and yet a broken thing. I am a sinner, of course. There is no perfection here. Shall I confess my sins to you? Command me and I shall.'

'No, no . . .' He held up his palm. 'I cannot absolve you, nor hear confession.'

I had him on the defensive, allowing me time to collect my thoughts.

The king knew a little. He did not know all. I suspected he was hinting at a great deal of knowledge, in the hope that I would admit more. Yet I was not a fool, nor a child.

'You are a very young man, Dunstan, a young man of great promise, it is true. That is clear to me. I will not throw you to the fire. I am building a kingdom, after all. I need strong backs and fine minds. Give me your hands.'

I rose from my chair and held out my hands in a sort of trance. To my dismay, he did take them in his. We stood there like lovers, looking into each other's eyes. I did not flinch. He could not see me.

'In his last breath, a man can turn to another path, should he so choose. If you have sinned, Dunstan. If you have sought a diabolical cure perhaps for your fits, if you have had thoughts born from pride and anger rather than the goodness of God, there is still time to cast your old life into the flames. Do you understand?'

His hands were very warm, though it may have been the sickness in him.

'Lady Elflaed has intervened on your behalf, asking for mercy. Your uncle too has begged me not to abandon you – to show compassion. I want to believe these hands were touched by angels, Dunstan. On that, even your enemies will not gainsay you. Now, tell me on your oath and on your immortal soul. Is it true? Were you carried down?'

I nodded at him, horrified at the stakes. The silence beat at me in great strokes, each more powerful than the one before, until I thought I might faint away. The king breathed again and I realised he had been perfectly still, weighing me, my hands against his.

'God be praised, Dunstan. He has found a good servant in you. Very well. You are freed of your service here, your oaths to me. Glastonbury needs an abbot. Go and do God's work in that place, far away from here. Far away from me.'

His voice hardened subtly and I wondered if he understood me perfectly well. A king will know many kinds of men, saints and sinners among them. Yet they must be practical fellows themselves, to hold a throne.

'I do not expect to see you again, Brother Dunstan. Do you understand? This is mercy from me – and the favour that comes from having such advocates to speak on your behalf.'

'Th-thank you, my lord,' I stuttered at him, beginning to understand what he was giving me. It was too much to take in and I could feel myself trembling. I felt as if I'd been dragged screaming to the edge of hell, then given my greatest desire. I sensed my inquisition was coming to an end, but still he held me by the hands.

'Thank your uncle and Lady Elflaed, if you wish.' Æthelstan made a twitching motion with his swollen hand that was almost obscene. 'I pluck you out, Dunstan, as one who is too much trouble. I choose not to waste your talents, but I expect you to learn humility. Let forty or fifty years pass now in peaceful labour. Work as God intended for you. Build the abbey Lady Elflaed desires. Grow into the role as abbot, as father to a community. Above all, do not make me regret my appointment. I sense overweening pride in you, Dunstan – and perhaps greatness, if you can master it. Either way, you will not return to Winchester.'

When he let my hands go at last, they felt stiff and cold, so that I flexed them. I bowed to the king in something of a daze, then backed away a pace before turning. Egill was there in my view, smirking. I did not respond to it, knowing that I was still observed.

In the hall outside, Lady Elflaed took me in her arms, tears spilling down her cheeks, the great soft bag. Uncle Athelm was rather more brisk as I told him what the king had said.

'Well, Dunstan, however it has come about, this is a great honour. You must strive to be worthy of it.'

'But I am too young to be abbot! And Simeon is still . . . How am I to remove him, even if they will accept me, which they certainly won't! Doesn't an abbot have to be at least thirty?'

'The king has the authority, Dunstan,' Elflaed said. 'The miracle of you being carried down gives him the right. Rome will not question it – and Lord knows that abbey needs a firm hand. Oh, you will do such things! I have been waiting for you to see your path ever since we came to Winchester. Since that regrettable business. You nearly broke my heart, Dunstan, but I see now it was all a test, of us both perhaps. Oh my boy, with my wealth and your strength, we will make the abbey of your vision. I swear it, though it cost me all I have and takes us a lifetime. But tell me, Dunstan. Did you say yes?'

I looked at Lady Elflaed, feeling a little wild and untethered. Her bosom heaved as she stood there, waiting. She and my uncle both seemed to be hanging on my word. It was a heady feeling as we stood together.

'I said yes. I will be an abbot.' I heard my own words in stunned disbelief. 'I will be abbot of Glastonbury,' I said again, as a breath.

The autumn had come by the time I stood ready to leave. My goods and books would be sent separately, cart upon cart, Lady Elflaed had assured me. I carried only a few of the ones I dared not leave behind, along with a satchel that made me walk almost like a hunchback.

In the shadow of the main gate, I was staring around at the king's estate, trying to hold it in my memory. I knew I might never see it again and the few years I'd spent there had been mostly happy. I'd seen war at its bloodiest and I knew that had changed me. The smell of the huge funeral pyres after the battle still came to me on the breeze at odd moments, as if it always would.

I turned at the clatter of boots, smiling at the sight of Edmund rushing out into the sun. He laughed to see me and we clasped our right hands, testing sword against hammer until our joints protested.

'I will miss our late-night talks, Dunstan,' he said.

We were both awkward. It is hard for some men to admit they are friends.

'I will miss them too,' I said.

He stood a little closer and dipped his head, so that I leaned towards him.

'My brother is a great king. Yet when he takes against a man . . .' He winced. 'He doesn't know you as I do. I tried to speak to him, to keep you here, but he would not listen.'

I was touched by that.

'I can't complain about being made to rise, can I?'

He chuckled and slapped my shoulder.

'You'll have them running around like chickens. Perhaps I'll come out and see that old place when you rebuild it.'

'I hope so,' I said.

'Have the monks mention me in their prayers,' Edmund said. It was suddenly enough for him. He raised his head to me and galloped off back to whatever he'd been doing before. I can see him as if he stood before me now, in all his youth and strength. God, I miss him still.

18

The boat creaked as Brother Guido poled his way across the salt marshes. I noticed his stare no longer lingered on me as it had in my youth, nor did he ask me to row for him while he sat back to watch young muscles work. I had grown forge-strong. I would have broken him across my knee if he'd so much as laid a hand on it. I actually hoped he would, and I think he sensed my anger, so that he stayed away from his scowling passenger.

As I'd stood on the scrub shore and struck flint and steel to light the torch to bring his little boat, I'd wondered how best to begin my work. I wore a black robe and a cloak over it, to keep me warm. The sun was a pale and reedy thing that day, smeared across clouds and damp. The air tasted of salt and samphire. My mouth had watered at the very thought, and then the boat had come and brother Guido was smothering the torch with damp rags, swearing as he burned himself on hot wool and oil, then poling back without a word, as if I were just a ghost and he had not seen me standing there.

The mists lay deep on the marshes as we eased through, following a narrow waterway. It seemed to last an age as I sat there on the thwarts, my hessian sack of books and my leather satchel clutched to my chest as the cold seeped in. Once more I heard the plop of frogs at our passing and the calls of birds that seemed to cry my memories as they beat into the air.

The little dock was deserted, though I saw it differently from when I had stepped out first, so many years before. I knew I would need dozens of boats and full barges for what I had in mind – and a thousand men to dig and cut stone. Perhaps the marshes themselves could be dammed and made dry, like Moses and the Red Sea.

As I tossed a coin to Guido, he seemed to shrug at me. He had not said a word and so I kept silent. I do not think he recognised me. He might have been rather more nervous if he had. I leaped out onto the dock with the shade of my father at my side, as if I was thirteen again, with Wulfric leaping about like a kid goat.

As I reached the abbey, the Tor loomed somewhere high above me, like a green tower. I felt my breath quicken and I had to stop as excitement swelled. I made myself remember the crowd who had stood around me as I scrabbled on the cliff edge. They had watched me, every one of them. They had broken my hands when I would not fall.

It was enough to douse my mood like the signal torch I'd left behind. I opened the gate with cold hands and cold eyes, ready for them.

I began to see men and women hurrying along, heads down and busy, as I walked through the abbey grounds. It was not quite the deserted place I had expected. In the years I'd been away, it seemed a few strangers had joined that community.

Some touched their forelocks as I passed, showing respect to the robe and tonsure. Among their number, I caught glimpses of faces I recognised – who had stood on that cliff edge and watched me cry out and fall.

The widow of Encarius was the first one I knew for certain. She looked weary, her hands red and gleaming, cracked and sore. I nodded to her and she only dipped her head in her little mob cap and hurried on.

I waited for a moment, holding my breath, convinced she would stop and denounce me. I watched her all the way across the great yard until she vanished into one of the embroidery houses, returning to her labours. I found myself obscurely disappointed and yet relieved at the same time, as if I'd braced for a blow that hadn't come and so found myself staggering.

I had changed, of course. I'd grown at least two hands in height and my face had lengthened. I reached up and patted the bald crown of my tonsure. That too would have changed my aspect. In the end, though, perhaps it was just that she thought me far away, or bones in a ditch somewhere.

I shook my head and chuckled, then turned, almost stumbling against Brother Caspar. He muttered an apology, looking me full in the face as he passed. He carried an armful of leather wraps, perhaps two dozen scrolls and quills, all protected from the damp as he took them to some new place. His old switch poked through the centre of the bundle and I wondered if it was the very one he had beaten me with, until I recalled how it had splintered. No doubt he replaced them regularly.

He walked two paces past me and then stopped as if he had been struck.

'Fetch the abbot for me would you, Brother Caspar?' I said to his back. 'I have grave news for him.'

I said it as if I'd never left, as if I'd spoken to him last just that morning, not three years and a great fall before. He turned slowly and I had the pleasure of seeing him pale as he did.

'I knew it was you,' he said.

As I waited in polite interest, he cast around for some place to lay down his burden. If you have not been eighteen and strong, I cannot explain how much I wanted him to attack me, how I welcomed it.

There would be many months and years of work to come, now that I had returned. I had a vision of an abbey to build.

One thing was certain, however, written in the stars. It would not begin with a beating from Brother Caspar.

I watched as he spotted a cart a dozen yards away, levering his armful into it and stalking back. I think he took a better look at me as he did so, for he wilted just a touch. I was taller than him, which does not mean much. I was broader than him, which meant more. I wanted to kill him, and that meant most of all.

'Call the abbot!' Caspar snapped to a gaggle of boys passing by. 'Quickly!'

'I asked *you* to fetch him, Brother Caspar, did I not? I suppose you cannot wait to talk over old times. Is that it? Did you miss me so very much?'

I was still a child then in some ways, to taunt him so. Back in Winchester, Lady Elflaed had wrinkled her brow at me when I'd said I wanted to go in alone. Those people had thought to kill me, where no one else would ever see. It was all too easy to imagine how it might have gone. I never let them see the fear I'd felt as I fell, the horror as Encarius broke under my weight.

I'd watched the life bleed from Encarius and felt only satisfaction at the time. Yet they'd gone back to their lives above, while I had been reduced in mud and filth and blood, crawling through the fields to the road and the lady's carriage. I think I understood how Lucifer felt to be cast down by such whey-faced, sanctimonious prigs.

'I knew you had lived,' Caspar said to me, his voice hoarse with emotion. 'I knew it when we found your trail, the marks of you crawling through the wet leaves. My friend Encarius dies and the rat who killed him survives, of course.'

'Ah, I see. Should I have gone meekly to my death, Caspar? Should I have blessed you as you murdered me?'

He flinched at my words, like a twitch. I saw the first touch of fear in his face as he truly looked at me. I was clean and tall and well fed. Had I come to accuse him? To accuse them all? He bit his lip in swelling worry and I smiled gently, chuckling. He backed a step from my expression.

'If I had come for vengeance, Caspar, you could not find a place to stand, not where you would be safe.'

'What nonsense is this? What boasting words are these?' He stepped forward in his temper and poked a finger at me. 'You come here as a mockery of a monk, tonsured and robed? Where is your shame, boy, your humility?'

'Ah, brother, where is yours?' I said, my voice rising to a great growl. 'Where is yours?'

I took hold of him and we struggled together for a time. He discovered he was not strong enough to break free and I waited until he understood that perfectly well. Then I dragged him by his robe to the cart and took up the switch he had laid down.

The bell in the tower began to toll then, as someone called a warning that could be heard for miles. I smiled at him. Caspar made an incoherent sound as I began to beat him with his own stick. I was thorough. I took my time with it. When the switch broke, I tossed the pieces down and left him at my feet, panting and bloody on the reeds and mud of the yard.

I took a deep breath and looked up to see a number of people I remembered with as much fondness as Caspar. They had come running in answer to the bell's warning. Aphra was there, gaping at me. Master Gregory of the workshop was staring at Caspar, no doubt recalling how he had broken my hands with neat blows of his hammer. Brother John of the gardens was there, though he had grown so frail and white-haired I wondered if he might have been a ghost. Abbot Simeon pointed a shaking finger at me, overcome. I smiled at him, too.

I turned around the circle of faces, showing myself alive and whole to each one of them who might have remembered me. I was tempted to bow, with Caspar on the ground before me, as if at a performance. I recognised that I was a little drunk on vengeance and so resisted that urge.

Abbot Simeon looked more like a wild hermit, with a long grey beard and hair grown thick with filth. Such men are said to be above the cares of the world, so that the pain of rotting teeth and flesh means nothing to them. In his case, though, it seemed mere madness rather than holiness. He worked his mouth at me, making no sounds, though his gaze passed from mine to the trembling monk who still lay dazed at my feet.

'You will be hanged,' Aphra said suddenly. 'By the law this time.'

It was a surprise to have the accusation come from her. She stood with her hands folded and her jaw jutting. I repressed a shudder of memory.

'I see. Of what crime am I accused?' I asked her, genuinely curious.

'The murder of poor Godwin, of Encarius, of who knows how many others!'

'Of Father Keats,' I prompted. 'He died while I was here, did he not?'

'You admit it?' she asked, her eyes widening.

'I admit to nothing, except Encarius who fell with me. When you gathered together on the cliff, I pleaded with you. I begged you not to kill me, a boy. Did you listen to a word of it? Or were you so certain I was a sinner that there could only be one judgement?'

They did not answer me, though our talk had given Abbot Simeon time to find his creaking voice.

'Gather him up once more. For all those he killed. For my poor son.'

There were enough new monks there to do it. They had come with axes and knives in answer to the bell, fearing a raid.

I raised my right hand, as if I might bless them.

'Hold,' I said. It is strange what works with men, at times. Merely saying a word should not stop them, but if the tone is right, it can be a wall.

I reached into my satchel and removed the leather wrap, a square in dark blue. I had the eyes of them all fastened on it, I could feel them. Certainly they did not rush me when they could have, though I felt a trickle of sweat running down my back at the possibility. I had cut it all rather finer than I'd intended.

'Gather him up!' Abbot Simeon screeched at them, pointing to me. I noticed he did not move alone to lay hands on me, so perhaps his madness was not complete. I would have broken his scrawny old neck with one blow, had he come at me.

I showed them a royal seal, the wyvern of Wessex in a wafer of blue wax, thick as a finger almost. Before them all, I snapped the seal in my hands – and of course I thought of the Host and Holy Communion. It had the feel of a ritual, a moment of perfection.

Rain clouds lowered overhead, threatening a downpour. I glanced up and frowned at the thought, wondering if I had felt the first drops. It would not do to see the king's ink made to run. Still, no one else spoke. They had seen the seal and it held them in chains. I held it up to them and began to read.

'"Be it known that Dunstan of Baltonsborough, son of Heorstan and Cyneryth, is named Abbot of the Benedictine Community at Glastonbury, under my authority as King of all Britain, to stand over all predecessors and in place of Father Simeon of Anglia, who has served well in the role these many years."'

I looked up at the open mouths and wide eyes all around me.

'There is not much more, beyond the signature of King Æthelstan and various titles. I think it is enough. I will make it available to anyone who wishes to see it. Perhaps away from the mud of the yard, though, eh?' I chuckled at them, though I hid the satisfaction that swelled in me. I wanted to laugh, to caper in dark delight in that yard, but I could not.

'I accept the king's appointment. Now, I will say this. I have returned. The past is the past.' I paused to glance down at Caspar, whose mass of livid stripes rather gave me the lie on that score. 'There are forty men arriving tomorrow to begin work – to break down the walls around us, stone from stone. I will reduce this poor stable to beams and spoil. Then we will build something greater in this place. I will see you all individually . . . What is it, Simeon?'

The old man came at me, almost in a daze himself, trying to rake me with his nails in great sweeps. I was pleased when one of the younger men gathered him up in a cloak, a kindness to him more than me. It took only that touch for his rage to become weeping, the sounds of it fading as he was taken away.

I heard a commotion then, from the rear of the group. A figure came through and I smiled in real pleasure to see Wulfric. He stood with his chest heaving and his hair wild. In his one hand, he carried an axe as if he was actually prepared to use it.

'You missed my speech, Wulfric,' I said, though I grinned at him. 'I'd not thought to see you here.'

'And there was I, thinking I was coming to save you,' he said, looking down in amazement at Caspar.

As he spoke, the monk tried to rise and I gave him a great kick that made him curl up once again. It was most unchristian of me, I accept that. Yet it served to demonstrate my authority. The Church must demand obedience. In that way, Caspar was a fine lesson.

Wulfric and I looked at each other, and I found much to like in the strong young man I saw before me. Sixteen months younger than me, I realised he was seventeen and resembled our father more than I did myself. Yet the 'T'-shaped scar on his scalp served to remind me I had also seen his skull laid bare. I shuddered.

'The king has appointed me abbot, Wulfric. He told me to clear out the old and bring in the new. I will need a reeve.'

'A reeve?' he said faintly.

'Well, what do you do here?'

'Our shop supplies the abbey. Cloth for embroidery, altar-pieces, robes and habits. I measure and I cut and we have looms in London to make it all. I . . . have a serving lad to help me when I need two hands.'

It was less than I had hoped for him. He looked at his feet as he saw my disappointment. I tried to imagine life without an arm, how hard it must have been. I felt my own anger kindling once again at the thought.

'You've survived then, Brother. I am sorry I could not do more for you.'

'Sorry? You saved my life, Dun! If not for you, I would never have lived to marry and father a daughter.'

'Truly?' I asked him in surprise. 'I am an uncle?'

He showed me an expression of such honest and simple joy that I stepped away from Brother Caspar and his miserable coughing to embrace Wulfric. It felt strange, but I had missed him.

When I let go, I looked back at those who still stood around me, like calves stunned for slaughter.

'Well? You have all heard the king's appointment. Go about your business. I will see each one of you in time.'

Aphra was among the first to turn on her heel and leave. The years I'd spent away had not been kind to her, I noticed. The rest drifted off in twos and threes, leaving Master Gregory of the workshop to stand alone, his cap in both hands before him. I was not surprised he'd remained, not really. Before smashing my hands with his hammer, we'd got on very well and I knew him for a straight sort.

'I don't . . . know all the truth of what went on,' he said, looking at the ground.

Wulfric stared coldly at him, though whether it was on my behalf or for his own concerns, I did not know. I had so much to learn.

'So I . . . um, I thought I'd say I was sorry,' Gregory said. He looked up at me through eyebrows that had only grown thicker in my time away. He seemed otherwise unchanged by the years. Perhaps I was weak. Perhaps I was just overcome with the emotion of the moment and seeing my brother alive if not whole. Or perhaps it was the power of Christ in me.

'I forgive you, Master Gregory,' I said.

'Thank you, abbot,' he said, dipping his head.

I watched him walk off with a lighter step than some of the others who remembered me. I was not completely sure I did forgive him, but I'd need craftsmen and he was a fine, skilled hand. My first thought of having him held down for me to break his fingers with his own hammer seemed beneath me, after just a moment's reflection.

'Come on, Brother,' I said to Wulfric. 'Broach a cask of ale with me. Tell me about this wife and daughter of yours. I'll tell you how I rode at the king's side in battle.'

I may have wanted to impress him, a little. The world called me a man and an abbot, but I was still young and unsure of myself. Wulfric looked awed by my words and I swelled a touch in pride. I had no wife and child – and I would not. Forgive me my small vanity.

I turned to go and started as I realised there was another standing in the gloom. I felt a shiver of fear as I saw it was Encarius' widow. Of all of them, she had the clearest cause to hate me. I saw it in her eyes as she sketched a brief curtsy to a new abbot. I remembered too that she had been happy enough to see my hands broken and for me to fall to my death. I stood tall at the thought. I would not be ashamed in front of my enemies. They had gaped upon me with their mouths, like ravening and roaring lions. Yet they had not broken me.

'Have you come to ask for my forgiveness?' I said. Perhaps I meant to goad her, preferring to have my enemies declare themselves. Yet she shook her head and gestured at Caspar, sitting up with a groan on the yard.

'He is my husband now,' she said, looking almost ashamed.

'Ah, I see. Well, you should go to him. Come, Wulfric. I want to know everything that has happened.'

We left Caspar to be tended by his wife on the ground behind us, bloody and swollen. As I walked away, it began to rain in a great torrent, which pleased me. I had come back to Glastonbury with a king's authority. There are worse homecomings.

19

I could not part the salt marshes like the Red Sea. I did not
have to. Lady Elflaed sent me the king's master mason, a
man named Justin whom I liked almost from the first. He'd
looked a little scornful while I interviewed him in the abbot's
study. I'd let him have his doubts for a moment, then begun
to question him on his understanding of geometry. It was
something of a pleasure to see him begin to sweat and get
out a slate to help him with the calculations.

'How do you know so much about triangle frames?' he asked.

'I read Pythagoras and Euclid. Did you think these things
sprang out of the air? They are the works of men, Master
Justin, not angels. Believe me, I would know.'

He had a particular genius for solving problems as they
arose, which made him immensely valuable to me. It galled
that he would not take my silver as his pay, however. When I
pressed him, he admitted to some attachment to the king's
purse. A man cannot have two masters, he told me. I told
him a simple man could not. An educated man could have
three or four. He raised his eyebrow at that and yet said nothing, choosing not to disagree. As I say, I liked him.

Caesar had built his bridge across the Rhine with trunks
driven into the mud by pyramid frames. One log raised above
another in the frame, drawn up on pulleys, then allowed to
drop as a hammer blow, driving in the bridge piles. That had
worked even in a rushing river, whereas we could lay great
depths of reeds in temporary beds. I told Master Justin we
had it easy compared to the men of Rome, and he looked
askance at me, raising one eyebrow again.

It took weeks just to prepare the track of the bridge we would build. With Lady Elflaed's coin, we put the word out and hired two hundred Wessex men, all young and poor enough to be willing to risk their lives for good pay. Master Justin was still unsatisfied. He developed a habit of throwing his hands up and saying some problem or other was madness, was completely impossible, then finding a way to do it that was both neat and clever.

By Laetare Sunday in Lent, we had a dozen yards of track at most, a pier to nowhere. Our workers had learned the vital skills – and made most of the worst errors. It went faster after that. By the time Pentecost was past, we had our bridge, our wooden road, our dry land across the marsh. Six hundred piles had been driven deep into the sucking mud. Thick beams and planking made a causeway across the marsh for the first time in all the history of the isle.

Four men had drowned when a frame tipped up and held them under. Another vanished into a hole and we never found him. One of the strangest days was when I was called across to witness a body pulled out of the thick mud that no one knew, a man so long dead that his skin was as dark as a saddle and shone, while strange things crept in him, living in his flesh. That stranger was reburied with his old bow and hunter's skins on the edge of the marsh, with Christian prayers said over him and a good wooden cross to mark the spot. Though we had no inkling of his name, I'm sure he knew his own when it was called.

Though I was but newly ordained, it fell to me to offer Mass for those lost souls. I compensated their families as well, when they could be found, but the truth is, construction is not unlike the movements of an army. Men die when they move stones and wood. That is just the truth of it. We spent only a little time in mourning and the work went on.

When it was finished, Master Justin and I were amongst

the first to walk the entire distance. Where once I had been poled through reeds and mists, now reached a stretch of new and yellow oak, as sturdy as a spire. Only Brother Guido seemed unhappy about the bridge and that was because he was made to dig the gardens rather than pole his little boat.

The true work began after that. We had already engaged masons and stonecutters at a great quarry near Bath. Huge blocks of golden limestone had sat uncomplaining for months, too heavy to travel over those marshes, though they do say the blocks for the old stone circles were carried by barge – bigger than anything we used.

I had to work to hide my happiness, so that others saw me as the abbot, a man of God and dignity, myself a servant. Yet I was home! I was back in my beloved Wessex, with a new workshop built alongside the chapel, with my own forge that puffed away at all hours of the day and night.

Once we could roll carts in and out of the site, the old abbey was reduced with extraordinary speed around me, the cottages rebuilt some distance from where we would create a great ark in stone. The design came first from my mind – from the visions I'd had. To those dreamed images, the masons joined an understanding of rubble cores and flint facings, of limestone and proper ratios in dimensions. From Master Justin, I learned that there is little mystery to why one building appears fine and graceful, while another seems short or a dull block. There are rules to their dimensions known to masters, but not to mere journeymen or apprentices. I learned at his feet for a time and my mind filled with the golden mean and the rule of thirds, a hundred new things.

In the evenings, I insisted the monks eat together. The refectory then was makeshift, the old one reduced to beams and tile. Yet it was always the heart of our abbey, with the chapel. We came together to break bread and that had more than a little significance.

I did little else at first beyond that single order to remind them they were one household, though of great size and with varied interests. I thought to let the monks settle for a while, accepting my authority over them – or perhaps the king's, over us all. Poor Simeon had walked away in the night, to join a community of hermits at Clewer. I did not see him again and I'm pleased for it. His mind had deserted him by the end.

I experienced the first rebellion from my little community when I placed sturdy fellows at the door to our refectory, turning away the women and children. It hurt me to do it, but I knew better than most what foulness can come from the indulgence of desires. Christ did not marry – and I saw one path writ clear for those who would reside in my abbey. Despite my youth, I would be father to them – *abba*, as it is in Aramaic. The rules of St Benedict were perfectly conceived, but not much observed. Prayer and work! There can be no better course for men to control their base desires.

We enforced the old rule of the meal as a time of silence after that, with just one voice reading aloud. I saw then how peaceful it became, just men alone in contemplation. I saw too how my mind would leap ahead as I nodded over my bowl, thinking of all I had to do the next day. In that way, I was not a fine example. We are all sinners.

The abbey ground was cleared before the Advent fast began, which was a relief. Enormous holes had been dug at Master Justin's order to make foundations, so that there were valleys where once had stood the old bell tower and the grain stores. I was peering into one of those when I saw Brother Caspar hurrying past me, head down and mouth set into a thin line. He had not spoken a word to me since I had beaten him, and I felt the pang of regret that is only possible in a victor.

'Brother Caspar, a moment!' I called.

He missed a step as he considered whether he could

pretend not to have heard, but I strode over to him. He flinched as I came into range, and it was that which made me decide to put it right.

'Brother Caspar, would you fetch me a whip?' I said.

He looked suspiciously at me and I saw he thought I would use it on him.

'It is for my penance, Brother Caspar. St Benedict's rule forbids us to strike one another in anger. I have sinned, Brother Caspar. I must suffer.'

He moved quickly enough then, I noticed. Nor did he return alone. Word spread quickly in that small place and Aphra was just one of those who came out into the evening gloom to see what I was about. I saw too that Master Justin was there, with a mug of ale and a piece of bread in his hand. His supper was forgotten as he looked on the concerns of monks.

Caspar returned with a whip I had not seen before, used to drive oxen when they are most stubborn. It had small brass pellets tied to the end of each strand. As a prick spur will set a horse to bleeding, I had no doubt they would be cruel.

I clenched my jaw over any censure. I had to pay the price of what I had done to Caspar, the humiliation I had given out. Most importantly, it had to be in public. My authority could not come from fear.

I stripped myself to the waist and took up the flail, feeling the weight of it.

'As a sinner, I ask for penance, Lord, for forgiveness, and the strength to endure. I ask to be forgiven my ill-treatment of Brother Caspar when I first arrived. He deserved better from his abbot, or from any man. I was cruel, Lord. I beg your mercy.'

I began to whip the flail across, left and right, over and over as I prayed aloud. It drew blood quickly and stung, though it was not too bad at first. I could feel heated lines dribbling down me, then saw bright spots spattering. I felt a warmth gathering over my back, almost like a healing touch, so that the pain dwindled away and I could gaze steadily at those who watched me.

Aphra looked afraid, as if she saw something she could not understand. Master Justin appeared amused at first, then troubled, so that he turned away. The blood rained from me in fat drops and the heat grew worse, becoming a different kind of hurt. I was striking myself with fire and I could not bear it.

I stopped, panting hard in choking, short breaths. My head was down and the pain was as bad as anything I have known. I held out the flail to Caspar.

'Lay on, brother,' I said to him. 'If you would forgive me my sin.'

A greater man might have handed the flail back to me. Instead, he took it up and laid on with such enthusiasm I was driven to my knees and thought I might pass out before he was done. I could hardly see for dizziness and agony, and it took some time for me to realise it had stopped. I staggered up once again to find him panting almost as hard as I was. Flogging a man is exhausting work. He held out the flail and I took it from him. Yet there was awe in his eyes and I reached out stiffly with my left hand and patted him on the shoulder. Then I handed the flail back to him and closed his fingers over it.

'Again, brother,' I murmured to him.

Once more I hoped for some decency in the old bastard, but instead he walked around me as I stood facing the crowd, by then every soul on the island. He began again and it was extraordinary how the pain soared and burned the wounds that were already there.

Caspar looked white as he came to face me. Some of the men in the crowd called out for him to stop, growling that I'd done enough. I noticed none of the women's voices joined them, but they have always been more cruel.

I could see indecision in Caspar's face. He sensed the mood of the crowd turning against him, but he was spiteful enough to want a third go at flogging me in front of them all. Yet always it was with my permission. That undermined him. If I had been a prisoner, or tied to a post, I'm sure he would have gone on all night. As it was, his own shame and the mutters of the crowd forced him to hand back the flail. I held it out to him, making sure they all saw, though when he shook his head, I was so relieved I could have wept.

'I forgive you,' Caspar said. He looked into my eyes and suddenly sobbed as he turned away. I was dazed from pain and loss of blood, and I could not understand the change in him.

Wulfric came forward to drape a cloak around my shoulders, though he had trouble with only one arm, so I had to help him with it. I could not walk on my own, but he suppported me as best he could, while I hissed at every touch. We went back to the infirmary then, where Aphra tended my wounds, stitching and wiping them clean without a single word.

It is quite extraordinary how my authority over that community underwent a change after that. Aphra did a fair job of keeping the wounds clean, and though I moved stiffly and could neither hammer nor gild nor stitch over the following month, most of my work was in planning and keeping the community out of trouble, which did not need another strong back.

I had achieved much by allowing Caspar to wield the flail, though I felt the single experience of it was enough – for him and for me. A few weeks later, he came to me with the flail in his hand and asked humbly if I wished for him to resume the labour. I'm afraid I was quite sharp with him.

Advent is the beginning of the liturgical year, in cold and

dark, in the sense of wonder that is Christ coming into the world. *Adventus* in Latin, or *Parousia* in Greek – it is a time of penitence and prayer, with only a little food and all the chapels and churches laid about with green boughs.

Much of the building work stopped as our labourers went home to their families. We were, once again, a smaller group, ready to welcome the birth of Our Saviour and endure the winter months that follow.

In that quieter time, I turned my mind to the problem that had troubled me almost since the moment we began work. Lady Elflaed had sent me back with a satchel of gold and silver that I'd thought would be enough on its own to build the abbey.

I had not reckoned on the cost of dressed stones of the size and quality we required. Nor had I understood how paying two hundred men and a dozen master masons could eat through a king's ransom in just a few months. Prayer had not kept that satchel full, though you may be sure I'd tried it, once I saw the way the levels were dropping.

As Advent began, I found myself sharpening a fresh quill to write to my patroness for another donation to the cause. I listed all the costs we had incurred, but it seemed not the sort of thing that might inspire Lady Elflaed to reach more deeply into her strongbox. I knew her well enough to understand she wanted glories and choirs and prayers soaring to heaven, not a list of tons of rubble and how many thousand dressed flints and bricks lay in our stores. Still, I had to ask. I sent three of our lads across the causeway with instructions to reach a good road and go thence to Winchester and the lady's house. With that done, it was a sombre group which came at my request to the new school we'd built.

I looked around at the gathered men. Caspar had come, though he did not glower so since our little adventure with the whip. I did not trust him fully, but I know I was less harsh with him.

Master Gregory of the workshop was there, waiting in silence and showing no sign of the cold that made younger men shiver. The ancient brother John sat at his side and Guido of the boat took a place on the high benches. I had ordered them built in the manner of a Greek theatre, or the Roman senate house, so that each bench rose in curving lines, with steps in between. I have no doubt it was my pride again, but I clasped my hands behind my back and hoped for wisdom as I let my gaze pass over some forty others. Not all of them were known to me even then, to my regret. I had been too busy with the bridge and my forge to spend time with each one, learning his strengths. The abbey needed time and gold and youthful labour to be born. I had no qualms about using the men before me to achieve that end.

I paused in my slow turn before them, as my gaze snagged on one I had not expected. Master Justin was on the benches with them. He'd been long accepted as one who heaved in the same furrow as the rest of us. He and Master Gregory of the workshop were like old friends. I was pleased he had stayed. I had no doubt the king's courtiers would be asking about him, but if he chose to look within for vocation, there was nothing they could do about it. Even Æthelstan might not order a man to other work if he felt God's call. Better still, if the master mason became a monk, he'd take a vow of poverty and I would no longer have to pay him. I smiled at Justin. He blushed like a boy and looked around the room, anywhere but back at me.

I began by leading a prayer together, as was our custom. In the end, though, I had to put my purpose to them.

'My friends, I have asked you here for the most sordid of reasons,' I began, clearing my throat noisily. More than one looked worriedly at those around them and I hurried on before their imaginations could do too much damage. 'To ask you to help raise the silver and gold we need to build this abbey.'

'God will provide,' a young fellow said.

I had to bow my head in response, though I'd rather have kicked him.

'Of course, but we must not be idle. We have taken down the poor place that stood here. We must build a far greater abbey, or we have done harm to a house of God. Did not St Patrick come here to die?'

Someone certainly had. I'd seen the bones. I'd heard he'd died in Ireland as well, which is impressive, even for a saint. Still, it had them nodding.

'I have asked the king for land to be granted to the abbey,' I said.

A murmur of excitement went through those gathered to hear. I had a strong suspicion my request would go un-answered, that the land would not be coming. Æthelstan suspected me of dark practices, which simply meant prac-tices he did not understand. Kings are often simple fellows. They must be led by the Church or they are likely to break their necks getting out of bed.

'I have asked also for great sums from Lady Elflaed, his niece, though she has already given enough for a dozen fam-ilies of high estate. We must do more in our need. Our lives are dedicated to God, and this abbey will be a hymn of praise on the land. Anything we can make or grow to be sold will go into the coffers.'

They became quite rowdy for a time as they discussed it. I let the ideas come thick and fast, though most of them were impossible. Monks, too, need to be led.

After a time, I counted off the best suggestions on my fingers, though they were the ones I'd wanted from the beginning. They had not been able to hear one another in the arguments and laughter.

'English embroidery is perhaps our greatest asset. There is our first. It brings in gold, but takes an age to make. I wonder if we might employ and train more young fellows from the villages around us. Who knows, but some of them might feel the call when they have lived here for a time.'

They smiled at that, led by those who knew the skills of close stitching. I could teach those who did not.

'Silverwork and gilding is our second – though we will have to find markets far beyond Wessex for those to buy such things – and we must purchase the metals before we make a single penny. It will still be vital, I do not doubt, but it will take some planning.'

'Stonework,' Master Justin said. He seemed to suspect I would not have listed it on my own and he was right to. For all my pretence of echoing their suggestions, I had not heard that one. I looked at him in silence, considering. He took it as an invitation to speak.

'I can teach a few bright lads how to dress stone. Or carve it with iron chisels, if a supply of those can be made and sharpened in the forges here. Every church in England and France needs fine stonework. Every guildhouse, every earl. If you can find the young men to learn, I'll make them masters.'

'Thank you,' I said, releasing a third finger. It was a handsome offer. God would provide indeed.

'My fourth, brothers, was to be simple ironwork – the old "pots and pokers" of a good smith, perhaps also the shoeing of horses, though we are not well placed when all men must come to us. I see better now that we need more to donate their labour. Men we cannot pay, who must come for the glory of God, for the great work of their lives that will earn them a place in heaven.'

I paused for a moment as that last thought blossomed within me. Master Justin would never have given up his evening to hear a mere guild of merchants talk. We were there to make a mark greater than our own selves. Whether he sensed it or not, Master Justin had come because he too heard the call. There would be many more. There had to be.

I made my voice ring to the rafters as I addressed them all.

'Building a church is a labour to forgive sins, my brothers. We must tell them that in the towns and villages this winter. We must go out from here and take word of a new, great abbey rising at Glastonbury, where all Christian men will be welcome.'

'And their wives,' one of them said.

My vision broke apart and I realised I'd been staring upwards, filled with excitement. I scowled instead at the interruption.

'Christ chose no wife,' I growled, though I was not ready to make the argument. A few of them began to object and I held up my hand. Bless St Benedict for his rule on obedience. They shut up and folded their arms at me.

'That is a discussion for another evening, brothers. For now, we have three, no, four strands of gold and dark months of winter upon us. Let us put it all to good use.'

We opened up the doors of the school onto a night of frozen clarity, with the moon and stars hanging so clear and bright I could have snatched them down in my excitement. It is not every day a young man sees the path of his life. I would bring them together and raise the abbey stone by stone.

I attended Matins after midnight, though there was no bell and tower to summon the monks any longer. I was pleased to see the makeshift chapel packed full of yawning men – and women too, with Aphra glaring at me, just waiting to see me slip.

I was yawning myself as I left and trudged back to my little dormitory, the frost crackling under my sandals.

I looked up at footsteps coming fast on the icy path.

'Who is it? Who's that there?' I demanded, suddenly afraid. In the moonlight, I could see a young fellow, reeking of horse and mud and sweat. As he came close enough to peer at me and take my arm, I could feel the heat coming off him.

'Are you Abbot Dunstan?' he said, looking doubtful. He was older than me, with a neatly tended beard that he may have thought lent him a semblance of authority. It did not.

Somehow, I knew it was bad news. I began to pray Lady Elflaed had not been taken. Without her, all my efforts for the abbey would surely be stillborn.

'It is the king,' the young man said. 'King Æthelstan is dead.'

'God rest his soul,' I said instantly, my mouth falling open. He dipped his own head in prayer.

'Is Edmund king, then?' I asked suddenly. 'His brother?'

The young man had the cheek to frown at me, as if the question would not come to every soul the instant after they heard.

'The country is in mourning, father. But yes, the Witan has called his brother Edmund. He will be crowned three weeks after the feast of Christ's baptism.'

'By my uncle, Archbishop Athelm, presumably?'

The messenger realised he should perhaps have been a little less full of his own importance. On impulse, he decided to release my arm to kneel and bow his head, though it was a bit late.

'I believe so, Father Abbot. Forgive my impertinence.'

I dismissed him with a wave of my hand, standing there in the dark and cold with my mind afire. I had been banished by Æthelstan, but Æthelstan was no longer king.

'I must return to court,' I said, in awe and wonder.

20

I did not go racing off into the night, though part of me wanted to do just that. Dawn and the Lauds service were some way off when I rang a hand bell and summoned our community to the refectory. As a show of goodwill, and because I did not have the patience for another argument, I made a point of allowing the wives and yawning children in, though they made a terrible noise, darting about like kittens, with no sense of dignity at all.

They settled down when I told them the news. It was a shock and a blow to all of us. Æthelstan was the first king I'd met. I'd watched him charge in with his horsemen like a spear. I admired him, certainly, but he had made no friend in me.

Perhaps because of that, I was surprised to see tears on the faces of many there. Master Justin crooked his head in his elbow and truly sobbed, red-faced. Honestly, I had not expected such a torrent of grief. It set the children off to see their fathers and mothers weeping. They began to wail until I thought I might have to wait outside, or just put the bar across the door and ride to Winchester while they bawled and keened endlessly.

I strode back and forth before them, then stood waiting, tapping my foot on the floor as they passed cloths to one another and embraced in family groups. After a time, after a veritable age, they settled down once more. I told them then what they must do in my absence.

That had them blinking red-eyed at me, you may be sure! Like sheep hearing the shepherd was going away for a time.

I told them I would leave to see the new king crowned – and to repeat my request for lands for the abbey. I had far more hope of it that day than the one before and I felt the thrill of it in my veins.

I saw my brother Wulfric had come to listen, standing tall and ruddy with health, if not for his missing arm. How I wished then that I might leave him in charge of the abbey in my absence! I could not. Not only had he not taken vows, or holy orders, but his work and his family were his concern. He had neglected it all for me, but his heart was not in Glastonbury.

I saw Brother Caspar's gaze was on me and I nodded to him, making the decision without more than a moment's hesitation. I had been appointed abbot in extraordinary circumstances, it was true, with Simeon gone mad in the post. Such events were rare, and no matter who ruled in Winchester, I would remain as father to them.

It fell to me then to make a grand gesture, the last proof of my forgiveness of them all.

'I will be back and forth in the months to come,' I told them. 'In my absence, I appoint Brother Caspar as prior. When I am not present, he will be my voice, my proxy.'

Caspar went such a pale shade, I thought he might faint. I have seen that once or twice on long services at Easter, where a monk suddenly falls as if dead, not even putting out his hands. The injuries can be extraordinary. Yet Caspar remained on his feet, disappointingly. He bowed to me, clearly too overcome to speak.

'There must be no respite in our labours,' I went on. 'The abbey . . .'

'Thank you, Abbot Dunstan,' Caspar managed, his voice thick with emotion, or possibly phlegm.

'. . . will rise.' I went on. 'You know these people as well as anyone here. You know the tasks that lie before us, the hard years. Do not sell yourself at short weight, prior. You will do God's work and do it well.'

I raised my head once more to address them all.

'I will plead our case for land and funds, you may be sure, but there will be a hundred others asking to dip their hands into the royal treasury, before Æthelstan is even cold.' I saw some of them wince at that, as if I had somehow struck a bad note. 'Though my uncle Athelm will . . .'

'You do me a great honour,' Caspar croaked as I tried to continue. I am afraid I lost my temper then. It had been a long day.

'And if you interrupt me again, I will take that honour back!' I roared at him. The room was really silent, the children huge-eyed and trembling. As they began to blubber and screech, I raised my eyes to heaven.

'O Lord, bless this flock, even unto the lambs. Keep them safe as we build in your name. Bring us the coins we need, Lord, to complete your work. Bring us, too, the strong backs and arms, the men who will raise our walls for us without complaint. In the name of the Father, the Son and the Holy Ghost, Amen.'

I swept out as they echoed me and crossed themselves. Caspar stood to address the crowd, but some of them were already leaving in my wake, streaming out into the night. Though it was petty, that pleased me.

I had left Glastonbury once before with nothing. At least the second time I had the horse I'd ridden at Brunanburh. I'd trained Scoundrel rather better than he deserved after my safe return, riding him regularly and accepting the advice of those who understood the strange animals. Scoundrel certainly knew me as a purveyor of carrots and turnip slices. He raised his ears like a dog when he saw me arrive at the stables in town, immediately kicking the door of his stall to come out. I cannot say I liked him – I have never liked a horse. Yet he was undeniably useful to me, especially with days of hard roads between Glastonbury and Winchester.

The old saying has it that lords ride and the poor walk, but an abbot cannot be expected to risk wolves and thieves in the service of the Church. I must have ridden Scoundrel a thousand miles back and forth over the years. He learned the route so well I found I could sit and read upon his back, letting the hours and the miles pass underfoot without my noticing. In that way, the wilful old nag was a marvel.

As I set off, the high king of Britain was being laid to rest at Malmesbury, the town whose men he had ordered free for all time after their service at Brunanburh. He and they shared a love of that rare and fragile state, it seemed, though I favour the yoke myself. Freedom is too much for most men. It frightens them and makes them anxious. Better by far to be calm and safe in harness, I have always said. Not for me, you understand, but for most men. I would always prefer the king's freedom, to freeze or starve, yes, by my own hand and by my own will. Yet I am a rare bird, a rare bee.

I am told the funeral was a great outpouring of grief, with thousands come to witness his passing. I doubt it was any more moving than those I have seen – particularly the services I have given myself for kings since. King Æthelstan was a great man, but he failed to see the worth in me. It follows that he was not without flaw then.

I came back to Winchester at the end of darkest January, with a fall of snow on the ground and more in thick white clouds above. It began to drift down even as I trotted Scoundrel through the western gate, so that it smothered sound like a held throat.

The city light was being hidden beneath a bushel in its mourning, with the drinking houses shuttered and the street criers all silenced. It seems the world will stop for a king's funeral, even one to which I had not been invited. That was the other reason for Winchester to be so quiet, of course. There was hardly anyone there.

I arrived at Lady Elflaed's home, a few streets away from the royal estate. I'd begun to worry I might have to find an inn for the night, but she'd left a rather wizened creature to answer my knock, constantly bowing or hunchbacked, I never did find out. There was also a stable boy to tend Scoundrel, who was steaming and mud-spattered after carrying me over stile and bracken. I found a room prepared for me and a dish of cold meat, salt cod and bitter beans in brine, all laid out. My lady Elflaed was always a fine hostess. I retired that night to vivid dreams, but they were silly things and no true visions, so I will not relate them here.

I have heard tales of men who dreamed a place not unlike the world they knew. They would see their own homes and towns, but either no soul was there, or the traveller moved like a ghost through places they knew well – not being recognised even by their own. I felt that sense of strangeness when I went to sleep in perfect silence, then awoke to hear the noise and bustle of the city around me once more. The royal funeral procession had returned from Malmesbury, on better roads than I'd found. The clean snow turned to brown slush by noon and the streets were filled once again with the smell and muck and noise of people. I felt upset by it somehow, though it may have been the form of my grief, it is hard to say. It strikes us all differently. I thought I felt only a vague sense of dismay at the king's passing, but maybe it meant more to me than I even knew myself.

Lady Elflaed returned to her home wearing drab clothes of dark brown and red, like an autumn leaf in her rustling layers. She told me every detail of the ceremony, once more conducted by Uncle Athelm, which actually was a pleasure to hear. An uncle called to both crown and bury kings is a power in the land – and mine held me in high esteem.

I was less pleased to hear of the extraordinary beauty of the abbey at Malmesbury. I felt as one man might on hearing another describe the virtues of his wife. What cared I for Malmesbury's heights and pillars? Its famous windows and tombs? My own creation would make it seem a shepherd's hut in time. Yet I endured, because the lady was my patron and I needed her.

They had brought the crown home, for Edmund to wear. That ceremony was still being planned and, yes, I saw my chance there, the fruit of the friendship I had formed before. No longer would I be scratching away at the door while the king feasted. Edmund was my friend, and I tell you true: he was a good man and a good king.

It all turned to ash after him, as youth and courage vanish – as virginity is sold cheap, as good wine sours, as towers fall.

PART THREE

Behold the Priest

AD 940

'But I am a worm, and no man; a reproach of men,
and despised of the people.'

Psalms 22:6

21

In the hush of a cold chapel, I watched my uncle raise the crown over Edmund's head. I held my breath as it rested in the air, then touched the young king. The choir voices soared out once more, like angels in the dark.

It is strange, looking back. We all knew how important it was, but Edmund had prepared for the throne his entire life. He was crowned in Kingston, just as Æthelstan had been. It sat on the border of Mercia and Wessex and meant all the more for that. When my uncle put Æthelstan's crown on him, Edmund was made king of all England, not just one part.

I had not enjoyed riding for two days on bad roads to get there. Yet I understood the reason for it. Edmund was no lesser man, but his brother's equal in every way. Such things matter.

When we returned to Winchester, it was no easy task getting within arm's reach of the new king. Hundreds of men and women, of high estate and low, seemed to sense their one chance to win favour for themselves. The petition hall was packed with people, from morning to night. I detested them, with their needs and their weeping, all the while preventing me from speaking to the new king. His thanes went armed and suspicious around him, guarding their own fortunes as well as his life.

Edmund might have kept Egill as his champion, but Æthelstan had paid the mercenary rather too well after Brunanburh, a king's whim. The royal champion appeared at the petition hall one morning with a huge sack of coins on one shoulder and a number of weapons about him, taking his leave of us to go home at last. He did not seem to think he'd need a guard.

My uncle offered to bless his journey and Egill shook his huge head and laughed at the very idea. I'm told he lives still, as old as I am – and still refuses Christ. Well, he was a wilful bastard and I don't doubt he will burn for it, but I liked his stubbornness even so.

I could not force myself into Edmund's company, of course. I think that is perhaps one reason to be king, that no one ever can. His thanes treated all those grasping hands as mere irritations, taking power unto themselves as I had predicted. It was disappointing to find that close group did not appear to include me, though I had fought at their side. I sent letters to one or two on fine vellum, a fortune in ink and paper, just to ask to be remembered to him. It had not been so hard to speak to Edmund on the battlefield! Now the whole world tugged at his sleeve.

The Witan took some of the brunt of the work, but that old vital safeguard remained: that any free man could put his grievance before the king. It was our way, older than his grandfather, when Wessex was all we had. Æthelstan had allowed petitions; Edmund could not deny them. He listened and ruled on disputes from before dawn to long into the night, sleeping hardly at all. Still they came, bleating, bleating at him.

I had kept my room at Lady Elflaed's and was roused in the small hours by a servant banging on the door and telling me the king had asked for me. You may be sure I ran through the cobbled streets, feeling the chill. I believe that is why St Benedict included the rule about monks sleeping in the robe, so that we can rise and be about God's business without delay. It has served me in that way a hundred times over the years, though they do have to be smoked out when lice or fleas bite especially hard. That night was not long after such a smoking and the odour of it was strong in my nostrils as I reached the royal estate and was taken through to the heart. I must have passed a hundred jealous gazes, even at that grey hour, all wondering why I should have been put ahead of them.

I arrived panting at the petition hall, passing through as the guards held back those who peered and pressed in. The doors closed behind me. It was almost dark within, though the sun rose outside. I confess I had a moment of worry, until King Edmund stood up from a seat by the fire and smiled. He did not wear the crown. I am certain he did not. Yet I see it on him. Memory is a strange thing at times.

'Father Abbot,' he said.

It was to be formal, then. I saw Edmund wore a new gold ring, thick and bright on his hand. I bowed to kiss it and felt it pass between my lips, as if I was trying to swallow his finger. He pulled back rather sharply, I thought.

As I raised my head, blushing, I became aware of the shadows of men in the corners. I squinted to make them out, but there was only the firelight and the dim gleam could not reveal them to my eye.

'Thank you for asking for me,' I said, bowing deeply. 'I imagine the whole world is after you for something.'

'You would not believe how true that is. I have all my own people sleeping outside to see me, but also sisters and cousins and lords in France asking . . . Ah, it does not matter. I will find the time, I'm sure. Mind you, how my brother did so much in his forties, I have no idea.'

'Practice,' I said.

He chuckled, though there was a sadness in his eyes. I realised Edmund was still deep in grief himself, for all the excitement of becoming king. Of course he'd dreamed of the day he would sit the throne, but he had also loved his older brother and expected him to live for decades longer.

It changed how I saw him, in that moment. He had not wanted to rule. He could still hardly believe he had been made to. I had come into that room full of life and laughter, ready for the easy way between us before. I put it all aside in a moment as I read the man he had become.

'He was a great king,' I said.

A sheen appeared in his eyes, called forth by just a few words.

'So they all say. Everyone. Æthelstan was an extraordinary man, a great man, a great ruler. They tell me of Brunanburh as if I hadn't heard every story of that day — and been part of most of them. And yet, Dunstan, what they forget . . . what they fail to understand . . .' He trailed off, looking past me to the dark corners of the room. I watched resignation settle in his face and I was suddenly determined.

'Would you like me to hear your confession, Your Highness? I'm sure we could find a private place.'

'I doubt it,' Edmund muttered, but he nodded even so. He gestured to a side door, away from the mob still waiting outside. I gave no sign I thought of them, so perhaps it was his own guilt that made him speak.

'Oh, they are always there, don't worry. They will be there when we return, just the same. Day or night, the faces change, but the queue stays.'

'From the Latin *cauda*, a "tail",' I said.

He paused, not sure if that interested him or not.

'Dunstan, you are a surprising man,' he said. 'If the king is the dog, they are the tail, yes.' He laughed, but there was still pain in it. 'Come on.'

I followed him out and endured the glare of his guards as he spoke sharply to them to make them stay behind. They were not happy about that! A king is hard to refuse, but equally, they knew their lives were the stake if they let him out and something befell him. I made no friends among them by taking Edmund out of that place. I began to realise he was as much a prisoner as the petitioners.

Without a crown, or some clear symbol of his kingship, Edmund was a stranger to almost all of his subjects. I hadn't given it any thought, but as we passed into the crowds, I was glad he was not recognised. Of course, it did mean we had to refuse traders and street rats holding out something to buy, just about every four or five paces.

Once more, Winchester surprised a country boy like me with its raucous clatter. The streets were thronged with people. It was truly the capital then, not just of Wessex, as it had been under Alfred, but of all England. There are men of Middlesex and Kent who prefer London, I know, perhaps for its closeness to France. I don't see it. Winchester has the great river Itchen, a royal mint, mills, monastic houses, merchants, all.

We walked downhill to the river bank, past the great timbered walls of Nunnaminster. The nuns were singing the 'Agnus Dei', the Lamb of God. Their harmony was softly beautiful, muffled as it was through beams and plaster. I find the voices of women can be somewhat reedy as a rule, but it suited our mood then. The sound of John's Gospel even stilled the yells of traders passing by. They crossed themselves and bowed their heads, and resumed their clamour only when they were further on.

At the wide river, great flat-bottomed barges were creeping through, taking bales of linen, bone goods, pewter and silver and stirrups, oh, a thousand things out to the world. Some of our spoons would end up in France or Flanders, or even Egypt.

The king's city was the great forge. It took in ore and tin and gold and wool. Iron gleamed, spindles and looms clattered – and the city gave back tools, horseshoes, rings and whole cloth. The clicking of looms was just one of the noises, like insects in the joists, all scratching a living, all making something. York and London were almost as busy then, but there was an excitement to Winchester – in ambassadors and retinues and gorgeous extravagance – that lies only with the royal capital.

Edmund looked sideways at me and I saw he seemed awkward.

'I do not know how to talk to you,' he said.

'What do you mean?'

'Well, you are Dunstan, of course, whose hands were broken when first we met, but who laughed even so. I saw you canter across the battlefield at Brunanburh, clutching your axe and shield while your horse went, well, wherever he wanted.'

'I hate that horse,' I said quickly. He chuckled.

'Yet you are also the abbot of Glastonbury, a man of the Church – though my own age, just about.'

I smiled to hear this.

'I think I know what you mean, friend Edmund . . . who is also king of England.'

'Perhaps we should remain friends first, as that came first – and abbots and kings after.'

I shook my head, a little sadly.

'You can leave your crown behind and still be king. Neither does this robe make me abbot. There are deeper hooks in us. But, yes, I am your friend, Edmund.'

He seemed unhappy at that, but he did not press me.

'Do you wish to confess?' I asked him.

'Only that I do not want to confess,' he said lightly. 'I was absolved of a lifetime of sins before my coronation, by your uncle. That was awkward enough. It'll be some time before I go looking for another experience like it. No, I just wanted to get away for a moment, from all those solemn men and women telling me what a great man my brother was, what a fine king.'

He turned to me suddenly and I stopped. We stood on the edge of the river, on a narrow path. A bargeman watched us about as amiably as any cow chewing its cud might have done.

'And he was, yet if he was, how can I match him? How can I keep England safe as he did? Eh, Dunstan? What do you say to that?'

'I say you have prepared for this your whole life. The torch has passed to your hand a little earlier than you would have liked — but you will not fail! You are your father's son, just as Æthelstan was. Are you a lesser man? No, just a younger one! You are your grandfather's grandson, as Æthelstan was. You, the grandson of Alfred the Great, the son of Edward the Elder, the brother to Æthelstan! There's no better line in England. You will not be found wanting.'

He seemed to take heart from my words, though he rubbed his nose on his sleeve as we stood there. The bargeman was pointing us out to his mates, making some comment that had them all cackling toothlessly.

'Come on, we're drawing a right crowd of yokels here,' I said.

One of them was miming something filthy that had the others slapping each other and guffawing. I was tempted to ask if they meant to offend the king of England, just to watch them swallow their own tongues, but I did not.

Edmund climbed up the shallow bank to look up the high street to the cathedral spire in the distance, dominating the city. He grimaced at the sight of two guardsmen much closer by. They stood awkwardly when they saw they had been spotted, but remained even so. He sighed.

'The meanest churl in England can put down his tools and take a walk as a free man. Yet his king cannot do the same. It is a strange thing, Dunstan, truly.'

'You are grieving still,' I said. 'Which makes you chafe — feeling the crown as a harness.'

He looked congested, with blood heavy in his face. I had never practised the doctor's art, but I knew as much as any of those I had met, certainly when it came to herbs.

'I don't want to let him down, Dunstan. I feel his gaze on me.'

'He'd be proud of you, I am sure, but more importantly, he would understand what burdens you now. Æthelstan wore the crown for fifteen years. He knew the weight of it, right enough. Yet he kept his oath to see you made king, did he not? He took no wife. I think he knew you would bear the crown well. Imagine if you had ruined yourself in drink and sin, if you had been a coward, an adulterer, or an oathbreaker! Would he have sat quietly then?'

Edmund seemed to take comfort from my words, which pleased me as they were clearly true.

'My father died when I was very young,' he said, 'my mother soon after. Æthelstan was brother to me, but also father. I loved him — and he was always there. Now . . .' He broke off and I saw that sheen return to his gaze as he looked into a distance I could not see.

The two royal guards followed us as I led the king to the same cart seller I'd visited so many times with Beatrice, years before. The old woman who made such a fine broth and ladled horseradish into it for warmth had not aged a day since then, as if age had given up and was just waiting in disgust for her to die.

Edmund took a bowl and raised his eyebrows when she offered one of the spoons on chains. I grinned at him.

'She doesn't know you. Can I vouch for him, Sally? He won't run, my honour on it.'

'For you, love, course,' she said, producing a long-handled pewter spoon from somewhere in the folds of her skirts.

Edmund bowed to her, but her attention was caught by the royal guards loitering on that part of the street. She turned away to keep her eye on such a strange pair.

'Thank you, Dunstan,' Edmund said. His colour deepened with a mouthful of the horseradish stew. 'I have enjoyed this. I'll go back to my tail of petitioners with renewed strength, I am certain.'

'There is satisfaction in duty, without glory,' I said. 'In work done quietly, a life's task.'

I hesitated then, but he only smiled, supping away at the thick broth and smacking his lips in appreciation.

'Go on then, ask me,' he said, between blowing on spoonfuls.

'Ask?' I said, though it was just to gain time.

'Everyone does, sooner or later. What would you have of me?'

I didn't like the idea of joining the vast number begging for favours, but I would have been a fool to miss such an opportunity. I saw then how lonely it was to be king.

'I ask nothing for myself, Edmund. I do need land, though, for the abbey. Land I can rent or use to raise crops and mutton to sell, anything to bring enough coin to complete the task. Lady Elflaed has been generous, but I need much more.'

'Very well, Dunstan,' he said. 'I'll have my seneschal go over the maps with you. I know you'd prefer something close to the abbey, though I'll tell him to pass on some farms near here to your care as well. It will give you a reason to visit me, perhaps.'

We smiled at each other and I realised with a shock that we truly were friends. It was a heady feeling.

'How much land are you after?' he said.

I had not expected to be asked to name a figure, so I pulled one out of the air. A hide of land was enough to feed one small family on its produce. My father had held twelve such and been a wealthy man. I multiplied Heorstan's land by ten and then hesitated, then tripled the result. King Edmund was enjoying my company and the broth, after all.

Old Sally seemed to have understood something was up. She turned back and forth between us, peering with one eye then the other, her wrinkled mouth closing and opening as if it worked on its own. Honestly, the woman could have charged a penny just to watch her face change expression.

'Three hundred and sixty?' I said, feeling my throat grow tight.

Edmund didn't blink, though he stopped smiling.

'That is a lot of land, Dunstan. A fortune.'

'For the Church,' I reminded him. 'For the first abbey to be built in your reign, in fact. You know, your brother was buried in Malmesbury. I could build a royal tomb and chapel at Glastonbury that would stand as great as any other.'

His eyebrows went up at my brazen offer – and I saw the same ambition that had touched me. He and I were alike in that. Why not? We have such a short time alive. Should we spend it drowsing in the sun? No! The sun goes down and each hour is more precious than a gold coin.

'Very well, Father Abbot,' he said. He handed the bowl and spoon back to the old woman, whose mouth hung open. Sally tried to bow and we both thought she'd fainted, so that we reached as one to hold her up.

'That was wonderful broth,' Edmund said to her. 'The best I've ever tasted.'

He left her babbling something in delighted squeals as we went back to the royal grounds. I knew I'd made myself a petitioner by asking, at least for a time, but still I was almost dazed as I walked along. Three hundred and sixty hides of land would be enough to fund a huge construction. I'd be able to order marble from Ireland, glass from Venice, master craftsmen from all over England. I bit my lip as I walked, though, wondering if I should have asked for more. The thought still haunts me, sometimes.

A month later, I travelled to London to see my brother's shop. With six servants, two armed guards and Uncle Athelm in tow, we took ship at Southampton. I had heard some men and women have delicate stomachs at sea. Mine was like iron. Uncle Athelm told me I should not be proud of nature and God's will, that some simply suffered and some did not. Of course, he was hanging over the stern at the time, green-faced and tied on by the sailors so he would not fall.

We spent four days hugging the coast as we made our way to the entrance of the Thames and from there, inland, until we saw the walls of London. I had seen France too for the first time as we'd rounded white cliffs, though that country had looked rather dark and threatening to my eye. I set foot on a dock by the Roman wall, close by the south-east corner and the single bridge spanning the Thames.

Perhaps I was too ready to dislike London on that first meeting. Too many preferred it to my beloved Winchester and I found it a shabby place compared to the royal capital. The river certainly stank and the streets, though some were cobbled, were hidden beneath a layer of human ordure. In my first moment after landing, I watched a man drop his leggings and squat by the docks, leaving a little pile, with the river just feet away. It was a strange welcome.

The Holy Church was served in London by a spired cathedral and another great chapel on Tower Hill – as much wood as stone, mind. The people of London protected the beams from burrowing insects with a coat of thick tar. That would prove a mistake, eventually, when it burned down.

It seemed to me a worn-out place, battered by time, though the river was busy enough. The Thames was the key, that black vein right through the heart. We went from a choppy sea to a safe berth at our London dock in a single day. It is true that we could have ridden across country from Winchester in less time, but then I arrived at peace, rather than scratched, torn, filthy and probably murdered on the road.

Wulfric came to meet us with a fine cart and another half a dozen of his employees. Good, strong-looking fellows all, they took up our bags and followed along in a great troop. Some urchins of the town began laughing and jeering and shying stones at us, until we put two men amongst them with horsewhips. It was not on my behalf, you understand, but rather for the dignity of the Church. Still, I enjoyed the way they screeched and wailed.

The Roman walls had ancient gates, old and much repaired. Wulfric's shop was on the corner of a street that ended at the eastern gate, a fine establishment advertising its wares in great bales of cloth, open to the touch of passers-by. There were many of those, hurrying along, busy little bees all of them. I felt a touch of worry at the sight, but Winchester held the king. That was what mattered.

I entered the shop proper and found myself astonished by the noise and clatter of the place – and the size. It went back and back and was filled with young men, cutting and measuring, calling orders to one another using words I had never heard. I took it all in, understanding that my brother was actually not the failure I had thought he would be.

Wulfric saw my surprise and chuckled.

'We bought out the last share this year. This is all ours now – and honestly, Dun, I'm thinking of buying another shop closer to the north gate. Just outside it, perhaps. It would be madness not to! Land is so cheap in London, more so than Winchester. Cloth needs looms and looms need space. We've room to breathe, here.'

'I can see that,' I said, a little faintly. The flush of excitement and healthy sweat on his skin was not what I had

242

expected and it disturbed me. His scar remained, to remind me he owed his entire life to my hands.

'I think Uncle Athelm has found the silk,' Wulfric said.

We both turned to see our uncle fondling a piece of blue cloth with something like awe or greed in his eyes. It shimmered.

'Dear boy, what is this?'

'From Cathay,' Wulfric said, raising his voice over the clatter around us. 'Two years of travel to reach us here. It is strong and yet fine. We don't have the secret of it yet, but I'm testing a dozen new threads to make those fibres. We'll match it – and then we'll make it better and faster than they can, you wait and see. London was built on trade, Dun.'

'Trade . . . I'm afraid my interest lies more in faith and prayer, Wulfric,' I told him, though it was petty and I felt sorry the moment his face fell in dismay.

'Of course, of course it does! I'm sorry, Dun, I was carried away showing it all to you. Oh, I feel a fool now. Uncle Athelm! I will make a gift of that silk to you. Will you come through to the back now and see Alice and your great-niece?'

The prospect was enough to drag the archbishop from his discoveries, moving amongst us like a ship passing smaller boats.

I took Wulfric by the arm as Athelm went through to the back.

'I am pleased to see you doing well, Brother, truly. I'm . . .'

He cocked one hand behind an ear to hear me.

'Come into the back, Dunstan. It's quieter in the rooms upstairs. I have a surprise for you.'

Away from the noise of the shop, we ascended a creaking staircase together. It seemed ancient and I was comforted that it had borne the weight of my uncle before me, proving its strength beyond all doubt.

A small door brought us through to a cramped living

room, with a brick stove of its own. I entered to see Alice sitting with my mother, dandling a baby between them. It could have been my life in that warm room above the shop, if I had not taken vows and holy orders. I think that made me colder to them than I might have been.

'Mother, Alice,' I said stiffly, bowing my head. Did the pink-cheeked young woman know about the bag of goose fat and its horrible purpose? I shuddered, feeling hairs rise on my arms.

My mother came to me with an expression of wonder on her face.

'You are a man, Dunstan! Oh, I saw you last when you were still a boy.'

She embraced me and some of my chill vanished. I was home, and my family was about me. I wondered what they would say when I took Wulfric back to Glastonbury.

22

'I won't go, Dun! You can't ask me to. You've seen the life I've built here. You've seen my wife and my daughter, the way the shop runs.'

'Pay another to manage it, or bring Alice and the girl with you. I need someone I can trust to oversee three hundred and sixty hides of land, Wulfric! Someone who won't steal half the rents.'

We were walking along a street thick with filth that defied description. I imagine the Romans were cleaner, honestly. The north wall lay ahead and, in our argument, I realised we'd walked at least a mile. I turned to go back, fed up with London's noise and reek. Wulfric took me by the arm.

'It's a life's work, Dun,' he said faintly. 'What you're asking. So many farms, the crops and mutton, timber, charcoal burners, hunting and poaching, quarry and fishing rights . . . I could not do so much and still run the shop here for my wife and our mother.'

'I have not asked you to,' I said firmly. 'I've said Mother can find someone else to run her . . . cloth business. Or you can persuade her to sell the share you own. I'll have a house built for you and Alice, don't fear for that. Or I'll buy our old home, whatever you want. I have won a huge holding for the abbey, Wulfric. I just need a good man to make it work.'

'You do it, then,' he said mulishly, surprising me.

'I cannot! I am an abbot – and my concern is the king. If I can leave you in charge, I'll know the work will go on, that I won't come back to Glastonbury and find the place looted and abandoned. Those are the stakes, Wulfric. Come home.'

'I can't do it. This is my home now.'

I didn't want to make my claim on him, but the 'T'-shaped scar on his head had darkened pink in his anger, so that it drew my eye.

'I climbed the tower and brought you down, Wulfric, in the rain.'

'Dunstan, please,' he said, groaning as we stood facing each other in the street.

'I cut that pulley out of you in pieces.'

He pressed the heel of his hand into his eye, making a sound more like anger.

'I let Encarius cut off your arm,' I said, 'because you were dead if I didn't. Because I made the choice to have you in the world, but wounded, rather than not in the world.'

'I know I owe you my life,' he said. 'But I have left all that behind. The shop is doing well, Alice is a fine wife and we hope to be blessed with more children. Alice wants a son as well. I'd like two or three, to be brothers to one another.'

'Wulfric,' I said gently, as if to a babbling child. 'I cut threads into iron. You bear the scars still.'

'And you killed Godwin in revenge,' he said. His eyes opened and he glared at me, though I felt sick and cold. 'It was all they talked of when you were gone, did you know? Caspar and Simeon raged together that you had survived. They searched for days in the fields around that cliff, looking for your body, for wherever you gave up and died. I prayed you would not be found – and you were not.'

'I fell on soft ground,' I whispered. I had never thought what it had been like for my brother. 'You went to London, though, to this shop.'

'Not for a month, Dun. I had to hear all their spite first. I've never asked you . . .'

'And I have nothing to tell you, Wulfric. I have acted always in the service of God. That is all. I served God when

I pulled up the bone of your skull, when I wept over you and washed you and spooned soup into your mouth and brought you back from the brink of death, over and over.'

I stopped, waiting, as his head sagged to his chest.

'All right, Dun,' he said. 'I'll come back.'

'Thank you,' I said. I was furious with him that he had made me plead for it. His life was mine own. He had no right to make another, away from me.

We walked back to the shop in silence. I could see a frown deepening in Wulfric as he considered how he would tell his wife she had to uproot and go back to Glastonbury. I thought I'd leave them privacy for that. I suspected Alice would blame me and I told Wulfric I'd remain on the street for a while, taking the air.

I felt trouble coming before I understood something was wrong. As I stood looking along the street by the gate, I saw people pull one another to a halt and talk with great vigour. I saw hands raised to cover mouths and eyes go wide, before I ever heard the urchins cry their news. I felt blood drain from my face as I understood what they were shouting. My breath seemed to choke me as I leaned in through the entrance to the shop.

'Wulfric! Come now. Wulfric! We've lost York.'

The shop fell silent, with every face turned towards me.

'Don't just stare at me. Fetch my brother!' I roared at them.

Rumours were wild things and I knew not to trust wild talk of Vikings and war when it was bawled on the street corners. We'd had scares before, of invasions and once of plague. There had been riots and great rushes of people, men and women falling underfoot as they ran like sheep in their panic.

The city of Rome had its news read aloud on the corners by senate heralds, while ours was three parts gossip, two of rumour and the truth all hidden within, if it existed at all. I could hear women shrieking nearby. They enjoyed the horror of it, the great emotions. I could always see it in their eyes as they wailed and had to be comforted.

The city had come to a halt as word spread. Clusters of people gathered, knots of them, swirling wherever someone claimed to know something.

I chafed as I waited for my brother, roaring 'Wulfric!' to the back of the shop at intervals. I kept my knife in my hand as well. There was that sense of panic in the air, as if the whole world might go up in flames at any moment. I felt my heart thumping and knew if it was true, I had to get back to Winchester and the king. If the invasion was actually happening, he would be making ready for war, just as Æthelstan had done.

I thought of the ship waiting at the docks, but it was too slow. It had to be horses. I knew I could make the ride in three days. I could do it in two with the wind behind me if I had to.

Uncle Athelm came out, pale and sweating.

'What's all this shouting, this madness?' he demanded from me.

'They're saying we've lost York. That a fleet has landed in the north.'

I watched him look along the street as I had done, trying to sift the truth from the sight of panicking crowds.

'Lord God, pray it is not true,' he said softly.

'You should go by ship, Uncle. Wulfric and I will ride to Winchester.'

My brother appeared at last in the doorway, wiping the front of his shirt with a cloth. I gathered some liquid had been thrown at him in his conversation with Alice and my mother. Yet we had other concerns then.

'The ship is too slow, Wulfric,' I said. 'We can do it in two days on horseback, but we'll need good mounts.'

'It's true, then? It's war?'

I just gestured down the street, to a hundred clusters of men and women, all afraid.

Wulfric paused only a beat, then began to issue orders to his people. I watched in surprise as he sent his employees running to arrange all we would need. With no warning, Wulfric snapped out his arm to collar a lad trying to run through our little group. The boy's legs flew up alarmingly as Wulfric grasped his coat.

'What have you heard?' he demanded.

'Vikings, sir. They've taken York, they're sayin'. Master says the king will call 'is levy and we'll all go and cut their froats!'

Wulfric let the lad run off and sighed to me as he turned back.

'His master has an ear for such things. Yet if we've lost York, truly lost that city, the kingdom is cut in half.'

'Is it Anlaf, do you think?' I asked. I wanted to remind my serious brother that I had experience of war. 'I saw him on the field at Brunanburh. I thought we'd sent him running for good, with his tail between his legs. We'll do so again, if he's come back.'

'We don't have Æthelstan now,' Wulfric murmured, staring off along the street. 'God help us all.'

I frowned at that, though I wondered how many others were saying exactly the same, the length and breadth of the country.

'Where are those horses?' I demanded. 'I need to get back.'

I heard the iron hooves clattering on cobbles before we saw them. I was ready and I leaped from the mounting block to the beast's back with some show of skill. It made my robe ride up, however, so that my legs were left bare to the thigh and my buttocks were suddenly chilled by saddle leather. I considered calling for a cloak to go over it all, but it still looked ridiculous. In something of a temper, I dismounted again, stalking back into the shop to wait while the tailors ran up some thick woollen trews to go under the robe.

By the time we were all ready to go, Alice and my mother had come out to wave us off. Neither looked happy at the prospect, and Alice was in tears as she embraced Wulfric and told him to come back as soon as he could. She said not a word to me.

I thought my brother would not have been able to mount with one arm, but he jumped into the saddle with something like grace. I said a prayer over our little group, asking God and St Christopher to keep us safe on our journey through deep country. We crossed ourselves and wheeled our horses, then scattered urchins like leaves before us.

We reached Winchester late on the second night. The roads were good in the last dozen miles to the city, so I insisted on going on in the dark, though Wulfric wanted to camp and eat.

The gate of the city was closed, of course, with the country all a-tremble at alarms and invasions. We'd lost time on the road when troops of royal soldiers held us at bay until they were certain we were not enemy scouts or traitors. From those men I learned it was indeed Anlaf who had returned to England.

It seemed the old wolf had moved just about as soon as he'd heard Æthelstan had died, making plans and calling the Viking Irish who settled around Dublin and all along that east coast. I heard later that there was a great knot of them at Limerick and they'd walked to join his fleet that year, for silver and women and a king's favour. They brought their old gods back with them. I fancied I could feel the unease in the land as the gate opened ahead of us.

There were soldiers everywhere in Winchester, ready to challenge and suspicious of all. Honestly, it is a wonder civil war did not break out on the streets, they were so ready for violence. Panic had spread amongst the people there and word was of the king calling all his lords. I wondered how many could possibly reach Winchester in time, so far to the south were we. For the first time in my life, with London dust in the buckles of my sandals, I wondered if the king's capital should possibly be a little further north than Winchester, God forgive me. Leicester, perhaps.

Lamps fluttered on every corner, burning money, just about – and in paying boys to guard them so poor households could not steal the oil. There was a sense of chaos on the air as Wulfric and I rode in as far as we could, then passed the horses to the care of a couple of our own lads. They'd ride back to London to return the animals, but they'd wait first for news, whatever they could learn.

It could only be war. That much I understood as I made my way into a thicker and thicker crowd, all heading to the Witan hall for the king's gathering. I came to a halt in the end and had to elbow close enough to catch the attention of two guards blocking a door.

'Abbot Dunstan of Glastonbury, here on the king's orders,' I growled at them. I did not have to point to my tonsure and robe. They were nervous of the crowd turning ugly, but the Church is not to be crossed. Heads bowed and Wulfric and I swept inside.

In the Witan hall, I grew hot and angry in moments. I found myself buffeted and pushed, at least as roughly as I had been on the street outside. I'm afraid I used my elbows and knees quite ruthlessly to give Wulfric room. He did not seem unduly troubled, but with one arm, I wanted to get him to a seat – and there was at least one free, as Uncle Athelm could not have reached Winchester before us.

'Watch it!' someone growled at me.

I pushed back harder than he had and a space opened, so

that we were out of the crush and able to signal to one of the king's officers who actually did know me. He waved us into a clearer place, for which I blessed him, truly pleased to be past the crush of people, in all their heat and stench. I'd thought my stomach was strong, but in that darkness, so many greasy heads and so much unwashed flesh had stolen my appetite all away.

King Edmund was there, his thanes around him, deep in conversation with one or two. I saw him cross the open floor at the centre of the hall to greet a newcomer, embracing a man named Dodd who had commanded horse with Æthelstan. Edmund clapped him on the shoulder and turned him as he exchanged pleasantries, almost displaying the man to the rest of those gathered there. I understood. The new king needed the magnates of the old one. Edmund needed the support of Æthelstan's earls and thanes as well as his own.

'My lords,' Edmund said suddenly. His voice carried well, though he was not yet twenty-one. 'The king's peace sits upon all of you who are here, though not in the north, not in York.'

Edmund would have gone on, but he had confirmed our fears and a murmur swelled across the room. He waited impatiently, then raised his voice further.

'You may have heard our old enemy has returned. Anlaf of Dublin, who has brought unchristian men to these shores once more, expecting weakness and fear. I believe we will surprise him.'

They cheered that, though I could not help thinking of Æthelstan and the way they'd roared for him. I swallowed nervously, exchanging a glance with Wulfric as King Edmund went on.

'Time is short and not all my lords have reached me. I call the levy even so, to march to York and wrench it from their grasp, to kick them back to their ships. To take the heads of our enemies and spoil all their fine ambitions, all their plans.'

They bellowed then, taking heart from his confidence. Edmund was proven in war, a king of the bloodline of Æthelstan and Edward the Elder and Alfred the Great. They would not fail him. Yet there were empty seats in the darkness, out beyond the lamps.

I did not get a moment alone with King Edmund until the following evening, though I sent letters to be handed to his steward at dawn and noon. I would happily have sent one every hour, but I did not wish to annoy the man whose favour I needed. Wulfric wrote to his wife and our mother, paying six silver pennies to the messenger – and agreeing as much again to be paid on delivery! That was my first understanding that war raised prices to an extraordinary degree. It was also interesting to see the trouble Wulfric had keeping the paper still with only one arm. I resolved to make him a long-handled clamp in oak and brass the next time I had a spare hour in the forge.

We passed the long hours of waiting at Lady Elflaed's house while she rested upstairs, laid low by some sickness of the lungs that made her cough and spit into a bowl. I made sure her servants knew how to prepare vapours of crushed rosemary and I made her up a draught of my own design: horehound, barley water, honey and the whites of eggs. It healed nothing, but soothed sore throats rather well. After I had instructed those who tended her, I paced up and down, just waiting and thinking, while Wulfric sucked the end of his quill. I asked him what subject had him frowning so and he said he was trying to write a love poem to his wife. On good vellum! I wondered if such a wastrel was the right one after all to trust with a great estate.

All around us, the city of Winchester prepared for war, with the clatter of running men outside keeping us on edge with thoughts of invasion. When I saw a servant in king's livery coming down the street, I suddenly could not bear another moment of waiting. I told Wulfric it was a private matter and rushed out to the road, turning the messenger around and telling him I was the one he wanted. I hurried the fellow along as if I'd caught a thief, but we made good time and it was not long before I was passing through the bands of royal guards and into Edmund's presence.

So great had the clamour of soldiers been that I was surprised not to see the king in mail, or armed with his sword and shield. Instead, Edmund wore a simple robe over a tunic, belted at his waist and with his calves bare. He did wear the crown, however, so that I could not help but stare at it as I halted and bowed.

'Ah, Dunstan! My appointments steward has been muttering about you for half the day. What is it?'

'I came to offer counsel, Your Highness. Would you like to give confession?'

He had not asked for the sacrament, but he remembered walking with me, not a month before. I saw him smile in memory, though once again it was touched with strain, as if he still carried weight too heavy to bear.

'I cannot stroll down to the river now, my friend.'

'Will you clear the room, then?'

He looked at me, more in confusion than anything. Yet I was not one of his lords looking for favour, nor was I his father or brother, for him to follow. In that moment, Edmund was quite alone. To my pleasure, he did not hesitate.

'All of you, wait outside for me. I wish to speak in private with Father Dunstan.'

They filed out and drew the doors closed behind them. I endured the hard stares of royal guards as they tried to promise terrible retribution without saying a word, if I was to anger or hurt their master. Yet as the door closed, I saw some of the burden lift from Edmund. He blew air out in a long, slow breath.

'I am in rare trouble, Dunstan. I don't know what I am going to do.'

I chose to keep quiet, to let him speak.

'This Anlaf has York – and half my court want me to go out like my brother before me. They rouse each other with talk of kicking them into the sea, of carrying the Wessex banners all the way to Ireland and setting Dublin on fire.'

Still, I said nothing, while Edmund paced back and forth by the fireplace, stopping only to warm his hands.

'Yet I've had no word from the new king of Scotland – and I doubt he has much love for my family, not after Brunanburh. The latest king of Cumbria killed the messenger I sent to him. It seems they would prefer to have York in the hands of Vikings once again, rather than as part of our England. They turn away from me.'

'Can you take it back? Do you not have the men?'

I knew we'd suffered losses at Brunanburh, but I had no real awareness of how armies were called. They seemed to me to come from the land somehow, rising almost like autumn mists. In truth, I'd meant to keep my silence. Yet the idea that I might be watching Æthelstan's Britain break apart in front of me was enough for me to blurt out my fears.

To my dismay, Edmund shook his head.

'The Witan says it can't be done. They say some will not march this year, that they want to settle it by treaty rather than fight. I'm told I might expect ten thousand in the field now – and that Anlaf will have twice as many, especially if he is aided again by the Scots.'

He paused, looking away. I saw colour come to him as he forced himself to go on.

'They do not believe I can lead, as my brother led. Who knows, Dunstan, perhaps they are right. I have called them, but the Witan says the mood is not for war.'

'No! That's not what I saw at Brunanburh! They weren't there, those old men.'

Edmund smiled wanly at that and clapped me on the shoulder.

'They want me to sign over York in exchange for peace, rather than begin a war that could see every town and city burn, from here to Scotland. They say even Æthelstan would not ride out against a host with so few, that my brother would not betray the hopes of those who just want to live in peace.'

'It seems the Witan have said a great many things,' I muttered, irritated with them. I had no idea if the fears of those men were justified, only that my friend and my king was in pain. I wanted to help him, but I had expected a young leopard readying himself for war, not a broken man, preparing to shoulder more shame than he could carry.

'You know your men, your armies, better than anyone,' I said. 'Better than the Witan. I saw you on the field at Brunanburh, the way you bled the enemy, tearing into the flanks. Numbers did not seem to matter so much then. Can you not do it again?'

'Would you?' he said, in despair. 'I never understood, you know, when my brother took us out. His life was at risk, but much more than that. His family, his honour, his line – everything. All of England was at stake.'

'Wessex,' I said softly, awed at the image of it. He sighed.

'It would make any man hesitate, but not him. Æthelstan threw the dice into the air and let them fall. Now I wear the crown, still warm from his head. I am called upon to do the same, or to make a shameful accommodation with that same enemy!'

Edmund began to pace, furious and frustrated. When his foot clipped a bucket of logs, he kicked the thing so hard it scattered the contents all across the floor. He swore at it and looked to me for counsel. So I spoke, though I understood the stakes as well as anyone. This king was my friend and my star was rising with him. If Edmund was killed on the battle-field, all my ambitions would come to nothing. The Christian faith in England might also have been in peril, but I must admit, I thought first of my own concerns.

'If you treat with this man, will he respect the oath he swears?' I asked.

Edmund shrugged.

'I doubt it. Men like this Anlaf Godfreyson have no sense of honour. It seems to amuse them that we do. No, he'll break his word if he sees a chance to take more land, in a heartbeat. Yet what does that matter if I cannot defeat him? Is my only choice a quick death or a slow one? Or should I do nothing and just wait as he creeps south, taking all of England?'

'You beat him before, Edmund. You are being rushed into this, I think. You just need a season or two to raise armies, to send out a levy, to train more horsemen. Your brother lost York once to Anlaf's cousin, did he not?'

'He did.'

'And did he not win it back? If I have learned anything, it's that there are times to rush in – and times to stand clear and catch your breath.'

'You think I should give up York?' Edmund asked again, challenging me.

'If you don't have an army to crush this Anlaf in one sea-son, then yes, you should treat with him! Give this little man the city he wants. Turn the other cheek, as Christ taught us.' I stepped close to him. 'Then build your armies ready for next year! Have faith, Edmund. This is a Christian country, not a Viking one. You will prevail.'

I was aware that Christ had not turned the other cheek just to give him time to get his dagger out. Yet I thought it was good advice then. Of course, fate would make a mockery of all our plans. It is strange how we keep thinking we can change the world, only to be revealed as smaller than the turning of the sun on a single day.

I went north later that year, with King Edmund and an honour guard of a thousand men. Anlaf came south with about the same number and we met at Leicester, in a host of tents by a stream. There was some bickering and wrestling between champions that became bloody and violent, as was common enough. There was little love shed between us. Edmund was tight-faced with his wounded pride, though he made himself smile and raise a cup in toast to a new friendship. Only those who knew him well saw how it hurt him.

I thought Anlaf too looked relieved, when Edmund sealed his Wessex ring to the treaty. Some tension went out of the Viking's shoulders as copies were folded and placed inside leather wraps. Anlaf Godfreyson had always been a big man, but he was a little grey around the mouth as he shook Edmund's hand.

I had seen it before in those whose hearts are labouring, a certain colour about them that suggests a weakness. Some of them last for years, which was why I did not remark on it. Some of them, like Anlaf Godfreyson, drop dead in the middle of a feast just a few months later, clutching their chest and falling face-first into a plate of grilled kidneys.

23

Every man's life is two strands — a dog with two tales, if you like. The first is all the small victories and disasters that go on around him: the friends and loves and enemies and servants. Yet at the same time, that man might be privileged to see the rise and fall of crowns and nations — the greater threads. Some of those are kings worth telling, while others are mere names on a tomb, unmourned. Still others are kings who broke my heart for all that could have been.

I was not there when Edmund took ten thousand men to York and reclaimed it. He certainly did not need me to slaughter Viking lords and their followers. I do not know if we are meant to show Christian fellowship to those who have raped our people and invaded our homes. No forgiveness was shown and I felt that was right. Christ offers a hard path to follow and there are times when I would rather not follow it to destruction.

Edmund took his enemies in their disarray, one town, one lord, one banner at a time, rolling them up across the north where they had crept down for a hundred miles. They had spread themselves thin after we'd signed our peace with them. Edmund made himself red-handed in slaughter, and earned the approval of us all. I offered him confession on his return and he accepted the forgiveness of his sins. I saw the lines ease from his brow afterwards. It is a wonderful sacrament.

All that occurred while my lesser tale went on. I established Wulfric and his wife and daughter that year at Glastonbury, though it was in a house in the local town rather than at the abbey site. Wulfric insisted upon that as a condition of accepting the work. I could not dissuade him, though some part of me still hoped he would put aside his wife to a convent and join me as a brother Benedictine. A man who has a wife whispering at his pillow each night can never be as predictable as one who does not, I think.

My difficulties were not with the abbey, which proceeded apace now that we had rents coming in. Three hundred and sixty hides amounted to over eighteen thousand acres and covered a fair part of Wessex. Wulfric was rushed off his feet with the work. He employed a dozen young clerks and another dozen to visit our holdings, his own little empire. I saw men and women of the town bow their heads to the great employer as Wulfric passed – the man of London, so they saw him. I thought it all a little grand myself and I warned Wulfric against pretension. All the while, his wife tutted at me as she rocked their child in her arms, as if she knew better.

Still, it bore fruit from the first quarter day, when our collectors brought so much silver and goods across the bridge that I thought we'd have to deposit it with a moneylender, or risk starting a war. I asked Wulfric how he could be sure they'd handed over all they had collected, but he just looked grim and said he took their word. I believe he had some system of checks, but he relied on trust for fair accounting. Some of the men had come from the shop to join him, it was true, but I think he was still too innocent of wickedness.

I was so delighted with the new funds and so busily engaged in discussions with Master Justin and our new masons and builders and everyone else who worked with us that summer, I hardly stopped to think where the money might have come from. That was an error. I just assumed then that the king owned all – as he did, in a sense. In another sense, though, the king's earls and thanes owned it on his behalf.

Two men had lost part of their estates when the king signed

them over to my abbey. One of them, Earl Talien, lost almost half of his family's holdings. He made some query with the king, I believe, but as soon as he understood it was for the Church, he asked only that we celebrate Mass in his name, as we have done on his feast day ever since, to the benefit of his soul. Not a whisper of protest did we hear beyond that, though the dear man lost a fortune.

The other was one I had met at Brunanburh – and thought little of, even then. Leofa of Kent had family lands along the south, many times as great as the small part the king had gifted to us. I imagine he had to be told he had lost those few acres, a couple of farms of poor hill grazing, no more. I believe the royal clerk included them only to grant us access to a river. On such small things, the sun grows dark. It seemed Leofa, king's thane, begrudged the loss of his farms as if we had stolen his first-born.

He came first to the abbey to protest, and as abbot, I went out to meet this nobleman who rode onto Church land with half a dozen men and then sat his horse, shouting at my brother. Wulfric was cowed by the threat of violence, and right to be. Men like Leofa were quite capable of breaking his skull a second time in their righteous anger. The law was weak when it came to punishing such acts. Yet I knew he would not dare to touch me. I stood between them and greeted my old comrade-in-arms.

'What an honour, my lord Leofa, for you to visit our home here.'

The Kentish thane was not pleased to see me. Perhaps he had not understood the monk he'd known at Brunanburh was abbot of Glastonbury. It must have made him think and consider how close I was to the king to have been given lands at all. I imagine it was not lost on him that I did not invite him to dismount or to take food and wine. He had sat his mount to intimidate my brother. Now he had to stay there.

'These acres you claim are yours,' I said. 'Are they not then the king's to disburse as Edmund sees fit? Do you not own them on behalf of the Crown?'

'They are my family lands,' Leofa replied, though he clenched his jaw and his voice sounded strained.

'Oh, no, no, my lord. That is a common error. They were the king's land,' I said. I wanted to prick his arrogance. He had come to my home expecting us all to kneel in the mud for him. I would not. I could not, with the dignity of the Church resting on my shoulders!

'Still, I do not understand your concern, my lord. They belong to me now, to this abbey, as it will be. The Holy Church now owns the land in question. Not the king. Certainly not your poor claim.'

'You should return them to my family, those fields where I trained as a boy,' he said. He had darkened in colour, I noticed. I was pleased to see it and I shook my head in sadness.

'Perhaps you could purchase them from us. I would be willing to sell them for ten years of income. I believe that is fair.'

For an instant, I wondered if he might suffer an apoplexy on that yard. He grew quite swollen and his men became restless, though I smiled at them still, partly to infuriate their master. I was not surprised when Leofa turned and led them away without another word, leaving just dust rising in their wake.

Wulfric wiped sweat from his face.

'He'll make life hard on the farmers and villages there.'

'Pay for armed guards then, if he does,' I snapped. 'This is your labour, Wulfric, not mine. I brought you in because I have other work. It is your concern! All I ask is that you make enough to pay the bills, as they arise. I do not care about the rest, nor how much you pay yourself. Live like a king, for all I care, as long as there is gold and silver for the abbey.'

'What if he makes trouble for our people?'

'We have the king's ear, Wulfric. Our Kentish lord will not dare to interfere in Wessex business.'

Ah me, it hurts to recall some days. If we had raised a hand against Leofa in that yard, he would have been within his rights to defend himself. Wulfric and I would not have lived, and I don't doubt his men would have rampaged then, looting and raping. For the life of me, I cannot see how I could have done anything differently with what I knew at the time. Yet my desire to see him humbled laid a seed of destruction that makes me want to weep in memory.

I spent a great deal of my time in Winchester and London over the next year, leaving the abbey to rise without my constant supervision. Even with the incomes from new land, I needed to make bonds of friendship with rich lords and churchmen, like any other worthy beggar with his hat in his hand. It was a little more subtle than that, but at times, not very much so.

I missed two letters from Wulfric as they followed me around the country for months. I moved with a small group of servants, taking road or ship up into the north or west into Wales, to hills so beautiful they might well have been Eden. When wealthy families offered funds for my abbey, I would leave the actual coin with moneylenders in York, say, knowing I could redeem the sums in London or Winchester. That is a nation, there, in trust for our institutions.

King Edmund had redeemed and proven himself. Anlaf was dead. York was ours once more. The Witan council were very quiet in those days – abashed for their lack of support of him. He'd nearly lost the north, it was true, but because he had won it back, they would never refuse him again. We had Jews arrive from Flanders and France when they heard how peaceful our land was becoming. They have always been a weathercock worth watching, those fellows.

Edmund's England began to thrive. I will not say the whole realm, as we heard nothing from Scotland – and no one wanted to poke the wasp nest by sending men so far north. Yet the new king's reign looked to be a golden age. My abbey was rising from the foundations, built row upon row by hundreds of artisans, trained on the job by our masters and journeymen.

My good mood lasted as long as it took for my brother's letter to reach my hand, a much-oiled packet by then, though still with his seal. I frowned at the Wessex wyvern, wondering if he was using our father's old code for trouble.

He was. It seemed Leofa had begun a campaign of intimidation of our people, as I had come to think of them. I could read the same outrage in Wulfric's descriptions. My brother demanded, not asked, that I take the case to the king.

I read with slow-building anger when I saw how many men Wulfric had hired. Two of them had been beaten almost to death and a third had been found hanged, though no one knew if that was by his own hand, or some other grievance, as it was not far from his own village. Worse news was the crop that had been burned, with tales of foxes running madly through the wheat, fiery brands tied to their tails. It seemed our Kentish friend knew his Book of Judges and the story of Samson.

Beyond the hanged man, the damage was petty enough, though I could see how it had become a misery for those forced to endure it. Wulfric painted a picture of bullying and casual beatings that cried out for justice. I read the letter twice more. There was no evidence – and even if there had been, there would be no punishment. The families of the beaten men might ask the Witan to rule, perhaps to make a payment from the king's purse in compensation. Such things were common enough then and hardly reached the notice of the noblemen in question. Their factors and servants paid off those who brought suit against them and the world went on.

I was, that night, at a house in Bath. My host was a Venetian merchant who traded in glass and refined metals. I had enjoyed a most stimulating evening with all the thoughts of what new things I could make with his wares. I had already fashioned the clamp for Wulfric's letters, a device that had him almost weeping on my shoulder — I could see the result before me that day in its clean written lines. I had plans too for both a new harp and a way of conveying the voice from one end of a hall to another, as an echo, but keeping its form.

Instead, I found myself discussing my brother's letter with my host. The Venetian spoke Latin as well as I did and we had both been drinking wine of such potency, a single glass made my head swim and my sight blur. We had finished a flask of the stuff. I even laid plans for vineyards at Glastonbury, but they refused to grow in a salt marsh, more's the pity.

By midnight, my host and I had agreed that patience was needed, not rash action. Time itself would scar the wound. In a season, in a year at most, Leofa would be distracted by some fair face, or some other grievance. If he was not, perhaps a private word in the king's ear would suffice, rather than a formal petition to Edmund or the Witan council.

It was the best course, though unsatisfying. Maturity is putting aside small spites, or understanding that they matter not at all. It has been a struggle for me at times. That night, I would much rather have paid men to kill Leofa in his bed, but I recognised a warlike spirit that surprised me. That drink called brandy made me quite ferocious for a time, though all my bloody dreams faded by dawn, as such things will.

I returned to Glastonbury to discover the monks up in arms and the bridge over the marsh guarded as if we actually were at war. It seemed Leofa had continued his campaign since Wulfric had written to me. Denied an answer, the Kentish thane had set himself on a course of increasing violence and intimidation, so that his men lurked in all our villages. Barns had burned, as well as crops. No young man could walk alone without being chased – and battered if caught. No young woman was safe from their lewd comments and grasping hands. It was an appalling state of affairs.

The abbey was in a state of siege, with monks wearing sword belts or carrying axes as they walked to chapel! We were protected by the marsh, unlike those in the town and the villages. I could hardly believe the sullen anger I saw in men like Caspar and Master Gregory. At their bidding, I went to the infirmary, dreading what I would see.

My first reaction was almost nostalgia, when I saw my sister-in-law Alice, bustling with a pile of clean cloths.

'Dunstan!' she said, dropping them all. 'Wulfric has been trying to find you for weeks. Didn't you get his letters? Where have you been?'

I went past her, irritated at being questioned so in my own abbey – and at being addressed by Christian name rather than my title. I stopped at the sight of full pallets in the main room, a row of injured men. Aphra was there, painting some yellow muck onto a stitched wound. She looked up only to purse her mouth and glare at me.

It made me shudder to see masons with broken hands, to the point where I wondered if Leofa had heard some rumour of my own past. No, it was just deliberate cruelty, meant to hurt us. Still, I was relieved Master Justin was not among them. We needed him, though even then it was not to build, so much as to plan and design.

I wondered if Leofa had bound himself so tight in rage that he'd forgotten all good sense. He was a fool. Even a cur will bite, if it is tormented long enough.

I realised I could not just bow my head and endure, not that year, not for him. Leofa's malice was too clear, his casual blows too much like a child. We had ignored him and he had raised the stakes.

Wulfric came in a few days after my arrival. I'd sent letters to Lady Elflaed, asking her advice, though she was ailing then and I thought she would not survive another winter. That was a grief to come that I dared not touch. She had saved me at my lowest and I'd repaid her with my youth, raising an abbey from the earth with my hands and my dreaming thoughts – and my faith, poor thing that it was.

When Wulfric returned, the cry went up for the abbot and I rushed out of the school, almost tumbling down the steps as I saw he was bloodied. They had broken his arm. I could only imagine the horror of that, though I saw it in his eyes.

Alice came past me, wailing at the sight of him, pressing her hands to each side of his face and pulling him down, so that he could kiss her. It made me think of my Beatrice and I felt a pang of envy. Wulfric was exhausted and in pain, so that he almost fell as he slid from the saddle to a mounting block, steadied by his wife. He cried out as his arm came loose, flopping from where he had held it nestled in his lap.

I looked at him and at the bruised and battered men who had come back. Their scabbards were all empty and they bore the marks of battle.

'Where is the quarter rent?' I said.

Wulfric shook his head, made pale by pain.

'Leofa's men took it.'

He began to smile as he spoke, despite the pain. I matched him, though Alice looked from one to the other of us in confusion.

'Have you gone mad? Why are you smiling like fools?' she said.

I ignored her.

'Are you sure it was his men, Wulfric? Be careful now, as you answer. You saw fellows you recognised?'

'I did,' he said. 'From a dozen times when they threatened me before. When they did not mind telling me their master. I knew them today.'

My brother was grim with satisfaction and right to be. He turned to answer his wife.

'I know his men, love. They stole silver from us. We can go to the king now – and, by God, put an end to this.'

'And what about your arm?' she said, running her hands over the swollen flesh so that he hissed.

'Injuries are nothing, love. I've said before we can't go to a magistrate or the Witan like children, saying they hurt us, they chased us. We could prove nothing, until today. The king won't stand for robbery on his roads. Believe me, Leofa will know he is finished when they bring that silver back to him.'

A thought struck him and he turned to me.

'We should not delay, Dun. The sooner we can put this grievance before the king, the sooner Leofa is in irons. I'll ride to London with you right now.'

'What about your arm?' I said. I must admit, I admired him then, for his stern manner. It is a strange and wondrous thing watching a brother grow up to be a man. It took long enough, mind.

'I'll have Alice splint and wrap it.'

'I mean, you can't gallop . . . with one arm, and that broken.'

I saw his excitement fade to frustration. It was all very well ambling along on a horse that knew its way home, but a three-day ride over rough country was impossible.

'By sea then,' I said. 'We'll put you in a cart for the coast. It will just have to be fast enough.'

Alice led him away to be splinted and fed. I watched them go, feeling rather sorry that there was no one to look after me in the same way.

24

When Wulfric and I had presented our tale to Edmund, Leofa was summoned to Winchester, to appear no later than Pentecost. He left it as late as he could, of course. Lady Elflaed died while we read our evidence into the records, so that I had to ask for a delay in the proceeding to preside over her funeral.

Edmund could hardly refuse my request. Lady Elflaed had been a great friend to his family and to the city. The king came himself to honour her, though he stood at the back of the cathedral in quiet dignity, leaving as the choir breathed the last verses. The benches were not filled, though they should have been.

Perhaps it did not hurt to remind King Edmund of my supporters, even as one of them fell away. Before the formal hearing with Leofa went on, I took an afternoon to visit the royal archives to read her will. The contents of it still make a shiver run through me. I had known the dear lady was wealthy. Elflaed had owned sheep farms in Somerset and a quarry of good iron ore in West Cumbria. It seemed she'd owned a number of ships and merchant businesses as well, a true fortune that had come to me. Not, you will notice, to the Church, or even to the abbey, but to Dunstan of Wessex himself, to spend as he saw fit.

Inheriting so much could not balance the grief I felt in losing her, but it eased some of the pain. I had taken a vow of poverty, which was awkward. I gave it a great deal of thought over the next few days, as witness after witness came to give evidence to the king on our behalf. I had not resolved the problem to my satisfaction by the time Wulfric and I were called in once more.

I put such thoughts aside as King Edmund entered the petition hall, walking slowly down the aisle to the throne. This was to be a more intimate event than the giving of evidence, with the king's interested subjects kept away. My brother and I had to be present throughout as accusers, giving oath that every word of it was true. Leofa might have done the same if he'd cared nothing for his immortal soul. Yet he had not challenged our account in a single instance, except to blame his men for their youth and rash action. He claimed no knowledge of any of it. I suspected the king knew very well by then where the truth lay, but I did not know how he would make his judgement.

Edmund had refused to allow my uncle Athelm to administer the oaths of our petition, given his relationship to us, so instead, a bishop I did not know had been summoned. Bishop Oda of Ramsbury was of Danish stock, though he grew to manhood in Wessex. He seemed a solid sort, of much the same build as myself and not one of those clerics who looked as if they'd never gone outside in all their lives.

On that last day, Oda and I bowed to each other when I entered, a courtesy between professionals. Wulfric leaned over to whisper something as I seated myself. I shook my head in answer, feeling the dignity of the moment and the king's presence strongly.

Edmund had found a new champion by then, a fellow who would have loomed over old Egill Skiallgrimmson. I'd love to have watched them fight bare-handed, mind. It would have been a rare bout. This John Wyatt was enormous and brutal, so he served King Edmund well enough. Even scornful, angry bastards like Leofa were respectful with Wyatt's gaze on them.

I felt Wulfric turn his head at the sounds of doors cracked open behind us. I kept my gaze forward, though I heard every step Leofa made as he came in. No one walked at his side, as he was only accused and no prisoner. Yet I felt his glare pass over me like the heat of an oven. He had listened to our complaint with no expression showing at all, beyond a slight boredom. It occurred to me that if we had failed to convince King Edmund, if Leofa was allowed to go free from that place, Wulfric was in real danger. As I considered the bullish quality of the man who knelt before the king as a penitent, I considered that I might be in danger as well.

Bishop Oda blessed the proceedings. He had a good voice, I noted, very rich in tone. We knelt and said the Pater Noster, then Wulfric and I rose to hear the king rule. Leofa remained on his knees, waiting for judgement with his head bowed. Oda finished with the sign of the cross cut in the air to us all.

Edmund let the silence swell. I saw his breath plume before him, showing the coldness of the air. When he spoke, it was without rising from his seat.

'My lord Leofa, Abbot Dunstan, Reeve Wulfric of Glastonbury, I have summoned you to this place to hear my judgement on this matter of disputed land.'

I hid a wince at 'disputed', feeling my stomach drop away and hoping it was not a prediction that things would not go well. I was only too aware that Edmund had fought alongside this thane at Brunanburh. One solution would be to give back the land to his friend. Leofa would be satisfied – and gloat at a victory. I wondered how long it would be before some rough fellows came in the night for Wulfric and me after that.

'I have heard testimony under oath, of violence, of destruction and of theft. It grieves me that men I respect could find no way of settling a dispute without bringing it to me. So I will rule on it. Dunstan, see my clerk. Sign over to me that portion of the land that Leofa claims. I will find an equivalent for you, of equal worth.'

My heart sank, though I bowed my head and did not dare look at Leofa.

'Thank you, Your Highness,' I said.

'And you, Leofa? Your men stole rents and broke the arm of an abbot's reeve.'

'I have had them punished, Your Highness. And I have offered to return the sil—'

'Do not interrupt me, sir!' Edmund roared at him.

Leofa dipped his head like a whipped cur, as well he might, with John Wyatt bestirring himself at the king's side.

'I cannot leave the terms of your punishment to you, Leofa. In your foolishness, you have brought my judgement upon you – and made sure that hundreds of my subjects are waiting to see if you are set free, if their hurts and losses will be ignored by their king. It cannot be so, Leofa.' He paused and took a deep breath before speaking again. 'Therefore, you are, by this judge-ment, banished from the realm and my kingdom for the period of five years, not to enter home or crown port, whether in storm or fair weather. I will give you six days to see to your affairs, then I will consider you oathbreaker if you are still in England. That is my judgement – and you have brought this on yourself in your childish rule. I thought better of you. Of you all.'

I gaped at that last part, feeling myself included. Neither Wulfric nor I had wanted to petition the king! We'd wanted to be left in peace. I half-wished I'd hired men to waylay Leofa on the way to his summons, but it was hard to keep such things from coming out. Tongues do wag and secrets spill.

Leofa bowed as Edmund rose and left. I was pleased to see the king's champion remained behind, as I was practic-ally alone with a man banished from the realm. Wulfric and I could hardly have defended ourselves, if Leofa had run wild. It occurred to me to pour a little oil on those waters while I had the chance.

'I am sorry it came to this, my lord,' I said. 'I wish we could have settled it in peace between us, as the king said.'

I will not repeat his reply, spat in anger. He too glanced at John Wyatt, resting his hands on the haft of an axe as he grinned at us. Leofa decided not to provoke that monstrous man and stalked out instead.

I heard Wulfric breathe in relief, though I was more worried than before. The problem with banished men is that they come back – and five years was not too long. It was why I'd been so reluctant to go to the king at all.

'I hope we have not stored up more trouble, Brother,' I murmured to Wulfric. For once, he was silent, his worry as clear as mine own.

That summer, King Edmund married a young woman of the court, making her his queen. He seemed happy and Elgifu was radiant, though she had either put on a great deal of weight or the wedding was more urgent than it first appeared. I was a little disappointed not to be asked to officiate at the ceremony. Bishop Oda was again the king's choice, as my uncle Athelm was then too ill to attend. It seemed a time of change was upon us all, though I was at least given a seat near the front and next to the king's own brother and two of his sisters.

I had not seen much of Prince Eadred, though he stayed close enough to his brother in Winchester. Eadred was a weak-looking, sallow creature. Every time I met him, I thought he would not last a month, as he coughed into a little cloth he tucked up his sleeve. Honestly, I have seen a dozen people die from ailments of the lungs, but Eadred somehow went on, coughing and spitting, but present all the same.

I tried not to play the toad-eater to him. I had Lady Elflaed's great fortune at my disposal, after all, never mind the abbey that was taking shape and growing greater and more expensive each year that passed. I did not need the favour of the king's half-grown brother, so I was merely polite to him. I felt his gaze on me and I suppose he was a little envious of my strength and size, my fine big lungs like bellows, compared to his little wheezing ones. I know now that very small men can be resentful of stronger, taller fellows. It encourages a spite in them, not a properly sanguine Christian outlook. Of course, we are all weak in the end, but some are never strong at all and grow quite bitter about it.

'Prince Eadred,' I said, bowing my head in greeting.

'Abbot Dunstan,' he said. 'How pleasant to see you once more. I heard about your trouble with Leofa.'

I frowned at the odd tone, almost of mockery, though I'd hardly said a word to him in the past.

'All forgotten now, I hope,' I said, though perhaps my worry showed.

'I suppose so. He was a very violent man, mind you. I recall he beat some poor seller of shellfish almost to death for giving him short weight. What a temper he had!'

I agreed, though I could see by then he was amusing himself at my expense. The trouble was that I could hardly prod Eadred in return, the king's own brother. I may have loomed a little over him, to remind him how much larger I was. I saw his gaze rise past me and I flinched as I realised I was being loomed upon in turn. The king's champion took a seat beside us, making the whole bench creak. My change of expression seemed to have amused Eadred, so that he coughed and laughed and ended up almost choking into his little cloth as I eyed him.

'My brother and I will go hunting at the end of the month, Father Dunstan. Not a great hunt, you understand, with hundreds of beaters and half the horsemen in England. No, just an intimate following. Hard riding through the wet ferns, that sort of thing. Too much drinking, usually, so that men fall off and break their necks.' He chuckled at his own humour. 'There have been sightings of a royal stag, actually not too far from you – near the cliffs at Cheddar Gorge.' He looked me up and down as if the idea had just occurred to him. I wondered then if it was no accident that I had been given a seat at his side. 'Why, you look fit enough, father. My brother

Edmund said you can ride. He said it was worth seeing. You should accompany us, if you have the stomach for it.'

I had no idea if Eadred sought to test me, or expected me to refuse. His expression was perfectly blank as he turned back to watch the crowd congratulating his brother and the new queen.

I'd gone hunting with my father when I was very young, though even then he was a little old for twenty miles of tramping over sodden ground. Our hare traps and bird nets were not quite the sort of thing kings and lords enjoyed. Yet the wonder was that this half-sized, coughing prince thought he had any sort of stamina or stomach that I lacked. I felt myself bristle at the challenge, for all I thought he was manipulating me. The brightest of young men will act like fools when someone queries their courage.

'I would be honoured, my lord,' I said. 'I knew Cheddar Gorge well, when I was a boy. There were deer there, great shaggy beasts. I have never seen larger animals.'

I caught his interest with that. He dropped the careless pose, taking my arm.

'In truth? I thought you would know the land there. It is, what, ten miles from Glastonbury? Any boys growing up in those parts would have gone to see such a wonder, of course. Now listen, father. I have huntsmen and dogs as fine as my brother's. Stay close to me and we'll find this monstrous stag. I'll eat his liver, still warm.'

His eyes glazed subtly as he imagined it, though whether he saw the blood or the triumph I could not tell.

'The local thane said he'd never seen such a spread of ant-ler, father. So I'll have that thicket, if I can.' Eadred shuddered and looked up, as if waking. 'Perhaps you'll be my luck, father. There is only one stag – and I would count you as a friend if you helped me to win it.'

*

275

I still had Scoundrel then, though he'd grown older as I came into my prime. He went lame rather too often to be out on rough ground in the half-darkness, but we had a local man guiding us, jigging along on a pony, so that he looked a child beside the great beasts Edmund and Eadred rode.

I was hunched and miserable, already wet through and so chilled in the drizzle and dawn cold that I just wanted to curl up until a warm fire and some ale presented themselves to my eyes. I had been warned by Master Gregory of the workshop to wear thick cloth against the biting flies, or clegs, as he called them. Yet they found me anyway, rising from the ferns and diving ceaselessly at my eyes and mouth. The sight of my sharp gestures seemed to please the local. He said there were more flies where the deer roamed, which made sense, though was no comfort. I glared at him for appearing to believe this would interest me.

I will say that watching the sun rise on the hills above Cheddar Gorge was an hour of extraordinary beauty. The great slice in the land can't be more than a mile or so long, but the cliff edges are sharp as a knife and drop hundreds of yards down to the ground below. I've never seen anywhere else like it in England, and as I shivered in sopping clothes and rubbed at the bites of horseflies, I never wanted to again. There is a reason man builds warm homes and churches. Yes, of course it is for the glory of God, but it keeps the wind and rain out as well, which is no small thing. All the philosophers of Greece and Rome had long sunny days to stroll and think. In England, we had to build roofs or freeze.

The king had vanished somewhere far off, though we could sometimes hear the barking of his dogs when they flushed a hare or a fox. He had his own local to guide him, while I rode alongside Eadred and our man. Our pony-riding fellow looked askance at me whenever I suggested one path over another, but the truth was I did know those cliffs and that gorge well. Ten miles is nothing to a boy, and Wulfric and I had walked that whole part of Wessex a hundred times when we were seven or eight.

It had not changed, though it took a while to come back. I'd catch sight of a rock or a boulder and suddenly know, just know, that there was a brackish old pond down the track beyond it, or that the copse of trees there leaned right out over the sheer drop.

Eadred looked to me constantly, as if I could conjure a stag from the air simply by knowing the land. At first, in the darkness, I was just pleased to find a path well away from the edge of the gorge. The drop seemed to be something I could sense, though it might just have been the way the trees and bushes came to an end into open air. The sounds and echoes were different and I could stay clear of it. That said, I was still relieved when the sun rose. It makes the world ours, that light. It banishes fear and we raise our heads.

As the light grew, I led us down a path between two huge rocks. I had climbed them as a boy and knew they would let me see far over the land around us. Scoundrel resisted being used as a stepping stone, but our local man held his reins and I went scrambling up. There was lichen and moss deep in the cracked surface. I dared not trust a single grip and I was aware of how much lighter I had been when last I climbed.

There was the sound of pebbles and scraping behind me and I saw Eadred had followed, climbing easily, though I heard him cough, a subdued sound as if he swallowed the noise. Still, he caught up to me on that slope, so that we stood together on the top, panting and delighted with our small triumph. It seemed longer down than it had been to rise, and I stared at our huntsmen, wondering if there was an easier way to reach them.

Eadred took my arm, turning me slowly to see the stag. It stood not two hundred yards away, on high ground. It was watching us, and as I gaped at it, it bowed huge antlers. I know now it was some kind of challenge, but at the time I stared at Eadred, wondering what it might mean.

'Move slowly now, father,' Eadred whispered. 'Let's get down without breaking a leg.'

He and I went to a crouch and I saw the stag turn sharply, sensing something on the wind before I did.

We heard the king's hounds, yammering away as they came closer. Eadred cursed and slid on his stomach down the rock, vanishing from my sight. He would have fallen badly if his huntsmen hadn't scrambled to catch him. He and they were kicking their mounts to a gallop in an instant, while I was still climbing down.

He had surprised me. His small frame and poor lungs had led me to believe he was a weak man, or not brave. Neither was true. Our dogs howled and bayed and Eadred galloped out of the shadow of those rocks. The great stag vanished from its perch. The hunt was on and I dropped into Scoundrel's saddle with a thump that jarred me all the way to my neck, yet I roared as I turned him, caught up in the excitement of it.

The noise of hounds tugs at something in a man's chest, a thread of old times that raises the blood and banishes all pain. I was off, riding like a madman, following the dogs, racing through small gaps without a care.

We pelted through wet woodland, so that I had to raise my arm against the briars that looped across the path, cursing as they snagged and hoping against hope I would not take one across the throat. I caught only glimpses of Eadred, and then the second pack of dogs was converging on my path from the side. I looked ahead and felt panic swell as I saw we had come back to the highest part of the gorge.

The stag was running there, as big as a horse itself, huge and thick with fur. I heard its snorting as it strove to stay ahead of both dogs and men. I knew that place. I had stood on that edge and looked over, scaring myself. I was already heaving at the reins as the stag reached the end of the rocks and leaped from instinct, as if it thought it could reach the other side of the gorge, far away.

It happened so quickly! The dogs were almost on its heels and in their frenzy they went straight after it, unable to stop. They screeched as they fell, the tone of their barking changing to terrified howls. I came to a halt and I saw King Edmund break out of the trees at full gallop.

'Stop!' I roared at him, waving both hands.

I saw him look at me and the drop ahead in growing horror. He was still the master horseman I had seen at Brunanburh. He heaved and turned all in an instant, throwing his weight to one side while his mount's hooves skidded and went splay-legged, whinnying like a scream.

Edmund could not halt in time. In the last moment, he dived out of the saddle and came to his feet, with the reins taut in his hand, pulling his horse to save it.

I watched him dragged one step to the edge, while the animal showed the whites of its eyes and scrambled with all legs kicking. It had no grip and I think the young king would have gone over if Eadred hadn't shouted to him.

'Let it go, Edmund! Please!'

Edmund released his grip and the horse went tumbling after the dogs and the stag, screaming all the way down until the sound ceased. I walked to the king with tears in my eyes, overcome. He was in agony and I thought he must have torn all the muscles of his back trying to hold an impossible weight. Six men could not have pulled a horse back from that edge. Later, his entire chest went purple under the skin. It was a foolish thing to do, but what is a king, if not a man who refuses to admit defeat?

'Thank you, Dunstan,' Edmund said. 'I heard you call. You too, Brother.'

As one, we three walked together to the edge. There were

still a few dogs there that had avoided going over with the rest. They seemed untroubled at how close they had come to death and wagged their stiff tails and panted as we peered at broken things below.

'I claim the antlers,' Eadred said.

Edmund chuckled and groaned at the same time.

'My back is sore. I've done something to it. Yet you will claim the antlers of the stag that nearly killed me?'

Eadred considered for a moment. He was the younger brother.

'I claim them to give to you,' he said.

Edmund embraced him. They knew how close it had been, both of them.

We made our way down, to that place at the bottom of the gorge. Perhaps twelve or fourteen dogs had gone over. To Edmund's astonishment, one of them had survived, though he had broken a leg and looked both scuffed and battered. He wagged his tail to see us and neither the king nor his brother could believe he had lived, looking up again and again to the cliffs high above. I had an idea how it was done. I suspected that dog had fallen on its fellows, or the stag itself.

The stag had indeed been a monster of its kind. It lay black-shouldered, dark with flies and blood, with a great spread of horn that made him a king of the breed. His antlers had broken in the fall, wrenched apart in two great pieces and with half a dozen tips broken off. Yet Eadred brought up his huntsmen and the local carpenter arrived, with saw and hammers and chisels to cut them free. King Edmund accepted the horns, and for all their battered look, they had pride of place in Winchester for all my life. They are still there now.

25

When Edmund's queen gave birth to a healthy son and named the little brat Edwy, there was almost a breath of relief from the hills of England, at least after the child had survived six months and the queen was showing again. It seemed Edmund found her tolerably attractive, enough to mount and bear his seed. The second son was named Edgar – and the line was secure.

Children are born, and beloved uncles die. It seems to me, at times, that I remember only great triumphs and disasters. The mere ordinary years of my youth, where the crops came in and the abbey rose higher, pass almost unnoticed. Yet a good life is made of such things.

When I offered Mass at Athelm's funeral in Canterbury, it was the first Thursday past Easter, with the spring sun burning colours onto the stone floor. I struggled to breathe, my grief came so strongly – and I remember how the incense rose in grey curls and how the words stopped in my throat.

I loved that enormous, kind man, though I've learned that one great grief will open a door in us that cannot be closed again. From my father, to Lady Elflaed, to Uncle Athelm – each of those we lose becomes a shadow for the next, an echo, a bell struck, that sounds in our lives until our own last breath. I was overcome by tears in my eulogy.

It did not help that a particularly beautiful young woman on the front bench looked up adoringly all the way through, snagging my attention. When I should have had my thoughts on the great coffin we would somehow carry to its tomb in the church of St John, I grew flushed instead at the way some unknown maiden bit her lower lip and stared up at me, dabbing her eyes and heaving in great breaths.

I was still tormented by desire in those days, on occasion. I punished myself in cold waters, though I might have made a river steam. Thank God such things fade with years passing. Lust goes to ashes in the end, like ambition, or honour, or hope.

It grieves me to have played a part in evil days and the bitter triumphs of the enemy, though I was innocent enough. The kingdom was secure, with a young royal family and two sons. King Edmund had ruled in peace for five years when he held a great feast for his noblemen in Winchester. The occasion was no more than a dinner on All Hallows' Eve, when old villages used to call back dead souls and interfere with graves. There were dark practices still in England then, you may believe it.

The nights were coming earlier and the fields were thick with mist as the sun went down. The air was crisp and cold with each breath, cleaner than the breezes of summer. Like a feast of Nero, the king lit the gardens with copper bowls of oil along the paths, so that his guests could stroll as if in the day. Half the city seemed to have come to honour his anniversary on the throne.

I saw Leofa standing without shame, returned and bold, holding a quart mug of ale and laughing with a group of hard-looking fellows. I'm afraid I stood rooted to the spot as I recognised him, filled with sudden fear and confusion. It had been just three years since I'd seen him banished.

It was true we'd had not a grain of trouble from his men after the banishment began. I suppose in part it was because we no longer owned the land Leofa had claimed. Edmund had been as good as his word to me. He had made a gift of some other hides of land to replace our losses. That time was long past then, a memory as far and forgotten as any other.

I wonder now if Leofa had decided three years was enough and had come to ask his old friend for a reprieve. I imagine Edmund might have granted it to him, even. Men who have fought together sometimes forge a bond that lasts a lifetime. In the right mood, Edmund would have laughed and embraced him.

It was not the right mood. Whatever Leofa had intended, it all went wrong before my very eyes.

On such occasions there are always hundreds who wish to be introduced, so that they can say 'I met the king' to their grandchildren, or 'This hand shook a king's hand'. As a result, Edmund was surrounded by well-wishers as he moved through the feast, his champion John Wyatt looming over all. Edmund had only to comment on the gardens and there would be a ripple of laughter from those who hung on his words. He had only to raise a cup to have a servant push through to fill it once again.

In the middle of the evening, the crowds had spilled right across the grounds, roving everywhere, inside and out. The mood was light and people were merry and clasping each other by the shoulders. There was some singing nearby as Edmund passed within a few feet of Leofa and looked right at him. I saw the king recognise a man he had banished, scorning him at his own feast. I saw Edmund's rage come.

If he had been less a fighting man, or twice the age he was, Edmund would have sent John Wyatt to lay hands on the impudent thane. Returning from banishment mocks the king and the law equally. Edmund was within his rights to have Wyatt strike the fellow's head from his shoulders right there, in the gardens.

Yet the king was twenty-three years old and at his greatest strength and vigour. Of course he did not summon his champion, or send a servant. Of course he went himself. Leofa turned away as he saw Edmund coming towards him.

I think perhaps he wanted to hand his great jug of ale to one of the others, but it might have looked as if he turned his back on the king.

Edmund laid his hand on Leofa, yanking him round. As well as his quart pot, Leofa had been eating some piece of fowl, his hands greasy with chicken – and his knife held in his right, to cut the meat. As Edmund heaved at him, the thane reacted as he might have done to a cutpurse, coming round with his knife out straight and hard, a punching blow. The ale pot crashed into pieces on flagstones at their feet.

I could only stare as Edmund went stiff. I saw enough of Leofa's horrified expression to know he had not planned it that way. His hand fell from the hilt of his knife and the king took a step back, his mouth opening in pain and surprise and hurt.

John Wyatt came through then, bellowing. He had been within arm's reach of Edmund, though no one could have stopped the king suddenly stepping forward and grabbing someone. We all froze as Wyatt brought his axe around in a huge sweep. It snatched Leofa from the world, so that he was there and then gone in an instant. The blow took Leofa's head off, with most of his right shoulder, going on to sink deep into the gravel and remain.

Edmund went down to one knee. I could see he was struggling by then, his face showing fear. I went forward to tend him, though I almost died for it as Wyatt reached to block me with a seax knife as long as my forearm.

'Let me through, you fool,' I said, though I'd thought I was done and my voice was a croak. Wyatt bared his teeth at me in his distress. No doubt he was afraid of his own fate for allowing the king to be struck.

I knelt by Edmund and he made no move to stop me as I felt for the knife's hilt. He heard my intake of breath and his eyes turned to me.

'Would you pull it out, please?' he whispered to me. 'I cannot . . . bear it much more.'

I saw him glance up at the crowd gathered around us and I realised the king's champion could still be of use.

'Master Wyatt, the king wishes to be alone here. Can you move this crowd away?'

The big man bent slowly to retrieve his axe, with Leofa's bright blood on it. Some of those who heard me speak were already moving when they saw him reach for that weapon. Wyatt raised himself up and put the axe on his shoulder.

'Leave,' he said to them all. 'Give the king room.'

It was crude enough, but it worked. Hundreds backed slowly away, their faces pale and stupid in their concern. Every one of them looked the same, wide-eyed and gaping upon us.

'Your Highness, the blade is in your heart,' I whispered to Edmund. 'The iron can seal its own wound for a time, but if you move sharply . . . or if I pull it out, you will be gone.'

He looked at me, that young man, breathing slowly. He understood at last and his eyes took on a sheen.

'I see. Would you fetch my wife for me?' he said in short breaths.

I could see his efforts to control the pain as he screwed his eyes closed. Tears ran from them, but it was awareness of death, not fear.

I looked up as a shout sounded and Wyatt stirred beside us, raising his axe. Yet it was not the king's wife but his brother Eadred who came running across the grounds. He skidded to a halt and looked down on us and the bloody pieces of Leofa.

'Who was it?' he demanded.

I heard Edmund's breath catch and I turned back to the king. His life was fading, but not quickly. His youth and strength held him there, though the pain built. He tried to pull the blade out. I had to grip his right hand in mine and I found myself weeping, unable to believe this was happening.

With a start, I remembered my responsibilities. I leaned closer to hear the king's last confession, though every word dragged slowly out of him. I made the sign of the cross on his forehead and anointed him with oil from a tiny silver box. I wept as I did so. I have not had many friends.

'Edmund!' came a shriek. His wife seemed to fly over the grass and she collapsed by his side, her dress billowing. To my surprise, Edmund smiled for her. He made a huge effort to speak in his normal voice, though the pain bit and tore at him.

'I am sorry,' he said. 'I thought we had longer.'

I could only stare as she looked into his eyes, an intimacy of such power it made me turn my own gaze. Her hands trembled as she raised them to his neck, curling her fingers inward, so that she touched him with the backs of her hands. It was a strange gesture, almost like a child and not one I had seen before. She kissed him then and he groaned as they touched.

'Pull the knife, Dunstan,' he hissed at me, looking over. 'It is too much. I must have it out.'

'It will kill you if I do,' I said. 'Please don't ask me.'

'It hurts . . .' He coughed and made a sound of pain that was cruel even to hear.

His brother Eadred reached down with no warning and pulled the knife from his brother's heart, throwing it to the ground then, as if it had stung his hand.

'Go to God, Brother,' he said.

Edmund nodded and smiled, and did as he was told.

I found myself wracked with sobs, though I had not cried like that since my youngest years of childhood. His wife cradled her dead husband in her arms as I rose and looked aghast at the slick of royal blood on my hands.

The king was dead. I looked at Eadred as he brought out his

cloth and coughed into it. My thoughts were dust in sunlight, spinning, falling. Edmund's eldest son was barely three years old; the other was still on mother's milk. It would fall to Eadred to keep the throne warm, I knew it in that moment. The Witan had no other choice, no cousin or half-brother worth the name. Yet I wondered if such a weak and sickly creature, such a very youngest brother, could ever be up to the task.

It made me weep again a day later to hear that Edmund had left instructions to be buried in Glastonbury Abbey. He'd assumed it would be long finished by then, of course, not the enormous worksite it still was. He was instead entombed in the same churchyard as my father, though we would not let him rest there. My Glastonbury needed kings as well as saints.

A week after Edmund's funeral, a huge wall fell at Glastonbury, killing poor Brother Guido. The boatman was crushed into the earth, every bone made dust by the massive weight of stone. Cracks appeared below another arched window and Master Justin called a halt to the work.

It seemed almost fitting, that my beloved abbey broke in the same year Edmund fell. My friend should have ruled for decades, like his father.

In some ways I blamed myself, for Leofa, though I still think it was mere accident rather than evil. When death comes so quickly, it leaves mysteries. Caesar pulled his robe over his head when he saw Brutus. Was it cowardice? Was it despair, or contempt? It did not stop those who wished him dead, and we'll never know. Did Leofa want to come home, to be reconciled? Perhaps he whispers it in hell. Who knows how the old enemy strikes at all that is good? However it came about, that year was a time of sorrow and of mourning – and the cost is still with us.

26

For a season, we were without a crowned king. No country is at ease then, just as sheep will cluster in the corners of fields and grow fearful if the shepherd fails to appear. Eadred may have wished to avoid any ill will and barbed comments about him leaping into his brother's shoes while they were still warm. Or perhaps it was because he was unmarried and did not want to make an oath as Æthelstan had done. His brother Edmund had fathered two sons, ahead of him in line. It was only their youth that prevented them.

I spent a little time wishing I had been more courteous to Eadred over the few years I'd been at court. I thought back to the conversations I'd had and, yes, if I'd known he would be king, I would have been more pleasant, more patient. One or two of those who had been rough or rude with him made themselves scarce and were not seen again in Winchester, as you can imagine.

My main concern was for the great cracks that had appeared in the walls at Glastonbury. I examined every part of the site to see if the walls had somehow shifted, but they were sound, the ground dry. It took me a month to have the lads dig down to the foundations in a dozen places. It was back-breaking work and all for nothing. We found no weak part, no new river come from beneath to wear all away, just our beds of broken oyster shells, more than stars in the sky, packed in by their own weight until they were almost brick. I even wondered if we should have built on the great Tor, but the wind howled up there, blowing hard and cold on a spring day. The winters would have been a misery.

In the end, I should be ashamed how long it took me to see what I needed to. The Roman arch is in every aqueduct and bridge, every window and door, every church and stone guildhall. I learned early on how they built their arches in equal sides, then lowered in the capstone, so that mere bricks became as strong as any natural shape, as an egg is hard to break in the hand. Those Roman curves could almost rival Atlas for weight borne from above. Yet they were not strong enough for the height and weight of our walls.

Windows are always a weakness, as any child can see. They pierce a solid wall and allow forces to act that have no place there. As I worked through one night to the dawn, I drew narrow windows, with a sharper curve that produced half the force to each side of a Roman arch. I took out my pair of compasses and drew arcs with the lead, spinning them around in growing excitement. When there was light enough to extinguish my lamp, I rolled up my sheets and raced across the yard to where Master Justin still slept with a dozen other monks, all exhausted. I banged on the door and roused them.

The master mason was wearing a black robe, I noticed. In the grey light, Justin saw my surprised expression and smiled, embarrassed.

'My own clothes were too scratched and torn,' he said. 'It made no sense to be having new ones made when there were robes here of good wool.'

'Of course,' I said. I was impatient for him to see what I had done, so that I missed the signs of conversion in him. Within the year, Justin would take an oath and my abbey would have brought another soul to God – and denied one more to the old enemy.

I shifted from one foot to the other as Master Justin looked over my sketches, raising his eyebrows. I saw a great stillness come upon him as he understood.

'There are secrets here I have seen before . . . known only to the most senior members of my order,' he said. 'Even I have not learned all there is. Yet . . . you have come upon them on your own.'

I felt his reaction like a slap. I had thought I might have been the first to see the strength of the shape, but I covered my disappointment with impatience.

'So will it stand, then? Will it hold? It seems to, when I add the forces, there, and there – where I have arranged them in columns.'

I pointed at the vellum. He looked at me and I could not explain the expression of awe on his face.

We discussed the new stone we would need as the sun rose over the site – and of course it would all cost a fortune. None of the stones already shaped with chisel and hammer would fit the new pointed arches. Justin strode across the yard to pick one up from a pile of balanced things, turning it in the light and talking in a torrent. I saw happiness in him and excitement. Like me, he wanted to build something for the ages, something that would stand long after we were gone. That abbey was our prayer and our mark.

Yet theories must be tested, or they are no more than wind. Lads ran with barrows of flint, sand, ash and lime, stirring great vats of the mortar, while others dropped the plumb lines and built us a wall. At the end of each day we had all worked until our backs and hands were sore and our red eyes peered from faces thick with dust. The lines of stone dried slowly over night and we ate like dogs, gulping down whatever our kitchen made, then falling into sleep as if we had been struck by a falling block.

I still woke for the Night Office in my exhaustion – and Master Justin came with me, to sing and chant the responses with more fervour than many of the monks who did so by rote, with all true feeling lost over decades.

After a week, we reached the height above that narrow window that had cracked the previous one. I stood before it, watching line after line of heavy flints added, cut and shaped. On scaffolds, more men poured rubble in from barrows.

The arch held. Justin and I stood before it as if we were certain it would stand for a thousand years. I brushed dust from my hands.

'There. It will do now,' I said.

I bowed my head and offered thanks to God, then returned to Winchester. It had not escaped my notice that the coffers were almost empty once again, with the whole project set back a year or longer by the fallen walls. The abbey community sold its goods all over the country by then, from silver cups to pork sausages. Yet the costs were immense and Wulfric was in despair whenever I broached the subject with him. We needed more funds, ideally in the form of rents from more land – and there was only one place I would find that.

In May of the year of our Lord 946, Prince Eadred was crowned king by Archbishop Oda of Canterbury, as Rome had made him. I grew to like Oda the Good, despite his Danish ancestors and strange customs. For all his faith, I think that squat and bearded fellow would have murdered his own mother for a plate of tripe, especially the sort so pungent that it curled the hairs on your arms and made strong men weak. I have never had any desire to chew on a cow's bunghole, but Oda seemed to relish it as a taste of childhood. I will admit he had fine strong teeth, well suited to the task. Yet despite his country ways, Oda was no one's fool and even rather lorded it over Archbishop Wulfstan, who had come down from York then for the coronation. Some men called Oda 'the Good', as I have done, while others called him 'the Harsh'. Which name you favoured depended on whether you had ever crossed him or not.

The same gold band that Æthelstan and Edmund had worn became the cock's plume on the brow of King Eadred, the third brother to wear it. As Eadred was smaller than either Æthelstan or Edmund, there was a rumour that the royal goldsmith had to put a crimp in it. I once ran my hand all along the edge when I saw it in the royal treasury and I do not think that was true, or if it was, it was polished smooth afterwards.

When I'd come to Æthelstan's court, I'd been very young, little more than a child and still feeling my way in the world. I'd grown into my strength with Edmund, as one of the same age and a friend. With Eadred, I saw for the first time how it might be when a younger king looked to me as one more experienced. I had found my role as abbot and priest.

The new king took his entire court from town to city to town in a great procession, so that his judges and his Witan might hear the voices of all England. Though it meant leaving Glastonbury once more, I went with him. Edmund had been my friend and I would not leave his brother to be overborne by others, not when he trusted me.

I'd seen that clamour of voices and outstretched hands once before, with half the country trying to reach the king or his officers, writing letters and calling out in their pitiful misery. Honestly, it was most vexing. Wealthy earls and thanes made offers of gold, actual gold, for me to secure a meeting with Eadred! Yet if I had done so, I would have lost a trust that was far more valuable. No, those close to the king could not ask him for anything – that was my rule. He had enough petitioners.

He summoned me while we rested in York, that faithless harlot of a city. Eadred had insisted we travel by road, though half the stones had been stolen and some of it was just marsh. Yet he would not go by sea and river as I'd suggested, saying he had to see the dust of the land he ruled. It was fine and stirring stuff, though I suspect he regretted it after the first few days. He could still have taken a boat then, but Eadred was stubborn – and proud.

Archbishop Wulfstan was hosting a feast that evening, with promises of some extraordinary acrobats from Constantinople. My suspicion was that they only claimed to have come so far, but we would see. If they had truly known the New Rome, I'd be delighted to meet them. I could only dream of such places then, though I suppose our York and Winchester were as strange to those who came so far.

Anyone who entered the king's presence was searched for weapons, though it was more a nuisance than anything useful. They left me with my eating knife, for example, no smaller than the blade that had killed Edmund in the gardens. The new king gave that up within a year and things went back to what they had been.

I noticed John Wyatt was still in Eadred's service. I'd half-expected the huge warrior to have lost his head, or perhaps been banished himself. It seemed Eadred did not blame him, which was the sort of simple good sense I came to think of as typical.

'Father Dunstan!' Eadred said.

I bowed to him, wondering if I should kneel and deciding an abbot would not. To my surprise, Eadred took my hand.

'You have been patient, Dunstan, I know. I saw your request for more land a month ago, but I've not had an hour to myself in that time.'

'Of course, Your Highness,' I said, looking as if such a matter was of no concern and not the key to the abbey. I'd begun to wonder if the steward had even passed it on, or was holding out for a bribe from my empty pouch.

'Dunstan, I need someone who understands the royal incomes, who can stand between me and every other hand outstretched. One who can oversee the mint here in York, as well as the ones in Lincoln, London, Bristol – and the great mint in Winchester.'

I stood still as I understood where he was heading, my mind running ahead. He went on, oblivious, his hands cutting curves in the air.

'He must be a man I can trust, so that all my lords know he is honest. If just one fears bribery or theft, he may act against my interests.'

I swallowed. I was not sure I trusted even myself in the role he was describing.

'I trust you, Dunstan. As an abbot of the Church and as a friend to my brother. I trust you to be my royal treasurer, if you agree.'

'M-my lord, Highness . . . what happened to the old one?'

Eadred grimaced as if something had bitten him. Though he was smaller than me, I did not resist when he put an arm to my back and guided me out of the hall.

On the green outside, there was a dead man slouched against a pole. His mouth gaped oddly loose and I could see the jaw had been broken. His flesh was marked in strange shadows, as if he'd been touched by dirty hands. One of his legs hung badly, clearly broken. I shuddered at that sightless gaze.

Eadred seemed less calm as he peered at that hanging figure. With a gesture, he summoned one of his guards.

'I left Master Oran with his mouth full of silver, did I not? Did you collect the coins? I meant them to be left, as a lesson.'

The serjeant looked at his feet, while I could only stare at the last royal treasurer.

'I was worried the coins would be stolen, Your Highness,' the guardsman said. He held up a heavy bag. 'I have them all here, every one. More than a score of them.'

The sight of such wealth in the mouth of a dead man had

clearly been too much for him. The big red-faced fellow was sweating, I noticed.

Eadred shrugged.

'Ah. Well, you are right, of course. I should have had the coins melted and poured down his throat. That would have been fitting. Master Oran held back silver from me, Father Dunstan, as it seems half the country is stealing from my purse. So, I find I am in need of that honest man to be my treasurer. Will you accept?'

I could only nod, though I made pleased noises that seemed to reassure him. He gripped my arm until it hurt, then brought his cloth to his mouth, so that he looked at me over it while he coughed. It went on for a long time and I could only wait and stare back at him. At my shoulder, the guardsman shifted uncomfortably.

'Well, serjeant? Hand Father Dunstan the bag of coins!'

I accepted it and the man seemed relieved.

I followed Eadred back inside and thought about what I had just done and whether I'd had any choice.

'Sit with me, father – and tell me what you will do in the office,' Eadred said over his shoulder.

There was a table with two chargers and a bowl of fruit, so I lowered myself into a chair, with rafters high above me and the room rather cold. The river Ouse wandered by outside our window and I could hear its passage, but all the time I was thinking, 'I'm to be treasurer of England.' I only wished my father could have lived to see it. Wulfric would be astonished, I knew – and perhaps for the first time, his wife Alice might consider she had married the wrong man.

Eadred talked of new coins and the supplies of silver ore and natural gold, brought up from Cornwall and Wales. We had some good mines, apparently, with rich seams, as well as purifying furnaces of the sort I understood very well. Other coins came from mountains in Brandenburg or Saxony in exchange for wool. As he talked I could hardly take it in. My appetite quite dwindled away.

I do not think I had ever eaten with Eadred before that afternoon. I would remember it, for it was a strange sight. He saw me staring and coloured.

'My stomach cannot bear whole food,' he said. 'I am told it disturbs my thanes, so I prefer to eat alone. Yet I have so little time. I needed to ask you if you would accept the appointment – and I am starving.'

I tried not to stare as Eadred chewed another piece of red beef for an age, then removed a flaccid grey thing from between his lips, putting it back on the plate. In that way, he sucked the juices from every mouthful, working hard at them, then placing or spitting the result back on a side dish to be given to his dogs. It meant he ate everything and nothing, which seemed a poor way to live.

Seeing that my scrutiny made Eadred uncomfortable, I addressed myself to the slices of beef on my own plate, eating with some pleasure until I looked up and saw how wistfully he was watching me. I paused with a big piece still wedged into a cheek.

'No, no, father. Please go on. I wish I could eat so . . . lustily. It is my curse, that my body is too weak to hold my spirit.'

He smiled and I almost choked as I tried to swallow.

'I know you see a small man of no great strength, who must chew his food to pap and juice or vomit it back. Yet I feel such things as ill-fitting clothes. They are not me, Father Dunstan. I am a greater soul than that! I will be a greater king, though I did not ask for it – and God knows, I did not want it in such a way.'

'Your brother said the same,' I told him.

'I know. Edmund told me. He told me too that you would be more than just a humble abbot – and I trust that judgement. I know you did not come to me today to be my treasurer, but I suspect you are exactly the man I need, to root out thieves and sloth and bribes – before I sink under my debts. Truly father, you have no idea.'

'Your Highness, it is a great honour. It is true I hoped only for another grant of land for the abbey, so that I do not have to spend so much of my year raising funds. If I can secure that grant . . .'

He waved a hand, as if it was nothing.

'Earl Enlac has just died without heirs. He had two hundred hides, not forty miles from here. Two villages, with a fine manor house and a maker of barley ale. I will seal them to the Church. Was there anything else?'

I shook my head and swallowed the lump in my throat, which of course was more than he could do.

27

By the rivers Tees and Tyne, by the mountains of the north, almost all the way to Scotland, lie the ancient kingdoms of Northumbria, Cumbria and Strathclyde. And those treacherous bastards have caused me pain about as far back as I can remember. They had supported Anlaf of Dublin when he'd taken York. It seemed the lesson of their oathbreaking had not been learned.

No sooner had King Eadred returned to London on his tour than we had news of a great rebellion in the north against his rule. The earls of Northumbria had thrown their allegiance behind another sea-raider, who rejoiced in the name of Eric Bloodaxe. They are like children with their names! Harald Dog-strangler might have been a better choice, or Magnus Cow-raper.

While I grappled with my new authority in the face of royal mint masters, none of whom would acknowledge my right to command them, King Eadred had to go forth once again. His entire army marched three hundred miles to face those lords of the north who refused to see the new century was English. There would be no more small kingdoms: no Mercia, no East Anglia, no York and Northumbria, no, not even my beloved Wessex. We were modern men, by God, with one land and one king.

Christ was with our cause. I am told Eadred destroyed great swathes of the land, tearing down halls and homes and setting them on fire in his royal rage. He made such an example to them that they abandoned Bloodaxe out of fear. The invader was sent running and Archbishop Wulfstan even languished in prison for a time, believing he would be executed for supporting a foreign invader. As he should have been, in my belief. I will not support a man of the cloth who turns against his king. There is no excuse for it.

I was pleased Archbishop Oda had kept his nose out, unlike his equal in the north. I asked Oda about it, bearing in mind his Danish ancestry. He said Bloodaxe was out of Norway, as if that explained all. They are quite mad, you know, those Vikings.

It seemed to me that four main mints was asking for trouble, never mind the host of smaller ones run by licence or just long use and tradition. I saw some respectable houses, but they had no right to claim the king's seal or put his face on their coins! I wrote my first assessment and sent it to the king, but Eadred was still busy in the north then and I had only my own authority. I told the mint master of Lincoln I was considering closing his works and he told me to 'try it'.

I could not go running to the king in a time of conflict, nor did I want to let Eadred see I had been thwarted by a mere mint master. Yet there were coins coming out of York then that had 'Eric Rex' on them. Mind you, at least the silver was good in those. Worse were the fake coins from forgers, made of polished tin, lead, goodness knows what – but not silver. The king's coin stampers were serious men on the whole, who both carved and thumped the royal presses, hammering and repairing them by hand at their benches and clipping off the metal waste to be melted down and used again. Yet there were some retired ones, or those who had been caught stealing and had run. They would often take the only skill they had and make a back-street forger's shop.

I could not discover the weight of silver ingots delivered to the mints, though they came from royal mines, or from land where the rights were claimed by the Crown. It was even harder to go back to the weight of mined ore and the expected results. Simple questions – how much pure gold or silver can be made from sixty pounds of ore, say – caused them to bristle and grow red. At every stage, there were men employed to guard and make life difficult for anyone prying too closely.

When at last I was shown records, there were such huge differences reported from mine to mine that I began to suspect a thousand small sins that added up to a great one. Nothing burns silver like a war – and Eadred had found his coffers almost empty when he set out.

As I had been turned away from almost all the mints in England by then, I went to see my brother Wulfric. It was not to ask his advice, but rather that I needed to talk it over with someone I trusted. I was in London then, so I sent a messenger to bring him to the shop where my mother still lived. I knew he'd kept that business running all the years he'd been my reeve and bursar. I cared not for that, as I warmed to my new responsibilities. No, I had other work for him.

I was both surprised and irritated when Wulfric arrived two days later than I had expected at the shop, with his wife and daughter in tow. He tried to forestall my objection by saying Alice and little Cyneryth would wait in the back, but even when we'd closed for the day, the shop was too small for anything like that to be practical. I could hardly send mother and daughter to wait behind a curtain – where they would still have been able to hear every word! My niece was also at that age where children exclaim on everything, in loud tones of amazement.

I had to endure them, so I gave in rather than appear spiteful. Such concerns were beneath me, though it seemed typical of Wulfric that he should test my patience in such a way. I noticed Alice looked rather smug as she greeted my mother and agreed to a dab of honey on bread for her daughter and a hot barley tisane for herself.

Determined to ignore my audience, I laid out for Wulfric the problems that faced me – four main mints, a dozen smaller ones, as many mines and no one willing to let me see their accounts. When I had finished, there was perhaps a single beat of silence before my mother joined the conversation. She wanted to know why I did not ask for a sealed letter from the king to open those doors.

'Mother, please! This is not just your gossiping, or women's conversation. This is serious. It's my suspicion they are robbing the king blind and I can't prove it . . .'

To my surprise, Wulfric turned to answer her, interrupting me.

'First of all, those who have something to hide will just claim the king's letter is a forgery – and gain time to conceal whatever they are doing. And Dunstan does not get in. Second, he does not want to go back to the king with the very first job he has been given and have to say "They won't listen to me!" – to a man younger than he is. To a man younger than us both.'

I could only wince at the description, but Wulfric was broadly right. I shrugged when my mother looked at me once more to confirm his words, hoping she would tend to her embroidery after that. I held up my palm to her, in silent command.

'Yet . . . all these mines and mints employ a great number,' Wulfric went on. 'We'll need to get men inside, who can see what is to be seen and report back.'

'Not you, Wulfric,' said his pert wife suddenly, looking up and biting a thread. Alice had been embroidering something with only reasonable skill and pretending not to hear a word, while clearly listening to everything.

Wulfric only chuckled.

'There's not much call for one-armed men in the mines, my love – nor the mints. That was not my suggestion. No, we should ask Master Justin at the site. He can recommend good men. Why not? We have score upon score of young fellows at Glastonbury. If he will not do it, let me select . . . a couple of dozen of them for this work. Clever young lads who'll know when to be silent and when to talk. I'll send one to each mint and two or three to each mine, to work quietly until we call them back.'

'Will they be able to leave?' my mother asked suddenly. 'Those men in the mines, I mean.'

Wulfric shrugged.

'They won't be thralls, Mother. Thralls work as they are told, purchased by contract. Yet there are free men as well in such places – working for pay. I suppose they do the same tasks, though they work for their own benefit rather than some master. That is no more than we all do.'

He grinned at me and I was struck once again at how Wulfric had grown up and somehow apart. There had been a time when I would have known exactly what he would say. Yet over the years, my little brother had become expert in places I had not gone, just as I could calculate the angle for a window arch, as not one in a score of masters could.

'I work for the glory of God,' I told him.

He frowned at that.

'You are well rewarded, Dun, though not in pay, I admit.'

I blinked at him, feeling anger swell. There I was on the king's work and he made it seem as if I was more concerned with tawdry pelf and status! I raised a shaking finger to point at him and my mother spoke over me.

'Settle down, Dunstan. Your brother meant no harm and you know it.'

I dipped my head and swallowed anger out of habit, as I

had done a thousand times before. She was the only one who could command me in such a way then. I settled my thoughts and spoke to Wulfric without quite looking at him, so that I addressed the empty air rather than meet his gaze.

'How do we know these places will take the men we send?'

To my dismay, Wulfric only blew air out and chuckled as if he were the teacher and I the student.

'Men get injured in mines, Dun. We've lost a few ourselves at the abbey site, with broken bones, or pulled joints, or fevers of the brain. As well as poor Brother Guido, we've had three deaths. Mines are dangerous places, so they will always need new men. The mints, though, will be much harder as a prospect. They won't let any new lad off the street go sweeping up the clippings, or stamping the coins. Those are skills they'll guard.'

'They may fear spies too, in the mints,' my mother said.

I tutted at her to make her understand it was unwanted, but she didn't hear and went on anyway, embarrassing herself.

'From one another, I mean. The York mint will know the men of the mint in Lincoln, of course, by sight even. If they are competing for the same suppliers and customers, they'll worry about spies as much as thieves. I imagine it is the same in London and Winchester.'

She went back to her stitching. I turned from her to find Wulfric exchanging a glance with his wife, as if she had a part to play as well! It was too much. In something of a foul mood, I excused myself and left the shop, walking the streets for hours in thought.

By the time I returned, the moon was up and I had the seeds of a plan – born out of Wulfric's idle chatter, as it happens. The whole country knew Eadred was short of fighting men that year. Vikings had ambushed royal forces at Castleford – a brutal battle from dawn till sunset, before Bloodaxe quit the field, running for the coast. Still, four thousand of Eadred's men had been killed. By all accounts, it had been a close-run thing.

I knew the king had returned to London and I made up my mind to seek him out there, to lay my plans for the mines and mints before him. In the end, though, I was granted barely an instant of Eadred's time as he prepared for war once again. Some other Olaf or Swein had landed in the north, welcomed by the thanes of Northumbria against rightful authority and their oaths. Some new cousin of Denmark or Norway to threaten all we had, no doubt as bearded and savage as Bloodaxe or Anlaf of Dublin. It beggars belief that our own lords can be so faithless, that they must seek always for something more and never see the grass we own is good enough – and better than most. This is our field, our England. No, better still: this is our Wessex.

Poor Eadred was rushing through his halls in mail and armour when his abbot and new royal treasurer tried to explain a plan involving mines and mints that interested him not at all.

'Act with my authority, Dunstan!' Eadred called, as I babbled at him. 'I gave you the position and I have faith in you. You have my trust.'

I noticed he used my Christian name. The little man was growing into his crown, which I was beginning to expect. On the first day, all men sit the throne as if they are a child in their father's chair. Yet as the months and years pass, they swell to fit the seat – and it becomes truly theirs.

In a line of carts more commonly used to transport coal, wood and stone, I accompanied twenty-two of our young workers over the marsh road at Glastonbury, clattering along the wooden planks. Wulfric joined me, for once without his wife on his arm, as well as Master Justin, who took a fatherly interest in the whole enterprise once he understood it. I do not know how the mason reconciled the trip with his usual concerns, either building the abbey or his joining of the Benedictines.

In the last cart, we had six soldiers of a sort, on loan to us from the king's estate guards. Those men had earned their posts as reward for long service. Very long service in some cases. Such white-haired veterans could not have been included in the king's forces marching away once more. Yet they made it very clear they were not delighted to have been given over to my care, either. I had asked for John Wyatt to be one of their number, but Eadred had refused and taken him into the north instead.

It was not difficult to find places for our lads in the mines, as we reached each one. We waited half a day for the first ones to come back, but no one did. As Wulfric had suggested, the foremen were all so desperate for strong backs that our lads hardly had to ask for work before they were in and wheeling a barrow, or hacking away at a seam.

It began to feel as if we were planting seeds. They had their instructions from Justin, from Wulfric – and a last prayer from me. As we came into range of one of the mines, they'd slip over the side, alone or in a pair, then vanish into the roadside. Such a strange caravan as ours would be noticed in the local area and we told them to wait a day until they were good and hungry before seeking out the foreman for work. We bore the king's crest on our papers, if some thane or shire reeve had brought us to a halt.

As it happens, we were not stopped, not once, as we made our way through the green lanes. Though we were at war, that was all happening too far away to disturb the peace there. We left two lads at the great mine the Romans had begun near Bath, one more at works just across the Bristol Channel, two in Shropshire, and so on. Wherever there was a royal grant to take silver or gold from Crown lands, we made our way. We left our seeds behind – to seek and to grow.

There were a dozen lesser mints than the four I wanted to test. I could have dropped a lad in every market town just about, and found some backstreet workshop that stamped its own coins. It was an almighty mess in those days, but then that was why Eadred had called me to the work. Wulfric took two lads to the London mint, with fine letters of recommendation from a goldsmith in Winchester who owed him a favour. My brother caught up on my own mount, Scoundrel, though that old horse was in his last days. Scoundrel turned away from the apple I offered him and I knew. When the appetite begins to go, it all goes.

The beauty of it was how desperate the mints were for men, like the mines before them. That was our doing, with all young men of sound appearance needed in the shield lines. It had been simple enough to send a dozen king's men up the road a week or so ahead of us. With a writ from the royal treasurer as their authority, they'd sneered at those who guarded the doors, then entered despite their objection, as real soldiers always will. I heard they'd made a show of peering at teeth and palms, then signed up half a dozen fine fellows in every mine and mint from Winchester to York.

When our keen lads arrived to replace them in their Sunday clothes, ready to work with a letter of recommendation from their last master – well, we are lucky they didn't lose the hands they stretched out in greeting.

Seeing the last of our seeds on their way left me with Wulfric and Master Justin and our veterans, though by then they slept through the afternoons. We'd ended our journey at York, and though the fighting was still a hundred miles or more to the north, there was a feel of it on the air. It was a world apart from those sleepy hamlets and villages back in Shropshire. The whole country seemed up in arms then, with fear of invasion in every mouth and boys and women going armed. Yet our job was done for a time, so we spent a most amiable couple of weeks wending our way south once more with the carts and Scoundrel on a long lead. I caught a fine trout on a line Master Justin had made. He showed us all the trick of it and half the old fellows joined us whenever we came to a river, so that we had fish most days.

Just outside the lovely little village of Bicester, with peaceful farms once more all around, my horse lay down and would not get up. I exchanged sharp words with Wulfric over his care of the animal, but it was loss making me harsh. The carts halted on the road and the veterans had their fires started quick as winking. They were old hands at that. They were old hands at everything, in fact, but they liked to be fed on time.

I sat with Scoundrel for a while, with his legs oddly splayed in the road and a wild look in his eye, as if he could see something bad coming. In the end, Master Justin cut his throat and butchered him, which took the rest of the day. Both he and Wulfric said how fortunate we were to have the carts there for the meat, that it would feed a village and that it could all have been wasted.

I let them chatter on in my grief. I had disliked that horse from the very start, but he had carried me when I was afraid at Brunanburh and he was mine own. I did eat part of him the following night, but it was tough and I wished I had not.

28

As the sun set on the evening of the next full moon, one by one, our lads put down their tools and walked out to the roads where they had been dropped a month before. It took a few days to collect them all – and one of them, name of Cerwen, we never saw again, though we waited a full day on the way up and another on the road back down. I found later he had asked too many questions, though I'd told them all not to.

We brought all our seeds home except that one. For the most part, we found them spry enough, though thin and battered. Some had been beaten, though that is the life of an apprentice and they seemed to bear no ill will for the marks, even to find the whole task amusing. I had expected to greet the lads with solemnity and thanks, but instead, they came back to the carts with laughter and stories. It was a revelation, as I had never been a carefree child myself.

As I looked around at them, I realised I had become a father after all. A father can be stern and harsh, indeed he must be, if he is not to turn out a milksop boy. Yet he can also take pride and show it. As I knew very well, that quiet moment of praise, that single wink or smile, meant a great deal to young fellows. They look for it in those they respect, to give them worth. And there is nothing wrong with that.

Though I had forbidden strong drink the first time, it seemed our veterans had brought supplies of their own on the return trip. There was some drunkenness like Noah, as well as some fishing where one lad was half-drowned before we pulled him out. Yet they were as good as their word, and our returning workers kept my scribes busy writing down everything they had learned.

By the time we reached Winchester once more, I had a fair understanding of the mints and mines of England. Most of it was unremarkable. If those fools who ran them under licence had shared the secrets of their trade, I might not have gone to such lengths. Yet as I sat there at a fine oak desk in candle-light, looking at two dozen sheets of vellum filled with tiny letters, I could only breathe and shake my head in wonder.

The following morning, I visited the king's prison, where two forgers waited to be hanged, alongside murderers, poachers, thieves and rather pitiful madmen or deserters from the army. There was only one scaffold in Winchester then and the king's executioners went about their task with the steady hand of those who know they will always be in work. No one minded if they were slow, certainly not those who peered out at the yard from behind good iron bars.

I watched in fascination as the guards pulled two dishevelled and reeking fellows from among the rest.

'Skinner and the boy Jones, father. These are the ones you want. It's lucky you didn't come tomorrow or they'd have been gone, and we don't have no other forgers in for hanging at the moment.'

'You will soon,' I murmured, though my attention was on the rough pair as chains were fastened around their ankles.

'Stand up straight, both of you,' I snapped. Both the forgers and the guards responded, which pleased me. 'Now, you must understand, there is no true liberty on offer. I wish only to speak to you about your crimes. After that you will be returned to the cell and, when the moment comes, hanged.'

'What will you offer us?' the older one said, squinting at me.

'I am prepared to offer forgiveness of your sins, so that you can go right to heaven and spend not one day in purgatory, or of course the other place.'

That caused a stir among the men in the cell, though the one I wanted seemed less impressed. He leaned over to the one they called 'the boy Jones' and they conferred. The guard lost patience before I did, reaching out and slapping them both around the back of the head.

'Answer the abbot!' the man snapped.

Skinner glared at him, then looked over at me like a crow, his head tilted and one beady eye fastening on me.

'All right, father. We'll take that. I'll tell you everything I know about the old trade – if you throw in a plate of ham and eggs, a bit of bread and a pint of ale for me and the boy.'

The air grew still as the guards goggled at his effrontery and everyone else waited to see what I might say.

'Very well, Skinner,' I said after a time, hiding my amusement at his boldness. It was not such a poor bargain, given what I hoped to learn.

He beamed at that, appearing to know the word of an abbot had to be good. I saw he was both toothless and surprisingly wrinkled, though paler than half the men watching us through the bars. The poachers were darkest, of course, from all those years in the heather and the open sun, watching for prey or a sight of king's men. Yet this fellow Skinner and his lad could have passed almost for scribes, having spent all their working lives tucked away indoors.

The guards brought out a small table from their own dormitory, setting it in the open yard not a dozen feet from the cell and placing three stools alongside. They made a great show of wiping it down as if for a valued customer, amusing themselves until I asked them when the food would be brought.

I saw dull resentment in the eyes of the guard I addressed, so I sent another with him, warning them both that I would know if they spat in the food. I saw their shoulders slump as they heard that part.

I seated myself across from the two men and watched as Skinner in particular looked all around the yard from the new angle he had been given. The boy Jones sat with his head drooping and said not a word, so that I began to wonder if he was simple.

'Would you like me to hear your sins now?' I asked after a time.

To my surprise, Skinner shrugged.

'We'll wait for the food, father, if you don't mind. I don't like to confess on an empty stomach and they don't feed us here, not when we're going for the hanging. Fair enough not to waste it, when there are so many starving fellows, as I see it.'

He settled back, apparently content to doze in the sun. I felt my own eyes growing heavy as it took an age for the two guards to return. Ham and eggs and bread should not have tested them too greatly, but they were panting as if they'd run a long way. I did not ask and I engaged in a little mummery with the plate and the mugs of ale, running my hand over them and saying the Pater Noster while I watched the guards. Simple men will usually give themselves away. Yet neither guard looked afraid and I pronounced the food was clean.

'Thank you, gentlemen. I will call you when it is time.'

They bowed as they backed away, in awe by then of one strange occurrence after another.

When I turned my gaze once more to Skinner, it was to find his eyes gleaming at me in surmise.

'Well? I have fulfilled our bargain,' I told him. 'Eat and drink your fill. But as you do, tell me everything you know about the forging of coins like this.'

I laid a good fake on the table in front of them, a coin in dull grey that might have passed for silver in anything but the best daylight. The boy Jones looked up as I did so, glancing at it. Neither man had made any sudden move to touch the food or drink. They watched me as mice might watch a cat as they brought their hands slowly to it, still suspicious that I might dash it from their lips. I waited patiently, seeing hunger hard on them both.

Skinner took such a draught of the beer, I thought he would finish it in one, though he put it down with a little still slopping at the bottom. He wiped his mouth and gasped in appreciation. The boy Jones fell to as well, shoving pieces of ham and egg into his mouth. I watched as Skinner eased the second pint of ale over to stand before him. He breathed beer across the space between us.

'Ale for me. The boy don't have the taste for it yet.' He looked aside for an instant, showing regret. 'Won't live long enough to know it, I suppose, not now. Still, you've served us well, father, and I am grateful.'

He picked up the coin and bent it hard between his fingers before he put it back on the wood.

'Pewter, I'd say, which polishes up nice but will grow dull. Poor work, though. Work I'd be ashamed to put out, meself.'

I'd seen Roman cups of the metal. Lesser forges often used tin and lead and I knew it was some combination of those. Any great forge that could make iron did so, scorning the poor metals of a crofter's oven.

'I thought it was,' I said. He looked askance at me, unsure if I knew the first thing about metal. 'I have worked iron, Master Skinner,' I said. 'I am a fair hand with brass and bronze as well.' I gave him the title out of habit, though it seemed to draw a more serious look from him.

'No one knows how to make good pewter no more,' he said in answer. 'Though I do. I know what the Romans added to tin and lead to harden it all up into good metal. You couldn't bend a coin I'd made. If that was one of mine, you'd never have known it was a fake even.'

'Is that common, then? The use of lead and tin?'

'And a few other secrets, yes. It's almost all tin, though. Lead would be too heavy in the hand, do you see? It doesn't matter much anyway. Tin melts as easy as lead just about. Not like silver. That takes one of your fine forges. For most, anyway. I've blown it hot enough to melt. I know the tricks of that an' all.'

'Master Skinner, you do understand that I will not take you out of this place? When our discussion is at an end, I will depart – and you will be hanged.'

'The boy did nothing, though. You might take him as a servant, maybe. You've seen the way he is. No wickedness in him, is there? Just look at him!'

We both did, to see the boy wipe his nose as he sat there, still staring at nothing.

'I am a king's officer, Master Skinner. I cannot aid or pardon those who have been sentenced to death for their crimes.'

'You are a priest, though, as well,' he muttered.

'I am, but I certainly cannot put the Church in opposition to the Crown. That is a path that would end in disaster.'

It was a strange thing to consider. I had the king's authority, and the truth was I could have taken him away and set him free to take up his old work that very day. No one would have dared say a word about it. Yet in my office, in that role as king's treasurer, I was the Crown. The king's authority and honour resided in my person as long as I acted on his business and in his name.

'I made you a bargain, Master Skinner, of confession of your sins – and food and ale. I was told you knew the tricks of coining and forgery. That if you didn't know them, no one did. So far, you have had the better of it. Now, put aside false hope. You will be hanged today, just as if I had not come to this prison yard. Say what you know and I will shrive you and leave you to your thoughts.'

'I've drunk the ale, though,' he said, cradling the second mug to his chest. 'And my boy has eaten his scran and that. I think we're finished here, father.'

'You place no value in the confession of your sins? You and this child are content to risk your immortal soul, to suffer eternity in hell for your arrogance here? You do not fear what awaits you when the curtain is torn and you stand before the archangel?'

My voice had risen in wrath and volume and Skinner looked in amazement at me, seeing perhaps a different side to the gentle man who would swallow all his lies. He raised his open hands to quieten me as I began to stand.

'All right then, father. Your point is made.' He settled himself as if there had been no raised voices between us. 'Now, there's clipping of true coins, which is done with shears. Some prefer to rub away the silver on a stone, then heat the stone to make it run, but the bigger firms clip. You'll have seen the marks of it, of course.'

I had, as almost every silver penny bore a straight edge somewhere.

'You collect your clippings and you have enough silver to make a fine new coin as good as any of the real ones. Now, you already know about the pewter coins . . .'

'What was the secret ingredient?' I asked him.

He sighed and blew out a great gust of beery air.

'Antimony. The Romans knew it well enough, though no bugger seems to any more. It hardens the tin along with lead. Nine-tenths tin, the rest lead and a few pinches of antimony, what they call kohl. Some women put it on their eyes, so they say. I'd have thought that would sting something fierce, but maybe high-born girls is different to the ones I know.'

He grinned at me, but I just gestured for him to continue.

'Tin and lead melt easily on a charcoal fire – and the ores is all over. Good shops have their own suppliers, who dig seams out in the wilderness, where no man has ever trod, well away from the king's mines and king's men. They know where to look, or they use the spots their father showed them. I must have seen a hundred of those mines. I could remember a few of the good ones if I was taken back there, as well.'

'You will not be,' I said firmly.

'Fair enough. So . . . however you get your metal, you have to cut and stamp it. The shears are harder to make than anything, as you need a blacksmith and he has to be one who won't ask no questions. You need good iron, though, or they won't cut. Now, the proper mints have one side of the coin set below and the other held in the hand. They put the sheet in and down comes the hammer – and there's both sides struck at the same moment. Most of my trade makes one side at a time, which is easier but slower. You can spot those if one side is cut deeper than the other, but it takes a good eye like mine. If I were set free to work as your faithful servant, I'd ferret out those rabbits like a good 'un. If I took an oath as a king's man, with the boy here, we'd find and stop every forger in the realm, I swear to God.'

'That will not happen,' I said. 'What else?'

He chewed his lip for a moment.

'Sweating? That's when a merchant takes a bag of silver coins, of wool, see? He shakes them or he gives it to a boy like mine to do it. They all rub alongside each other and the dust that comes off is good silver. No one can tell it's been done – the coins look cleaner, if anything. Do that with every coin that comes through and you'll have enough metal dust to make a few spare pennies.'

He sat back and folded his arms across his stomach. The animation faded from his face and when I raised an eyebrow at him, he just shook his head.

'I'm sorry, father. I think I've done enough now. Maybe I

hoped to convince you that me and the lad would be useful. You being a believer in forgiveness and all. All I wanted was a second chance for my boy – and maybe to put right some of what I done wrong, by closing all the forgers in Winchester and London and round the country. It's a small world and we all know each other, see? They'd be gone if king's soldiers came knocking, but I could tell you . . . Ah, it doesn't matter. I'm done, as you say. The boy and me will be hanged. I'll ask you to hear my sins now and not take any more time tormenting those who are to die.'

I sat and thought for a long time, using my second and third fingers to pick at the broken nail of my thumb. The guards hovered when they saw the talking had ended, though none of them dared approach.

'I can't take you out,' I said firmly, cutting the air with my hand.

'We ain't murderers, son,' Skinner murmured. 'You can bring a great triumph to the king if you give me a second chance.'

'I know far more than you realise, Master Skinner!' I retorted, stung. 'I have heard testimony and seen more mints and mines than you can possibly know.'

'I don't doubt it, father. You seem a thorough man and a clever one. Though my world ain't in the mines or the king's mints. I'll bet they have a hundred ways of robbing the Crown, ones that me and my boy ain't even dreamed of. That's your world, maybe.'

He leaned forward then, fixing me with his gaze.

'This is mine. I've offered you my fair service and you won't know it, but my word is good. I want to walk out of this yard with my son, to give him the chance he should have had. If you pardon us, I swear I am your man for ever. That is my oath to you, father, by Christ and my eternal hereafter.'

I stood and made the sign of the cross over them both.

'Are you sorry for your sins?'

Skinner nodded, though I saw the despair in him.

'Very well.' I raised my hand once more in benediction. *'Ego te absolvo a peccatis tuis, in nomine Patris, et Filii, et Spiritus Sancti.'*

They crossed themselves as they heard the Father and the Son and the Holy Spirit, just as they had in every service of the Church all their lives. I could see resignation in Skinner's eyes as I called the guards over to me once more.

'All done, father?' one of them asked.

'I believe so,' I said. Without making a decision, without changing my mind, I simply went on speaking, so that I was almost as surprised as the guard helping them to their feet. 'These two have knowledge that is valuable to me. I will not leave them to be hanged, but instead I will take them as thralls. I am a king's officer. See who you wish to see. Summon . . . whomever you must summon. I will speak to the magistrate who condemned them.'

It took the rest of the day until those chains were struck off. Skinner said not a single word except to confirm his name to the judge who came out and demanded to know what I thought I was doing. Only the royal warrant smoothed his hackles, though he took me aside as man to man to persuade me against such madness. I was half-inclined to agree with him, but I'd gone too far to turn back and I was as stubborn as any one of them.

'I answer to the king,' I said. 'Pray direct your complaints about his royal treasurer to King Eadred. I wish you luck of it.'

In the end, they could not refuse me, though the rest of the men behind bars howled and entreated as they saw Skinner and the boy Jones would not be returned to them. I do not know what they thought I was about, but they screeched and wailed and pleaded as I led my two new thralls across the yard to the gate of oak and iron.

I watched Skinner as the gate opened and he saw the city beyond.

'You are mine, Master Skinner, you and your son. Your labour is mine until I choose to free you, or until I sell you in the great market at Bristol. If you run, it will be at the expense of your immortal soul and your honour – and I will hunt you down and see you broken to get the rest of what you know. Your son too will suffer greatly before I am satisfied. Is that understood, Master Skinner? You gave me your word and now I will give you mine. If you run, I will find you and you will wish I had left you to hang today.'

He looked across at me and, to my surprise, he put out his hand to shake. I took it, and for the first time he felt the strength of my grip, so that his eyebrows went up.

'I understand, father. The boy and me have been given a second chance. You will not regret it – and we will not run.'

29

I cannot say exactly why I freed Skinner and his lad. His sentence of execution was right and just, and yet perhaps I heard his entreaties even as I denied them. I have always liked a rogue, for some reason. Some men are cruel and thick with it, but if they can smile as they sin, there is a part of me that admires them, just a little.

I had judged one thing correctly, at least. Skinner did not run the first time I left him alone, though I wonder now if he knew I had guards waiting to snatch him up if he had done. As far as I know, he hardly looked up from his labour creating a forger's workshop in the king's private stables, near the smithy. We built a secret room with its own forge, joining it to the chimney off the blacksmith. It was the only way to show the tricks of Skinner's trade, though I was very careful about those I allowed to speak to him.

I made my plans and, for a time, King Eadred resumed his duties hearing the cases of poor men and overseeing the works and ports and trade of his battered realm. I saw him only once in Winchester the following Christmas, when he appeared suddenly in the petition hall and stalked down the aisle. Wulfric and I were there with the king's steward, arranging to withdraw the royal licences from the main mints, so that they all had to reapply or be closed down. The steward had either been dropped on his head as a child, or he'd been bribed, but whatever the cause, he refused to understand what we insisted had to be done.

In the middle of that furious argument, the door came open and Eadred entered, clasping and unclasping his left hand. An axe swung idly in the other. He wore a mail shirt that covered his head, leaving his face bare. I don't think he saw or heard us as he reached the great table where the Witan sat for their meetings. We had fallen silent, of course, while the king breathed over that table, swept up in some emotion. I was ready to speak when he swung the axe in a great arc and hammered the blade into the oak, leaving it stuck deeper than I would have believed possible. He stood back then, with a wince at the damage he had done.

He looked over at three gaping men and saw I was one of them.

'I just wanted to destroy something, father,' he said.

Whatever temper had controlled him before seemed to resurface and he wrestled the blade out, heaving at it, then swinging it again. The table broke, its main plank snapping right through. I saw it afterwards and noted the tiny holes of woodworm that had stolen some of its strength, but still, it was a fine blow.

I heard later that Eric Bloodaxe had returned to the north – and those men who had sworn their submission to the house of Wessex had not fought as they had promised they would, but instead run to their Viking lover the very moment he landed ships on their coast.

Eadred, who was not the warrior either of his brothers had been, who coughed and had perforce to suck the juices from his meat, would spend more years in the field than Æthelstan or Edmund together. It fell to Eadred to chase raiders across the land, to see trails of smoke in their wake, that script in the air that said he was a ruler who could not protect his people.

It was not what most men meant when they thought of a crown. Eadred grew stern and harsher than I remembered. He came home once with a thick red line across his broken nose and two snapped fingers. I tended those for him, as it was a hurt I knew well.

I could not give that young man the gentle life he might have had. I could not stop the raids, or lend strength to those who bent for each breeze and had no honour. I knew it cost rivers of coin to provide for an army on the march. I recalled the axes and shields at Brunanburh, ready for any man who wanted them, the blacksmiths and the leatherworkers, the lines for food at every stop. War means the king and his lords turning the world on its head. No more do their tenants pay them. Instead, Eadred and his thanes bled silver for them all. To save his father's kingdom, I knew Eadred would need more silver and more gold than had ever come in before. In that way, I could be of use to my king.

I came to accept that Skinner was as good as his word. I do not believe he ever truly saw himself as a thrall, and I understand it was too much to expect him to act like a servant. He had been a free man all his life, as he said. It would be a cruel master who punished a man for the manners of freedom, when we all aspired to it.

I took Skinner and the boy Jones to my mother's shop in London, where Wulfric and Justin examined him for hours on what he knew. Master Justin came out looking a little pale, I remember, at everything he had heard. When I asked him if he was well, he gave a great sigh.

'It is a wicked, wicked world,' he said.

We set Skinner up with a new workshop and once more I built the forge to my own design. I was pleased to have Skinner asking questions at my elbow as I worked mortar and stone. He exclaimed at every new thing, at the angles and the iron sheathing. I am afraid I left him rather more able to make a high-temperature bloomer on his own than he had been before. I do like to talk and he was a very good audience.

His boy said nothing and I assumed he was a simpleton of some poor union, or one damaged as a child. There are so many rashes and ailments that leave the poor mites deaf or slow. Yet he was loyal to his father and he was silent. I remarked on that to Wulfric as a wonder in a young lad.

We began our great task in London, as it was a place where we were strong. Skinner had argued for Lincoln, and he wasn't wrong to want to practise. Yet the king's treasury was empty. I'd seen it. From that moment, Eadred was going to war on loans alone, which meant the moneylenders could ask for almost anything and he would have to grant it or lose the crown. I would not let that happen while I lived.

We struck the first blow in the smaller workshops, the forgers that had no licence from the king, who made their coins from tin or clippings and never paid a penny to the royal treasury. I will not say it began well, as Skinner had warned it might not. We had enough men to close down six different places. Any more and we would have been spread too thin. Yet as soon as the first couple of doors were kicked in, boys yelled a warning from the rooftops and there were men scrambling everywhere to get away – in places we hadn't even spotted before. It seemed for a while that half the city was forging coins, though some of them were just ordinary thieves and criminals, believing the law had found them at last.

Still, I saw some thirty men bound in good chains I'd made myself. Most of them were just workmen, but I wanted the ones with a touch of wealth to their clothes, who wore rings of silver or a fine belt buckle.

Those men struggled and raved until we showed them the hangman's nooses we'd strung in the open street. It was a brutal business, but then so was war and so was the survival of the kingdom. We lined them up and we all watched a few kicking their last, back and forth like children on a swing until they fell limp. One of them held up his hand and said he'd talk if we swore we wouldn't hang him. The sight of it had stolen his nerve.

'Any others?' I asked.

One of the rest cupped his hand and muttered, as if he could not understand my accent. The rest of them laughed until I had him hanged next. They were surly after that, but we did get two more volunteers.

We hanged sixteen men that first day. Some of their friends came out and I thought we might be overwhelmed. Stones were thrown, but our lads took up cudgels and rushed the crowd, driving all before them. Before they returned, we broke the forges and took away the tools to a local smithy. I watched as all the carved cedar dies, the shears, all the little punches and even wool bags for sweating were thrown into the furnace to become ash. It occurred to us that the local blacksmith would hardly be innocent. Yet he claimed to know nothing and he did a vital trade. I may have been a little too merciful with blacksmiths.

The one thing that did not go into the fire was the silver. I had no use for tin or lead, but some of the shops used clippings and dust and had true silver coins already stamped and still waiting to be cut out. It was not a fortune – no more than a few hundred coins that had to be melted down once more into ingots by weight – but it felt like a victory.

The following days were harder as word had gone round the city. I worried news of our raids had spread further, but we were too few to do more. Our results began to dwindle as forgers across London dismantled their own places and waited for us to pass like any other storm. The men we had taken told us whatever they knew once they had been leaned on a little. Yet time and again, we found empty rooms and storehouses. At first it looked as if we'd missed them by just hours, with the bricks still warm. As the days wore on, we found them all cold and I began to worry. We had collected barely enough silver to cover our costs and spent almost half of that to feed the lads.

I was dejected when our little group came together for an ale that evening.

'I can feel it slipping away,' I said. 'They've all shut up, or gone somewhere else. I can't walk down a street without eyes following me now, paid to watch us.'

Skinner seemed unworried as he downed his ale. I suppose a thrall should have eaten later and served us at table, but I felt as if we served the same cause and he was more the expert than any of us.

'We should touch the mint, then. Get all the lads in mail and with swords and that. Take the whole place down.'

I wanted to. The London mint master was one of my father's generation, name of Unmere. He was one of those who had refused to accept my authority, though I'd shown him the seals. He'd known I was not lying, but he had closed iron gates in my face even so, waving me away like some clerk. I had intended to visit him last, to enjoy kicking him onto the cobbles while we searched his accounts. Yet as I looked around at the others, they slowly grinned at me.

'It's not slipping away,' Justin said. 'It's just getting started.'

Iron is the strongest metal. Yet it must be anchored, and that had not been properly understood by Unmere at the mint. Two brawny lads went through his gate with hammers in as long as it takes to describe it. They broke the stone sills and smashed the locks, so that we were facing an appalled mint master in his private office in just moments. He called for help, but I showed my royal appointment to the guards who came trundling up to challenge us. They saw the sheer number of armed men and just bowed and scraped their way right back out again.

'I don't know if you remember me, Master Unmere,' I began.

He was swollen up, brick red and bristling. He still thought he could bully and shout over us.

'Get out! Get out of this office!'

He had a good voice and I wearied of it.

'Be quiet. I gave you a chance before to let me see your books. I did not trust you then. I do not trust you now.' I turned to the men watching. 'Take him into another room and ask him if he wishes to tell us anything before we find out.'

'How do you mean, "ask him"?' Skinner said.

I turned back to Master Unmere, by then watching our exchange in horror.

'I mean first treat him like a man of good estate and ask. If he will not answer every question with perfect clarity, come and find me. I will tell you how to ask him then.'

Unmere shouted for help as he was bundled out of the room. By then the noise of the mint had gone silent.

I sat at the desk and looked up when a clerk was brought before me. He stood shivering and wide-eyed as Wulfric prodded him forward and inclined his head to me where the man could not see. Someone of use.

'Ah. Your name?'

'Bayliss, sir.'

'You work for Unmere?'

'I do, my lord, for ten years now, yes, my lord.' He was laying the titles on thick, but I could understand his desire not to offend.

'I am an abbot, Master Bayliss. You may address me as "father".'

'Thank you, father. God bless you, sir.'

'Yes. So, Master Bayliss, would you say you are loyal to this fellow Unmere, even as he goes to his deserved retirement?'

It took a moment. The fellow thought it through and looked around at what the new day had brought. I made sure my royal warrant was in sight on the desk. He came to the right conclusion.

'I would say . . . I am more loyal to the king, sir – and to the mint herself.'

'Herself?' I asked him. He coloured.

'She gives birth to the coins, sir. It's just my fancy.'

'I see. Of course, you know the king owns the mint – and it seems a huge number of ingots enter this place, which is not then reflected in the number of coins produced. Would you say that was a fair assessment? Think hard now, Master Bayliss. You seem like a young man who knows this place well. It is not beyond a possibility that you will find yourself mint master before the sun sets today, if you impress me.'

He took even less time to make that decision.

'I would say that was likely to be true, about the ingots of silver, sir, yes. I cannot say for certain, as I have no knowledge personally, of course. Yet I did hear rumours, and . . .'

I held up my hand.

'Bayliss, I care not. My task is to stop up the holes where the king's wealth drains out. This is one of the holes. If you are of use to me, I give you my word no harm will come to you. Will that suit you? I do not have the time or the interest to play games where you pretend you were unaware. I cannot hang every skilled man in the mint, Master Bayliss! Who would run the mint tomorrow if I did? So consider your answer once more. This is the moment your life takes a new path.'

I had judged him well enough and he breathed in relief.

'Thank you, father. Yes, I would like to accept your kindness. I have seen the accounts behind the wall there. You'll find they read quite differently to the ones Master Unmere presents to the king's officers.'

I found I'd frozen as he spoke, not quite able to believe I had been right. There may have been some sort of clever catch to reveal the brick hole behind the wall panelling. I was in no mood for that, so I had one of our lads hammer it to pieces, revealing a leather wrap of sheets.

'Wulfric, would you please take Master Bayliss to observe the conversation with Unmere? In case it brings anything else to mind?'

I saw Bayliss looked afraid at that prospect.

'I have given you my word, Master Bayliss. You will not be harmed.'

There are different kinds of criminal, of course. Some like Unmere I could hang as an example, while others had to be persuaded, or shown a light to strive towards. By the time I left the London mint, it had a new master. Wulfric and six of our lads stayed behind for a month to oversee the repairs and to be sure the new king's master of the mint settled in without getting a knife in the back from one of the other employees. I drew a loan against my funds at Glastonbury, leaving my name to it in the mint office. I was on the king's business, after all, and we had to eat.

The mine at Bath had been the chief supplier of the London mint, which surprised me. I'd have thought the old Roman pit would have given its ingots over to Winchester, but these were arrangements going back for centuries, right to when the legions tramped up and down the country on better roads.

The mine master had learned somehow of our London work. I rode there with around forty men, ready for anything. Yet when the fellow came out, he took one look at the two young lads we'd sent in months before and gave up any pretence or resistance. He escaped the rope as a result, though he did lose the manor house he had built. His wife stayed with him, which surprised me.

There was more than one such revelation at Bath – and more at our second stop in Shropshire. Silver and lead are often mined together. The simplest theft was that the royal treasury never knew how many pounds of ore had been dug each year. Almost all the mines declared less than they dug out, then sold the extra silver to forgers and illegal mints the length and breadth of the country. The sheer scale of it all staggered me when I began to understand the numbers. I don't think half of the gold and silver mined had ever reached the royal mints. There were more bad coins than good ones that year, though it began to change as our efforts made their mark.

It took me another eighteen months before I felt happy with the results. We had to employ men as overseers and king's officers in each mine, as well as making scales more accurate than any that had existed before, in high-quality brass and iron. Each set was identical and I made thirty of them for the royal office of treasurer, to be sent around the country. Finding so many good men was the hardest part of it, even after all the preparation we had done. I considered putting more men on our rolls to watch the first ones, but *quis custodiet ipsos custodes*? Who guards the guards? There would always be corruption around gold and silver. My job was not to cut it out completely, but merely to reduce it to a level that did not leave the king having to go as a beggar to the monasteries and moneylenders. It took me a long time to understand that – and longer to accept it.

I think I knew even then that I was working to an end, that I could not be royal treasurer for the rest of my life. The work raising the abbey at Glastonbury suffered badly while I laboured for Eadred – how could it not when I took all the men from the site? I felt a sense of shame when I returned to the abbey with Wulfric, seeing it almost abandoned, with weeds growing through the muddy yard.

I did not give up my post as treasurer, however. I confess I tried to, but King Eadred was so pleased with all the gold and silver flowing into his treasury that he would not hear of it. He offered to make me bishop of Winchester and I refused, saying I would rather serve as a poor monk than as a prince of the Church. I think money meant even less to me than it ever had, after seeing it dug from the earth and made into coins. Every coin had some blood on it, but then this world is the forge where the metal of our souls is tested. It is not a land of milk and honey, but a dark field of battle. Some will show clean and good and they will be rewarded. The rest will be cast away to burn.

Rather than own a thrall, I drew up papers to free Skinner and his son, returning them to the world in a rather better state than I had found them. I even arranged for a small pension to be paid to the man who had helped me overcome impossible obstacles. It was within my gift, but as I told him, my reason was to let him retire in small comfort. If I heard he had ever shared our adventures with another, or if he returned to his old work, I would visit much worse on him than he could imagine. He seemed to understand I was serious and he smacked his idiot son across the ear to make him show some respect.

With that behind me, I returned to Glastonbury, to gather our little community around me, to bring them at last into the light.

30

The community of monks at Glastonbury had tripled in size in the years since I'd been a boy there. In part, I am sure it was because we fed the workers rather better and more regularly than they had known before. Some of them stayed for that, or turned their labours into a common feeling that led them to take vows. Not all have souls aflame with desire! The world is mostly made of sensible men. We cannot all be saints; most do not have the strength of will. They get by – and that can be enough for them. Yet those who lead them need passion and strength far beyond their followers. The shepherd must climb after every lost lamb. It is both exhausting and exhilarating at the same time. There have been years when I was weary, when I wished I could just hand it all over to another, but then, without exception, I remembered my path and I raised my head.

When I returned to the isle, I recalled my vision from years before, of scores of monks in black robes, going in and out of grand cloisters. The cloisters were still unfinished, but King Eadred's generosity meant the work would be completed. I'd lost count of the number of times I had been called upon to witness laws and papers or even discuss the king's policies. I stood high in Eadred's esteem and I took that confidence back with me to Glastonbury. It felt like home to me, as it always had, just about.

I'd walked to my father's house once or twice in the years since we'd left. My half-brother had fallen on harder times when some portion of his wealth was lost. It seemed Aldan had invested his trade success in some part of a silver mine, which may not have been quite properly owned. It had been confiscated by a right bastard of a royal officer, apparently. I hadn't told him who it had been. Aldan was content enough on our father's twelve hides of land. Old Threefingers had lost his mind and died not long after, with no one able to look after him in his rages and weeping. It is a sad thing when we are taken like that. I have always thought it is worse than death.

I did not expect my task to be easy, when I told Brother Caspar I was considering enforcing the true rules of our founder, after centuries of neglect. St Augustine himself had been a Benedictine and established the first monastery in Canterbury on his arrival. Our order was the bedrock on which English Christianity was founded.

It was within the bounds of my authority to order married brothers to turn their faces from their wives, yet even in my certainty, I suspected it could not be done with force. If I had to lose those men, it would be the will of God, but I wanted to persuade them first.

I called them to the rough school hall we had made together. On the night I set aside, it was crammed to the edges by those who came to hear the discussion, including all the women who would be put out if I were successful. It seemed Prior Caspar, or more likely Aphra, had spread word of what I wished to discuss. I objected to the idea that the women might attend, but there were so many voices raised against me that I subsided. Very well. I would overcome them. I have always relished such a fight.

Winter was upon us and the day grew dark as they shuffled and muttered to one another. I'd agreed to allow Caspar to speak for married men, though I had not seen he would stand as my equal and oppose me in front of a crowd that favoured his view over mine. We had the structures of Athenian debate to fall back upon – points and counterpoints, rebuttals, conclusion and the all-important vote.

I cracked my neck and my knuckles as Caspar stepped up to a rostrum. I resisted the urge to pace behind him and remained seated, genuinely interested to see what he would say.

'Brothers, we stand at a crossroads tonight,' he began, his voice shaking. 'We can go forward as we are, or take a path unknown. Our abbot, Father Dunstan, will argue that Christ was not married, that women are a distraction. I am sure he will make a dozen other points to build his wall to keep them out. To keep the mothers out, and the daughters – and of course the sons who might have been born to this monastery. It does not matter that the abbot is unmarried. Nor does it matter that I have a wife. Our small tales are nothing as we contemplate the Rule of our Benedictine order – and the future of all such orders. Yet perhaps it matters that the apostle Simon was married. In the gospel of Mark, we have the detail, so often overlooked: ". . . but Simon's wife's mother lay sick of a fever." And Christ went to her and raised her up well, so that she could tend to them. And much later, he called Simon and said unto him, "Thou art Peter and upon this rock I will build my church – and the gates of hell will not prevail against thee." Simon Peter, who had a mother-in-law, who was still Christ's choice to be the first pope, the rock on which the Church is built, whose bones lie in Rome this hour. What greater sign can there be that priests and monks might marry without sin? What greater authority?'

Caspar paused then and indicated me with his outstretched arm. 'Abbot Dunstan will make clever and powerful arguments against, I do not doubt . . .'

To my fury, someone in that place hissed at me! I searched the rows for whoever had dared, seeing only a lot of bowed heads. Poor Caspar was unaware of their insolence and went on in that amiable way of his, never realising he had not moved the crowd as I would.

'He will make his arguments from reason and from faith,

yet in this I believe he has missed the path Christ chose for us when he raised Peter. That is my first point – I reserve my right of answer.'

He sat down to nervous applause, no more than a crackle of it as I went to that same rostrum, looking out on the packed hall that stretched away. I had built half of that place with my own hands, sawing and hammering and cutting joints. I knew it as most of them did not, deep into the bones. I had intended a more scholarly debate, but I sensed that Caspar had done well. If he somehow forced a vote, I could lose. I changed plan. I led them in prayer and they bent their heads in silence. Perhaps they also remembered I was their abbot and father to them all.

'This hall,' I said at last, indicating it with a grand sweep of my arm, 'that sits above the schoolrooms below, was built by us, by this community. It was the labour of months, with a year of seasoning the great beams before that, so they would not warp. And it was made in faith, for that thread that binds us all together in this ancient and holy place, that justifies the relicts we own, that makes us one: the Church. We are not a village, here! This island is a place of prayer and devotion. St Augustine brought the faith to England and he was Benedictine. It is those rules that give us the right to look kings in the eye – as I have done with three. I am no great thane or king myself. I am the humble abbot of a monastery dedicated to our patron. Yet I think if another abbot came here and saw how we live, I would be ashamed. We took a vow of poverty, yet eat our fill and live in comfort! The abbey is incomplete, but instead of working every hour to finish it, I see slackness and sloth everywhere I look. I see brothers of the cloth strolling hand in hand with wives, their children around their feet. Where is the silent prayer? The mortification of flesh? Where is the dignity in our order? Can you not see we have lost the path?'

I became aware I was haranguing them, that I had grown red-faced and angry in my passion. I cooled myself with deep breaths and went on.

'A brother of the order must dedicate his life to the worship of God. The Rule of St Benedict concerns his behaviour, yes, saying he should visit the sick and bury the dead, that he should not provoke laughter or take oaths he might break, and so on. There are hundreds of such commands, though not a single one, not one, is intended to frustrate or restrain, but to focus our hearts. The Rule says, "As soon as anything hath been commanded by the superior they permit no delay in the execution, as if the matter had been commanded by God Himself."'

I let a natural pause develop as they swallowed that particular morsel. It did not hurt to remind them.

'Devotion to God cannot be shared with a wife,' I told them. 'We are about God's business in this place. For this is his abbey, rising around us.'

I sat down in triumph, though they were too stunned or moved to applaud me. We sat through another hour of Caspar speaking and my replies, each answer striking down his points like arrows, littering the ground with them. Yet he endured. It was getting late and I was wearying of their resistance when a whisper of childish terror went through that place.

It began as a groan almost, a low sound like an animal in pain, spilling out across the rafters so that we all heard it in the same instant. We sat like statues as the voice spoke, clear as if the words were whispered by our ear.

'Blessed Father Dunstan knows my will and my way,' it said, three times.

Silence flooded back in and scores of men crossed themselves or touched beads or relics to their lips and murmured prayers.

I began to rise, determined to call a vote, knowing the

moment of triumph had come at last. Yet Caspar was still there at the rostrum and, to my astonishment, he shook his head.

'Was that the voice of the enemy?' he called across the hall. 'If you will speak, Lord, speak to us now, that we may know you. If not, we must believe it was the devil himself.'

I bristled, but the whole room went silent again, listening. Nothing came, as I had rather suspected it might not. The extraordinary awe of the moment had been lost with a simple question. I began to regard Caspar as a threat I could not ignore.

'There is our answer, then,' he said: 'that the devil himself wishes to banish women and families from the holy orders! I suggest to you that goodness lies in retaining them!'

I looked to my right as a great creaking began. Once more everyone sat as still and as afraid as mice. I took one great step to my left and then the hall went crashing down. Before my eyes, the entire floor dropped away, sending screaming men and women into a chaos of broken timber and so much dust we were blind. I alone remained standing there, balanced on the single beam that had not given way. It was a great miracle – and proof that I was in the right and that the voice had been God's and not the devil.

Three men died in the crush that evening, found pale and broken when the rest clambered out. Caspar survived, though with a broken ankle. In all, it was a high price to pay, but I think it was important to deny them a vote which would have tarnished their souls.

When I made arrangements to return to court, it was with the understanding that Prior Caspar would deny any newly married monks from then on – and encourage a more disciplined approach from those who resided with us.

The north had settled down by the fifth year of Eadred's reign. Eric Sore-axe and a whole host of Olafs had been put into the ground, or set afire. The main walls of the abbey were finished in the summer, so that a host of glass-men and lead workers crawled over it then. It would take another year before I was finally satisfied with it, when the Te Deum could be sung and the air lost some of its chill behind the great doors. Yet it stood – the greatest abbey in England. My vision had been made real, each stone upon stone. Whenever I was alone there, I would put the palm of my right hand on a column and thank God for helping me to bring it about. It will stand when I am dust – and that is not a small thing to contemplate.

Though the grounds were still rough and unkempt, we held a great ceremony there in the spring to exhume and re-inter the body of my friend, King Edmund. That royal tomb was in cream marble, polished to a high sheen and bearing an extraordinary likeness of him. I had overseen the work and even taken a little breadth off the nose with my own hands when I saw the mason could not understand what I was describing. Our choir sang to the wooden beams high above.

The life of the abbey settled down to a routine that sustained us all. Master Justin wore the black and the number of our monks had reached one hundred and eighty or thereabouts, with another forty-two lads learning their letters and their Latin in the school. The community was thriving.

King Eadred had commissioned a new palace in London, and Master Justin left us for a time to oversee the work. As always, the entire royal court moved from city to city – from Bath, to Norfolk, to Leicester, to Wales and so on, always in sight of the people, always watching for insurrection. The king staged great tourneys in some places, which was a rare entertainment but also served to remind his subjects that he had a large number of warriors at his command. I liked Eadred, I really did. I might easily have gone with him, but I was working on the best harp I ever made – a thing of great beauty. I loved to run my hand along the sweep of grain, though I was no musician. Having failed to draw any great music from my previous attempts, I understood the flaw lay in me rather than the instruments. Yet I had an idea to create sound without my having to touch it at all.

I was lost in my work, with a long summer evening drawing to a close. From old habit, I'd chosen the smaller forge we'd built up against the side of the chapel in the earliest days of the abbey being torn down and rebuilt. It was a snug little room, not six feet by eight and uncomfortably warm when the forge was hot. When I rested from my labours, the only sounds were the clink of metal cooling, or a hiss of my sweat falling on some part of it.

There was a window and I had the shutters back and the evening breeze coming in to give me relief. I looked up from a perfect iron string, drawn fine but strong, to see a face I knew leaning in on me.

'I told you to go back to your retirement,' I said.

Skinner raised his head in a sort of challenge or a greeting. I frowned at him. He had been drinking, I could smell it.

'You did, father. You did that. But you made me a free man again . . . and free men don't always go where they're told.'

I put down my tools, though the heat of the forge beat at me. I liked neither his tone nor the way his eyes gleamed in his drunkenness.

'You have no business here, Skinner,' I told him firmly. 'Not with me. Go back to your son in London. I have treated you well and I owe you nothing.'

'Maybe you do owe me a little more, though,' he said. 'After all I've done for you. Me and the boy.'

I felt illness creep across me, almost like a chill, though the forge seemed to thump heat in time with my heart.

'You think they would believe you, against my word?' I said softly.

'That we helped you saw joists in the old school and rested

it all on wedges that me and the boy could hammer out? I heard three poor monks died in the crush, so I think, yes, they might be interested in that. But if I had a little gold, perhaps . . .'

He was an old man and he could not move fast enough to stop me. I reached into the forge and swept up tongs that were yellow in the charcoal. I grasped him by the back of the neck so he could not pull away. With my right hand, I closed those iron jaws on his nose and held him as he screamed and boiled. Voices called in fear nearby, asking who could be making such a clamour, or whether it was some animal.

Those voices turned into running feet, coming closer. I let him go as they reached my little forge. I put the tongs back to heat again and the monks who came with cudgels heard Skinner screaming in agony as he ran away into the darkness.

'Who was that? What was that?' they demanded.

'The devil,' I told them in my fury. As I'd once been carried by an angel, I began another tale attached to my name, one that has stood the test of time more than any other part of my works and the years granted to me. The devil came for Dunstan and the abbot took him by the nose with red-hot tongs. It has a life of its own, that. Yet in a sense, it was true. Skinner had threatened me. I made him regret it. I am not proud of the truth, nor how it was twisted around me, against my will or my intention.

31

My harp played itself. Now, yes, it was the wind, but saying that as if it explains all is not the half of it. Mere wind unclothed can howl around eaves and whistle like a beggar, but it does not make a chord or a tune. It sings not, it plays not, it only moans. I tuned my harp strings to make music — and the wind brought forth the notes. It was a wonder. King Eadred was certainly entranced by it, so that I made it a gift to him. If the abbey was my first great work, the harp was my second. I had made a dozen of them over the years, but that was my last. I had mastered the craft and I had no more interest.

It was around that time that Archbishop Oda asked me to create a robe for him to celebrate Mass.

As the priest stands with his back to the congregation, the only thing they have to rest the eye upon is the long stole he wears. It can be the work of years to embroider scenes from the Bible or the lives of the saints in rich colour. I had seen the vestments King Æthelstan had given to the tomb of St Cuthbert, rich with gold and silk and filled with colour. I could not do less. I will not hide my light under a bushel. As I said to Wulfric once when he remarked on it, 'Where would I find a bushel big enough?' It was in jest, of course, but also a great truth.

It helped that we were not at war. If I'd known then what was to come, I might not have spent so long learning English embroidery.

I remained the royal treasurer, and as I entered my thirties, I was well known at court, in Winchester and in London. The sheer weight of coin that came from my efforts to root out corruption made me a favourite every time King Eadred spent time in his treasury. I did not travel much beyond those places, as I had my workshops and my libraries there. I was also illuminating a Rule of St Benedict then, in fine gold, blues and red. I had ground the very best encaustum ink and overseen vellum so well cured and dried as to last a millennium.

If perhaps I have a tendency towards pride, it is humbling to think of my greatest works being read long after I am gone.

King Edmund's sons had grown into strong lads in the years of their uncle's reign. Their mother had fallen into sickness early on, snatched away in the night with some female ailment. I was not called to tend her, which is why she died. The two boys looked to King Eadred as a parent, but of course that poor man had spent half his reign out hunting raiders and burners.

I will say the oldest of those two boys was spoiled by all, as an apple can rot at the heart though the skin is clean. Edwy was an orphan, yes, deserving of our compassion, but there was a spitefulness in him, a slyness. Becoming the darling of the court only allowed that side of him to grow. I did not like him then. I cannot say I ever grew to.

In part, it was his confidence that grated on me. From his days of playing with wooden soldiers, he knew he would be king. I smiled at first to see him placing real guards in a great hall, marching them up and down and ordering them about like a general in his high, childish voice.

The knowledge of power to come is what corrupted him. It is too much for some, so that they learn no curb, no character from being refused. Edwy was never refused, in anything. Whenever I stopped him racing past me at full cry, or snapped at him for pissing in a corner rather than leaving the room to find a pot, he looked at me with a little smile on his face, as if he alone knew what lay ahead. I have to say he quite unnerved me as he grew older.

Part of the problem was that he was as fair as the devil himself. There was an almost unnatural beauty to that boy. His teeth were white, his skin unmarked by pock or pit. His features were very regular and his hair was as blond as his father's had been. The young ladies of the court sighed at his passing when he was still only a child, fanning themselves and rolling their eyes like Jezebel, telling one another what a dashing young prince he was.

I found his younger brother Edgar much more amenable, a boy of quiet prayer and kind disposition. The Witan had placed him in the home of an ealdorman in Worcester, an old Mercian family. Those two boys had been our kingdom's main assets while Eadred ruled. It was an old practice to keep them apart, though as a result, they could not have been more different.

When I went to visit Edgar, I found him serious and charming, the opposite of his laughing brother. He asked for stories of his father Edmund and I told him a dozen, over and over. Edgar had inherited his father's sense of duty, without which all the talent in the world can be wasted. That was what his brother never understood.

If only Edgar had been born before Edwy. So much would be different. Archbishop Oda agreed with me about the pair – that one was mere dross, while the other bore the signs of his noble father. Only one could be king, and as Eadred's health worsened, we felt that day rushing upon us, closer every month. At least we knew it was coming, so we had time to prepare.

I do not think Eadred was ever truly well, in all the years I knew him. His stomach ate him up from the inside and became, in the end, his master. He was always in pain.

Eadred asked me to be bishop of Worcester when that post came free and I could not refuse him a second time. From the start, he had raised me up and seen my worth – and I loved him for it.

In the ninth year of his reign, I was dosing Eadred with mugwort every day, though it hardly eased his poor ulcerated stomach. He was thirty-two years old. He could not bear even beef juice then, never mind solid food of any kind. I saw him mark his little cloth with blood sometimes when he coughed, so that he had to change them twice or three times a day. As he could not eat, he lost weight alarmingly. It was not long before the whole court knew he was fading. His nephew Edwy would be king before the year's end.

The boy learned it himself, of course. He had many servants and thanes who saw their futures entwined with his. At first, they only whispered in his ear and hoped for favours. As his uncle began to fail, they were more open in their support of him.

In a different lad, the prospect of great responsibility might have tempered him, at least while his uncle slipped away in agony. Instead, that fifteen-year-old bantam cock strutted about Winchester. He rode to hunt rather than keeping a modest demeanour. While the court whispered and waited for the passing of a beloved king, Edwy roared with laughter and drank until he vomited with his coarse friends, eyeing the maids and noble ladies who fluttered at them. Doing a lot more than merely eyeing them as well, if half the rumours were true.

In contrast, young Edgar came to Winchester in a great riding party of Mercian lords, rushing in with the smell of wind and earth on him to his uncle's bedside. There was no laughter in him, no wildness – only solemnity and dignity as he gave honour.

I made a promise then, in the vault of my private thoughts,

as Edgar knelt and prayed for his uncle's return to health. He would make a better king.

Edgar's prayers would be disappointed. His uncle had ruled for a few months shy of ten years and he was a gasping, withered thing at the end. He asked to be buried in the Old Minster at Winchester.

'Or perhaps Glastonbury, Your Highness,' I murmured to him. 'Where your beloved brother Edmund has his wonderful tomb.'

Eadred turned a look on me, I remember, that was full of indignation. Death steals our strength, but also our authority.

'I said Winchester and I meant it,' he said. Pain took him away for a time and he was silent. In all that ending, I do not recall him weeping or crying out, though death clutched at his face and buried its claws in his gut.

'Where is Archbishop Oda?' Eadred said at last, when he could speak again.

The archbishop stepped forward from the servants arrayed around the king's bed. Kings die in a crowd. Never alone, even if they wish to be.

'Here, lord,' Oda said. 'Would you like me to administer the last blessing and confession now?'

Eadred breathed out and out. I thought he had gone, but it was merely acceptance. The worst of the pain seemed to leave him as he gave way to it.

Oda said the last rites over him. We waited a long time for the end. When it came, I closed the king's eyes. As the news was carried away from his rooms, I felt the return of old fears.

You have to understand our kingdom is a flame in a storm gale, guttering, flickering, struggling to survive. To the west, we still had the Vikings who had made their fiefdoms in Ireland. To the east and north, we had the might of all those small kings who saw our coast as a challenge – the Danes,

343

the Swedish kings, the savage Norse. To the south, all along the coast of old Gaul, more Norsemen gathered, peering across at us. They waited all around us then. We had no chance to survive, some said. Yet we fought even so, whenever they came. Some men will.

We fought, because not to fight was to be destroyed, but also because we'd glimpsed something in the land, in the rivers. Our fathers and grandfathers had found a good place, a sweet valley, with wolves on every hill all around us, just watching. We were farmers and soldiers and princes and priests. They were mere cruelty.

When a king died, they came howling down the hills. So I was afraid, not least because I knew Edwy would be king – and he was no friend of mine. My star had risen with Edmund and Eadred. It fell with Edwy. More, it crashed to earth.

PART FOUR

Behold, a Prince of the Church

AD 954

'A bee of genius, that flies over divine meadows.'

Vita S. Dunstani

32

I went along when the Witan gathered. They came in dark colours for the king's funeral, showing mourning and giving him honour. Yet they came also to choose a new king. When the funeral was over and Eadred had been placed in his tomb in the minster, his Witan walked in procession to the great hall, taking their seats around the central aisle.

Prince Edwy and Prince Edgar took places on the benches there, with every noble earl and thane from Winchester to Scotland. Both young men wore black and bore swords at their waist. Edwy stared around with one eyebrow raised, as if we bored him, as if he owned us.

I was there as royal treasurer, but also as witness, bishop and abbot. I had no proper seat on the Witan as I had not been elected to one. As a result, I had no vote that day, though I could still address the gathering and play a part. We were without a king. The whole country waited for the good word to come out of that meeting.

We all knew the Danes would hear in a month or two, if they had not already. I am sure they had spies in that hall. There are always some whose honour can be purchased. No one else had any great desire to see the Vikings return. If they did come, we needed a king on the throne to lead our men to battle. A man of the line of Alfred and Æthelstan.

Yet it was not so simple. Edwy was the oldest boy, but he was neither warrior nor scholar, nor man of God. He was just a minstrel gadabout, and I will not say worse of him, though I could.

Before King Eadred was in his tomb, I had visited

Archbishop Oda at his private home in Winchester. He'd welcomed me to a study that contained models of ships, to my slight surprise. I examined them closely and he explained how he had made them from memory, recreating the vessels he had known as a boy. He had food and wine brought and settled himself to hear me. All priests are familiar with men and women seeking them out, overborne with some great problem. It is part of our role as shepherds, and he expected something like that from me.

'You are the foremost man of the Church in England, Your Grace,' I said to him – for archbishops and cardinals are addressed as princes, and given the same courtesies when they travel to a foreign court. I was a mere bishop of Worcester, though I still hoped for a position in London or even Winchester.

'Your Grace, this cockscomb prince, this headstrong boy, has no real faith, no desire to rule well, beyond his lusts and his greed. I have met a hundred men and found not a single one willing to speak well of Edwy.'

'Truly?' Oda asked. He tutted in dismay as I confirmed it.

'If there was no other, Your Grace, I would say it was God's will, but we do have a better son, in Edgar.'

'He is too young,' Oda said immediately.

I shrugged.

'He is fourteen – older than I was when my father took me to the abbey at Glastonbury. Older than you when you came to England. The Mercians speak well of the lad and he has impressed me. They would follow him and that . . . that is what matters. The king does not have to wield a sword if he has the confidence of his lords. Edwy cannot command that confidence.'

'Yet Edwy will be king,' Oda said.

'The Witan chooses the king who will be best for the land,' I said patiently. 'Not always the eldest of the line – just as Eadred wore the crown while these boys grew. They chose King Æthelstan only because he gave an oath not to marry. Edmund was their first choice. Father, Your Grace, we have one chance here, to turn the path of history. If we say nothing, if we do nothing, a spiteful, cocky boy will wear the crown for fifty years. Yet if you and I speak for Edgar, the Witan will be forced to listen. To me, as abbot and bishop, but more to you, as archbishop of Canterbury. You are the voice of the Church in England. They will not turn away from you.'

'Who will Wulfstan support, do you think?' Oda asked. The archbishop of York had spent some time in prison under Edmund and learned some valuable lessons from the experience. We'd heard nothing from him after that.

'He will not speak,' I said, though I did not know. 'You and I can persuade the Witan, together, no other. If you agree Edgar is the right choice.'

'I will pray on it,' he promised, but I knew even then. Oda too had seen Edwy's lies and thefts and cruel games. An old hound, half-blind, had snapped at the prince a year before. Edwy had kicked it to death in rage for that slight hurt. No one cared about one old cur, but the public temper, the childish, spitting fury, had disturbed many.

Oda needed only the faintest push to be persuaded. He had wanted to hear what I had to say.

The Witan was made of earls and thanes and shire reeves and old members of the court, elected when a place came free, which was rare. England had more than a million souls, so they said. In representing such a number, the Witan was a great gathering – the voice of the subjects. When those men came together as they did that evening, their greatest and most sacred role was to choose the king to rule them.

Edwy was smiling to himself, I saw, like a sly cat almost,

with his head half dipped and his blond curls catching the last rays of the sun. Perhaps that beauty was what ruined him. There is honesty in ugliness, I have observed. An ugly woman is often a faithful one, with no temptations to draw her from the path.

I had made up my mind to stand between Edwy and the crown. Though I could feel my heart beating so hard as to make me faint, I signalled my desire to speak. The room fell silent. I drew myself to my feet and, though they were all around me, I could feel Edwy's gaze.

'It is my understanding, as one who has counselled kings, that the Witan chooses the best of the bloodline to serve the land. That is our way, from older courts than this, to times our fathers and mothers would not recall. We choose who rules us – and that is their power over us all, that they know they were chosen. It is our honour, bound into one decision and never challenged again until death or betrayal.'

I looked around at them all and a part of me was surprised at how closely they listened. In some ways, I still thought of myself as a callow youth, but the truth was I had advised kings, especially Eadred. All men there knew me, and most respected my judgement. I had assumed I needed Oda in support, but to my pleasure, I realised that I might not. Somehow, through some combination of mere age and the seam of my talent, I had become a man to whom others listened. It was a moment of giddiness in that place and I gripped the bridge of my nose and took a slow breath.

'A king must have strength and wisdom – or the seeds of both, in two candidates so young.'

A stir went around the room at that. Until that moment, Edwy had been the heir apparent, unchallenged. I had not even told Edgar of my intention to speak. I could almost feel Edwy's smile slip, replaced by a scowl in the gloom.

'I fought at their father's side at Brunanburh,' I said. 'I

have known battle in all its blood and noise. I saw the greatness in Prince Edmund then – and I guided him until he was taken from us as king. I saw then how the trials of the north wore at King Eadred and how much of his strength he bartered away, to kill those who tried to steal the land. I have known kings – and I know now what makes a good one. I see that strength in one son of King Edmund, but not the other.'

The stir was louder then and a few called for me to sit down and be quiet, no doubt the defenders and friends of Edwy making themselves heard. I had to wait for a time before they were still, or close enough to it for me to say what I had come to say.

'I have witnessed weakness and spite in one son, dignity and honour in the other. Therefore, I urge the Witan to choose Prince Edgar over his brother.'

There was pandemonium for a while, as if they'd all drawn in a breath just to howl at me. When I sat down it was to a great roar of noise. Yet when it died away, both Archbishop Oda and Edwy himself were on their feet.

The prince looked at the older man in contempt. He might have had the sense to give way if he hadn't been exactly the spoiled brat I'd known he was.

'Sit down, Your Grace,' Edwy said softly.

Oda did so immediately, though he wore a dark look as Edwy went on.

'I have heard enough from whining clerics. Some of you may not favour me as your king, though I am. Yet before this Witan votes, I remind you that I am first-born of my father, Edmund, who was your choice and would rule now if his life had not been ripped away. You know what his will would be in this. You know my right.'

He had the cheek then to turn to his own brother. I think we all stopped breathing for a time.

'I'm sorry, Edgar. I would choose you in all things, but not in this. In this, I must be king.'

His brother gazed back, watched by everyone there. If Edgar had nodded or agreed in any way, I think it would have been settled then and there. He did not. I saw the muscles of Edgar's jaw clench. The younger brother knew Edwy better than anyone.

Edwy resumed his seat, red-faced, his climax missed somehow. In his place, Archbishop Oda rose and spoke in his halting English. He was as good as his word to me and threw his office and the Church behind Edgar. The archbishop even acknowledged my gaze as he took his seat. Edwy had gone such a dark shade and was so tight-lipped, I thought he might condemn himself in a tantrum.

A dozen others spoke after that, in support of both princes. Some were too full of their own importance to make much of a mark, while others argued well. My feeling was that Edgar's supporters were of a better sort, but they were mostly from Mercia, and perhaps their words did not have as much weight in that chamber. It was hard to know how it would fall and I began to wish I had waited until later, in case my words were forgotten. That would have been a coward's path, though.

It was some hours before the speaker for the Witan finally looked left and right and received nods. They had heard enough. The royal guards cleared the hall, ushering us all out. Oda remained to represent the Church – and to cast his Witan vote, which was why I'd approached him in the first place.

As I left in a crowd, I found myself almost alongside Prince Edwy and endured the flicker of anger passing across his face, though he knew better than to say anything.

I suspected something was wrong when neither I nor the princes, nor any other witnesses, were summoned back that day. I confess I grew nervous with each passing hour. If the

Witan chose Edwy, though the whole world could see he was not suited for the crown, I would have thrown away twenty years of work. I'd be lucky to keep the abbey I had built. There had been something very personal in the slow way his eyes had drifted across me, a promise of retribution.

I'd never heard of the Witan taking so long to discuss the succession. I passed a few coins to the servants taking food and wine into the chamber, but all they could tell me was that there was a very heated argument going on. The council of the Witan preferred to keep such things to its private self, so they stopped whenever they had a break or summoned servants.

In the morning, they gathered again and when the sun was high in the sky, the doors were thrown open and all those who waited rushed back in. The two princes walked first among them and I noticed by then that each brother had his own supporters around him, almost as twin armed groups. I found myself glancing to the closest door in case fighting broke out. If the council refused Edwy, there was a chance I would have helped to begin a civil war.

The speaker for the Witan stood and held out a piece of fine vellum, nicely cut, with a proclamation followed by the witness names of all those present. We craned to read the choice, but it was impossible and he merely teased us with the sight of it before he read.

'"We, who have sealed our names below, make this judgement in the matter of succession, that Prince Edwy shall be king . . ."'

I felt it like a blow over my heart, that stole away my breath. I had gambled and lost. For once, I had followed my conscience and acted not for my own good but for the good of the country – and I had destroyed myself.

The man stopped reading as a great shout went up from all Edwy's supporters. I exchanged a glance with Oda and he gestured sharply towards the speaker, so that I looked back as the man bristled.

'Silence! Be silent, by God!' the speaker roared at them. 'You have not heard all!'

He had to pick up a staff and rap the floor with it for an age before they subsided. I did not know him well, but he had a fine voice, I remember that. His name was Capell, or Capet, something like that.

'"Prince Edwy will be king of all land south of Cirencester, that is the kingdom of Wessex and all the south, including London. Prince Edgar will be king of all the north, including Mercia and York. In suchlike way, two brothers will rule England, both of the line of Alfred the Great, both the choice of the Witan."'

The old fool then read the names and titles of all the half-wits gathered there who had come to such an extraordinary decision.

There was more muttering than stunned silence, as the crowd asked one another what it could mean. Slowly the noise grew once again, like a shout on the battlefield almost, a great chorus of jeering and anger from all sides. The members of the Witan were protected by guards, but those men had to look sharp to stay on their feet as the crowd pushed and shoved.

Prince Edwy reacted badly, his blood fired by the noise around him, the press and the heat of that place. I saw him go from shocked stillness to bawling anger, while his friends tried to hold him back. The guards had spears and swords, and they were nervous. We were an eye-blink away from bloodshed.

I looked to Edwy's brother on the other side of the hall, in time to see Edgar exchange a glance with one of the Mercian earls. Both men shrugged and gave equal half-smiles. They were not too displeased at the judgement.

Edwy drew his sword. It was a line of silver that flashed in the gloom before his friends grabbed him and it went skidding across the floor underfoot. The young man might have been king in Winchester at that moment, but his own lords held him rather than let him run berserk.

All those who had spoken against Edwy taking the throne left at a good pace, not quite a run. As his roaring faded behind us, I saw Oda was alongside me. We all streamed away like rats, looking back to see if we would be followed.

'The Witan are fools if they think this will stand,' I said, bending close to his ear. 'Could you not stop it? They gave Edwy reason to hate his enemies and the power to act, in the same moment!'

I swallowed as I considered the truth of my own words. Edwy had lost half a kingdom because of me. No. I let blame fall from my shoulders. I would not carry it. Edwy had lost half the kingdom because his conduct and his manner were cruel and petty and venal.

I was grim with foreboding as I made my way to Lady Elflaed's old home, still then my own possession as her inheritor. I washed myself with slow deliberation, though it was not spring. It has been my habit for each coronation and I found it restful and calming.

Prince Edgar came to see me there before he rode back to his Mercian keeps and fortresses, now as their king. I went out onto the street to greet him, though he sat with a dozen armed men on horseback. I had no fear of that young man and I wondered then if I should ask to accompany him to his new court. If I'd had a horse, I might have done.

'I wanted to thank you, father, for what you said in the Witan hall. It was a brave thing to do – and I did not expect their answer to take that form.'

'You are not displeased, though,' I said, reading him.

Edgar smiled and once more I was struck at his dignity. He was a man to follow, for all his youth.

'I am not displeased. I thought I would leave that place with nothing, father. I came away as king of the north. Better still, my older brother has had a right blow to his self-esteem. That should not please me . . .'

'. . . but it does,' I finished for him. I sighed. 'I wish you well, Your Highness. Perhaps I might call on you when I am next in Worcester. I am . . . a bishop of Mercia, after all.'

'Yes, so you are! Of course you may. You will always be welcome wherever I am, for my father – and for the service you did me. I will not forget it.' He thought for a moment, unsure in his youth how to end the conversation. 'I do not think I will attend my brother's coronation, Father Dunstan. He would not like to see me there, not while his temper is hot. Still, I would like to hear it described when you come to see me next.'

'I would be delighted, Your Highness,' I said.

He inclined his head and rode off. One of his lords nodded to me and I returned the gesture, pleased to be well thought of in at least one part of the country. I was a hero in Mercia that year, though for a Wessex man, that is not a particularly grand ambition.

The coronation of Edwy took place a month or so later, at Kingston. In a gesture of reconciliation, Archbishop Oda was asked to crown the prince and did so to a cheering crowd. I was surprised at the numbers who turned out to see him, but then Edwy looked like the idea of a king, almost, the perfection of a man. I heard him called 'King Edwy the Fair' almost immediately as the crowd cheered and raised cups to toast a long and happy reign. I could not help thinking of his father, who had been called 'Edmund the Magnificent' for his battle victories and his manner.

The coronation feast was to be held in the great Guildhall in London, as it was just eight or nine miles away. I did not remark on the fact that Edwy's father and uncles had been crowned in that place because it stood on the border with Mercia and so demonstrated the reach of the Crown. He could no longer claim that kingdom as his own. I wondered if that ate at him as the crown was lowered to his head.

The huge crowd accompanied us in procession as we walked. I stayed close to Archbishop Oda as I considered my future. I thought once more that if I left that night, I could appear and be made welcome at Edgar's home, yet it was not something I liked to contemplate. I did not want to leave all I had made! For fear of some gilded boy on the throne?

I told myself I'd rather spend a few years of peace as abbot of Glastonbury, creating relict boxes in silver. All that work awaited me. Yet I enjoyed being where power lay, though it should not have been my concern. I have, on occasion, lost sight of the object of true contemplation and fallen instead into the concerns of the world.

On the night of the coronation feast, I destroyed myself. Standing close to kings is like leaning in to a great fire. One who has a spot in a royal hearth can be warm and dry, even as others shiver in the darkness outside. Yet step an inch too close, or see a spark alight on your robe and pierce a hole to grow and grow – and all is undone. I tell you, over the passage of a single hour, I tore down a whole lifetime.

33

The London feast hall might have been the nave of a cathedral, just about. No king can celebrate his crowning with an intimate dinner for his closest friends. They have a duty to be seen – to reward those who supported them and perhaps to heal the wounds of those who did not, if they care to.

The table stretched sixty yards, with three or four hundred lords and ladies and about as many to serve or prepare the dishes. I had never seen such fare, in such strange combinations. Edwy had a particular delight in animals having eaten other animals, so we had eels stuffed with sardines, and roast pig with pigeons peering from between its jaws. I recall a great pike filled with ducks. It was all for show, but there was one fellow near me who made a point of trying all the unusual meats on offer, so that he could tell his children he had eaten vole and red grouse, rooks and dormice. Oda drank only water and when I asked him why he avoided wine and ale, he said it made him angry, that he had never been a happy drunk. I was intrigued as to what damage Oda thought he could do, but I have known other Danes who did not drink for the same reasons. For myself, both ale and wine have always been a blessing, lending wit and laughter like light in a dark room.

You'll understand, after my adventures in the Witan, that I was nowhere near the head of the table. Perhaps that explained Archbishop Oda's melancholy that evening, as he was near me and as far from the light and noise around King Edwy as it was possible to be – he, the churchman who had actually crowned the king. Not that Oda was good company at feasts. He had a tendency to recite poetry and it was hard to forgive him for that. Heard once, there was always the chance of it happening again.

Still, on that night, I felt rather fortunate to be included at all. I looked for others who had spoken against King Edwy and found none, which I confess gave me a cold start and filled my mind with the most horrible imaginings. Was I to be humiliated, or murdered?

Perhaps I drowned my fears, I do not know. The lamps burned low and were refilled and some of the men passed out on the straw. Others vomited in the corners, then came back refreshed, calling for wine. It ran like a red river. I wanted some sort of peace between us, or a quiet moment to mend what I had broken. I watched for Edwy to rise, either for air or to empty his bladder, but I missed him in my bleariness.

When I half-stood, I saw Edwy's seat was empty.

'Did you see the king leave?' I said to Oda.

He shook his head and his eyes were scorched. He had been drinking after all.

We waited for a time – and a new course of steaming suet steak-and-kidney puddings came in. It was met with groaning, and though it was perhaps my favourite dish of all, I wondered how I could eat even a spoonful of it and not pass out.

Oda took me by the elbow, frowning.

'The king has been gone a long time,' he said.

I saw that end of the hall had grown quieter without a crowned head to impress. Perhaps that said more of them than of their host, but his absence was still a petty rudeness. I found myself growing annoyed once more at that golden boy, with all the world given to him, who could not even act with grace to his guests on his first night as king.

Had I been sober, I believe I would have left him alone. In my drunken confidence, I thought I could just shake his hand and say a few words and it would all be as it had been before. I patted Oda on his broad shoulder and winked to him. Much of that night is a blur of memories lost, but I remember that. My hour began.

I do not know exactly how I found myself in a wood-panelled corridor, with the noise of the feast just a distant murmur. The cooler air sobered me a touch, so that I had the sense not to bawl for Edwy. I listened instead for him, suspecting that I would hear his voice or his laughter and then choose my own entrance.

A woman began shrieking and I pressed my ear to a door. I believed the worst and madness surged, so that I knew neither fear nor caution. I burst the lock as I put my shoulder to a door, then stood gaping at the scene before me.

The sixteen-year-old king was not murdering the young woman. As she sat astride him, the advantage could only have been with her. Neither one was fully naked, as they had pulled up their garments, so that I saw a great length of her thigh as she came to a halt and turned to see who had broken in their door. Edwy smiled, a lascivious, satisfied expression like a cat who has murdered a helpless thing. His crown lay on its side on the floor by him, untended. I saw all that, and I could only blink at the third person in that room. An older woman knelt by the king's head, naked as a child and with great fat bosoms that hung like heavy fruit. They shone somewhat, so that I had the sense he had been nibbling greedily at them. Mother and daughter they were. I had been introduced to the young one earlier in the evening, before we took our seats. Lady Elgiva had been placed close to the king, within reach of him.

If Edwy had scrambled away, or jumped up and slammed the door back in my face, I think I would have remembered our relative stations. Yet he just raised one side of his mouth and waved his hand in the air.

'Shut the door, father. I won't be long.'

I saw fool's white flash across my eyes, the madness of rage that ruins men. I felt mocked by their nakedness, their lack of shame. I could see Elgiva's pink nipples trembling in the firelight as she stared at me, her eyes huge.

'Fornicator!' I shouted at him. 'Sinner! How dare you, on the night you were crowned! After you gave oaths to rule in Christian dignity and honour, then this . . . !' Words failed me and I came further into the room. Elgiva squealed and her mother finally – finally! – covered her breasts with some garment thrown over a chair. I laid hands on the king. I took the wrist of King Edwy and dragged him to his feet, spilling the harlot in a tangle of legs. Edwy was bare-chested, with some golden loincloth pulled up around his waist for his foul couplings. He tugged it down over his thighs, the work of a moment. He glared at me as he tested my strength.

In drink, in rage, I did not see the signs of his own fury building. I pulled him out of that room and halfway down the corridor, until I found suddenly that he was pulling me, so that we were moving faster and faster and I could not keep up. I was stronger than him, but I was swollen and slow from all I had eaten, while he was sixteen.

As we reached the feast hall once more, I fell forward, or he threw me down, I don't know. I landed on my stomach and all other noise ceased.

Edwy stood before them all, half-naked, uncrowned, an angel made flesh, but nursing a worm in his heart.

'This man has given grave offence!' he shouted to the stunned guests.

In the silence, something fell off the table in a crash. One by one, they all rose slowly to their feet. The few who were lost in drunken sleep were kicked awake, their grumbling quickly stifled.

I had barked my knees on the stone floor, so that pain

seared from them and I saw thick beads of dark blood as I pushed myself up. I knew I was in trouble, but I tried to summon my authority, as I had a dozen times before. I should not have tried it with a king. I should not have tried it with a young man. They are all fools in one way. They can roll the dice on anything. They can throw their lives into the air without fear of consequences.

Edwy strode back and forth before us all, seething with rage.

I rose to my feet, still taller than him.

'As abbot of Glastonbury, as bishop of Worcester, I cannot see the crown stained in sin,' I said.

Some wisp of sense and horror entered me then, too late. I really did not want to denounce the king in front of his guests on his coronation night. Most of what had gone on would still be unknown to them, if I did not describe it.

It had been a mistake to mention my titles, however.

'Abbot of Glastonbury, was it?' he roared at me. 'No more! Bishop of Worcester? Gone! I will find better men than you, Dunstan.'

'You will not, as God is my judge. You cannot take those things from me, Your Highness,' I said in fear.

He came close and stood looking up into my eyes.

'Perhaps I could not, before you gave me reason. You gave me reason.'

I felt my senses swimming and my jaw sagging open like a halfwit as the king strode over to the feasting table once more. He spread his arms wide.

'I had thought to begin my reign with a feast, but instead I will begin with the banishment of a sour priest. Gather whatever you wish, Father Dunstan. My guards will take you to the coast and put you in a boat. You will not return to England.' A thought struck him and I saw the old spite, the old fury. 'Do not think to find safety with my brother Edgar.

If I hear you have found a space under his wing, I will ask him for your head. No, father. Live free and far from me. Go to France. Go to Flanders. Go to hell if you wish, but go from here and go from my sight!'

He had a fine turn of phrase, that vicious cur. I thought to argue with him, but the feasters were delighted with their master's display. They hooted at me and cried out over my protests. The king had spoken and they would not allow me to answer.

I was taken by the arm and ushered towards the night. I struggled in that grip to look back, seeing Oda's appalled expression and then the two rumpled strumpets coming back into the hall, their hair restored, their delight visible. The young one dangled the crown in her white hand. I roared that they were whores and jezebels, but those at the feast table all howled again like demons, as if it was all just a great game.

I saw the daughter bend her head to Edwy and whisper in his ear. She put the crown over his curls, pressing it down. It reminded me of Salome asking for the head of John the Baptist. I had a terrible sick feeling steal upon me as King Edwy looked up once more.

'Wait a moment,' he called.

His men halted and turned, making me face the king and his harlots.

'Lady Elgiva reminds me that she too suffered this evening, Dunstan, at your hands and at your word. Hold him!'

I had begun to struggle as that concubine came drifting over the floor towards me. I have never felt so vulnerable as at that moment, when she leaned close enough for me to feel her breath upon my neck.

'I saw you watching,' she whispered. Her voice sent a shiver through me.

'What restitution would you have, my love?' Edwy called

to her. 'Shall I make him bark for you like a pretty dog? Or kiss your feet? He bruised you with his rough words and his accusations. Shall I have him flogged for it? Would you like to hold the whip?'

I heard Oda shout in outrage, but that crowd were drunk on cruelty, even aroused by it. The devil himself sat in that room with us.

'He was so proud before, Edwy,' Elgiva said. Her voice was warm. I saw then how beautiful she was, how red her lips were. 'I think I would like to see him crawl.'

'You are the great enemy,' I said, spitting out the words. 'The more you rejoice, the more you will have to regret, when it is your turn to be judged.'

'Possibly,' she said, leaning close once more. 'But tonight, it is your turn.'

Edwy gave the order and I stood as long as I could, while his guards beat at me. I fell in the end when they kicked my legs away, so that I could not rise up and saw only my own blood on the stone floor. I remember Elgiva laughing as she beckoned to me. I came up to my hands and knees and she told me they would stop if I just crawled to her.

I tried to curse her, but there was laughter on all sides and I could only mouth my pain, blind to them all.

I lost some part of that evening, or rather it was stolen from me. It took the cold of the night to revive my senses as I was taken outside at last. The doors slammed at my back, shutting off light and sound and laughter. I spat blood.

The king's guards ambled along to dark horses, waiting with dozing boys in the gloom.

'Can you ride, father?' one of them said.

I tried to nod, but there was not enough light for them to see me and so I cleared my throat and said I could. My teeth were loose and my face felt extraordinarily swollen, as if my lips and cheek and eye had grown together. I spent some time touching the most tender parts with my hands, then cursing as I felt at least two of my fingers had been broken. For a time the world swam.

'We gave him a right hiding inside,' the guard said. 'For peering up the lady's skirts or something. Dirty old bastard.'

I moaned in response and he pulled me to my feet from where I had slumped.

'Still with us, then? Good,' he said. 'I'll tie you on if you can't stay on, see? You're in my care now, until I put you in a boat, just like the king told me to.'

'King Edwy? He won't even remember in the morning,' I murmured, struck by the change in my fortunes and beginning to gather my poor spilled wits. 'Don't you see? He'll regret everything he said. He'll ask where I am. What will you say then? Just let me at least wait until the sun is up, to apologise. In the name of God, man! Just let me stay for a while, right here with the horses!'

To my astonishment, the guard struck me again, twice in quick succession. The fresh pain helped to sober me further, though the second blow made me vomit at his feet, so that he cursed me. As if I'd done it to annoy, rather than because he'd punched me in the gut.

'What is your name?' I asked him.

He only snorted at me.

'I'm the king's man, father, not yours. That was just a last taste, if you understand me. You go to the boat without any fuss and you'll get no more. I'll wave you off, see? But if you struggle or argue with me, I will take you somewhere quiet and I will finish what we started in the hall. I'll kick your teeth in.'

He peered at me, looking for resistance. I turned away from his bright malice to mount the horse, though I had to stifle a cry as I stretched bruised ribs.

As I breathed deep of the night air and closed my eyes, my

mind felt clear for the first time since sitting down to the feast. I was appalled at the suddenness of my change of fortune and I could only moan as moment after moment of it flashed before me. I had been a fool, but I had not deserved such treatment, such bitter humiliation.

I made no further appeal to the king's guards. They were not the Witan, or a magistrate, able to decide guilt or innocence. Their role was to be obedient to the king's wishes. I had no words left to turn them aside from that duty.

We rode away from London, crossing the river over the deserted bridge and heading south to the coast as the sun rose. There were a few carts coming the other way, but no one hailed us, three men out riding in the dark.

The sea was some fifty or sixty miles to the south, so a messenger rider might have done it in a single day. At our ambling pace, we did not make it before nightfall. It meant we had to stop at a tavern till morning. For the first time, I was back amongst respectful Christian folk, who bowed their heads at the sight of my tonsure.

There was no question of escape. The guard who had struck me slept in the same narrow bed while the other laid himself out in front of the door. One or the other was always awake. Yet they did not stop me writing letters, paid for from my dwindling purse. I bought paper and ink and wax and spent the night writing to Wulfric and Oda and Prior Caspar and King Edgar in the north. I handed them all to the innkeeper as I left, with a few coins to take them to their destinations. The act gave me hope.

At some fishing village on the south coast, perhaps Worthing, my nameless guard found a merchant captain who would give me a berth. The man eyed my swollen face and demanded twelve pence to take me to Flanders. I refused to pay him. I could hardly see it was a cost I should count as my own! There was a struggle and the angry guard struck me again as he wrestled my pouch away. He handed the sailor six pennies and then pocketed the rest, leaving me with nothing. He just sneered when I demanded it back. I had known humiliation before, but I had lost the habit of it. I had forgotten the appalling frustration of justice denied.

I saw the white cliffs bright in the morning sun as I left Wessex, heading for the continent, with all my life in ruins behind me. My Wessex, my home. I think I did weep. I can say it was because I stood too close to the king's hearth, but the truth is, I had brought it on myself in my pride and my righteousness.

Not that I was wrong, of course, though that did not make any of it easier to bear. I imagine a few saints felt as I felt that morning. Wounded, wronged and broken by the world, but still, in the final accounting, in the right. It was not much comfort as the wind blew up and I began to shiver.

The captain answered me only with grunts and curses at first, but when we were out at sea and I still stood at his elbow, he told me Ghent was our destination. He was happy enough to boast about the fortune he would make that trip. On that subject, he was willing to talk all day. England had more wool than anyone could make into cloth, while the cities of Flanders had more looms than they could find thread to fill them. He was a rich man, so he said. I wanted to tell him I'd spent gold and silver by the cartload on my abbey, more than he would see in a dozen lifetimes. Yet I had learned to keep my mouth shut. I said nothing and he thought he had impressed me.

We were a week at sea and then three days on barges coming inland to the city along a river as wide and deep as the Itchen in Winchester. As soon as we moored, I stepped onto the shore and walked away without looking back. The captain shouted something, but I did not return to find out what it was.

Ahead of me, on a fine hill that overlooked the city, was the walled abbey of St Peter, just as I'd heard. I had never visited Flanders before that day, but I spoke fluent Latin and Greek and I could find a welcome in any monastic house or church for a thousand miles. Our community was greater than the boundaries of nations, with Rome guiding us all, no matter where we were born. I had welcomed 'stranger monks' at Glastonbury from as far afield as Aleppo and Jerusalem. I would be welcomed in turn, as a brother.

My steps were light as I strode up the hill on good cobbles, seeing signs of wealth all around me. It was not perhaps as wide as Winchester, but there were only a few beggars and the city seemed busy and prosperous. There were new houses and warehouses being constructed all along the docks there, where the rivers met.

At the gate of the monastery, I pulled a small bell and waited for an age for the door to be answered. I was a little surprised to find it shut at all, but I suppose I was more used to Glastonbury, where the marsh meant fewer visitors.

When the door opened at last, it was to reveal a tonsured man old enough to be a grandfather. In Latin, I told him I was Abbot Dunstan of Glastonbury and bishop of Worcester. I begged him to let me enter, as I had fallen on hard times.

He raised his hand and I flinched like a beaten dog, after all the rough treatment I'd endured. Yet it was only to pat my arm and reassure me. He reached out then to take me by the chin, turning my head back and forth so he could examine my scrapes. He said nothing and I wondered if he had taken a vow of silence. Still, he smiled and patted my arm once more. I felt my gut unclench and some of the fear leave me. I was taken in and fed and shown to a small cell with a clean pallet and dried herbs strewn to make the air sweet.

The old man turned to face me as I sat down on the only

chair. His Latin was very clear, though the voice was an old man's piping note.

'I am Brother Favager. You are welcome to remain as long as you wish. Please rest, my son. Abbot Reynault will want to see you, but he is away in Antwerp and he will not be back for a week or two. We do not get many visitors from England and he will be delighted when I write to him. I should think Count Arnulf will ask you to dine with him as well, when he hears. Until then, eat, sleep, pray. We are a quiet order. You will find peace here.'

He patted me on the arm for a third time, and if that sounds like a small thing, you have never felt quite as alone and abandoned as I did. Brother Favager drew my attention to the pot beneath the bed and the jug in the corner. He blessed me and left me to think on my old life – and my vengeance.

34

I learned to like the Flemish, in the time I spent among them. They were tall and serious Christians for the most part, without too much frivolity. They prided themselves on being good hosts and seemed to take more of an interest in food than I was used to at home. Even the simple fare provided at the abbey was most varied. They made a superb broth of chicken and leeks, and a hare in red wine that was so good as to be almost indecent.

Ah me, like the sunlight of my youth, or the odours of flowers long ago, I cannot go back. My mistakes have been made and cannot be unmade. That is why I can write them now, when there is nothing to be done. The pain is more distant, the wounds become scars.

I had been fortunate in the destination of that ship's captain, I will admit. Not only did he find me a city where I would be made welcome as a fellow Benedictine, but ships travelled between Ghent and England in unceasing procession. My letters could go out and be answered within a few weeks.

I wrote again to Wulfric, knowing I could trust him. His reply reached me before the abbot of St Peter's returned, as the fellow was delayed in Antwerp on some business of the order. Abbot Reynault acted as a private moneylender to noblemen of Flanders, providing a vital service and gaining more than a little influence.

I clutched Wulfric's letter to my belly under the robe as I swept along the cloisters there. Every monk I passed bowed or smiled to me, though I saw them each day. That sense of welcome had begun to grate a little, I will admit.

In the privacy of my cell, I opened the outer packet and drew out thick folded papers, sealed with a circle of wax — and impressed with a wyvern ring. My heart sank as I snapped it in two and read.

It seemed King Edwy had learned the lesson of his father's short life and shorter reign. He had married his sweetheart just a few days after wearing the crown. Elgiva, whose name seemed to burn into my eyes as I saw it in my brother's letter. The woman I had called a whore in front of hundreds of guests. The harlot who had smiled as I was beaten to my knees in front of her, who asked sweetly for me to be made to crawl, who pouted her red lips at the king. She, who was my queen. She, who was mine enemy. I would have brought the world to ruin to bring her low. I was still a young man — and they will roll the dice.

When Abbot Reynault joined us, he brought some life to that sleepy little abbey on a hill. He was a large, pale man who used his hands to express whatever his words could not. Yet his Latin was clipped and strange in places, as if I heard words from another age. I told him so and he seemed delighted. I learned he adored Cicero's style and tried to mimic it in reverence to that great orator.

More importantly, the abbot heard my poor tale and showed all the disgust and anger I hoped he would. I did not share every detail with him, only that I had been ill-used in front of a great feast by the new king — and that the woman had become queen. My humiliation made his eyes glitter in fury. He understood well enough that I did not want my whereabouts to be reported back to the royal court, especially that I had found a place where I was welcome. I had no idea how far King Edwy would go in his spite, but I didn't want armed men climbing those abbey walls in the night, looking for me. A king can reach across the sea. But he was not the only one.

If I had been poor, I dare say I would not have been able to set anything in motion. Yet I had been the royal treasurer for ten years, and had amounts left with moneylenders as far apart as York and Winchester, in my name, no other. More, I had Wulfric, whom I trusted.

The difference between having a friend and having a brother comes when a man has to deal with a body. Wulfric would never betray me, I knew. Every time he hugged his wife with one poor arm, or kissed his daughter Cyneryth, he owed it all to me. I wrote to him, reminding him of an old game we'd played as children, replacing letters so that it became a jumble to anyone else. The Greeks had tattooed their messages on the scalps of soldiers, then let the hair grow back. Julius Caesar had used a simple cipher in his letters and I adopted it. It would not have survived the attentions of a clever man, but it would not give all our secrets to a quick and stolen glance either. That was enough for me to begin. I added shifts and codes within codes later, so that Wulfric began to complain it took him half a day to read my letters.

I have never cared for wealth, though some will spend their lives in its pursuit. Yet Wulfric was apparently astonished by the amounts of coin I owned. I will say only that I hardly noticed such sums in my daily work.

I have said I trusted Wulfric and I did, but my business was destruction. I could not put some things in ink or on vellum. Some things had to be said face to face, with no one to overhear.

He said he could not come, when first I summoned him. The winter rushed upon us and the smallest merchant ships rocked in port, gelded by storms along that coast. I worked my codes and made my plans — and even drew designs for the master weavers, when they asked about English work. Ghent was cold in winter, the whole city locked in ice and quiet, so that a man could hear only the crunch of snow and his own breath as he walked the streets.

All I could do was endure the cold and the grey. I attended the services and the meals. I spent entire months without saying a word to another, lost in my own contemplations. I thought for a time that the silence would swallow up my anger, but it seemed to beat it on a forge, so that it gleamed as yellow bar. I told myself it was for the dignity of the Church, that my humiliation was a sin that cried out for justice. But it was for me.

When the thaw came, the barges began to vanish and return again, filled with scores of bales to start the looms all over Ghent and Bruges. I went down to the docks and waited with my arms folded, shivering as they loaded and unloaded. One or two of the sailors made mock of me at first, until more devout members of their crew bade them be silent. They had no desire for bad luck, those crewmen. No appetite for my curse.

I continued to write my letters, of course, but as the spring warmed, I began to despair, certain somehow that Alice or my mother was preventing them from reaching Wulfric. I was alone and Abbot Reynault's conversation had palled. Over the winter, I had endured a number of meals with Count Arnulf, who was perhaps the dullest, most earnest man I have ever met. An evening in his company was like a glimpse of eternity, with no chance to repent.

In all, I had begun to weary of Ghent and I was homesick. Perhaps I understood then why Leofa had come back after just three years of his five. It can be a cruel thing, especially when English voices can be heard on the boats, calling to one another. I imagine it is more bearable to be a Frenchman.

I stood on that dock in rain and sun whenever there was a

rumour of an English ship unloading closer to the coast. Most of the vessels that came in were huge, slow barges, laden high with goods and a few passengers.

I was there when Wulfric stepped ashore with a companion, looking around him in wonder at the strangeness of a port that was not home. I gave a great shout of joy to see him and I ran across the cobbles, though there was a drizzle and they were slippery under me.

I am not usually given to open displays. I keep my secrets well and prefer them not to be shouted to the rooftops. In that way, I fitted in with the Flemish, who are much the same. Yet I could not help myself. I embraced Wulfric and crushed him to me, feeling his single arm batter me on the shoulders in happiness. I was not alone.

I turned to the fellow he had brought with him, who stood wrapped in a thick cloak and layers beneath that reeked of old sweat. The face too was covered, as children will tie scarves over their mouths on cold mornings. I waited as Wulfric's companion tugged it loose and then I just stared, raising my hand as if to ward him off.

Skinner's face was a mass of scars, with a huge hollow where the nose had once been. I could see into his skull, where brown teeth moved and raw skin glistened and seeped. As I stared, frozen, he coughed long and hard into a cloth, his eyes never leaving mine.

'Why . . . what is this, Wulfric?' I said. 'Why have you brought this man here?'

I did not take my eyes off the forger, in case he went for a knife and his own vengeance, right there on the Ghent dock.

'I think perhaps this is too open a place for idle talk,' Wulfric said with false cheer, looking around him. 'Where is the abbey?'

'No. I'm not moving a step until I understand this. Did you ask Skinner how he came by such terrible scars?' I said.

Wulfric frowned at me.

'He said he was burned.' My stunned expression had begun to worry my brother. 'That's right, isn't it, Skinner?'

'It's right, yes,' the man said. I winced at the way his voice slurred, the damage I'd done with my forge tongs. 'And your brother was the one what burned me.'

Wulfric looked back and forth between us, his eyes wide.

'What? I swear, Dun. He didn't say anything like that to me. I didn't know. You asked me to find someone and I thought of him. I went to him, Dunstan. Why . . . by God, Dunstan, why did you burn him?'

'Don't blaspheme, Brother. What do you want, Skinner?' I asked. 'Is it vengeance you're after? You won't find it here.'

'Your brother came to me and asked me if I'd be interested in paying work. He mentioned silver. So I came with him.'

'I'm sorry, you have been misled. I can't trust you, Skinner. Do you understand? You came to me before, with threats . . . and lies, wanting money to be quiet. I can't buy a man who won't stay bought, I'm sorry.'

He took me by the arm suddenly and I almost pulled away.

'Don't send me home. I got nothing, father! Not a penny to my name. My burns went bad and I nearly died. No one wants a man who looks like this, understand? They throw stones and kick me out of every place I go, like a bleeding leper. But my boy has no one else, so I'll work till I'm dead for him. You fill my pouch with silver and I give you my oath on the life of my son you won't see me ever after, unless it's to visit my grave.'

'Dunstan, I'm sorry,' Wulfric said. 'I had no idea this was between you.'

'No, Brother. You were right to bring him.'

I saw something in Skinner's eyes that I needed. I think it was desperation. I understood that better than most.

'You must have hated me, when I hurt you,' I said to him.

'I did, I won't deny it! I went mad for a time, with the pain and the fevers. I realised I brought it on myself, that I'd gone to you. You who'd rescued me once, didn't you? And the boy, which matters more. If you'd said to me, Skinner, I will save your boy, but burn you worse than you've ever known, I would still have taken your hand in that yard.'

It was true I had no other choices, but I saw truth in him.

'Kneel then, Skinner. Give me your oath on your immortal soul and the soul of your son. Swear you will be obedient to me, no matter what I ask of you.'

'I will,' he said, dropping down. 'Thank you.'

I took a silver locket from around my neck and handed it to him. He eyed it almost in fear.

'You hold a piece of the cross on which Christ died. It is stained in his blood. Do not lie, Skinner. Do not dare to. I ask you again. Will you swear on your immortal soul and that of your son to obey me in all things? To never speak of what we are about here? To keep your word?'

'I do, sir. I do!' he said.

I took his hand and found it cold and shaking. I raised him up. The docks had grown still around us as the sailors with their bales and goods had come to a halt to watch the strange scene. The noise came back as I glared at them.

'I gave you both your lives. You, Skinner, when I took you from the scaffold, on the morning of your death. You, Wulfric, when I put the screws into your bones and cut your arm from you. I saved you both – and now I have a task for you. Come with me. Let me show you St Peter's Abbey.'

Wulfric was visibly relieved at my forgiveness. As he strode along at my side, he was fascinated by everything he saw and some part of his mind was intrigued at the possibilities. He had the shop in London, after all. Wool and cloth was his business.

I listened to him exclaim and comment, but walked every

step under a cloud. I knew what I wanted to do would hurt him. He was an innocent, in a way, a good man. My work was cruel and it would mark him, as I had marked poor Skinner.

I could have turned away then, before I had gone too far. Yet I clenched my jaw and told myself it was already decided, that there was no going back. My enemies had brought me to that point, beyond all endurance. My feet were steady on the path ahead.

Abbot Reynault was uncomfortable with my desire for privacy, he made that perfectly clear. I had to add to my sins with lies about family matters to be discussed with Wulfric, just to get a room to ourselves. Reynault was as hungry for news of England and Glastonbury as I was, but there were other matters I did not want him to hear. In the end, Wulfric, Skinner and I ate lunch speaking of very little. Perhaps it was too much caution, but I became convinced I could be overheard and said nothing of consequence until we were alone in the abbey gardens.

'Brother, I am sorry,' Wulfric said. 'I hate to bring you such news.'

'In truth? It is just one more small hurt. I am already banished, Wulfric, without limit. Thieves might get five years, but not for me, an abbot and a bishop, who merely tried to stop the king's lust corrupting the court! Of course he gave my abbey to Caspar! I see her hand in it, Wulfric. Elgiva is the witch who drives him. She is our enemy, the one bad tooth that will kill a man.'

Wulfric frowned at me, understanding from my manner that I did not speak lightly.

'She had you beaten, at the coronation, I know. Can you not put it behind you?'

'No. The king's whore had an abbot beaten. She had a bishop bloodied at the coronation. I do not speak on my own behalf, Wulfric, but for God. When she is punished, it will be for her injury to the Church. Although I will take some satisfaction from it.'

Wulfric and Skinner watched me as they might have a wild dog, waiting to see if I would snap at them.

'Why did you summon me here, Dun?' Wulfric said. 'What was it that could not be written in your codes, which I can barely read myself?'

I gestured to a bench and they both sat down. I could not join them as my anger swelled, so that I paced up and down while they watched and listened to me talk.

'I have lost the abbey I built. I have lost my bishopric. I am no longer the royal treasurer.' I saw Skinner frown. 'Oh, I have more gold and silver than I could ever spend, Skinner. Do not fear for your reward.'

I leaned forward.

'I do trust you both, or I would not say this. Edwy may reign for fifty years. I will not spend that reign in Ghent! His wife is the poison. We will draw her out, take her from the king's side. He will find another. Perhaps he might even become the king he should have been. We could do some good here, Brother, for Wessex and for England.'

'What do you mean, draw her out? I won't be involved in murder, Dunstan, not for you or anyone. I won't do it.'

I smiled at him in affection.

'You are a gentle fellow, Wulfric. I know it. I would not ask you to do such a thing.'

'I would do it,' Skinner murmured. He gave a shrug when we looked at him. 'If you say the word, I'll cut a royal throat, as easily as you giving me a pouch of silver.'

'No, Skinner,' I told him. 'I won't kill that young woman. I would prefer her just to be taken away from the king, to be lost to him, so that he might always wonder whether she abandoned him or if she was taken.'

'Where could she be taken?' Wulfric asked.

'Ireland,' I said. I had considered a dozen places, but Ireland was far enough. 'If she was sold as a slave there, she would vanish into the hills as if she'd never been born. Let her wail and scream as she scrubs the floor of some peasant's hut. Let her never see home again, exactly as she wished for me.'

'I won't do it,' Wulfric said. 'I don't even know how it could be done! This is not some washerwoman, Dun! Elgiva is the queen.'

'It should be in daylight,' Skinner said. 'Somewhere she feels safe, where she won't have too many guards. At night, she'll sleep with the king, safe and sound, like. There'll be men, walls, all sorts. In the day, though, I could take her with a couple of lads.'

He was talking as if we were hunting hares or setting traps for birds. I was grateful Wulfric had brought him to me.

'You will work with Master Skinner, Wulfric, because you owe me your life – and your loyalty.'

'It's too much. I can't. Have you any idea what the king would do if we were caught?'

'It would be the end,' I said. 'The end of the life I gave you: the wife, the daughter, the shop, the respect of other men. The fine house you built for your family in London. When I stood over you and your blood was on my hands, I just wanted to save your life, that's all. Now they have hurt me, Wulfric. Worse, they have mocked the Church. This is my answer for them – and this is the question I have to ask you, though it twists my gut to do it. If I could keep you out of it, I would, you know that! I would dirty my own hands. Yet I am too well known in Winchester. If I set one foot in that place, I will be taken up. So, Brother, all my choices are made. Will you do this for me? Will you pay your debt to me at last?'

He bowed his head and I knelt before him, looking up at his eyes as he rubbed tears from them.

'All right, Dun. I'll do it.'

'Thank you. Skinner? I took your word, but I'll fill a sack with silver if you act for me as well.'

'I am your man, sir,' he said, bringing out his cloth and touching it to himself almost delicately.

I closed my eyes for a moment, feeling some of the weight I carried lift away.

'Very well. Then we three will bring it about.'

I am not proud of that day in the garden. My anger and shame and hurt overwhelmed me. I have always forgiven my enemies, but only when they have been punished.

35

It does sound a terrible thing to have sold a queen into slavery, when I write the words. I cannot defend all I have done, but I will say that when a woman persuades a king to tumble her – with her mother, mind – it does not make her a queen, not in the greater sense. Even if he calls her a queen, she merely sleeps in a king's bed and gives birth to princes. That is all that changes.

Wulfric stayed for a month in Ghent. He tried a score of times to dissuade me, but in that one thing I would not be moved. I could not forgive her.

I waved them off at the end of April, then waited, helplessly. I'd given Wulfric permission to draw on my deposits – telling him where they were and what words he needed to say as his bona fides. It was his task to provide whatever Skinner needed and even to accompany him.

I hated that I had to depend on another for something I'd rather have done myself. I have always been that way. Yet I had not lied. I could not wrap myself like a leper on a summer's day and walk the streets of Winchester. Men and women were too afraid of plague. They would demand to see my face, and then I would have been recognised and snatched up, perhaps to slavery or execution. I did nothing to Edwy's queen she would not have done to me, given the chance.

No news came that summer, though I had letters from Wulfric saying they were watching our bird build her nest. It seemed too that Archbishop Oda was making complaint about my treatment to the Witan, the dear old Dane. Wulfric wanted to wait, to see if Edwy would relent, or be forced to bring me home. My brother was too soft-hearted. Edwy could not be overruled. I had seen his face and known his venom when I laid hands on him. He would not call me back, not while that woman whispered in his ear.

I wrote in fury to tell Wulfric not to delay, that the nest should be struck down. I received no reply and my second year of exile was as dull as the Flemish. It rained almost every day, and when I did receive a letter, it would be read and read a hundred times before I sanded it clear to be used again.

That winter I spent illuminating and drawing mechanical illustrations for a work of Diogenes. That was a comfort to me, as he was a Greek who had been exiled and even sold as a slave, yet made a virtue of needing nothing from the world. I wonder how it must have been to know such men, back when the world was young.

I worked in a little scriptorium with some thirty other monks, all scratching and painting from sunrise to sunset. I used my English silver to pay for new lamps for us as the days became too short, in part because I would have gone mad without work to fill the hours. The monastic life is in repetition and ritual, and it creates a great peace in a man. I could not feel it that year, with all my plans and all my waiting for my brother to find his nerve. I did not fool myself. I knew his softness could undo us all.

As Christmas passed and the new year began, I sent Wulfric a single, stern command, then waited, setting aside new work and instead walking deep into the countryside around the city. I had learned a few words of the Flemish tongue, though I was still mostly a deaf-mute where Latin and Greek were not spoken. It was isolating – and Latin is a cold tongue in some ways. The structure of it seeps into the mind and reorders, I think. I missed the old words, with all their Wessex richness.

In March, a single ship came in from home, showing a

lashed and splintered spar from some storm endured on the grey. I went down to it from the abbey as soon as I heard bells sound. The first one was always an event each year, as it was the herald of work and wealth for the merchant houses. It woke the whole city, just about.

This particular ship was barely bigger than the barges, which might have explained why it was limping into harbour. I was just one of a crowd that gathered, waiting for news or letters, or trade goods they had ordered the previous autumn and waited for all winter.

I had begun to understand some of the words they spoke to one another in their excitement. Yet I stood like a crow amongst those people, dressed in black. I felt their glances alighting on me and sliding away like snowflakes on cold cloth. I was not of them and I wore my dignity like a cloak.

The captain himself stepped across to the dock, if that name is not too grand for the master of such a small craft. He fetched out a bundle of letters and called each one, often collecting a few coins for his trouble. I passed over a couple of silvers and took a single letter away with me. I could feel the cold wrap against my skin as I went.

I could not wait, so I undid the cords and looked for the wyvern crest. Wulfric and I had agreed a different seal for success, a Wessex oak. I sank back against a wall when I saw it, as if I had been struck and lost my wits. My vision swam and I could not see. I hardly dared to open it after so long spent staring, but when I did, it was just three lines.

'The poor bird has gone from our garden. It is a great sin to hurt innocent creatures. I wish we had not.'

Wulfric had not put his name to those lines, though I knew his hand well enough. I felt irritation at his mealy-mouthed regrets. I knew only satisfaction at having brought her low.

I have said I cannot defend all I have done, but as I write,

I feel I should. Slavery was not unknown to me, though the thralls on my father's farms were well treated. I think the truth is that I hated without limit, as a child can wish his parents into the fires of hell.

That is the comparison. When I was six or eight years old and my mother refused some sweet, or smacked me, I would lie in the darkness and clench my fists and wish such vengeance upon her that I thought I would burst my heart. No one hates as a child can hate.

I read those three lines from my brother a hundred times, but I could tease no more meaning from them. I think I ran to my cell in the abbey there, to write my reply. Before I began, I readied my codes and tables, then took a deep breath to calm my nerves, holding out my hands before me. They were steady, I was pleased to see. Yet I knew I had to be careful, that I had to write every word as if it would be read by my worst enemy, aloud, to a vengeful king. With those bonds on me, I composed my answer, the work of an entire day. I was still banished, still in exile. I had not regained my abbey, nor was I bishop of Worcester once again. Yet I knew joy, and I gave thanks.

It seemed at first that Wulfric would not reply to me, as if our business was done. I wrote two letters a day and sent them out on every ship that left for London, but for weeks no response came. In the end, I wrote in clear that I needed to see him once more – and to my astonishment, I received a pert little note from his wife Alice, saying that he wished to hear nothing more from me. As if I would be satisfied with that!

I wrote to my mother for news and included a letter to Wulfric in case his little wife was throwing them in the fire. It was a risk, so I wrote without code and used the most innocent of terms, knowing my mother would not be able to resist running a hot knife under the wax seal. There are ways, if you are curious and have time enough.

Still Wulfric did not answer. My mother wrote back and forth to say she'd handed him the letter and had I heard even in my exile that the queen had vanished? The king was in tatters and believed she had run off with some other man. My mother's indignation was a pleasure to read, so that I hugged her sheets to me and laughed. I knew better, even if my younger brother had turned his face from me.

I settled into my life with a greater sense of peace than I had known before, though I will admit I found Ghent somewhat stifling. I began to make plans to travel to Rome, to see the tomb of St Peter there and the heart of the Church. I had heard of Roman ruins too that intrigued me.

I felt almost free, somehow, with all my responsibilities torn away. I had funds and my health. I was still a monk and a priest – no mere king could cut those knots, once tied. With my vengeance against Elgiva behind me, I was able to look forward at last. It was a rebirth, and I found myself whistling as I worked and planned to see the great centre of Western Christianity. From Rome, Emperor Constantine had spread the true faith across the world, to places of beasts and giants.

I still went to the docks when a new ship came in, though my business then was as bursar for the abbey, to bargain for the best cloth and seamstresses. Abbot Reynault had been impressed with my work and he too seemed to sense a change in my fortunes, my mood, so that he smiled now to see me.

I did not notice Wulfric at first. I was buying a loaf of fresh bread from the market stalls there, when he stepped off a barge and took me by the shoulder.

I turned and felt delight that he had come, at last. I did not understand his pale skin, his frowns and look of strain. I embraced him there, and those who knew me by then all smiled in response, at the sight of such honest affection.

'Brother, I thought I might never see you again,' I said.

'It is not for love of you, Dunstan. We are . . . I do not know how to say it. Walk with me and I will tell you.'

I took my basket in the crook of my arms and walked the streets of the city. I did not worry about being overheard. English was not well known in Ghent, after all.

'Are we betrayed?' I asked him, suspecting the worst from his grim looks.

'We might as well be,' he said. 'I had a letter from one of my suppliers in Dublin. He had no idea of my interest, but he told me the extraordinary news that a slave girl claimed to be the queen — and that she had been believed. We are undone, Brother!'

'Pax, Wulfric. Be calm and tell me all. Was there more?'

'He puts in the small events of the city at the end of his accounts. Murders and raids, usually. It is an old habit with him. Of course, I wrote back immediately, asking for more detail. He said only that he'd heard it in a tavern, that a girl with a brand on her cheek had convinced a family she was the missing queen.'

'She was branded?'

He nodded, looking away.

'They do it when a slave tries to run.'

I breathed out. There were apples in my basket and I offered him one. He would have refused, I could see, but hunger changed his mind. We leaned against a wall together in a quiet road, after looking to see we were not below a window.

'It won't be long before someone offers to bring her back to her husband,' I said. 'Will she know you were involved, Wulfric? Or me?'

'I can't say for certain. She saw my face, but she may not have known me.'

I eyed him, with his one arm and the line of pink scar on his forehead.

'I think she might have heard of you, Wulfric,' I said.

To my surprise, he grabbed me by the front of my robe suddenly, pressing his knuckles painfully into my chest.

'Tell me what to do, Dun! Alice and Cyneryth are all I have. They will not be spared for what we did! If this gets out, if it becomes known . . .'

I saw his desperation. He shook me like a terrier with a rat until I gripped his wrist and pushed him away, my own temper rising to heat at his treatment, no matter the cause.

'Be calm, Brother! Walk with me, before the whole town comes to hear who is shouting.'

I led him further away, into the fields around the city, though some were about as wet as our Glastonbury marsh that year, after all the rains. Still, there was a raised track, so I could be sure we were not overheard.

'Is Skinner around?'

'I know where he has a room with his son, above a foundry.'

'I paid him enough to buy land and live in peace,' I said, almost indignant at the way that man wasted the chances I gave him.

Wulfric shrugged.

'He says he paid his debts. He seems less . . . hunted and better fed. Yet he remains, with that son of his who never speaks.'

'Good. Because you know how this will end, Wulfric. Oh, don't pretend now! You are my brother. If someone comes to threaten you, should I stay quiet? Do you expect me to remain in the shadows while they put your wife and daughter in irons? Will it be you who tells your daughter we could not save her? No, Wulfric. I brought you into this. I will tell you how it must be, now. Give the task to Skinner. Offer to fill his mouth with gold. Where do the ships from Ireland come to shore? The main port.'

'There is more than one, Dunstan. There must be a score of fishing ports where they could land.'

'They won't try to hide,' I said gently. 'If your friend is right, they'll take her to Dublin and then to Winchester or London. The Irish will hope for whatever reward she promised, so they won't sneak about like thieves. If that witch has persuaded them, they'll come like glad hounds at her side.'

'Bristol then, perhaps. Yes, I'd say Bristol. God, how can we be sure?'

'Don't blaspheme, Wulfric! I will pray and they will come to us. Skinner will do whatever has to be done. Ireland was not far enough before. Perhaps he'll put her on a ship to Greece. There are many slaves there – and they do not speak her tongue. Yes, that is what we should do.'

I stared into my brother's eyes, wondering if he understood. Knowing is not a simple thing, like a torch lit or dark. A man can hear something, but want so desperately not to understand it, that it is gone, in a breath, like frost by a fire. We are a valley of shadows, I sometimes think. No one knows how far down we go.

For me, I felt my course was clear. I might have wished to walk a different path, but I could not go back and make a better choice. No. All I could do at that moment was save Wulfric and his little family.

I saw the relief in him as he passed the worry onto my shoulders. I think he did understand the king's whore could not be allowed to reach her husband once again. All our lives were forfeit if she did. It was a tragedy worthy of ancient Greece in the end. Each step took me deeper into regret, but I could not turn away and let Wulfric and his dear wife and child be destroyed.

I had begun that path to answer an injury to the Church. I pressed on to protect my brother and his child. I suppose the most terrible events can be woven from honest threads. An evil man would have ordered her killed and spared himself the worry and the work. I tell you, it was my own kind nature that pulled me into that sucking marsh – and once I was in, I could not escape.

I wrote my letter to Skinner, including a handful of coins as proof of my intention. I had paid him before and I promised to make him a rich man, if he completed the work. As I took Wulfric back to the docks, I reminded him to have bags by the door, to be ready to run with his family, if our plans went wrong.

I wanted to go with him, but I had seen what happened to a man returned from banishment, when Leofa was killed, years before. Fate was a fickle woman – that much we knew. Wulfric promised to pray each night and write when it was over. All I had done was take command and give my blessing, but that was enough. I had made his decision for him, taken the burden. I waited then, left behind. Alone, in Ghent.

I heard nothing for months as my third year of exile wore on – and wore at me like a whetstone drawn over my skin. It did not sit easily to have events unfold without my eye on them! Skinner knew his letters – as a forger, he'd learned them early, of course. Yet I dared not write to him, even if I'd known where to send it. As a scorching summer baked the monastery, I still did not know if Wulfric had been taken, so that I might expect soldiers to come for me, or perhaps that he had been killed. For all I knew, Skinner was singing in a cell, telling King Edwy that Father Dunstan was behind it all.

I gave up my previous thoughts of visiting Rome. The Dunstan who had dreamed of seeing ancient temples was lost to worry. I bit my fingernails until they bled. I picked at my toenails as well when I lay down, until they were taken with such swellings and pus that I could hardly walk. I spent some time with the herbalist then, preparing poultices and using a fine pair of shears to cut my nails. They had no forge of their own in that abbey, but there was a first-rate smith on the outskirts of the city. He spoke neither English nor Latin nor Greek, unfortunately, while I could only ask the simplest of questions about his health.

The letter that came at last was from my mother. She had sealed it with the symbol of a Wessex oak, but I had no idea if she knew it meant victory or disaster. I opened it with shaking hands and read.

It had not gone well. Skinner and his son had hired an old soldier to attend them. I don't suppose Skinner had explained in much detail – and I knew his son had not. The three of them had spotted the lady in question, branded on the cheek as a thrall, just as we'd been told. The queen stepped off that boat from Dublin with two men. She'd walked like a free woman despite the brand, without even a rope on her. Skinner had followed them away from the docks at Bristol, where there had been too many witnesses. They'd kept them in sight as far as a lonely stretch of road, not far from Gloucester, some miles inland.

The two men with Elgiva had not given her up without a fight. Yet Skinner knew how to cut and the soldier was an old hand. The Irish had been down in moments. Of course, the queen began to scream for help. It seemed the soldier had put a knife in her as well, in his panic. In return, Skinner cut the fellow's throat and then he and his boy ran, just raced away into the woods before they found themselves hanged by a mob or taken by the local reeve.

Skinner and his son had lived like wild things for days while bands of men from the port searched for the murderers, yet never found them. I wish I could say such grisly deeds were rare, but the roads are dangerous and always have been. Man is a fallen creature, born of sin. The wonder is when we are more, not less than our natures. Wolves can be cruel and so can we, but only man raises cathedrals and paints in gold.

It took over a month for the pair to make their way back

to London, with Skinner hot with fever and exhaustion when he reached the shop. He'd crawled through a ditch, my mother said. Some brackish water had got into his open face and swelled it to a great yellow boil.

My mother and Alice had treated him and heard the whole story. I was not pleased at that. It was not that I thought Wulfric or I were in danger; more that a boy of any age likes his mother to be proud of him. I could read her disappointment in every line, her dismay and her hurt. She had been delighted in me before, when I was made abbot, bishop, treasurer. All of that had been taken. All of that was gone.

I read the letter a dozen times. Then I put the cursed thing in the fire, took up my purse of silver coins and went into town to drink myself to oblivion. I do not remember much of the night, though I had been badly beaten when I awoke in a gutter, without a single coin left. I might have frozen to death and it would have been my ending. Perhaps I would have welcomed it in that moment.

The news reached London that the lost queen had been found. King Edwy rode to where her body had been wrapped and had her brought to a church nearby. I heard he spent the evening with her, brandy in hand, with candles burning.

They found him creaking on a rope in the morning, his life gone from the world, his soul gone to hell. It was another month before I heard the news from Wulfric's shaking hand. I wrote one last letter, to King Edgar, then collected my small bag of belongings, bade farewell to Abbot Reynault and made my way down to the docks. I turned my back on Ghent and went home. I will admit I wept when I saw the white cliffs once more. I am not ashamed of that.

36

I'd seen King Edwy crowned; I saw him buried, three years after. I did not think I'd be in time to witness his funeral, though I hurried back and we had fair summer winds blowing west along the Channel. I wonder now if the Almighty aided my return, so I could stand unabashed before all those toad-eating lickspittles who remembered me. They knew only too well how I'd left them and in what state. I could see it in their eyes and in their flushed faces as I came in and took my place. No one dared say a word about my banishment. You may be sure there was no cruel laughter as the screen closed and the sacred mysteries began.

I was not used to being in the congregation in those days, blind to the Mass. At least I could understand the Latin, denied to many of those in that cathedral. I did not need the sound of bells to know when to kneel and pray. I thanked God for my deliverance, like Jonah from the Whale, like Joseph from slavery.

Edwy had lain for weeks in a chilled crypt while Archbishop Oda argued with other bishops as to whether they could give a Christian burial to a hanged man. The strain of it wore at the archbishop and he fell ill with a summer cold that reduced him terribly. He was delighted to see me, but I saw how he had aged in the years of my exile. It shocked me, somehow, as if I'd expected them all to remain exactly as I remembered them.

I imagine Edwy's body was beginning to turn, by the end. The solution was a hard-nosed Wessex compromise, of course. He was a king, after all. No one mentioned the manner of his death and we chose not to recall it, or make note of it in the parish record.

King Edwy was buried in hallowed ground, rather than outside the churchyard wall as perhaps he should have been. The rules are not the same for kings as for ordinary men. I might add that his brother Edgar made huge donations to the Church. It is not the first time such a thing has gone on. It will not be the last. Suicide is a mortal sin, but judgement lies beyond, not in this world.

When the funeral Mass had been said and the 'smells and bells' were at an end, I came out into the sunshine and just breathed. I filled my lungs with air my ancestors had known for as long as the world had lived.

'That was a fine service, father,' came a voice.

I jumped a little, so lost in thought had I been. King Edgar had come out and I tried to look surprised, as though I had not waited for the right moment and done my very best to be seen as he left. He was sixteen or seventeen then, as blond as his father had been, with broadening shoulders. His eyes were clear, his breath sweet. He looked more at peace than I remembered.

'I will pass that on to Archbishop Oda,' I said with a smile. 'I hope you are not offended I am here, Your Highness? I wanted to show your brother's soul I had forgiven any slight, any injury against the Church. I wanted it to be seen that I did not scorn him in the end.'

It was fine, high-minded commentary and he seemed pleased by it.

'I will have the Witan rescind your banishment, when we meet tomorrow. I would have sent for you, Dunstan, before the month was out. I know what my brother did. Believe me, I have heard every detail of his cruelty – and that of his wife. Well, they have their answer.'

I began to protest and he held up a hand to speak over me.

'I know, father, I should not say such things. God judges

at the gates, not before. Yet there is a part of me that thinks he would not look kindly on those who bruise his bishop, his abbot. My brother . . . was a cruel boy.' A shadow came across his face and I wondered what he recalled to make him frown so. 'He barely lived long enough to become a cruel man. I should pretend I am bereft, but the truth is I feel only relief.'

There were tears in his eyes and I did not know whether I believed him. The ties of blood run deep, as I know only too well. In my desire to witness the funeral, I had not yet gone to see Wulfric. Yet I knew London lay in my path and I almost feared what I would find there, what our schemes had done to him.

It is odd, is it not? When victory is absolute, it brings a sense almost of dread. Great fortune only makes us more afraid of the reverse. I will say that prayer is the balm in such a case. God does not like pride, but prayer will ease the wound.

'I wish I could have been here, Your Highness. I spoke for you first in the Witan. I knew even then that you would be a great king, just like your father Edmund before you.'

'I . . . do not remember him,' Edgar said. 'Not more than a few moments.'

He looked at me in sudden thought, tilting his head. His guards had come out and the congregation milled around on the street, unwilling to go home while the king stood there. Yet it was just the two of us.

'Walk with me, father, would you? I would like to hear the stories you used to tell about him. You were about the same age, were you not?'

He walked alongside and the crowd parted before us as we walked down the hill to the river. I had done the same with his father Edmund and I described that day, which seemed to bring some small pleasure.

While the capital rushed and hurried around us all afternoon, I told that young man everything I could remember about his father and his uncles Eadred and Æthelstan. It seemed to ease some tension in him – and the strange result was that I became calm myself in the retelling. I kept my secrets, of course, but it served to remind me of all the things I had made and created in the world. Glastonbury Abbey was just the finest of them. I made a point of describing the labour and the personal fortune I had inherited and then spent on that site, only to see it given away to Caspar.

Edgar stopped by the river, staring out at the barges and small boats bobbing, all laden with goods. I was thirty-seven years old and he was twenty years younger, but I did not smile when he rested a hand on my shoulder. He had grown tall and he was, in that moment, the king unchallenged. We all knew the realm was his, from coast to coast. The Witan had endured three years of his brother for their foolishness. They had the chance to put it right.

'You have been ill-used, father,' Edgar said at last. 'So I give you my oath, as king: I will make amends. If I return your abbey to you, will you run wild?'

'No, Your Highness. I have learned peace.'

'Then I will put my seal to an order making you abbot this day. My father's tomb needs its guardian, father. You will be restored to your old offices, such as lie within my power. There will be another Witan in October. Come to that, as my guest. I will make further amends then for your cruel treatment.'

His hand fell from me. I knelt and rejoiced.

My years in Ghent seemed another life as autumn came. It has been my curse that I must remember all, so I cannot say they faded. Yet I was able to put them aside, as a door closed on the past. I made mistakes. All men sin, of course. The difference between us is that I worked for years afterwards to make restitution.

Trees flamed red, gold and brown across the country. For once, there was no news of an invasion. It was cold very early that year and the frosts spread quickly, snatching the old and the young in their beds. Still, we knew the Vikings would come in the spring. They always did.

King Edgar was busy grinding ploughshares into swords in London, establishing his presence there after three years of his brother. It was Edgar's decision to assemble the Witan in Bradford the next month, in the territories of York. He was happiest in the north, with people he knew and understood. It is not a small thing to know a man is yours, to know how he thinks.

I attended the Witan as Edgar had asked. He honoured me in front of men who would have been kings in a previous generation, but were his great lords instead. They applauded when Edgar confirmed me as abbot. More, they voted me a bishopric, though there was not one ready. My old place as bishop of Worcester had been taken up by an elderly fellow. There was a suggestion he would never last another winter, that he was on his last legs. It was an exciting time.

Of course, Archbishop Oda would have to confirm any appointment, but he and I were old friends. Edgar went out of his way to raise me in front of thanes and earls, to undo the hurt his brother Edwy had caused. As the trees flamed brightest and leaves began to fall, I felt a great knot of worry uncoil in my chest. I had come through dark years and I was home, among my people. I was honoured where I had been despised, praised where I had been scorned. Such things should not matter to a man of God, but I confess they did to me.

After the Witan had proclaimed him king of all England, Edgar's first task was to be seen all across the south, to show the people of Wessex and London that they had another son of Edmund to rule them. At the same time, he was learning about a realm he hardly remembered from his childhood. He was the king of the north. He knew Vikings better than his own people, some said of him.

While that went on, I made my peace with Wulfric and persuaded him to come with me to Glastonbury, in memory of our childhood. I found him bruised of eye, morose and afraid of nameless punishment. I saw his hand trembled and his head ached most days, causing him to groan and curse. He was always the weaker of us. I told his wife Alice a month or so in the old abbey would be a holiday for him, almost, a break from his labours. Wulfric had not been able to put the events of those grim years behind him, perhaps because he'd been closer than I had.

I saw my mother there, in the rooms above the shop, up above that creaking old staircase. So much was the same; so much was not. She looked at me with great sadness, until I felt anger for her. While she mopped at tears and tried to take my hands, I refused to talk about my exile. I would not dwell on what we had done and threatened to leave when she tried. I was home, that was what mattered! I was once more an abbot and a bishop, though I'd heard nothing about royal treasurer. I could continue my work and I would find a way to absolve myself from sins committed. I only hoped it would not take as great a work as the abbey of Glastonbury.

She could not remain angry with me and I did mutter that I was sorry to have disappointed her. I was not sorry, not really, but I remember my last sight of my father and my regret that I did not say more. It had influenced me in dealing with my mother since then. I thought each time might be the last and so I comforted her and promised her whatever she needed to hear. I mention it because one time was the last. I held her hands and kissed her cheek. She died the following night, passing peacefully in her sleep. I read the eulogy, though the bishop of London conducted the service. I miss her still.

Wulfric and I took three days on horseback to reach Winchester, then two more until we stood by the bridge across the marsh, with mists lying thick and white. Three servants had come with us, laden down with all my tools. Apart from that, it could have been the day of our first visit. It was hard not to think of my father and the little boat, with Wulfric bounding off ahead.

I looked at him, at the changes time and injury had made. He seemed more bowed down than I remembered. There were tears in his eyes as he looked out, perhaps in mine too.

'Come on, Brother,' I said, gripping his shoulders in a great hug.

We walked together across the bridge, hearing it creak. Our servants brought the horses behind, the sound of hooves echoing strangely.

At the far side, we entered the grounds of the abbey through a well-made gate of oak, still yellow. I could only stare at the changes that had been wrought in my absence. The gardens were stripped for winter, but the beds were once more laid out in perfect rows. A new wall of flint and brick stood twenty feet high and three thick, with alcoves for beehives, sheltered from the winter's cold. Apple trees stood in stark rows, with barrows and sheds and tilled soil showing black and frost.

There were monks in dark robes and one of them saw us open the gate and came over. I did not know him and I saw him take in my tonsure and black wool.

'Are you expected, b-brother?' he asked.

I smiled at him.

'Do you not give names now in greeting? Are we to be strangers?'

The young man coloured and stammered in reply.

'I'm sorry. I am P-Peter.'

I decided not to give him my name.

'Well, Brother Peter, perhaps you would fetch Abbot Caspar for me, would you? I am on the king's business.'

He looked dubious, but left us to do as I had bidden him. I cannot say exactly how my feelings ran then. I had entertained myself with fiery imaginings, of kicking Caspar all around the yard for taking my abbey. Yet I felt I had grown wiser in my exile, somehow, as all men will. It had matured me and I showed no great triumph as Caspar appeared at last, though he made me wait too long. His eyes widened in a very satisfying manner, however.

'We have a new king,' I said.

'I see,' he replied. His eyes flickered to Wulfric and the servants. He understood.

It was a moment to be dignified, and for once, I saw it coming before it had passed.

'Can you serve, brother?' I asked him. 'I am to be abbot once again, by royal appointment, though it does not sit well with me that our service of God can be given like a jewel.'

To my pleasure, Caspar went down onto one knee and bowed his head.

'God favours you, Father Abbot. I do not always comprehend his plans, but I bend before his will.'

Perhaps there was a little spite in me, for the man who had not refused the abbey I had built.

'And will you put aside your wife? I mean to follow the Rule of St Benedict here.'

I saw his jaw clench.

'I . . . cannot. You can't ask me to just . . .'

I shook my head. 'Then I release you from your vows, Caspar of Glastonbury. Make your trade in the town, or work here, as a member of the laity. You cannot be monk and husband.'

He was white with anger as he rose, but I took no pleasure in my victory. I could only regret the mistakes I had made before. I made the sign of the cross in the air and he sagged as if something had been drawn from him.

I swept past Caspar, calling to the young monk who had met us.

'Come along, Wulfric. Brother Peter. Show me the way to the abbot's rooms. You will have to store the belongings of Abbot Caspar for him.'

Brother Peter seemed to have lost the power of speech. He continued to stammer and I thought at first it was panic, until it went on too long. I rolled my eyes at that. I have known a few so afflicted. They require a patience I do not have.

When Wulfric and I had overseen our goods and chattles being unpacked, we went to the church proper and knelt. I was home. I was back.

The bishop of Worcester died that winter, which made me rejoice. I was appointed to the bishopric I had known before and I felt my coin had fully turned, that all my ill fate had been reversed. Yet before we saw spring, Archbishop Oda was taken with a great spasm, so that his face sagged and he could not breathe. He must have been sixty, so it was not a surprise. I am told it was not too hard, in the end. They found a dozen flasks of glass and pewter in his rooms, all filled with some strange aqua vitae. It seemed the old Dane had liked a drink more than I'd known.

I waited, recalling that King Edgar had said he would put right all the wrongs against me, that he would make amends. I did not know whether to hope or not. I concerned myself with the abbey and the services, yet I waited each day of winter silence to hear news of the greater kingdom and my own star risen.

I was to be disappointed that year. Perhaps Edgar thought

me too young, or perhaps he had other favours to return as well as the one to me, who had given him his kingdom. I had done more than anyone to unite England once more, but in fairness, that was not an argument I could make.

I had to be patient, and when Aelfsige, bishop of Winchester, was chosen, I took heart from the fact that he was not a young man either. I did not grow resentful I had been passed over. I knew I enjoyed the clear and public favour of a very young king. My turn would come.

An archbishop raises priests to be bishops, but in turn, he is raised by the pope himself in Rome. A pallium is placed upon his shoulders as a mark of favour – a great cloak of extraordinary beauty. I confess I looked forward to seeing it. I waved goodbye to Bishop Aelfsige somewhat enviously. He would see Rome before me.

I was wrong about that, as it happens. He froze to death in the Alps. It was spring before his poor servants made it home again, and by then, Edgar was busy with the north, though having more success than most of us had expected. There was no Viking invasion that year, perhaps because the lords of the north did not call them in, though they always denied such whispers. Edgar went to York to charm them and remind them he was as much Mercian as he was Wessex, as much York as London. It seemed to have an effect. He had a gentle manner, but he always managed to get his way even so. It was a rare ability, as he was a rare king.

I found myself almost disappointed as no news came of an attack. I'd grown used to the raids on the north, the Olafs, the Anlafs and Sweins. It seemed strange to hear tales of peace. Edgar was the high king and perhaps the northern lords had glimpsed chaos when he'd ruled alongside his brother. Perhaps they saw at last that England might survive us all, not just as a motley collection of small kingdoms, but as a great realm, from sea to sea.

Edgar returned to Winchester by the end of summer. He had been burnished by the sun and a life of hunts and feasts. He looked even more like his father. When I asked to see the king, I was not left to wait and chafe for a week. He made it easy, another sign of his regard for me that year.

I came to what was for Edgar almost a private meal, with just four other lords and a small table. They all stood to greet me and Edgar raised a cup in my honour, letting all there know I was in his favour still. A great fire crackled away and wine flowed without restraint. I tried not to beam too obviously, but if you'd recently spent three years in Ghent, you would have been delighted as well.

'I was telling my lord Immin here about the last Witan at York, father. If those men keep their word, perhaps we won't be called to ride out this year.'

'I pray for peace, Your Highness,' I said, applying myself to a roast chicken.

'Yet I should be crowned, father. There is that. The lords of the north may call me king today, but if I go too long without a crown, they will squabble and fall out, I know it. I wanted it to be Oda, who crowned my father, I really did.'

I put the chicken down, my stomach tightening in anticipation.

'Now that Archbishop Oda has gone from us,' he went on, 'and poor Aelfsige was overcome by the winter blast, I have another choice in mind.'

I tried not to smile, which was fortunate.

'Father Dunstan, I wanted to ask you about Bishop Byrthelm. He is most senior bishop now that Aelfsige has died. What do you know of him? Would you give your blessing to Byrthelm as archbishop of Canterbury?'

I took a drink of wine to give me time to think. I barely knew the man, even by reputation. I'd heard of him as an amiable sort and struggled to find a way to turn that against him.

'I know him, Your Highness, of course. Byrthelm is much loved in the Church. He is said to be a kind and decent man, generous with his time and unstinting in his devotion.' I had it. 'It is said of him, Your Highness, that he forgives almost before a sinner can repent. He gives and gives of himself to the point of exhaustion, shaming his priests by his charity and good works.'

I had judged it finely, I thought. The king's open expression had developed a line on his brow as he considered my words.

'Father, does a bishop not have to command respect? Must he not be stern in the faith, as well as kind in it? Please understand me, I do not mock his good qualities, but if you recall, Archbishop Oda was an iron hand with wayward priests.'

The eyes of everyone at that table were on me. I found myself flushing, but it was as if I was uncomfortable discussing another man, as if I knew his weaknesses but sought to excuse them. It was, I think, superb.

'I . . . have heard some of his priests are a little lax in their work, my lord, yes, but Bishop Byrthelm forgives them their shortcomings, as a shepherd must forgive his errant sheep. He turns the other cheek, Your Highness. I cannot fault him for being too forgiving in Christ's example.'

'No . . . no, of course not,' Edgar said, but the gleam of his announcement had gone from him, replaced by a frown. 'I will think further on it, father. Perhaps there are others.'

I sought to change the subject and he had given me an opportunity.

'My lord, I know you will wear your father's crown, but I have some small craft with metal. I wonder if I might be the one to remake it for you. It would be a great honour.'

Only the fire crackled for a moment. I had seen before how weary a king became of being asked. No doubt Edgar had already experienced a thousand different friends working themselves up to some request or other that only he could grant. It must have been tiresome, but of course my offer was for him. I knew my own skills – and I knew I could make a crown that actually looked like one. As he gazed across at me, no one dared to speak until I went on.

'I . . . could keep your father's crown, but make it . . . more, make it a symbol of a high king of all England.'

He made the decision quickly, just as his father used to do. I could see Edmund in him and it almost brought tears to my eyes.

'Very well, Dunstan,' he said. 'Make me a crown.'

I do not know how long King Edgar considered Bishop Byrthelm before he ruled against him. Perhaps he made up his mind that evening, or perhaps he sent men to learn more of Byrthelm and decided he did indeed lack the stern dignity an archbishop must have. I imagine I was in his mind then as he looked around. I had stood for him in the Witan. His brother had beaten me and banished me. There was a debt there. Perhaps that was it, or perhaps I was simply the best man he had.

King Edgar came to Glastonbury that winter, as a penitent, with only a few servants. He ate with the monks in the refectory and attended the services. We did not ask him to rise in the small hours, but he was willing.

I showed him the sketches I had made for his crown. The materials alone would cost eight hundred pounds, and he only said he would examine them further. I showed him too our scriptorium, where monks laboured by day and night to copy works that would have been lost. Our task was first to worship God, second to preserve. If it is not exposed to damp or mould, vellum lasts an age, but we had copies of ancient works there, three or four thousand years old, each page cracking as it was turned. Our worship was in the work, in the beauty, in the peace of hundreds of hours.

Edgar saw the quiet discipline of our abbey. He saw our gardens and heard our hymns. He stayed a week with us and, at the end, he asked me to be archbishop of Canterbury. My abbey won it for me, I think, in the end.

Like Aelfsige before, I would be going to Rome to collect my pallium from the hands of Pope John XII. As I wept and thanked the blushing king, I reminded myself to wrap up warm for the journey.

37

I travelled to dear Roma overland, though it was hard going. I considered a route by sea, around Spain and through the Pillars of Hercules, as I believe they are known. Yet in the end, I chose dangers I knew over dangers I did not. I could bring thick cloaks and blankets to cross the Alps, but at sea, I had no control over my fate. No matter how I prepared, I could still be taken by pirates or a storm.

King Edgar had returned the lands of Glastonbury Abbey to me. I passed them once again into the care of my brother Wulfric as prepositus, or steward. I hoped the old wealth and influence would bring him contentment. I had asked if Wulfric wanted to accompany me to Rome, but he refused, saying he preferred to remain at home and devote himself to his family. My brother had become a quieter, less vital man after my exile. He and Alice never had another child.

Unlike poor Bishop Aelfsige, I waited until the year was well advanced before charging across Gaul and up through the high mountain passes. We felt the cold, I will not deny it. Yet the road remained clear and there was only a little snow.

I saw neat rows of graves up on the heights, poor lost travellers buried under mounds of stone with no markers. I prayed at them all, though briefly, then rushed down onto the great plains of the north, as Hannibal had done before me. We had asses and mules with us to bear the weight of our goods, though they were lightly burdened on the way out. My intention was to use some of the gold I had brought with me to purchase works of great rarity. There could be no better source than Rome, I was certain. I hoped for another piece of the True Cross, or perhaps a bone from one of the apostles.

I confess I was caught by surprise at the way the sun scorched us. I had known hot summers before, but in Italy I understood why the old legions marched a mere twenty-five miles a day, even on good roads. The heat was a trial and we were always parched, it seemed, so that we had to stop at all hours to fill our bottles or let our gasping beasts drink. We learned early on not to cross a stream without dipping our beaks to drink of it.

In the evenings, I read aloud from my volume of Virgil, or Cicero or Livy, or declaimed from memory. I could recite thousand-line sections of the *Iliad* and I did so, to the delight of my servants as we made our way south. In those places, I met the ancient peoples – I saw history written in their noble faces, their wide, peasant smiles. It was a joyous time. More than once a great crowd gathered, though it was more for novelty rather than to gain true learning from the greats. Still, I recited for them, beginning to wonder how such minds could have come from among their number.

Ah, Rome! That city is the ornament of my life, the brooch upon my sleeve. I came into the outskirts of it after three months on the road – and I stayed a year. I saw the columns of the Temple of Saturn, the great senate house where Caesar sat and debated. I saw the Colosseum, which was taller than the great tower of my abbey. I went to the Pantheon, with its extraordinary dome that was a wonder all on its own and held me transfixed before it. There was a man there who told me the dome formed a sphere that would graze the floor on which I stood. I paid him a silver penny and felt I had the better of the bargain.

With two hefty lads in tow to keep me safe, for Rome could be a little rough on the unwary traveller, I wandered through the forum and over Capitoline Hill, retracing the steps of Caesar's murderers as they left Pompey's theatre and walked back to the senate house, holding up their bloody hands in triumph. I can hardly describe the awe I felt to be in that place, to feel that sun on my skin, to smell that ancient air.

I presented myself at the glorious Lateran Palace on Caelian Hill when I first arrived, though it was some time before Pope John was ready to receive me. His cardinals arranged it all, visiting me in my lodgings and explaining the manners and the rules of meeting their master. In the end, they seemed to assume I would be so overwhelmed as to remember nothing of what they had said, so I was bustled in and whispered at.

I knelt to receive the pallium cloak of an archbishop and kissed the gold ring held out to me, the ring of St Peter. Pope John raised me up and invited me to lunch with him. His cardinals did not seem pleased at that, but the dear man waved them away like wasps.

I liked him. He was no fainting cleric, but had led men in war to reclaim papal land. His grip was certainly that of a soldier, as mine was of the forge. I have heard since that the fellow sometimes visited a widow in the city, though he was discreet. Well, I too am a sinner.

There seemed to be a great deal of bustle around Pope John, so that dishes of food were whisked in and away again with barely time to dip a spoon. Perhaps I was a trifle dazed to be meeting the direct representative of Christ on Earth, the descendant of the Fisherman of Galilee, I don't know. I actually remember very little of the lunch and it was over much too soon.

Pope John wished me luck and long life. I kissed the ring again as he dabbed his mouth with a white cloth, then finally allowed his cardinals to move him on to whatever task they had in store for him. I was left alone for a time, staring around me at statues in bronze and marble, lost in wonder. Rome was vivid, somehow, with colours that glowed red and brown and full of life. It was a city of eternal autumn, perhaps.

I visited the tomb of St Peter in the crypt of the cathedral built in his name. That was a fine stone building, I saw, the equal of my abbey. I noted the pointed arches of windows and wondered what else I had been forced to conceive on my own, that might simply have been told. I wonder sometimes what we have lost over the centuries.

The best of us add something to the knowledge of man, but they do not keep it to themselves, like those master masons. I made some sketches of the dome of the Pantheon, which I knew no one would believe when I returned home. Even now, I cannot imagine mortar strong enough to hold the weight of itself. That is the way of things, of course. Iron rusts and great minds are dimmed through the generations. The world knew giants once. I hope we will again.

I lived as a Benedictine for part of that year, though I took rooms when I travelled beyond the city. I must have walked a thousand miles, either as a monk alone, or if I wanted company, with my servants alongside like disciples. I saw the Via Appia and followed it south to Vesuvius, where the ash had settled into mud and stone and buried ancient towns a thousand years before. To stand there was to know Spartacus had hidden on the slopes of the volcano, that Roman galleys had rowed up and down that sea, under that sun. My skin darkened like a peasant and I learned to like the rough wine they made. It was a simpler life, but it was not mine.

It was not too many months before both my imagination and my hands began to itch. My conscience was like one of the beggar children who tugged at my sleeve and asked for coins. That little voice spoke of home, of duty, of a king's trust. I was archbishop of Canterbury, responsible for twenty bishops – and who knew how many priests. I was their shepherd, and yet I had lost myself in glories of the old world, not the new one. I felt the sting of that when I understood it. That night, I bought and drank a fat skin of red wine, warmed through by the sun. I felt tears streaming down my face as I finished it and I wiped angrily at them, leaving trails of dust.

My hands itched because they were idle, which in itself became a torment. When the seasons turned to autumn and winter, my wandering life became less pleasant. A black robe is cold when it gets wet. It slaps at the legs and chafes the knees raw in just a few miles.

My servants and I took a boat to the ancient island of Capri, where Augustus and Tiberius had palaces, high on the hill. The day was cold and while the others shivered, I found myself bracing against the wind on a hilltop, closing my eyes and tasting salt in the air. I needed to go home. I understood it then.

When I look back, that year too has parts I do not recall, which is a strange thing for me. I wonder if somehow grief or shame dulled my senses. Death is a part of life, I knew that well enough. I had lost friends and those I loved, my mother, my father. I had endured blisters and storms that cracked thunder and lightning across the hills around me, while I sat and watched the sheer majesty of God's creation. I took such things home with me, but I could not recall the name of the town where I stayed, or how I had reached that place.

I returned to Rome to collect my belongings and retrieve the asses and mules. They were rather more heavily laden than they had been before, I will admit. I'd spent every last penny I'd brought, so that we had to hold begging bowls on the return journey, just to eat.

When you are accompanied by three servants and mules groaning under the weight of statues and books, asking for alms becomes quite the challenge. We starved for most of that journey, but there was always cold, clean water, and I endured.

Once more I waited for spring to be established before I crossed the Alps. There were blizzards up there that beat at us, so we could hardly see the pass at all. I wanted to tell my servants that Julius Caesar must have known the same route when he set out to conquer Gaul for Rome, but they were surly with me by then and I said nothing.

I arrived home in the year of our Lord 962, sailing into Portsmouth on a fine day, with the sky as blue as Tuscany. I had to give a fine bronze as the price of our passage, which irritates me now.

Somehow, I felt almost a stranger in Wessex, with my dark skin and the dust of a thousand miles in every crack and crevice I owned. I went first to Glastonbury, where I was greeted with some affection. I took enough silver from our bursar to pay my servants what they were owed. From there, we went to Winchester, heavy with gifts. The king was in the north, however, so I prevailed upon my men to escort me further, which they did with no good grace at all.

I put down my packs and bags in Canterbury, in the county of Kent, where Caesar landed, where Augustine brought the faith back to these islands. The cathedral was empty and still that day. Intricate beams formed the ceiling high above and I could hear bats squeaking. In all, it was a fine wooden building.

As I stood there, with the colours of Rome behind my eyes whenever I closed them, I knew I could raise it higher and in stone. I would build a great cathedral, with a dome and an apse at one end. I saw it all, as another St Peter's. In that moment, I sank to my knees and gave thanks. I had looked for the forgiveness of my sins and I had wandered lost for a time. In Canterbury, I had my answer. I had found my third great work.

King Edgar had married the daughter of the earl of Strath-clyde, so I heard on my return. It was not a union of love, but of influence and land. I do not believe they had ever met before Edgar made her his wife. Like his brother, perhaps Edgar felt the shadow of his father's short reign hanging over him. By the time I returned, his wife Fæltha was heavy with child and consumed with the desire to suck a piece of coal she carried in a cloth. It stained the side of her mouth and she made such a performance of her discomfort that I took against her, a little.

Perhaps I was still raw from memories of the last queen. Poor harmless Fæltha died in childbirth, not three months after I had returned from Rome. She gave a son to her husband, for which we blessed her memory, but honestly, in retrospect, she was a very plain woman.

Edgar wore black and would not hunt for a month, but I think it was more for the look of the thing rather than true grief. Who knows, though, really, the heart of a king? We live in the midst of death, as I have always said. It is why we carve skulls on doorknobs and posts and the walking sticks of old men. We see death in the loss of sweet daughters and wives and fathers and old friends. Yet the world does not end, even in our grief. The sun comes up, the spring returns – and other families risk all their happiness to bring life into this vale of tears.

The young prince Edward was as blond as his father and grandfather. His nurse was a great fat slattern of a woman, but she was amply provided with milk. Looking at her, I would have thought a full-grown calf would not have gone hungry. She had no teeth at all and when she wanted a baby to feed, she would shriek 'Grip it, grip it!' and make a face remarkably like the features of a young child, folding in on itself until I feared she would disappear entirely.

I saw the little prince at intervals, but my new duties had me rising at dawn and working deep into the night. I found I could survive on two sleeps of two hours for six weeks at a time, but had then to lie abed for almost a full day to recover. Sleep! It has always been mine enemy. I detest it as I detest the devil. We are given so little time and yet made to waste part of it senseless and snoring.

On the one hand, I was archbishop of Canterbury, with bishops under me who had to be met and examined closely for error. There were too many priests to see – I felt they were like chickens, there were so many. There were accounts to judge and expenditure to examine. I removed three men from their bishoprics and had them flogged. One I sent to his relatives, two were banished. They confessed their sins when I sat in the quiet with them, with their guilt spilling out as if it had been held by straw. I forgave them, but excommunicated them also. King's officers took them to the coast.

I made a point of beginning with that show of my authority, so that I would not have to do it all again. I had learned that much from King Edgar. Yet my true labours were with the abbeys, such places of slackness, lust and sheer sloth as you would not believe. I had not known what a shining beacon Glastonbury had become among them, compared to the rest.

Even as I engaged Brother Justin to design my cathedral in Canterbury, I set out to visit each of eighty monasteries and abbeys in the kingdom – though barely half were communities worthy of the name. I saw monks and priests living with their wives – and many who were not their wives. I dismissed twelve score of men from whatever vows they claimed to have taken – and you may believe they did not all go quietly! I made the mistake only once of thinking my pallium protected me, on which occasion I was almost killed by a baying mob. I see their red mouths still, as they roared and surrounded me and brandished sticks. They were not so brave when I asked the king for help. He sent forty armed men to my side and I returned like Christ in the temple, scattering their tables!

I cleaned a stable that Hercules might have recognised, a great steaming pile of ordure and sin that I could not endure. I thought it was the labour of a lifetime, to make every abbey in England follow the Rule of St Benedict. Perhaps that was my fourth great work, I do not know.

By all accounts, King Edgar kept himself as busy as I was. He was concerned with keeping the realm safe and rode each year into the far north for three or four months at a time. Fully half his Witan councils were held in York or beyond, so that the old kings of Alba could come and heed his words. He was a clever and subtle man, was Edgar. He preferred to talk and discuss, though he could be ruthless if he needed to.

If news came of a raid, even if it was just a single boat with a few men creeping in, looking for gold cups and virgins, he would answer it. His reeves and thanes across the country knew he would forgive them a great deal – but not if he heard they'd ignored a call of that kind. If they had only six servants, they were expected to ride out in arms. A single bonfire on a hill might bring forty or sixty men from miles around. It helped to bring us peace, I think, that we came so quickly with iron in our hands.

Edgar seemed to spend his life riding north and south and everywhere his fancy took him. Every king I have known has taken a court and a council around the country. It is the only way to remind some folk they are ruled at all. Yet I swear Edgar was never out of the saddle. He and his most dangerous thanes were all whip-thin, like the hunting hounds he took out whenever a good stag or a boar was reported. For news like that, the king would pay a gold coin, so half the country kept a lookout for him – either for Vikings or for deer.

On one such trip, the king cornered a pack of wolves against a fallen tree they could not leap. He'd been roaring and galloping after them, and suddenly there they were, jumping right at his horse and making the beast rear in terror. That had been deep in Wales and he decided that very night on a novel scheme. From that point on, he offered to excuse the Welsh the gold they dug from the mines each year, in return for four hundred head of wolf. The Welsh lords shook his hand and I am sure those men were delighted by that bargain. Though he was their feudal lord, they did not pay him another penny for twelve years.

There were fewer wolf attacks after that, which is all he'd wanted. In a sense, Edgar had paid the Welsh to make their own roads safer, though they should have done it themselves. As I say, he was a clever king. There was a reason he was known as Edgar the Peaceful – though it was for his reign, not his own manner. If you'd met him, you would have looked away from those cold, grey eyes. Edgar was not a man to cross. I knew that after what happened to his great friend, Allwold, in the sixth year of the king's reign.

I had met Allwold many times, though I did not know him well. As archbishop, I had a vote on the Witan council and I was jealous of my right to it, after so many years gazing in from the darkness. I put my name to witness laws and deeds and new thanes made by Edgar's hand. I understood Allwold to be a loyal fellow, a friend of the king's from years before, perhaps even from childhood by the way they talked and laughed. Allwold was not a clever man, however, not at all. He was as sword-thin as the others Edgar trusted, but there was very little actual thought in him.

I felt no envy of that friendship. I would like that to be clear. Edgar had given me more than I had ever dreamed of as a boy, so that my life had become three parts ritual and incense, with staff and palaces available to me. Even the king rose as I entered a room. Of course, I knew Edgar showed respect to the Church I embodied rather than the man, but it was still gratifying.

I do not wish it to seem as if we were gossiping, but in the midst of a dinner after a long day of petitions and judgements, Allwold said he'd heard of a great beauty in his part of the world. He described her in terms that would have suited a swan or perhaps a milk cow better than a potential queen, but

I could see Edgar's eyes gleam. He seemed ready to go charging off into the night to see this wondrous young woman, but there was still a crowd waiting to see the king and he had promised the Witan six days, with only one complete. I saw him wrestle with the demands of duty and carnal interest. I was pleased when he slumped in his chair and waved a hand.

'You go, Allwold. Seek out this fine-bosomed bird and see if the talk of her is true. If she is beautiful, tell her I am in need of a queen. If not, give her a gold coin and beg her pardon. It will be a fine quest.'

Allwold thumped his fist on the table and swore he would do it. He looked at me as he did and I could see he was considering asking me to join him. I shook my head. Not only was I no judge of female beauty, I was longing to get back to my forge. I had spent months polishing rubies to fit the crown I would make, studying with master jewellers until I could produce work as fine as any of them. I had asked Edgar how soon he would be crowned and he'd looked away and said I should take all the time I needed. A crown could not be rushed, he said.

I do regret not going with Allwold, now. I had to hear from Edgar what happened. I relate it here because it reveals much about the king.

Allwold went to the area where he'd first heard the rumour, going from village to village, then house to house, looking for the 'dark beauty'. Those two words alone seemed enough for farmers and old men to point further down the lane, or across a field.

When he found her, he was smitten on the instant. He discovered her as she was picking apples, with a flush on her cheek to shame the ripe fruit. Allwold declared he was a king's thane and that he would marry her and feed her grapes and have sixty servants tend her – all before he had asked her name.

Her name was Audrey of Wessex and she was of a fine

bloodline, daughter of a shire ealdorman. I believe her father had died by that point, leaving the family a little closer to poverty than they might have liked. Either way, the dashing young Allwold swept her into his arms, down the road to her village church to be married, and into the long grass before the sun set, the way I heard it.

There were some who later claimed that she remained a virgin, despite his attentions. As one who met both Audrey and Allwold, I would say that was very unlikely.

Quite how Allwold thought he would get away with such a rash act, I do not know. He did not mention the king's offer to her, for fear it would eclipse his own. Yet Edgar was expecting him to report back to the Witan. Allwold spent barely three days with his new wife before he came to his senses. He took her to a manor house he owned and left her there. Allwold then went galloping across country, in a fine sweat to reach the king before the end of that council.

I was there for his return to Winchester, though I was busy with Brother Justin and the plans for the new cathedral in Canterbury. We had cleared the site and built a small chapel nearby in the interim. It is my least favourite part of any great build, somehow. It feels as if we have taken stability away, that we have summoned chaos into the world.

In that chaos, I heard Allwold had returned. I left Justin with his compasses and lead markers and went to the king's side. The guards allowed me to enter, of course, announcing me as I swept in. They say it is a grand thing to be king. As I wrote so many months ago, it is better to anoint them. I did not have to go out riding on patrol, for a start.

Allwold was sweating, I noticed, as I took a seat. Edgar turned away from him and there was a look of honest puzzlement on his face. Yet he was always patient with his friend.

'So she was not the great beauty you heard reported. Why would such a thing be said, then?'

Allwold shrugged. He was as stiff as a board. I knew in that moment he was guilty of something.

'People can be cruel, my lord. Or perhaps they meant another.'

'If they meant another, you did not find her. I'd have thought you'd still be searching.'

'No . . . no, Audrey is the one they meant.'

'But no beauty, you said. A plain woman.'

'Very plain,' Allwold replied with more confidence, feeling himself on safer ground. He wasn't, though.

'Yet you married her, this plain woman. This very plain woman is now your wife.'

Allwold's eyes had widened, so that I could see the whites of them. His plan had fallen apart with just a few sharp questions. I know now that he'd intended to put Edgar off with talk of an ugly woman, but the king was not a fool.

'Yes, my lord,' Allwold said, as if he could not quite take a full breath.

'I see,' Edgar said. 'You were so taken with her plainness that you married her that very morning.' There was a coldness to his manner, but he smiled even so. I believe he did see.

I watched as the king stepped off a dais and laid a hand on Allwold's shoulder.

'My friend, I am sorry I missed the service. I will make it up to you. I will bring the hunt to your door and stage a great wedding feast for you.'

'Your Highness, there is . . . n-no need for . . .'

'It would be my honour, Allwold. Go now and tell your new wife the king is coming. This council is at an end. I will be with you by noon tomorrow.'

I watched Allwold leave and I saw in him the look of a condemned man. He was a fool, and fools should always tell the truth to kings.

38

Consumed with curiosity, I accompanied King Edgar into Kent, where Allwold had his lands. The king had summoned only his favourite huntsmen and companions. They rode good horses, and dogs milled and yelped around us, baying whenever something went crashing through the under-growth. Dogs and men went out and rejoined us, all panting and red-tongued, cheerful and savage. Before we had ridden twenty miles, they had speared two wild pigs and heaved a small doe across a saddle-horn.

It was a light and breezy day, yet the king's men wore cowled mail shirts that stretched right to their knees, with a padded jacket over all. Over that hood of iron rings, they wore simple helmets of polished steel. We resembled a war party more than a hunt on a fine day. I do not think that was by accident. Edgar was in the heart of Wessex, and though there could be brigands and thieves on any stretch of road, he could have gone lightly armed to Allwold's home. Instead, his thirty men wore iron.

Poor Allwold had understood he was in real trouble. Racing home before us, he knew he had to tell the entire sorry tale to his new wife. Yet when the moment came, he merely paced up and down, growing more and more nervous. In the end, he waited until King Edgar's dust could be seen on the road and the hunt was coming down his drive.

In a torrent of words, he told his new wife what he had done. He pointed to the dust rising and begged her to make herself plain. If she rubbed dirt into her cheeks, wrapped herself in old clothes, pissed on her skirts, anything, she might still save him from the king's anger.

Audrey rushed away to the private rooms at the back, while in his yard, we all saw him come out, red-faced and breathing hard as he knelt to the king.

Edgar dismounted, leaping down easily, though he too wore mail. The wyvern of Wessex was gold on his surcoat, I remember.

'Where is this new wife of yours, then? Show me this dear woman who caught your heart in her skirts.'

He spoke lightly, but there was no lightness in him, if you understand me. I dismounted outside, though I was the only one who did. The others waited as if they expected to be called upon to charge at any moment. There was no laughter or talk amongst them. Though they had known Allwold for years, their loyalty was all for Edgar.

The king refused when one of them offered to go in with him. He did not fear Allwold, or perhaps Edgar wished to test his courage, I don't know. When a young man has never known the pride of a father, he will sometimes push on, to show himself he is not afraid. I think there was a touch of that. Edgar's father had been murdered, but the son would still duck his head and enter a home without a flinch. Outside, we waited.

King Edgar accepted a cup of wine warmed on the hearth with herbs. He did not drink from it, so he said later. It was one thing to scorn attack, but he was not so trusting as to be made a fool.

The king asked to see this Audrey and then waited, ignoring every attempt Allwold made to draw him into talk. As one who stood outside in the silence, I can say it felt like an age to me. I stroked the nose of my horse, which was very pleasant to the touch. I wondered if anyone had ever made a bag or gloves from that part. I had seen a purse fashioned from a bull's scrotum that was very useful, lacking seams as it did that might have let in water.

When Audrey appeared, curtsying to her royal guest, she had combed her hair into great lustrous locks. Her face shone, Edgar said later, though with youth or pride it was hard to say. She wore the best dress she owned, which was dark red and of some fine cloth. A gold pendant hung from her throat.

She was exquisitely beautiful, with fine teeth and neck, lips she had bitten red, and wide, dark eyes that seemed to find wonder in the young king.

Allwold sagged as he came in. I'm told she didn't even look at the man who had married her. Her eyes and her blushes were only for Edgar. Oh, she'd understood what Allwold had done, all right. Her beauty was her rebuke.

Yet she was married – and that was where Edgar showed his bloodline, or so I believe.

He stood and bowed to her, taking a hand in his and kissing it.

'My lady, your husband did not do you justice,' Edgar said warmly. He turned a colder look on his friend.

'Well, Allwold, I came to hunt. Come out with me now.'

The earl made no protest, as I heard it. He knew the end was upon him and he only nodded rather sadly to himself as he went out.

Outside, I was still there to see King Edgar come back to the sunlight, with a miserable-looking Allwold at his side. I began to make preparations to mount once again and King Edgar's attention drifted over to me.

'We'll be riding rather hard and wild, Your Grace. Perhaps you should remain. If you would be so good as to instruct the servants to gralloch and prepare the meat we have brought, I will return before too long.'

That 'perhaps' from Edgar was an order from anyone else. In truth, I was relieved. I have never been a great rider and I was not then as young as I'd been at Brunanburh. My hands ached when I hammered with them and the knuckles seemed stiff in the winters. Age takes all, in the end. It is the same for everyone and I do not complain. In that, we are all equal.

When they were gone, I was left alone with a small pile of carcasses. I wrapped the reins around a post and knocked on the door. The house was much larger than my father's had been, perhaps three times the size, with walls and even corridors within.

'Hello?' I called.

I saw her then, when she came. I almost flinched at her beauty, which I cannot explain. Some women are so fair of face that men will follow them and gaze upon them, drinking them in. She was one of those, and yet I was a priest and an abbot, an archbishop as well as a man. I had still not been restored as treasurer, though Edgar had appointed me bishop of London, which brought me great prestige in that city.

I will not describe Audrey as I might a prize heifer, with talk of lips and teeth and ears and clear skin that knew no pox. She listened, I will say that much. When Audrey wished to flatter a man, she listened as if the whole world could fall and she would not care, as long as he spoke. I saw her do that to Edgar, but also to me. With me, she took one look at my tonsure and my gold ring and decided I was one to encourage. I could almost see her make the calculation, so that I was not fooled or drawn in. While Allwold's servants dragged the animals away to be skinned and disembowelled and jointed, I took a seat and we waited together for the hunt to return.

I look back now and realise I talked for a long time, as the sun certainly moved across the sky outside and the shadows lengthened. I told her of my childhood in Glastonbury and even how I had fallen from a cliff and broken a man under my weight. I made her gasp and laugh, and I could hardly believe the way old words tumbled out of me. I had almost to bite my tongue in the end, before I ruined myself. Such is the power of a beautiful woman's attention on a man. Thank God they do not know, most of them. Audrey did, though. She knew exactly.

We heard the hunt long, long before we saw even the dust of them on the long road leading to that estate. The dogs barked in constant chorus, never ceasing while they ran. The men rode much faster than before, at least to my eye when I went outside. Believe me, it is a difficult thing to remain seated while the king and thirty horsemen come thundering up to your door, never mind that baying pack.

Edgar dismounted, looking grim. In turn, I looked for Allwold in the crowd, but I could not see him. I think I'd known, from his expression. The man had been resigned to his fate, almost at peace.

'My lady,' Edgar said. 'I am very sorry. I'm afraid there was an accident. Your husband was killed in the deep woods.'

She did very well, I think, looking back. There were tears and a hand held to the mouth. There was a gasping prayer for his soul. They had left Allwold's body at the boundary of his land, rather than bringing him to his door like a bad surprise. Audrey walked out to where her husband lay sprawled in the grass, his ribs all red on one side where a boar spear had pierced him.

I went with them, wondering whether I should remain quiet, or whether duty demanded I should speak out. A king was writing his own tale as I stood there, bending the arc of the world towards him. I chose to say nothing, in the end. I had not seen the events of the deep wood. Perhaps another man would have cried out against it, or condemned the king in front of them all. Edgar was my friend and I did not.

There had to be another period of mourning. Allwold's body was interred in the family tomb and his weeping widow waited an entire month before accepting the king's hand in marriage. Her beauty had played a part, of course, but it was not the whole of it. When I look back, it was her ruthlessness that made her fate. Women are soft-hearted creatures, most of them. How many would have heard Allwold's plea and gone to make themselves plain? All but one in ten thousand, perhaps. She had given oaths at her marriage, and in that moment when he laid his foolishness before her, she had broken them all. For the fourth time in my life, a woman crossed my path. From Aphra and my Beatrice, to Queen Elgiva, to Queen Audrey, in the end they brought me only pain, only trouble. Audrey was the worst of them. Yet her fairness hid her from my sight.

I cannot understand why it should be so, but men link beauty and goodness together. An ugly woman is more likely to be called a witch, though it makes no sense at all. What form would evil take if there was any choice? It would be fair, and sweet and soft to the touch. It would not be withered fruit.

I conducted the marriage service in Winchester and sat near the king's right hand at the great feast afterwards. I raised a cup in toast to the happy couple and they both smiled and were pleased. Perhaps I was a coward not to speak out, but as I say, I liked him.

It was not long before Edgar's second queen was heavy with child. Audrey spent her days in the comfort of the royal estate at Winchester, waited on hand and foot and enjoying rather more status than she would have known as wife of Allwold. Still, even then I sometimes felt she was a strange bloom. There was no doubting her beauty. Her neck was long and slender, so that it always reminded me of a swan. The line of her jaw grew on me, somehow, so that over time it became more pleasurable to gaze upon her, rather than less. I do not know how that can be, as most things dim and jade through use.

When the gravid state was well advanced, I came to the palace to ask for a loan from the king – one I hoped he would simply grant as a gift, if I am honest – for the Irish marble I wanted to use at Canterbury. It had to be the first church in England, so the materials could not be poor stock. There was peace still, so ships sailed between us with trade goods rather than armed men, but the prices were extraordinary. As I explained to the king, a cathedral on that scale was the labour of eight or twelve years, but it would stand for a thousand, admired by all. It would impress all those foreign lords who visited the court. What price can be put on prestige of that nature?

Edgar was in his private rooms on that particular day. Even I would not sweep into those without some warning. I announced myself and waited for Edgar to be told I was there. As I stood in restful silence, reciting prayers to ease my mind, the door crashed open. A little boy came staggering through, almost falling, weeping and red-faced.

Before my eyes, I saw the queen erupt from the same doorway with a switch in her hand. Audrey was stronger than Prince Edward even in her state. I watched open-mouthed as she grabbed hold of the boy and beat wildly at him for a long time.

At last, he squirmed free and went away wailing down the corridor. Now, do not mistake me. Boys need to be beaten, or they grow snide and weak in spirit. Yet it must be done in stern reproof, not for enjoyment. It is not a pleasure to be savoured, but a reluctant duty to be endured!

I saw flushed triumph on her face as she looked after him, only turning to me when she felt my gaze. She was breathing hard and her dimensions reminded me rather of the apse I had designed at Canterbury. Lost for words, I almost said so and bit my lip.

'He said I was not his mother,' she told me.

She was still angry, but also bright-eyed and thrilled with herself. I felt a pang of dislike for her, despite her beauty. She seemed to me to be a plum too long on the branch, for all she had clearly been plucked.

'He did not know his mother, the lady Fæltha, of course,' I murmured. 'I imagine he longs for some comfort he cannot name. All boys need discipline, my lady . . . but also kindness.'

I do not know why I said the last. The queen was preening at my agreement, but then I had to spoil it, so that a hard look came into her eye. Men did not correct her, I realised.

'Are you here to see my husband, the king?' she asked, as if I might have forgotten his title. 'He is not here today.'

I stared, unsure what to say to that. I knew the guard had gone to ask Edgar if he might receive me. She raised her chin a fraction and I wondered if I wanted to make an enemy. The idea was quite intriguing, like ashes stirred for embers.

'I believe I shall wait,' I said.

She pursed her lips at me and glared, but I had not said she lied. I only looked peaceably at her, with one eyebrow raised in gentle question.

Without another word, she went back inside. A servant closed the door behind her and I was left with a single guard, a man very careful not to meet my eye. I was interested to see if the queen might let me win a small victory, or somehow interfere with his companion when he came back.

The other guard did not return, so I knew he had been stopped and sent somewhere else. What an interesting woman she was, to take such pains over something so small! I found myself humming an old tune as I walked away.

I left a written note to be passed to Edgar – rather than allow his wife to spin whatever tale she chose into his ear. Yet I was careful in the words I used. It does not do to come between a husband and his wife, still less a king and his queen. I only had to think of poor Allwold's fate to know that.

When I had sealed my note and passed it to a steward I knew well, I went out into the open air. I had put aside the afternoon to spend with the king and I was free. It was pleasant to feel no other work looming for once. I exchanged a few light words with the guards on the gate and stepped out onto the street. There, I found the heir to the throne and royal prince leaning against the wall like any urchin of Winchester. Edward was perhaps six years old then, as blond as his father and, on this occasion, dirty with dust and the trails of tears.

'Ah, Prince Edward, I was looking for you,' I said, though it was not true. 'I was worried you were lost somewhere. I don't know what I would have done, what I would have said to your father if I'd lost you.'

'He doesn't care. All he cares about is her now.'

He didn't need to explain. It was true to a degree. King Edgar had somewhat devoted himself to his new wife, though that is not uncommon, especially in young men. I could hardly explain that to the son of his first marriage, however.

'King Edgar has . . . a lot of duties,' I said, dropping into a crouch at his side. 'His own father was king for just a short time and left a lot of work undone. Did you know that?' The boy shook his head. 'And his brother Edwy kept making bad choices, so he left a great deal undone as well. Your father feels the weight of all of that on his shoulders – as well as being a husband to a new wife whom he loves.'

'He doesn't love me,' the boy said.

'No. No, I won't have that, Edward Aetheling! He adores you and he has said so to me, many times. I am his friend, Father Dunstan, and I do not lie. Is that understood? Why, I am the archbishop of Canterbury. I cannot lie!'

He sniffed and rubbed his face, taking some comfort from

my words. I knocked on the door and ushered him in past the shocked stares of the guards there.

'Take heart, sunshine,' I called to him. 'You are very young, but you know, one day, you will be king.'

I saw his smile return at that thought as the door closed once more.

She gave birth to a son, of course, calling him Edmund. He did not live beyond his first years and died of some pox rash before he could speak or walk. The queen took that rather badly, I thought, growing somehow harder, more a woman than a girl, though if anything, more beautiful. It was said of her that a troop of soldiers could not ride past where she stood without at least one of them falling or crashing into another. She made men fools to themselves, which is not such an achievement as it sounds, I sometimes think.

It was not long before Queen Audrey was great with child once more, this time blessed and washed with holy water on a daily basis to protect the child from disease. Her husband had been on the throne for ten years then and I sometimes felt like an old man, though my cathedral was not yet finished and had proved to be a task even greater than my abbey.

Even so, I was at the height of my strengths. It should not have been a surprise that King Edgar came to me to organise his coronation, at last. It seemed his wife wanted to see him crowned. She had plans for how it might go, with a grand ceremony and small kings from all over England, Wales and Scotland coming down to honour the high king and acknowledge him as their lord. He would be anointed by the Church, by me.

While his queen was confined to give birth, Edgar called me to his side. He had a slightly harried look, I remember, as all husbands have at such times. The crown I had made for him was in his hand and he was staring at it as I came into the petition hall in Winchester. I looked around and saw only a few guards at the doors, so that we were about as alone as it was possible for him to be.

'I could crown you now, if you like,' I said lightly.

He looked thoughtful.

'I have never worn it, father. Not once.'

'Truly? There is no law that says you may not, Your Highness. Not that I know. If you wish, I will place it on you today.'

'As archbishop?' he asked. His face was in shadow, his head bowed.

'As a friend, if you wish,' I said. I could not understand his reluctance.

'You are kind, father. But I think I will wait. I have waited a long time.'

A king does not have to give up secrets. He cannot be made to speak by any man, or even any woman. In the bedroom or before the Witan, he can say: this is my concern alone – and all questions cease on that instant.

I'd wondered a thousand times why there had been no coronation. His brother had been crowned within weeks of becoming king, his father also. I'd wondered if it had something to do with those men, of course. I'd even asked the question, twice, over the years. Both times, Edgar had just pursed his lips and looked away, as if a shadow had fallen over him. I hadn't tried to force an answer. A king will not be forced.

In that quiet hall, with Edgar dangling his crown from his fingers like a child's hoop, I wondered if I might hear why we were so many years into a peaceful reign but had somehow avoided a coronation.

'When I became king, it was in tragedy. My brother dead after just three years, his wife killed. I ruled half England, father. I had no desire to rule the rest as well.'

He looked up at me, but I know when to be silent. I heard him sigh.

'You asked for their crown to be remade and I gave it to you, in part so that I did not have to put it on. I was not ready then. I was, what, sixteen? I would have had to pad the band just to wear it. My father's crown, my brother's crown. No. And if there was a perfect moment to be crowned, it went by. I was king! The realm was under threat and I spent years forming alliances, breaking faithless lords, taking heads and oaths to keep the great peace.'

He smiled suddenly and looked up at me from under his brows.

'I had a gift for it.'

It was true and I felt a glimmer of tears come to my eyes as he spoke. What a strange creature, to have tears drawn from me with just a word and a smile! I rode to war, once. I made a harp that played itself. I did not expect strong emotion, just in echo of his old insecurity.

'My first wife brought me pain – but gave me a son. I know, Dunstan, you have your bishops, your abbots – you are father to them all. You have done well, with all I gave to you. Yet I had a boy in the world – and I saw him grow, as once I did. And I thought, if I wear that crown, it will all end. If I wear that crown, I will die. It fixed in me, somehow, for years. I did not want to speak of it, even. I had so much to lose and it could have ruined me. So I was harsher with those who broke their word – and I drew iron on them, where once I would have laughed. I clung too hard to the crown, do you see? So that it hurt me.'

I could only blink at him. I heard the words and the revelation that it had been more important in his life than I had known – and that I had missed that deep current in him, seeing only the good king, the friend.

'Why now?' I asked softly.

430

He smiled, almost as a man will when he is in pain and cannot bear to move.

'Because she asks me to. Because I told her I would, if she bore another son. Because I am king and I do not need a crown, but I will not be afraid.'

I reached out.

'It would be my honour to crown you, Your Highness.'

'It might not happen yet, father,' he said with a grin. 'I have prayed, but perhaps there'll be no answer. Perhaps the child will die again, before we bring my lords to one place.'

I sensed great pain in him, more than I could understand. Children died all the time. He would have other sons, other daughters, other wives if he needed them. Yet I patted him on the arm and spoke to him, an older man offering comfort to a younger one. We are sinners, all, but we can be kind.

39

She bore the king a son and they named him Ethelred. I was given the task of organising a coronation for a king who had ruled for what seemed an age of peace. Some men will talk of Alfred the Great, for his navy and his works of valour, or perhaps Æthelstan for bringing all Britain under one throne. Without Edgar's reign, it would have fallen apart once more and been lost. He was Augustus to Julius Caesar – the long years of peace and growth and trade that meant, by the end, we were England and not Wessex or Cumbria.

To put a crown on such a man is not the work of an afternoon. In the end, it took me almost two years to bring it about, and though I should not take too much pride in such worldly endeavours, I hold it dear in my memory, as my fifth great work. No mere pressing of a crown on a royal brow, this! It was to be a culmination of an age and a promise for the future. I had no limit on my purse and you may be sure I did not stint. My cathedral was finished in Canterbury, so that choirs sang day and night in constant prayer for the realm and the king. I made a crown for Edgar's queen as they sang, so that my hammering became the rhythm of the world.

My brother Wulfric died a few months into that year, in March. I had expected him to outlive me, as the younger of us, though I knew his old wounds and the loss of his arm made that less likely. Such things wear on a man. I'd wanted a fine tomb in Glastonbury for him, but his wife refused and I chose not to overrule her. Instead, we held a simple family service in Baltonsborough and he was put in the ground next to our father and mother.

As I stood there, looking down into a hole that held the boy who had run and leaped and wept at old enemies, I was surprised to feel his wife touch my arm.

'He was always grateful to you,' Alice said.

I looked at her, trying not to squint to see the young girl she had been. It was too hard, with so many years passed. Alice blessed me for the life I had given him, which was only right. She did not mention my time of exile, of course. Families have secrets and perhaps that was ours.

I had made my peace with them. I had been given time to. When I think of the young boy who fell through open air with Encarius, full of hate and rage, I am pleased I was not taken then. Age softens and that is not a bad thing. There were times in my youth when I might have chosen death, when I might even have welcomed it. I would have been wrong, each and every instance.

We chose Chester for Edgar to be crowned, where the king had a fine royal estate. There was a great river there and a huge crowd lined the banks, standing and cheering by the thousand. Edgar was rowed across the river Dee by eight kings and princes that morning, all in their finery, all willing to bend the oars to show he was the high king, whose reign had been a summer's gold. It makes me weep to think of it now. King Kenneth of Alba was there, Malcolm of Cumbria, Donald of Strathclyde, Magnus of Man and the Isles, Iago, Hywel, Ithel and Siferth, all of Gwynedd. The sun shone and the waters were calm as they rowed Edgar to where I waited on the bank. The ground was thick with meadowsweet, while flags and tents and carts made a field like a county fair for miles all around us. A choir of six hundred sang harmonies so fine they shamed the birds.

I put my crown on Edgar and I said Mass, with heads bowed as far as I could see. I anointed him with holy oil, as Æthelstan and Roman emperors had been before him. At

433

his request, I anointed and crowned Queen Audrey at his side, so that they stood together.

I do not think anyone who was there will ever forget it. It remains in my mind in every detail, so that I can close my eyes and hear the trumpets blast and see the reflection of the royal barge in the waters, a golden shadow.

It was the culmination of my life, and when I look back, I wish I had been taken then, struck down at that moment of happiness. Yet I had one more tragedy ahead, one great error. If I have lived a life of five great works, some have had their own shadows. For my abbey, I have my sin with Beatrice. For my vengeance upon Edwy's queen, I made my cathedral at Canterbury. For the glorious coronation of a high king, perhaps I engaged the attention of the old enemy of mankind. It was a moment of perfection, and such things are a challenge to him. This is a world of flaw and dust. I think it brought about his hatred of me, the petty, childish spite of Lucifer, of Samael. He saw what I had done and he had always been a creature of envy.

Of course, the queen was at the heart of it. If I am to be judged on one mistake, I pray it will not be that one. I saw her beauty and I did not truly know what it concealed.

PART FIVE

Behold the Death of Innocence

AD 975

'And I am old and grayheaded; and, behold, my sons
are with you. I have walked before you from my
childhood unto this day.'

1 Samuel 12:2

40

King Edgar died, as all men will, though he was younger than me. He stayed out one night in the deep woods to hunt deer and went to bed on his return, complaining of aches and pains in his joints. Some fever had its birth around the ponds of stagnant water where he had lain in wait and it got into him. He was scratched and scraped as well from briars, which became fat with lymph and pus as his agues took a grip. He was thirty-two years old and it was just two years after his coronation.

I prayed over him on his deathbed, and his son Edward stayed at my side the whole time. That boy was only twelve himself. He tried to be brave, but in the end, he crumpled. He wept and sobbed and took up his father's hand in his. I saw the last breath leave Edgar and the great stillness come. I knelt to him. I was the first to tell Edward he was king.

The Witan would be summoned, of course, but for once, there could be no doubt. His younger brother Ethelred was barely six years old.

As I promised Edward I would crown him, Queen Audrey came into that chamber, wrinkling her nose in distaste at the smell of sickness. I think she heard me speak to her stepson.

'What herbs are you using to stain the air so?' she said to me.

I mentioned meadowsweet and lavender, though I knew she was covering her grief with rudeness, as some will. I saw her gaze flicker over her husband's corpse and she nodded to herself once, as if closing a book.

I do believe she was loyal to him in her fashion, but as

soon as Edgar was gone, she was about her own plans and designs. Her loyalty vanished at the instant of his death. I believe she was cold at the heart, somehow, as if all she did was in mimicry of life. If I had not seen her blood on the cloths of childbirth, I might have believed she was a succubus – those demons of female form that have no kindness in them and will drain the life from a man until he is just a husk. She was certainly beautiful enough. Even there, as she leaned over her dead husband and drifted so close to his face I thought she might kiss his lips, I was struck by the perfection of her. She was the fairest woman I have ever encountered, though she was rotten within.

Ah me, I do not want to tell this part. It is too recent and too raw a pain for me. Perhaps I should end this packet of papers on the river at Chester, with eight kings rowing Edgar to be crowned. It was my triumph and his – just getting those proud men to that place, with feasts for days and every manner of diversion. It is my hilltop, my harp, my lamp in the dark. Yet it is not the end. The end rushes upon me.

I have known seven kings in all. Three were brothers: Æthelstan, Edmund and Eadred. Two were sons of Edmund: rash Edwy and Edgar the Peaceful. The last were two sons of Edgar: Edward and Ethelred. I am an old man. It breaks my heart.

As I had done once with Edwy, Queen Audrey spoke before the Witan. With her stepson watching her, with all men watching her, she said Edgar's first wife had been taken quickly, leaving only memories. Did anyone even remember her name? She should not have asked that. It was but one small part of her misjudgement, though I delighted in it. Prince Edward was no coward. I felt my heart leap as he stood up.

'I remember it. My mother's name was Fæltha. She was a

daughter of Strathclyde and her father bent the knee to mine. She was a queen.'

He sat down again and I saw the lady pause in the lamplight, marshalling her thoughts after that misstep.

'She was, as I am now,' Audrey said softly.

There was no noise and her voice was almost a whisper, I recall, as if the rest of us held our breath. Whatever else she was, she was indeed queen. That could not be denied. To my delight, Edward rose again in challenge, thirteen then and red-faced, but of all of us, perhaps the only one unmoved by her fair form.

'As I am king, my lady. There, we have named ourselves. Now, will you yield the floor, so that my Witan can vote?'

'You are still a child, Edward,' she said, coldly. 'Will you bluster so when Vikings land on our coast? When armies march? I have ruled at my husband's side for years. I have seen every treaty and deal and punishment King Edgar ordered. Half the men in the Witan owe their seats to my judgement!'

There was a mumble, though whether of dissent or astonishment, I could not say. From me, it was certainly dissent.

She glared at us in the gloom and the shadows, and I had to struggle not to grin. If she'd ever had it, she had lost the tide of the room. There is a moment in the affairs of men where they can be swayed. I knew better than most how persuasive women could be – but not in anger. The moment she grew angry, I knew she had lost. There is just something comical about anger without the threat of an attack.

'So,' she said, 'I tell you all what you already know. Some of those days of peace came from my decisions, made for the highest stakes. King Edgar, whose reign was sixteen years without war, trusted me. I ask only that the Witan trusts me in turn, that they consider my son Ethelred as heir to the throne. That if they will have Edward as king, they also demand an oath of celibacy from him, as Æthelstan took before. I am willing to guide Ethelred until he is fully grown. Let me be his guide, as I guided his father before him.'

As she had guided poor Allwold to an early death, I thought to myself. Someone made a scornful sound, as if the very idea she proposed was amusing. The same man chuckled in derision. I had to look away when she turned to seek the source.

Whatever part I may or may not have played, I think the dowager queen had misjudged the earls and thanes and reeves of the Witan. It was true Edward was young, but in speaking so to her, he showed that was a weakness that would pass in time. He had the will to rule, which is no small thing and not given to all, by any means. That will had made his father so feared that others would not dare to rebel. It had meant Æthelstan could keep thousands of men on the field when they wanted to run. Edward had that in his blood.

As the guests and observers filed out, Queen Audrey among their number, I remained as archbishop, to cast my vote. We did so by raising our hands, as soon as we were alone. Of the ninety-six landowners and two archbishops in that place, forty-eight chose Edward. Seven abstained like the lickspittle cowards they were, and forty-three voted to make Ethelred king.

I do not know what promises she had made before the council sat to get so many votes. I was pleased to see the archbishop of York raising his hand with me, though we had discussed it before the meeting. Oda's nephew Oswald had been my choice, though he was not long back from Rome then. It was my way of paying a debt of friendship to the old Dane. Either way, the church must be unified in such things. I had learned that much from the disaster with Edwy.

It had been closer than I'd have liked, but it was settled. I told myself I would be damned if I ever let that exquisite harpy any closer to the throne than that.

She did not take the news particularly well, as I heard it. A rumour went around Winchester that the queen had smashed plates and broken chairs, then gathered up a vast fortune from the royal treasury and taken herself away with her son to one of her husband's fortresses. If I had been treasurer, she would have been sent away with a tin penny.

I do not think she feared murder or some retribution. I imagine her husband's death had simply come too soon for her plans and ambitions. If her son had been sixteen, he'd have had a much better chance of standing before the Witan on his own. For a time, Audrey took herself away from the world, and I am afraid I thought little of her, or the king's second son.

The peace we had known came to a sudden end. I cannot say for certain that Audrey was behind it, but there were rebellions in favour of her son in East Anglia and Mercia. Two earls of the Witan rose up, both of whom had voted for her cause. They hanged their shire reeves and marched armed men through the towns, with torches and spears. Worse, they pillaged Benedictine monasteries from one end of the country to another, taking gold and relicts, throwing my monks out into the snow.

It was a brutal time and there was murder everywhere, so that the roads were impassable. Each town had to fend for itself and we felt that isolation even in Winchester. Every messenger who risked his life to make it through brought worse news: from the north, from the east, even on the borders of Wales.

I advised the king as best I could, but the truth was I had never been a man of war. I had relied on thanes and tacticians to know when to ride out, when to build walls and retreat. It seemed like chaos, and sometimes in the evenings, I could see red light in the sky from many miles off, as some home or fortress burned.

As I say, I cannot be sure she was behind it, though I think, like Eve, she could have made those men rise. She had always been persuasive. What matters is that she benefited from the unrest, so that the whole country knew King Edward's reign would not be as peaceful as his father's had been. Thanes and ealdormen began to lay in the stores for a war – in spears and mail, in shields and axes. Coin that had gone on cutting new land from the forest or on merchant stock, now vanished into weapons and the furnaces of smiths.

The lords who had voted against Edward in the Witan were not shy, or unwilling to suggest we might have chosen the wrong son. Again, I wonder how much gold she spent to make their tongues wag so. I'd have had them torn out of those faithless men.

King Edward summoned a levy, and most of his lords brought men to his banners, though there were some who failed to attend. He rode the length and breadth of the country and found only charred timbers and peaceful men willing to kneel and praise him. Yet as soon as his army had gone back to farms and homesteads, the bonfires would be seen again. There are some generations who need no Vikings to bring destruction.

For two years, it was the same, so that no one knew if murderers might creep in from the woods to kill, rape and steal what righteous working men had made, or monks had built with their own hands.

It was a time for savagery and I wondered aloud if Edward might forgive taxes in exchange for their heads, as his father had done with wolves in Wales. He refused, though I think that was a mistake. Every town has its bodies by the roadside or in the marketplace, swinging as a warning. Every child has been taken to an execution or a branding. My father made me watch a man struck dead, and it stayed with me for years as I tried to sleep, keeping me firmly on the path of good works.

I think Edward should have sent his judges and his army to take the heads of every lord in rebellion against him – and pinched the vein closed by doing so. The churls would have thanked him. A king must be feared – and rough men fear only soldiers. I will turn the other cheek, but I prefer my enemies to be dead when I do, so they cannot strike at me.

In the third year of his reign, King Edward turned sixteen. He was the image, not of his father, but of his grandfather Edmund. That winter had been quieter and he'd received lords from East Anglia and made some sort of peace with them.

It is the last drop that brims and spills the wine, not all the ones before. I'd warned Edward his stepmother had played a part in the rebellions. Though I had no proof, I'd seen the names were those who had voted for her. I'd heard her own whispered.

He did not believe me, or if he did, he didn't take that threat seriously. Instead, he worked, to pour oil on troubled waters, to break the backs of traitor lords, to bring calm to a troubled kingdom. Yet it was not all milk and honey. He sent a dozen men to murder one stubborn lord, I recall, taking the old fool in his bed. The whole realm was at stake, remember. Edward may not have decided on mass burnings and slaughter, but neither was he a weak child, not any longer. Yet he was still too trusting, too innocent.

He had been crowned immediately he was king, you may be sure. He wanted to be seen, a younger version of his father. It was true he lacked that man's hard stare, but it would have come in time. If I had been younger, I would have spent more days at his side, but my eyes and legs had grown weak and I'd never ridden well. When a sixteen-year-old king summons up a great hunt in the spring, he does not want old men like me trailing around and panting in his wake.

Royalty is first and foremost about youth. No one feels his

heart beat hard at the sight of some thin and wrinkled king. No, we see them flashing gold in their strength, clear-eyed warriors charged with the safety of the flock. God bless them all, those brave young men.

I delay, I delay. He was the age I was when first I came to court. I do not want to cross that bridge again. I was not there, I was not there. I heard it all from servants and from her.

41

If there had not been the first stirrings of peace, I don't think Edward would have hunted within a hundred miles of his mother. Corfe fortress in Dorset had become her refuge when the Witan rejected her offer. She might have lived a quiet life there, raising Ethelred to manhood. He could have become a powerful earl for his half-brother, a prince at the court.

The queen had done her best to bribe and pluck up Edward's enemies against him. Yet as I have said, in that third year, her plans were failing. Edward had made peace with East Anglia. Some said a truce would follow on its heels with Mercia as well. I gave him advice when he asked for it, which was often. I am proud to say he trusted me. I asked him once if he remembered the time I'd spoken to him in Winchester, when I'd found him by the gates, in tears. He looked at me then with the strangest expression – part pain, part sadness – and said, 'Of course I do.'

Despite his youth, Edward was no fool – and all men still remembered his father. He called on their oaths of fealty to King Edgar and his descendants. There are always a few for whom oaths mean nothing, but for most, they are the thread that binds, the cup that quenches thirst. Without our oaths, after all, without our faith, we are no more than beasts. I think Edward would have restored his father's peace in just another year or two.

He left the Dorset hunt as it ran west, when he realised he was just a few miles from Corfe. Over rough ground, hunters ride alone for miles at a time, finding their own way. I don't suppose it was more than a whim that turned him from the sound of dogs and horns.

There is a line of chalk hills around Corfe – the name itself means a cut in the land. The fortress there had a fine defensive wall, though it was all wood. Edward had sat the throne for three years without once seeing his younger brother. I suspect that was the heart of it. He may have wanted to greet the dowager queen, the woman his father had loved. I know Edward wanted peace, in his household and his kingdom. He was always a kind lad.

Now, his father would have surrounded the fortress and burned it to the ground if that woman had stood against him. Never mistake the peace of Edgar for gentleness.

Yet Edward was a forgiving son – and I think, a rather lonely one. I'd seen it in the years of his youth when his father had been besotted with the new wife. I'd seen it in the years since. Edward had no friends of the sort who could clap him on the back and mock his moods. He trusted me, but if I pressed too close, he would look out into the distance, or become guarded. I'd know then he was thinking of them – and particularly his little brother.

Edward felt a responsibility there. They'd played together, of course, with Edward carrying Ethelred around Winchester on his back. The thought of that little boy alone and far away troubled the king. I knew he'd sent messengers to Corfe, making some offering of peace and forgiveness. She had never answered.

It was late in the day, almost at twilight, when he came to her gate alone. Edward sat a very fine stallion that was yet as meek as milk for him. There was always danger on the roads, so Edward wore mail and a surcoat, with a good sword on his hip and two spears lashed alongside his leg. It was madness to have left his hunt. He had scores of brave men willing to die for him, but they were crashing through the undergrowth after boar and deer, miles from their master.

He was sixteen and the bulky strength and savagery of a warrior had not yet come upon him. He was brave, though – reckless, to be there at all. I know Edward still thought hatred could be turned aside with a word or an open hand. He trusted me when I told him so and he was the closest to a son I have ever known. I delay, I delay, because it hurts me so.

The dowager queen had a dozen guards on her wooden wall, as many servants to tend her. I think she had around eighty hides of land there. She did not want for food or comfort in that place, even without the gold she had brought away with her.

She would not open the gate to him. In her suspicions, she could not imagine the young king might have come on his own. She feared some trap, some trick to get her to come out. Queen Audrey climbed the stairs to the walkway by the outer wall instead, so that she appeared above and looked down on the king. Her son had come with her and stood holding her hand, then nine years old with a mop of black hair and wide, dark eyes, an innocent.

As I heard it, Ethelred cried out with pleasure at seeing his brother. They had been three years apart, but the little boy remembered. He tried to pull away from his mother, but she held him hard enough to hurt.

'What do you want here, Edward?' she called.

'Only to see you, to raise a cup. To greet my brother. May I enter as your guest?'

'No. Though I will throw down a cup and a skin of wine.'

She gestured to one of her men and the man appeared with those things, lobbing them down. Edward caught them both and laughed. Perhaps he feared poison then, I do not know. It would have been an odd thing to have tainted wine waiting.

He poured the cup full and tossed the skin back, then raised the cup.

'I give you honour as my father's queen. You too, brother. I have missed you.'

He had not heard the man who crept up behind his horse. As Edward drank, he stiffened and gave a cry of pain. The cup fell to the ground, and on the battlement, Ethelred shrieked his name.

Edward twisted in the saddle to see what had bitten at him. He saw a man still there, clinging to him, ramming a punch dagger through a hole in his mail over and over into his lower back.

The king heaved on his reins and kicked in, making his horse scramble to a run, leaving his tormentors behind. He rode a dozen miles or so before he fell. His horse was wet with blood and he had grown pale without it, his eyes bruised dark.

I heard it all later on. How the queen thrashed little Ethelred on that walkway, for showing weakness in his tears, for his wailing. She was the one who had made him weak, but all she could do was scorn him and show him her contempt. She ruined two kings in all, I think.

The Witan had no choice but to choose Ethelred. There was no one else, and though I spoke against it, no one could say for certain that King Edward had been killed at her order. Audrey claimed it was a brigand, a thief on the road who had tried to steal a gold cup.

The man was never found. I know, because I sought him out for years – and spent a fortune learning every word and whisper about that day. I did not want to see her triumph, but there it was, even so.

I did make sure the story spread, of King Edward the Martyr. I would not let his tale be forgotten. We are all dust, but he was a good boy.

I was born the son of a thane of Wessex. I will die an arch-bishop. I have raised an abbey and a cathedral – and a king to manhood. I have made England Benedictine, in all honour.

The Vikings have come in force this year, so they say. I only wonder how King Ethelred and his mother will deal with those crow armies, those violent men. Perhaps they will meet the same end as Edward, I do not know. *Ethelræd* means 'noble counsel', but I tell you he is *unræd* – 'badly advised'. His was a great vine and I can hardly bear to see it fail. I weep too easily in old age – for my youth, for my father and mother, for all those I have lost. I shall see them again. In the name of Christ, I will.

Dunstan

Historical Note

The year of Dunstan's birth has never been known for certain. It is a useful marker to have it started here as late as AD 920. That should have made him too young for certain age-limited appointments, but it's hard to know if such rules would have been applied to a man of extraordinary ability, any more than they were to Julius Caesar.

Dunstan appears to have been one of the rare, great minds of history – a Leonardo of Glastonbury, a Newton of Wessex. His birthplace is claimed by the village of Baltonsborough, a few miles from Glastonbury, in Somerset.

In the tenth century, Glastonbury Tor and Abbey was more island than hill, surrounded by vast and dangerous salt marshes that would not be drained to golden farmland for centuries. Dunstan first visited with his father Heorstan and was apprenticed to the monks there. To find a community with knowledge of art, sculpture, engineering, metallurgy, carpentry and architecture must have been like water to a dry soul. The boy Dunstan absorbed it all.

He first appears in the *Anglo-Saxon Chronicle* as part of King Æthelstan's court. Æthelstan's own birthdate and place are unknown, but his father, Edward the Elder, and of course his grandfather, Alfred the Great, turned Wessex into the kingdom of the south, and then the kingdom of the English. Æthelstan ruled from AD 924 to 939 – just fifteen years. It was Dunstan's first experience of a royal court – and he made his mistakes early.

*

Godwin is an Old English name, common enough in England before the Norman conquest. He is, however, a fictional character. Nothing is known of Dunstan's early schooling, beyond what he must have learned as judged by his adult skills – and the subjects all Christian monks learned in those early years, such as calligraphy, herbs and medicine, and the lingua Franca of Latin. Greek was usually the second language of scholarship, though not everyone had the ability. St Augustine of Hippo found Greek almost impossible.

Note on spelling: The entire concept of spelling is fairly modern. Even four hundred years ago, Shakespeare spelled his own name in different ways. A century before that, the Paston letters might contain the same word spelled differently in the same document.

I have simplified Dunstan's mother's name 'Cynethryth' as 'Cyneryth', because it's a little easier on the eye. As with Boadicea/Boudicca a thousand years before Dunstan, no one really knows how it would have been said.

The character of Elflaed is a simplification of the name 'Æthelflæd'. It may also have been Elfgifu or Ælflæd. She was King Æthelstan's niece and visited Glastonbury with her spiritual adviser. I have not been able to discover which of the king's sisters was her mother, however. I chose the spelling also to save confusion with Æthelstan and a much better-known Æthelflaed, Lady of Mercia.

It is not known if Elflaed sought out Dunstan or he her, but their friendship – that of a mentor and sponsor with a young talent – would prove vital to his ambitions. King Æthelstan himself came to visit Glastonbury, even then famous for its relics. Not only did Elflaed introduce Dunstan to her uncle's royal court, she also left him a huge fortune in her will. When he became abbot of Glastonbury, he would make it the richest abbey in England.

*

The scene of Dunstan predicting the death of an otherwise healthy monk and then seeing him die within three days is from near-contemporary accounts of his life written in the 990s. It is the sort of thing that made Charles Dickens suspicious of Dunstan as a saint. Either he had the vision and saw it come true, or he made it come true – and saw his status raised as a result.

Dunstan's earliest miracle set the pattern. It is too easy to suspect skulduggery in every aspect of his life – some there certainly was – but we only have a few mostly admiring descriptions from the period and must read between the lines. It was said that when he was still very young, he had a vision of the great abbey he would one day oversee. He climbed a tower and walked along scaffolding in a trance. Instead of falling to his death, however, an angel brought him back to the ground.

I will not say his version was impossible. I will only suggest that a master artificer, a man who could make a harp worthy of a royal court, for example, or an entire upper floor drop away and yet know exactly where to stand, might not have had too much difficulty with an arrangement of pulleys. From my first encounter with Dickens's suspicions about Dunstan, it has been my delight and sense that Dunstan was a very unusual man indeed. That should not be such a surprise. A towering intellect born to that age would have sought out the Church – and thrived, going to the highest post in England. There has only ever been one English pope and perhaps that highest honour was denied Dunstan, but what a life he made for himself otherwise!

Note on titles: At the beginning of Dunstan's life, senior men of power appointed by the king were known as 'ealdormen'. Towards the end, a more recognisable contraction, influenced by the Danish *jarl* was more common: 'earl', or 'eorl'. I've used that version for simplicity. We know so little about Dunstan's family that it is hard to say if his father, Heorstan, was an ealdorman, but the balance of probability is that he was. They were certainly a high-status family, with two bishops, court connections and some degree of wealth.

I have also used 'prince' for its root in the Latin *princeps*, over 'ætheling', which was just too close to some of the names.

Although his exact age is unknown, we know Dunstan appeared at Æthelstan's court before AD 937, when the battle of Brunanburh took place. A 'burh' was a hill fort and market, the seed of a town. They were the creation of Alfred the Great, his son, Edward the Elder, and of course Æthelstan himself, as launch points to repel the 'Wicingas', the 'robbers': the invaders better known as 'Vikings'.

The location of Brunanburh is lost to us, unfortunately. In fact, very little is known at all of that day, except that King Æthelstan faced a great host: Viking forces landing from Ireland, the warriors of King Constantin in Scotland and the men of King Owen of Strathclyde. In essence, these were small kings rebelling against the idea of a high king – of Æthelstan ruling all Britain.

Æthelstan took a great army north and won. Until Towton, five hundred years later, this was said to be the bloodiest battle on British soil. I recommend the hundred-page book *Athelstan: The Making of England* by Tom Holland. It does rather well with the few facts that have survived a thousand years from that time.

Egill Skiallgrimmson is not a fictional character. An Icelandic berserker, he was at Æthelstan's court and fought for him at Brunanburh. It has always been one of the great pleasures of writing historical fiction to come across characters who deserve a book all to themselves, for the sheer fascination of their packed lives. Egill is one of those.

As well as his uncle Athelm, who was archbishop of Canterbury, Dunstan is said to have had another kinsman at court: a bishop known as Ælfheah the Bald. For fear of strangling the tale with too many characters, I have conflated two uncles and given the story to Athelm instead as the lead – though he died rather earlier than I have it.

Ælfheah the Bald was briefly involved in Dunstan's life as one who supported Dunstan taking holy orders. Dunstan refused at first, preferring instead to become engaged to a young woman. He was then struck down by such terrible 'swelling blains' that he thought he had leprosy.

For a man who would have seen lepers, that is no small item of description. There could of course be a number of causes, but some sort of sexually transmitted pox would explain it neatly. Unfortunately, the name of the lady to whom Dunstan was engaged is unknown. I chose 'Beatrice' because the name existed in some form from the fourth century onward – and bore no resemblance to all the names beginning with Athel, Ethel, Aelf, Ath or Aethel.

It is true that King Æthelstan was his father's first-born son, but royal inheritance was more complex. His father openly favoured the first-born of a second marriage, to a mother of royal blood. That son was named Ælfweard, but he died before he could contend for the throne with Æthelstan – a death that does appear to have been from natural causes, all too common then.

Æthelstan was the only son of fighting age able to resist the Vikings in the north. It is not known if he swore not to marry or have children in favour of his brother. It is interesting that he and Edmund remained on excellent terms for the fifteen years of Æthelstan's reign and Edmund fought at his side at Brunanburh in AD 937. The evidence suggests Æthelstan really was that very rarest of creatures: a great king and a decent man.

All that survives of Brunanburh is a poem in the *Anglo-Saxon Chronicle*. We know Constantin of Scotland escaped, as did Anlaf Godfreyson (sometimes called Guthfrithsson), king of Dublin. He would return. Their armies were left for the crows and wolves that had learned to follow armed men to battlefields.

Æthelstan had triumphed. The stakes were simply the survival of England as a nation. In later centuries, distance and the Normans would mean Scotland became an independent kingdom, before the throne was eventually reunited by James I and VI of Scotland – and then the formal Act of Union in 1707.

Brunanburh is said to have involved a great cavalry charge by Æthelstan's forces. He would have faced Viking berserkers, Irish mercenaries, Picts who had never been troubled by Roman legions in their highland fastnesses. They would have been followers of pagan gods and Odin (or Woden) in particular. In comparison, Æthelstan was a devout Christian king, though in those years, following Christ in war was proven by victories. Those who lost battles did not live to tell the story – so the spread of Christianity is often a tale of victors.

Battlefield numbers are always exaggerated in poems and song – that is in part the purpose of poems and songs. Yet Brunanburh certainly involved thousands and perhaps tens of thousands: 'Never before this, were more men on this island slain by the sword's edge' (*Anglo-Saxon Chronicle*).

William of Malmesbury wrote that Anlaf, king of Dublin, spent the night before the battle in the camp of Æthelstan, pretending to be a 'skald' or bard. As unlikely as that sounds, the rest of Anlaf's life suggests that was something he might have done.

To the Romans, Winchester was 'Venta Belgarum', 'town of the Belgae tribe'. To the Saxons who settled the area in later centuries, it was 'Venta Caesta', which as the years passed became 'Winchester'. I have used this spelling, though Dunstan would have known it as an earlier form: 'Wintancaester'.

It may have been King Edmund who appointed Dunstan abbot of Glastonbury, rather than Æthelstan, who had no affection for him. Though Dunstan spent some three years at Æthelstan's court, he was expelled from it, probably for practising sorcery of some kind. Whatever it was, he does seem to have made enemies easily – he would later be briefly expelled from King Edmund's court as well, before being banished by King Edwy.

Æthelstan died of natural causes in AD 939, just two years after Brunanburh and at the age of forty-seven. In those pre-antibiotic days, he could have developed sepsis from any scratch or minor cyst, but the exact cause is unlikely ever to be known. He was the first king of England and had a good claim to have been the first king of Britain.

King Edmund was on much better terms with Dunstan. Records survive of land given by Edmund to Dunstan as abbot of Glastonbury. Numbers vary by source, but one figure was 368½ hides of land, a vast holding.

Dunstan did indeed appoint his brother Wulfric as a 'prepositus' (a bursar), to administer those estates, trusting him completely to provide the income and funds without oversight. Wulfric turned out to have quite the knack for gathering wealth and lived till AD 951, dying a very rich man indeed, owning over a hundred hides in his own name – though it is likely he left a lot of it to the abbey in his will.

Anlaf Godfreyson, Viking king of Dublin, did indeed come back after Æthelstan's death in AD 940 and take the city of York. Aged eighteen, King Edmund was not the renowned battle king his brother had been, though he had done well at Brunanburh. He felt he had no choice but to give up the city. The treaty was immediately followed by a land grab by Anlaf of a hundred miles of territory in the heart of England, including Derby, Lincoln and Leicester. Anlaf was an insatiable enemy for the young king of England to face.

However, fate intervened. Anlaf died in AD 941, just as he was getting going, presumably of a heart attack for its suddenness. King Edmund did not need the full might of his brother's army to take back the north in the chaos that followed. He acted quickly and surely, giving some sign that if he had lived a full life like his brother, or certainly his father, he would be much better known.

The scene in Cheddar Gorge is from the earliest sources, though I have told it a little differently. King Edmund had fallen out with Dunstan after a group of courtiers took against the monk and told many and various lies about him. The young king actually banished Dunstan for a time, sending him home from a hunt around Cheddar Gorge.

The following day, Edmund chased a great stag to the edge of the sheer drop. It went over the edge, followed by his dogs. He could not stop and apparently promised God that he would make his ill-treatment of Dunstan right if his life was spared. The king's horse stopped and Dunstan was back in the royal favour.

It is possible that the story is exactly accurate, but it seemed to me that Dunstan being present as a local lad and calling a warning that saved the king is just as likely.

Edmund was killed after only five years on the throne, at the age of just twenty-three. He had two sons at the time, but they were too young to succeed him. Once again, a brother would wear the crown.

He was indeed killed by a banished thief named Leofa. There is nothing else known about Leofa, so the rest – being a thane and fighting with Edmund at Brunanburh – is my own invention. There is a story of Edmund grabbing hold of the banished man at a feast, which I've used. The exact sequence of events is unknown, unfortunately.

Edmund's early death set off a sequence of relatively short-lived kings: his brother Eadred, his sons Edwy and Edgar, his grandson Edward, who was also murdered, and finally Ethelred the Unready, who paid the Danes to go away and lost everything. Dunstan was there for all of it.

Note on Gothic arches: The pointed arch which became the hallmark of Gothic architecture in the great cathedrals was first seen in England around 1093, in Durham Cathedral – so a century later than I have it being used here. That said, the ruins at Glastonbury have many examples of the pointed arch that moved architecture on from the Roman forms – and the abbey was destroyed and rebuilt two or three times in the thousand years since Dunstan. No one knows for sure, and he was the sort of man who would have understood such an innovation. Glastonbury is worth a visit, for the ruins – and for the Tor and the views from the top.

Edwy and Edgar: Quite how a country, previously united under one king, came then to be divided is not clear. I wrote it as a decision of the Witan, based on Edwy being unfit. It is mentioned in the *Anglo-Saxon Chronicle* as if it was unremarkable – 'And Edwy succeeded to the kingdom of the West Saxons, and Edgar his brother succeeded to the kingdom of the Mercians . . .' – though their uncle Æthelstan had taken oaths of fealty from the king of Alba in Scotland and claimed to be 'Rex totius Britanniae'! The earliest written lives of Dunstan describe a period of unrest in the country while Dunstan is banished, so that by some alchemy, the north chooses to be ruled by Edgar. I'm afraid there are too many gaps in the records here to be certain of the chain of historical events.

Dunstan being banished from the court of King Edwy is one gossipy part of the historic record that is well attested. Edwy (Eadwig/Edwig) left his own coronation feast to sport himself with a mother and daughter. Archbishop Oda asked for someone to fetch the king back and remind him of his duty. Dunstan and the bishop of Lichfield went, finding the king and both ladies in passionate embrace, with the crown rolling on the floor. It seems Dunstan lost his temper. He told off the women, laid hands on Edwy, put the crown on the sixteen-year-old's head and marched him back to the royal company.

The young woman was Aelfgifu ('Elgiva' as I have written it) who was, if anything, more furious with Dunstan than the king. She was certainly involved in his banishment and in his losing Glastonbury and all the lands around it. It is not difficult to imagine how hot she burned at his public humiliation of her. It was unfortunate for Dunstan that the woman he had called a whore in front of the king should then go on to marry King Edwy and become his queen. Such mistakes can curtail the most promising careers.

Dunstan's exile in Flanders is mentioned only in the *Lectiones* of one Adelard of Ghent. He spent his three-year exile at a

Benedictine abbey called St Peter's, built on a hill in what is modern-day Belgium. Interestingly, very rich gifts were made to St Peter's a few years later, by King Edgar of England – as thanks for their hospitality to the banished Dunstan.

The historical story of King Edwy's queen being sold into slavery and then killed cannot be known for certain. It does not appear in the earliest accounts of his life, though in fairness, it would not. The difficulty of thousand-year-old sources – particularly the lives of saints – is that some things would simply not have been written. Yet the tale persists and appears in many histories.

The manner of young King Edwy's sudden death is unknown, which goes to show some of the difficulties of incomplete records. A suicide would not have been recorded, so I have filled that gap in a way that would not have appeared in the history. We do know the marriage was annulled by Archbishop Oda, on grounds that Edwy and Elgiva were too closely related. It is not clear exactly when this happened. There was no heir born of that brief marriage, so King Edgar took on the mantle of the entire realm once more. Depending on the source, the country was split between those two brothers either in the beginning or after unrest in the north. However it happened, it is interesting to consider that this run of kings begins with three brothers, continues with two brothers – and ends with two brothers.

When Archbishop Oda (or Odo) died around AD 961, there were a few candidates to replace him, but Dunstan was not senior enough. The bishop of Winchester was put forward to receive a pallium in Rome and it is true he froze to death on the journey, somewhere high in the Alps.

*

King Edgar married twice. His first wife was Æthelflæda, or Ethelfleda, which was just too close to many other names. I changed that to 'Fæltha', which at least does not begin with Aethel or Ethel. She was mother to the boy king known as Edward the Martyr. She then drops out of the historical record so quickly there are some who still think Edward was illegitimate and Edgar never married her. Such things are possible, though Dunstan supported the boy to be king. The exact truth, however, is unlikely ever to be known. Edgar's second wife was a real find – an extraordinary character for any century. Her name was Ælfthryth. I used 'Audrey' because that actually is the short form. The story of her first marriage to one of Edgar's lords has a chequered history, denied or embraced through the centuries as true or apocryphal. I believe it to be true as it matches the lady's ruthlessness rather well. Audrey/Aelfthryth was mother to the last king of this book – Ethelred.

King Edgar's long-delayed coronation actually took place at Bath, though the pageants and celebrations of that event included the river scene at Chester as I described it. The imperial style of the ceremony devised by Dunstan is said to form the heart of the modern event in Westminster Abbey in London – which would make it Dunstan's longest-lasting achievement. Even cathedrals and abbeys do not last as long as some traditions.

This is not a well-known period of history, in England or anywhere else. It is pleasing, however, to be able to begin and end with the only two names that have a claim to being part of general knowledge: Æthelstan, first king of England, and Ethelred the Unready. In the end, Ethelred ruled to 1016 and is famous mostly for trying to pay the Vikings to leave his kingdom alone. It was not a successful tactic and King

Cnut, son of Swein Forkbeard of Denmark, took the throne from him in that year.

The facts are that Æthelstan to Ethelred is a period of eighty years in which the idea of 'England' was created, with Edgar's peaceful reign the high point that allowed the idea to settle and become real. The Vikings were constantly prowling the edges for all that time, with a dozen different attempts to break it up and establish their own fiefdoms. Kings were required to fight for the people then, over and over, in what was a losing cause. The Vikings came in the end. Yet the idea had settled and an island kingdom had become real.

Dunstan's work on the cathedral of Canterbury did involve design aspects that were similar to St Peter's in Rome, no doubt because of his experiences there. Yet it had a square tower, as I have said. The ingredients and proportions of ancient Roman mortar, which included volcanic ash and lime, were lost for centuries, before being rediscovered. Roman mortar was incredibly strong and had the peculiar property of being able to set even underwater. It is used today. Dunstan's tower and church in Canterbury were taken down and rebuilt completely in the eleventh century and later.

On a final note, the fact that the name of Ethelred the Unready actually meant 'Nobel counsel' (*Æthel-ræd*) the 'Ill-counselled' (*Un-ræd*) must be one of the earliest jokes, if not the earliest, in the English language. 'Old Good-Advice, the badly advised' is a fair approximation.

In 1066, a vast invasion of Viking Norse launched from France. To some extent, the modern age began in that century, but the torch was lit on the bones of great kings, at least in Wessex. The people remained and endured and suffered and worked and thrived – and in 1497 sent a ship under John Cabot to Newfoundland and began the largest empire the world has ever seen. All such empires fall away, leaving stories behind: from Plato's men staring at shadows in a cave or Horatius on the Bridge, to Sir Francis Drake playing bowls and a thousand more. It has been my privilege to tell just one.

Conn Iggulden
London, 2016

He just wanted a decent book to read ...

Not too much to ask, is it? It was in 1935 when Allen Lane, Managing Director of Bodley Head Publishers, stood on a platform at Exeter railway station looking for something good to read on his journey back to London. His choice was limited to popular magazines and poor-quality paperbacks – the same choice faced every day by the vast majority of readers, few of whom could afford hardbacks. Lane's disappointment and subsequent anger at the range of books generally available led him to found a company – and change the world.

'We believed in the existence in this country of a vast reading public for intelligent books at a low price, and staked everything on it'
Sir Allen Lane, 1902–1970, founder of Penguin Books

The quality paperback had arrived – and not just in bookshops. Lane was adamant that his Penguins should appear in chain stores and tobacconists, and should cost no more than a packet of cigarettes.

Reading habits (and cigarette prices) have changed since 1935, but Penguin still believes in publishing the best books for everybody to enjoy. We still believe that good design costs no more than bad design, and we still believe that quality books published passionately and responsibly make the world a better place.

So wherever you see the little bird – whether it's on a piece of prize-winning literary fiction or a celebrity autobiography, political tour de force or historical masterpiece, a serial-killer thriller, reference book, world classic or a piece of pure escapism – you can bet that it represents the very best that the genre has to offer.

Whatever you like to read – trust Penguin.